PRAISE FOR THE IN...

THE INVI...

#2 on the *Indepen*... Novels of 2015 List

On *Library Journal*'s Best Science Fiction/
Fantasy Books of 2016 List

"Satisfyingly complex . . . a book in which to wallow."
—*The Guardian* (UK)

"Ms. Cogman has opened a new pathway into our vast heritage of imagined wonderlands. And yet, as her story reminds us, we yearn for still more."
—Tom Shippey, *The Wall Street Journal*

"A dazzling bibliophilic debut."
—Charles Stross, Hugo Award–winning author of *The Nightmare Stacks*

"Surrender to the sheer volume of fun that appears on every page . . . thoroughly entertaining."
—*Starburst*

"Fantasy doesn't get much better. . . . If you're looking for a swift, clever, and witty read, look no further."
—Fantasy Faction

THE MASKED CITY

"This witty fantasy also includes a Holmesian detective, a wondrous magical train, some fascinating Fae politics, frequent funny moments, and a very limited time for Irene to rescue Kai, all making for a thrilling and deliciously atmospheric adventure."
—*Locus*

continued . . .

"Series fans will be thrilled to learn more about dragon-kind and the capricious Fae, and will be eager for Cogman's third in the series." —*Booklist*

"Another fantastic adventure . . . fast-paced and entertaining. The books in this series make for light, fun popcorn reads." —The BiblioSanctum

THE BURNING PAGE

"Funny, exciting, and oh so inspiring, this is the kind of fantasy novel that will have female readers everywhere gearing up for their own adventure[s]." —Bustle

"As with the previous two books, *The Burning Page* is action-packed from start to finish and will keep you hooked until the very last page." —Nerd Much?

"Imaginative and suspenseful with a touch of magic and science fiction, the worlds of the Invisible Library are ones I want to visit again and again. . . . What makes this series magical are the incredible scenes and creative imagination of the author. The creatures, portals, attacks, and investigation are all surrounded by a feast for your mind's eye." —Caffeinated Book Reviewer

BY GENEVIEVE COGMAN

THE LOST PLOT

AN INVISIBLE LIBRARY NOVEL

GENEVIEVE COGMAN

ACE

NEW YORK

ACE
Published by Berkley
An imprint of Penguin Random House LLC
375 Hudson Street, New York, New York 10014

Library of Congress Cataloging-in-Publication Data

Names: Cogman, Genevieve, author.
Title: The lost plot: an invisible Library novel/Genevieve Cogman.
Description: First Edition. | New York: Ace, 2018.
Identifiers: LCCN 2017031710 (print) | LCCN 2017037915 (ebook) | ISBN 9780399587436 (ebook) |
ISBN 9780399587429 (paperback)
Subjects: LCSH: Librarians—Fiction. | Secret societies—Fiction. | BISAC: FICTION/Fantasy/
Historical. | FICTION/Fantasy/Paranormal. | GSAFD: Fantasy fiction. | Alternative histories (Fiction)
Classification: LCC PR6103.O39 (ebook) | LCC PR6103.O39 L67 2018 (print) | DDC 823/.92—dc23
LC record available at https://lccn.loc.gov/2017031710

Pan trade paperback edition / December 2017
Ace trade paperback edition / January 2018

Printed in the United States of America
1   3   5   7   9   10   8   6   4   2

Cover art: border courtesy Shutterstock; wolf illustration by Adam Auerbach
Cover design by Adam Auerbach
Book design by Laura K. Corless

ACKNOWLEDGEMENTS

Sometimes at this point in a team meeting at work, someone makes a joke along the lines of "You're probably wondering why I've called you here today . . ."

This novel is only here—and only good, if it is good—because I've had a lot of support from people. My agent, Lucienne Diver, and my editors, Bella Pagan and Rebecca Brewer, who are marvelous at their jobs and fantastic people. Thank you very much.

Thank you also to all my beta readers: Beth, Jeanne, Phyllis, Anne, April, Unni, Petronia, Caroline, Iolanthe, and everyone else. Thanks to all my supportive friends at work who put up with my muttering about dragons and Prohibition and other non-clinical topics. Thanks to Charlie and Stuart and Walter and Jeanne for advice and help about such topics as traffic speed, elevator mechanics, what happens when you set fire to large amounts of alcohol, and DVDs of Wo Xin Chang Dan. Thank you to my friends and readers online who have encouraged me to keep on going.

Thank you to my family for all their support. At some point in the future, I will manage not to freak out if you bend the spines of any books you borrow from me. (This day will probably not be anytime soon.)

My appreciation also goes out to all the authors whom I read while doing background research for this book. If any details are incorrect, then it's entirely my own fault.

Thanks also to Damon Runyon, more than somewhat. Because the race is not always to the swift, nor the battle to the strong, but that's the way to bet.

Unless Librarians are involved.

THE
LOST
PLOT

Kostchei,

We have a problem. Yes, I know we always have problems, but this one may derail the peace conference before both sides have even formally agreed to meet.

I've just had word (it was a "polite notification," but you could read between the lines) that Minister Zhao's dead. He was one of the dragon candidates for the upcoming Paris summit. I find it impossible to believe that the timing is an accident. And no, there wasn't any information about how this happened. "Tragic loss to us," et cetera. But this is a significant problem for them.

The Queen of the Southern Lands is going to have to send another dragon representative. And she's having to scramble to fill Minister Zhao's post in her own court. He was extremely senior. It'll be at least a few weeks before the final candidate's settled. But let's be honest—for high-ranking dragons, that's unseemly haste.

The Fae aren't trying anything yet, but they'll be on the situation like sharks on steak if they smell blood in the water.

Any weakness amongst the dragons is an opportunity for them. Our best course of action is probably to stay well out of the whole business. We must concentrate on our side of the deal, and we absolutely have to maintain our neutrality. If either side decides we're biased or that we're playing both of them against the middle, then the whole plan goes out the window. And I don't need to tell you what might happen to the Librarians in the field. Besides, we're understaffed. We need a recruitment programme (as I've said before, repeatedly) and we need it now. Alberich's actions during the recent crisis only made things worse; the problem was already in existence.

Hopefully this current mess won't involve any of our people, as it's making the political situation potentially explosive. As always, it's our duty to stop the Fae and dragons from turning a mere disagreement into a world-destroying war. Let's try to maintain the balance where we can.

Catherine, Librarian

PS—Will someone please show me how to turn off the automatic signatures on this piece of software? You all know who I am.

PPS—Kostchei, you still have that copy of T. H. White's *The Book of Mordred* signed out to you. Would you kindly finish reading it and pass it back into general circulation? Some of the rest of us would like a look at it too.

CHAPTER 1

"My dear girl," the woman sitting next to Irene sniffed, "if you haven't opened your veins before, then do let Mr. Harper do it for you. He's had a lot of experience with nervous young things like you."

Irene looked down at the scalpel lying in the saucer next to her cup of tea. She was trying to think of a way out of the situation—one that wouldn't involve her fleeing the house and slamming the door behind her. She'd visited multiple alternate worlds in order to obtain books. She was capable of dealing with different customs and knew all sorts of polite manners. But she didn't want to serve herself up as the dish of the day. "Nobody actually said there were going to be vampires attending," she said mildly. "I wasn't expecting this."

"Bah!" another of the elderly women snorted.

Irene was the youngest person in the crowded room, trapped in a nest of chairs and little tables that were encrusted with ornaments. The thick curtains were drawn tightly against the night outside. The tea was cold. The cakes were stale. The atmosphere was thick and heavy, and if it hadn't been for the fragrance of the log fire, Irene had a suspicion that it would have smelled even worse.

"I don't wish to sound harsh, but in my day a young woman knew her duty! If this Miss—Miss . . ." The woman trailed off, trying to remember Irene's name.

"Miss Winters," Mr. Harper said. His hair was a grizzled white that retreated in a pronounced widow's peak, and his eyes were black as coal, sunken deep behind half-closed eyelids. He hunched in his chair, tilting forward like a vulture scouting for prey. And whenever he spoke he bared his fangs. The one highlight of the evening so far was that he wasn't sitting next to Irene. He was apparently one of the minor vampires attached to the household; the more powerful ones hadn't risen yet that evening. Small mercies. "So nice to have some young blood present at our little soirée."

Of course, if Irene had known that it was going to be a soirée, let alone one with vampires present, she wouldn't have attended. Which was probably why they hadn't told her. She'd thought this was going to be just a straight book exchange. The negotiations had all gone through smoothly, and she'd been looking forward to collecting a new book for the Library's collection—without violence, drama, or running down corridors screaming. Apparently she'd been mistaken.

"I had absolutely no idea I'd be mixing with such important people when I called," she fluttered, putting on her best air of innocence. "I only wanted to exchange these books, as we agreed—"

"The books, yes. As we discussed." It was the first time the woman at the far end of the room had spoken. The background whispers fell silent at her voice. She touched the red leather binding of the book in her lap; her pale fingers were thin and wrinkled, given an artificial colour by the firelight. "Indeed, I think we should discuss that in private. If you will all excuse us for a moment?" She didn't bother pausing for any possible disagreement. "Miss Winters. Do take a little stroll with me."

Irene put down her cup and saucer—and the scalpel—and rose to her feet in a rustle of skirts, picking up her briefcase. She'd dressed politely and soberly in response to her invitation, in a dove-grey jacket and skirt with dark green trimmings. Given the circumstances, she was wishing she'd accessorized the outfit with garlic, silver, and running shoes. "Delighted," she murmured, and followed the other woman out of the room.

Along the corridor and up the stairs, old-style gas lamps burned, rather than the newer ether lamps. Dark portraits gazed out from gilded ornamental frames. Irene could see the family nose and brows in many of them, mirroring the haughty face of the woman ahead of her.

She really wished she hadn't come here. She'd just wanted to *exchange* a book, rather than stealing it, for once. Her virtue was not being rewarded. Quite the opposite.

Mrs. Walker—referred to as Lady Walker by the rest of the household, even if Irene hadn't come across any trace of a title when she was researching the family—came to a stop in front of a particularly dramatic picture. She turned to look at Irene. Her eyepatch hid her right eye, but the left eye was considering, thoughtful, evaluating. Since Irene preferred to be underestimated and ignored, this wasn't welcome.

"So, you are the notorious Irene Winters," she said. "How convenient that you've come to me, rather than my having to come to you."

"Really." Irene decided to drop the act. It seemed she'd acquired a reputation, so she might as well throw any plans to dissemble out the window. Which was where she'd like to be right now. "Might I ask your sources?"

"Family connections." Mrs. Walker shrugged. The jet ornaments on her dress shivered and danced in the gaslight. "Just because I prefer to spend my time up here rather than running off to frivol in the fleshpots of London . . . But I digress. I assure you, Miss Winters, I know more about you than you might think."

"Oh?" Irene said, in the conciliatory tone of voice she'd had the chance to practise in the past. *Do tell me more,* it implied. *You're so clever.*

"Good." Mrs. Walker looked positively approving. "Just the sort of thing I'd have said, in your place."

Damn, Irene thought. "Perhaps we should skip the preliminaries and get to the point," she suggested.

Mrs. Walker nodded. "Very well. Here it is. I know you're part of a power play by one of the other families. I want to know what is going on. I want to know who you're working for. And if you hope to leave this house alive, you will tell me."

Irene blinked. She'd been ready for various possibilities, ranging from *I know you work for a secret interdimensional Library* to *I have evidence of your criminal acts and plan to blackmail you,* but this was unexpected. "Dear me," she said. "This is so sudden."

"Your cover story was quite impressive," Mrs. Walker granted. "Claiming to be a freelance translator and book-collector, and suggesting an exchange. A copy of Marlowe's lost play *The Massacre at Paris* in return for our copy of John Webster's *Guise.* Both of us would have profited by the deal. And it seemed credible enough to be genuine. But an offer that tempting seems like a fairy story, doesn't it, Miss Winters? And we all know that fairy stories don't happen."

"They happen more than you might think," Irene said. In a high-chaos alternate world like this one, narrative tropes had an unfortunate way of coming true. Unfortunately the traditional heroine-gets-trapped-in-household-full-of-vampires story seldom had a happy ending. At least, not for the heroine. "Honestly, I don't understand why you think I'm an—er, what do you think I am?"

"A spy," Mrs. Walker said.

"A spy?" Irene said in tones of mild horror. What precisely did Mrs. Walker *know*? Irene was an agent of the Library, and it was her job and her duty to retrieve works of fiction from alternate worlds. Bringing them back to her interdimensional Library home created links with these places. And thus did the Library help preserve the balance between unfeeling order and uncaring chaos, across a multitude of worlds. It was a noble calling and a lifetime commitment, and it allowed her to use the Library's special Language to command reality. It also often involved her stealing books and running away. So technically, yes, "spy" wasn't entirely inaccurate. But it sounded as if her cover might still be in one piece.

Even if her chance of obtaining Webster's *Guise* was looking less feasible by the second.

"Yes, a spy. Scheming for one of the other families," Mrs. Walker elaborated. The gaslight flickered, making her look even more like a barely preserved corpse than before. She was thin enough that, in her heavy black dress, she resembled a marionette from the sort of Punch and Judy show that ended in a zombie apocalypse. "Weren't you listening? Personally I suspect you're working for the Vale family in Leeds. You've been seen associating with Peregrine Vale in London. He's supposed to be estranged from them, but that could be just a cover story. Or maybe I should look more closely at the Read family in Rotherham. I've been wondering about them for a while. They'd be delighted to have a spy within my walls."

Irene had known, in a technical sense, that the north of England had its share of vampires. Vampirism wasn't actually illegal in this Great Britain, though killing people by draining their blood was still classed as murder. She'd even been aware that this household she was visiting had some vampires in it. But she hadn't expected quite such a convoluted nest of plotters or network of feuding families.

"Mrs. Walker," she finally said, "you are completely wrong. I'm not some sort of spy or secret agent, or a minion of your enemies. I'm not involved with your family's affairs. I just came here to make the exchange." She indicated her briefcase. "And I have my share of the deal."

"You're wasting your time," Mrs. Walker said. "We don't have the Webster here, in any case."

"Then I might as well leave," Irene said coldly. She made a mental note to find out where they *did* keep the Webster, and then remove it. Without offering payment this time. She didn't appreciate being jerked around on the end of a string, even if the bait was books.

Ignoring her statement, Mrs. Walker looked Irene up and down assessingly. "There are ways to bind you into the family, if you know too much. It might be the best option."

Irene gave in. Sometimes it was easier to play along with conspiracy theorists than convince them they'd got it wrong. "And if, hypothetically, I was to decline this honour?"

"You are in a house full of vampires, several miles out of town, surrounded by countryside, and it isn't even midnight yet." Mrs. Walker's lips curled in a thin smile. "The rain outside is getting worse. No tracks will be found. It'll be days before anyone even realizes you're missing."

"Yes, they'll probably assume I've locked myself away with a good book and didn't want to be disturbed," Irene agreed. "Might I ask what makes me particularly suitable as a member of your family? I'd honestly never seen myself in that sort of position."

It would probably have been more truthful on her part to say *No, thank you, not in a million years. Excuse me while I kick the door down and leave.* But she was curious.

"You're intelligent," Mrs. Walker said. "You've proven your abilities—and we can't allow you to leave now, anyway. You needn't worry about your job either."

"Really?" Irene said.

"Of course not. Once you swear loyalty to my family, you'll be far too compromised to keep up your current job. You can leave it to the colleague with whom you share rooms. Incidentally, where is he?"

"Out of London," Irene lied. Kai had gone to a family party. And given that he was a dragon—even if he was currently in human form, and working as Irene's assistant—that party was in an alternate world. It was a relief to know he was out of reach. Mrs. Walker might appreciate an extra hostage in order to persuade Irene.

"I'm honoured to have been, um, invited into the family like this," she dissembled. "But I have other responsibilities, which I need to discuss with my colleague—"

"Of course. After you've sworn an oath of loyalty in our basement chapel," Mrs. Walker broke in. "And made the usual formal pledge of blood. I wouldn't want you changing your mind between here and London."

Awkward. Irene was quite capable of lying, but the "formal pledge of blood" sounded potentially dangerous. Besides, she didn't want to see what sort of chapel a houseful of vampires had in the basement. "I'd like a few minutes to think," she said. "It's a very big decision for a young woman to make."

Mrs. Walker didn't look at all convinced, but she did nod. "Yes, Miss Winters. But I'd advise you not to wander around the house on your own. The inhabitants receive their food from the local hospital's blood depository, but there is such a thing as provocation. Your wrists—" Irene looked at the lacy cuffs of her blouse. "Are what I would call indecently exposed."

Irene decided to give reason one more try. "Let me ask you to reconsider before this goes any further. Please don't put us both in a . . . difficult situation."

"Begging will get you nowhere," Mrs. Walker said coldly. "I will expect you downstairs in a few minutes. If not, we will be coming to look for you."

She swept along to the head of the staircase, her watered silk skirts hissing against the thick carpet, then turned to give Irene the sort of measuring look that counted every drop of blood in her veins. "And that includes my husband."

Irene watched Mrs. Walker glide down the stairs and considered her dwindling options.

The Webster had been her latest assignment from the Library, and this swap had been the quickest and easiest way to get hold of it. Losing this opportunity was inconvenient, but not disastrous. Her priority now was to get herself safely out of here. She put down her briefcase; it would only be a hindrance to her escape. She'd obtained the copy of the Marlowe play that it contained in an alternate world, where the play was commonplace. So that wasn't a significant loss.

The portrait they'd been standing beneath seemed to frown at her, its imagined gaze a cold spot on her back. She turned to return the glare. The dim lighting and the picture's age made it difficult to judge when it had been painted—or, indeed, what the figure was wearing, or even what the features were. There was an impression of swooping brow, beaky nose, dark mantled clothing, and terrifying eyes.

Like everything else in this household, it showed the signs of age. She crossed to the window and dragged back the heavy brocade curtains.

Behind the curtains, in front of the glass, were heavy iron bars.

Irene finally smiled. Cold iron could stop a human. It could seriously inconvenience a Fae. But it was nothing at all to a servant of the Library.

Rain slapped against the window from outside. It was night, it was raining, she was several miles from the nearest town, and she was probably going to be chased cross-country by vampires the moment they realized she'd left the house. And the river Ouse was flooding again—apparently a regular occurrence in these parts—so there wouldn't be any traffic on the roads.

She should just stick to *taking* books in the future, rather than trying to make a fair exchange. Quicker, quieter, and less trouble with vampires.

She leaned close to the iron bars, keeping her voice low, and addressed them in the Language. **"Iron bars, bend apart quietly, wide enough for me to pass through,"** she murmured.

The bars quivered in their sockets for a moment, then slowly curved like warmed wax, dried paint flaking off them to rustle to the floor.

The windows were locked—but again, that wasn't an issue for the Language. **"Windows, unlock and open, as quietly as possible."**

The lock scraped as it released itself, the dry tumblers grating as they fell into the open position, and the hinge rasped as the window swung back.

There was no drainpipe, but the thick ivy running down the side of the house would do.

Irene bundled her skirts round her waist—quite indecently for this time period and culture—and climbed out of the second-floor window. The ivy was sodden wet, making it treacherous. She paused, hanging outside, to murmur, **"Iron bars, resume your former shape; window, close and lock,"** before starting to climb down. The longer she had to make her getaway before they realized she was gone, the better.

Half a minute of heart-in-mouth scrambling later, she stepped on something wet and squishy, lost her balance, and sat down in the mud. Rain poured down on her. It was very dark.

The problem, Irene decided as she struggled through abandoned lavender bushes—she could tell by the scent—was that she'd become far too used to having backup. As a Librarian, she shouldn't expect that. But oh, right this minute it would have been so useful.

Lightning flashed overhead, and thunder rumbled two seconds behind it. Irene listened for pursuit. Hopefully the weather would obscure her trail.

Something called in the darkness behind her. It was a hollow sort of call, somehow lungless, avid, *thirsty*. Another cry like it answered the first one, farther off. The hunt was up, and she was the quarry.

Rain soaked through her pinned-up hair and dribbled over her face, ran down her jacket and skirt, and did its best to get into her boots. North to a probably empty road, or south to a swollen river and more fields?

Right now the river was the fastest means of transport around. Her research on the house had mentioned a boathouse . . .

A convenient flash of lightning showed her a shed-like building, positioned on what would have been the riverbank. It was now a foot underwater.

It also showed her a dark shape crouched between it and her. "You're not leaving," Mr. Harper snarled, drawing himself up to his full height.

"Get out of my way," Irene shouted, angry now, raising her voice to be heard over the wind. "I'm declining Mrs. Walker's request."

"I don't think so." The water trickled down the vampire's long bony fingers and dripped from his nails, and his eyes glowed like coals as he gazed at her. "I don't think so, Miss—"

"**Earth, open and seize his feet and ankles, and hold him fast,**" Irene ordered. "**Boathouse door, unlock and open!**"

The muddy ground beneath Mr. Harper's feet gaped like animate jaws, and Irene felt the Language draw energy from her as the world adjusted itself to her words. As Mr. Harper sank shin-deep into the mud, she dodged past his furious grasp.

The boathouse opened onto the river, and there was just enough light to see by. Rowboats previously dry-docked on rails now balanced just a few inches above the shimmering flood-waters. Irene splashed towards the closest one.

Behind her, outside, Mr. Harper called, "She's here! She's *here!*"

A good solid shove had a boat off its rails and into the water. Irene grabbed an oar and clambered in, just as Mr. Harper came staggering through the door.

He grabbed for her. She swung with the oar. It cracked solidly into his chest, sending him staggering backwards. The force of the swing almost tipped her out of the boat as it skidded towards the open river. Then the current caught it.

Shrieks came from the shore. Through the rain and darkness, Irene could make out Mrs. Walker, and other shadows behind her, painted in whites and blacks by the lightning.

"You'll regret this!" Mrs. Walker screamed after her.

"Enjoy the book!" Irene called cheerfully as the river carried her downstream towards York.

CHAPTER 2

It was nearly midnight when Irene walked into her hotel. Her skirts and boots left a sodden trail on the carpet. She'd expected to have to tip the desk clerk, but he merely shrugged and asked, "Caught in the floods, madam? They can take visitors a little by surprise."

"It was annoying," Irene agreed, glad to have a convenient excuse. The river had washed her all the way through the centre of town and out the other side. And then she'd been scolded by a policeman for going pleasure-boating by night during the floods. Explaining wouldn't have helped, so she'd just looked stupid and apologized before getting directions back to her hotel. "I'll have to be more careful next time," she added, and headed towards the lifts.

"Excuse me. Are you Miss Winters?"

Irene's only excuse for turning, without checking the lobby mirrors to see who was asking, was that she was wet and tired.

She'd heard a young female voice, rather than an elderly vampire's, but it was still rank carelessness for an agent of her experience.

The woman rising from one of the lobby armchairs almost glowed under the ether lamps. Her hair was a rich gold—not the sort of bleached yellow that was considered fashionable at the moment in this alternate world, nor even the ash-blonde shade that looked golden under moonlight, but a heavy warm gold as bright as buttercups. Her dark coat was subtly out of fashion: it was expensive, of good quality, but the collar was cut too high and the waist too low. Her gloves were silk rather than wool or velvet, and the veil pinned to her hat was clearly an afterthought, rather than designed as part of the outfit. But most of all, it was her face that gave her away: its beautiful serenity was unconcerned by what lesser beings might think of her.

She was a dragon in human form.

She began to walk across the lobby towards Irene, as casually as if they already knew each other. The fact that they were representatives of two factions, whose actions could influence the many worlds of the multiverse, seemed a mere afterthought. Her power ran ahead of her, an invisible thrill in the air that Irene could feel against her skin. She wasn't as dangerous as some dragons Irene had met—but she wasn't a lightweight either. "I don't think we've met," the dragon said. "But I've been told a little about you."

"I'm afraid you have the advantage of me, madam," Irene said politely.

"Well, at least I know what you do for a living." The woman smiled graciously and extended her hand.

Irene manufactured a smile of her own. She rejected the offered hand. She could sense the other woman's leashed energy beneath her human appearance, and it made Irene distinctly wary. "I'm so sorry," Irene said. "I really don't know who you are or what you want. Under these conditions . . ."

The woman withdrew her hand. For a moment her lips pursed, but she smoothed them into another smile. "That's very sensible of you. Perhaps we should talk for a bit—I have something important I'd like to ask you. I think this establishment's bar is still open?" *And even if it isn't, it soon will be,* her tone implied.

Irene reminded herself that she didn't need *more* enemies. "I'd be delighted to sit down and chat, but perhaps the nearby tearoom might be more welcoming? And if you wouldn't mind, I'd like to change my clothing . . ." She gestured at her dripping skirts. "And if I might ask your name?"

"Of course," the woman said. Her smile widened a little. "I'm called Jin Zhi."

Unfortunately Kai had never mentioned a Jin Zhi. Nor had the grand total of two other dragons (his uncle, Ao Shun, and said uncle's personal assistant, Li Ming) whom Irene knew personally. And Irene couldn't get at the Library's files from here, which meant she had no way of checking up on this Jin Zhi (assuming it was the dragon's real name) and whether she was dangerous.

It wasn't as if the Library and the dragons were hostile. They were generally on polite terms, with the worst disagreements being over the ownership of particular texts. But the dragons, representing the forces of order and reality, and the Fae, representing chaos and fiction and unreality, *were* enemies—constantly and violently so. Irene had wandered into the fringes of that conflict, having a dragon as her personal apprentice and student, and didn't want to get more involved.

The Library didn't ally itself with either side. Librarians weren't supposed to get involved. Being the allies of one side would mean being the enemies of the other side. The Library survived as neutrals; any other position would be far more dangerous.

So why was Jin Zhi here, and how did she know who Irene was? And what did she want from her?

Irene changed her clothing and towelled her hair dry as she considered possible implications. She didn't mind making new friends—allies, whatever—and she had no objection to drinking tea with dragons. Yet if this particular dragon thought Irene was going to follow her orders, or that Irene's loyalties were for sale, then matters were about to become . . . awkward. And what was *this important thing* that she wanted to ask Irene about? The words hung in Irene's mind, more of a threat than a promise.

She sighed. She would just have to go and find out what the dragon wanted. So much for a nice quiet evening with a good book.

Jin Zhi was waiting for Irene in the tea-room, already seated at a table. She had a small notebook open and was writing something, but when she caught sight of Irene she slipped it into her handbag.

The tea-room was well lit, and its ether lamps glared out onto the dark wet pavement outside. Mirrors faced every wall that wasn't already set with a window, and the overall impression was one of bright clarity edged with expensive dark wooden flooring. Waiters and waitresses glided silently around in plain white and black clothing, as blank-faced as dolls. Vale had mentioned the restaurant as a place where most of the local spies met up for off-the-record conversation. Vale knew the most interesting facts. It was to do with being London's greatest detective. What Vale didn't know, he had absolutely no idea about, but what he did know was usually fascinating.

Irene let the waiter pull out her chair, and sat down opposite Jin Zhi. The two women studied each other across the menu. Again, Irene felt that touch of underlying power. She tried to decide whether she was *meant* to perceive it and be afraid, or whether Jin Zhi simply lacked practice at keeping it under control.

"Having tea with me won't place you under any sort of obligation," Jin Zhi said. "That'd be a Fae trick. We can split the bill."

"That sounds fair," Irene agreed. "What would you like?"

"The high tea for two sounds reasonable. Tea, sandwiches, macaroons—"

"It's past midnight."

"So? They're still serving it."

Irene nodded and let Jin Zhi give the order. She glanced at the other people in the room, studying their reflections in the mirrors. There were very few people alone: most of them were in pairs or trios, gathered at their own tables, heads close together as they spoke quietly. A piano in the corner of the room tinkled sweetly, not enough to be intrusive, but loud enough to blot out whispers.

"Let me start this again," Jin Zhi said, once the tea had arrived. "I'm sorry that we got off on the wrong foot. My name is Jin Zhi, and I serve the Queen of the Southern Lands. I hold only a small position, having dominion over a mere dozen worlds. I am grateful you allowed me the courtesy of this meeting."

"The honour is mine," Irene said, matching the other woman's formality. "I am Irene, a servant of the Library, though a junior one, and I am Librarian-in-Residence to this world. I don't know why I've deserved your attention, but naturally I'm delighted to receive you here." And how had Jin Zhi known where to find her? A question for later. "How do you take your tea?"

"A little milk, no sugar," Jin Zhi said. She waited for Irene to fill the cup. Clearly her gestures towards equality only went so far: the inferior person poured the tea. "Do you think that fulfils the requirement for professional courtesy?" she added.

"Probably," Irene said. She added a splash of milk to her own tea. "Though a 'mere dozen' worlds? I hope I'm not taking you away from anything important."

"It's all admin," Jin Zhi admitted. "There's very little actual involvement in ruling them, and only from behind the scenes. None of them are actually at risk from the forces of chaos. But to get to the point . . ." Jin Zhi gave Irene what was obviously a well-practised smile of friendly sisterhood. It pinged every single one of Irene's mental alarms. "It's about a book."

Irene folded her hands around her cup. "I may not have it personally in stock, but I know most of this world's major libraries by now, and a fair number of the best bookshops," she said. "Can you tell me the author and the title?"

Jin Zhi snorted. "If I'd just wanted an *ordinary* book from *this* world, then I could have sent a servant to find it. I wouldn't have needed to discuss it with a Librarian."

"Then what *do* you want? And where do you want it from?"

"I'm interested in a version of the *Journey to the West*." Jin Zhi sipped her tea. "No doubt you know the work. It's from a specific world—and not this one. I can give you the details. I'm sure you must have many different versions in your Library . . ."

"I'm afraid that we don't lend them out," Irene said flatly.

However, she did indeed know the *Journey to the West*—it was one of the four great classical novels of Chinese literature in many worlds. It was a sixteenth-century work of semi-history, semi-mythology, and semi-philosophy, about one monk's travels to bring back Buddhist scriptures from India, with his supernatural companions. It involved hair-raising adventures, shape-changing, beating up monsters, and flying around on clouds. The monk's contributions tended to involve standing around being useless—or being on the dinner menu for the monster of the current chapter, while his companions did all the work. The Monkey and Pig characters had all the interesting moments. Most Librarians would at least have recognized the name, even if they hadn't read it.

But some requests had to be refused, however dangerous the person requesting it. "This simply isn't possible."

"Not even if you have more than one copy?" Jin Zhi's eyes flashed with an angry light, like sun glinting off a sword.

"It's a strict rule. We don't make exceptions." Irene kept her expression calm. Showing fear would only confirm her as an inferior entity. "Though this does refer to the Library's *own* copies. If what you're looking for is a transcript of the text, then I could have someone make a copy—"

Jin Zhi was already shaking her head condescendingly. "No. An original edition is required. Preferably Ming Dynasty, though later would do." Even though Irene had just refused, Jin Zhi didn't look discouraged. "Perhaps if I explain why?"

Irene noted that Jin Zhi's phrasing was extremely cautious. Not once had she actually asked Irene to obtain a copy for her, or even suggested that she wanted it personally. It was all *I'm interested in* or *It is required*. Very curious. "Bedtime reading?" she suggested.

Jin Zhi laughed, surprised for a moment into genuine amusement. She helped herself from the tiered trays that had arrived at the table—laden with sandwiches, scones, little cakes, and macaroons—and gestured for Irene to do likewise. "Nothing so simple, I'm afraid. You see . . ."

She paused, as if not sure where to begin, but there was something a little staged to it—as though it was all part of a demonstration of nearly human fallibility. *We're just women together. You can trust me.*

"The Queen of the Southern Lands is one of the four great queens who rule the inner dragon kingdoms. Or should that be queendoms?"

"I understand that there are four outer kingdoms ruled by four kings, and four inner kingdoms ruled by the four queens," Irene said. She'd managed to get that much out of Kai. "And the outer kingdoms lie closer to the worlds of chaos, while the inner kingdoms are closer to the worlds of order."

Jin Zhi nodded. "Recently Minister Zhao decided to . . . retire. And Her Majesty has decided to offer two of her junior servants a chance to take the empty place. So she has set us in competition with each other."

"She wants you to find her a book," Irene said. And yes, perhaps Her Majesty the Queen of the Southern Lands had also set her servants trials of rulership and administration, and so on. But if not, Irene could only admire her. *Go fetch me this book.* The woman— the dragon—the queen—clearly had her priorities right.

Jin Zhi dissected a cucumber sandwich. "Yes," she finally said.

"She wants us to find her a very particular book, in order to demonstrate our abilities. The courtier who brings her the book will get preferment. The one who doesn't . . . will pay the price. Those who aspire to high office must accept the high risks of failure."

Irene buttered a scone thoughtfully. "I understand why you considered going to a Librarian," she said. "But I can't give you a copy from the Library, and there are so many different versions of that particular book out there, in any case . . . I wouldn't even know where to start looking. You said you knew which world it was from, but I don't think dragons and Librarians use the same terminology for alternate worlds. Even if we did take commissions . . . which we don't. I'm not even sure where you heard my name in the first place." In fact, that last point was making Irene nervous.

"A friend of a friend," Jin Zhi said, "knows Kai, son of the King of the Eastern Ocean . . ." She stopped. "Forgive my formality, but it's hard to break the habit. Anyhow, I heard that Kai was spending time in this world and that he had a Librarian serving him. I wanted to ask a Librarian some questions. I'm sure you can see my logic."

"Absolutely," Irene agreed. Her inner alarm was rising to a low boil, but she didn't show it. Jin Zhi knew far too much about Kai, Irene, and the Library. This was not good for Irene's safety, and might be dangerous for Kai as well.

But why did you visit while Kai was elsewhere? the cynical part of her mind commented. *And why didn't you go to him first? This story does not hold water. It positively leaks.*

Irene kept her expression neutral. She couldn't call this dragon a liar to her face. Dragons were not generally concerned about collateral damage when they took offence. "But I'm afraid I'm not actually working for Kai. I'm also surprised that you found me here—in York."

"I employed servants to locate you," Jin Zhi said with a shrug. "I'm not one of those people who tries to do everything herself. I prefer to employ experts."

"Like a Librarian," Irene agreed.

"Well, exactly." Jin Zhi leaned forward. "Now, naturally I don't want to make any sort of arrangement with you. It would be highly inappropriate. I'm glad to hear that you're so definite about your independence."

Irene's danger signals were going off all down the line. Was this some sort of test by the Library, to see how she'd react? No, that had to be too paranoid. But was Jin Zhi skirting around asking for help so that she could claim innocence in future? And if so, what did she want from Irene?

Jin Zhi had admitted that this was the pivot for an internal power struggle in the dragon court—but had avoided saying how important it was. Which suggested it was very important indeed. As such, Irene—and all Librarians—needed to stay well out of it.

"I'm glad to hear it," Irene said briskly. "Because I really am neutral, the Library really is independent, and we absolutely do not get involved in dragon politics—let alone dragon court politics. I appreciate the tea and sandwiches, but anything more is out of the question."

Jin Zhi's eyes narrowed as she sat back in her chair, her mask of civility gone. She picked up a biscuit and snapped it between her fingers, and for a moment her nails were longer and claw-like. "How *interesting*," she said, making the word sound like a curse. "And I'd thought I was just evening the scales."

"I don't understand."

The door blew open as a group staggered in from the night, hats and umbrellas drenched from the pouring rain. Even at this hour of the night, past midnight and with the rain coming down and the river flooding, York hummed with activity.

"I understand that my competitor has already secured a Librarian's assistance. Apparently not all Librarians are quite as principled as you, Irene."

Irene shrugged, but a chill ran down her spine. "I know nothing about that," she said. She didn't keep track of most Librarians' schemes. Apart from them all collecting books, of course. That went without saying. But surely no sane Librarian would get involved in something like this? It would mean drawing the Library into dragon politics. And that could make other Librarians in the field easy targets for any dragons with a stake in the situation. As for the Fae reaction, if they found out—or even if they just *suspected*—that the Library was collaborating with dragons . . . Kai was apprenticed to the Library, possibly the only situation where a dragon-librarian working relationship was permitted. Even so, Irene had been scrupulous about not involving herself and Kai in dragon politics. Anything else would not be tolerated.

"Really." Jin Zhi's tone was edged metal. "Don't you talk to each other at all?"

"We probably aren't as well-organized as you dragons are," Irene said, obfuscating. She needed more information. "And I'm surprised you're so well-informed about your competitor's actions."

"Well, if *I* fail to get the book due to Librarian interference, I won't forget it. And I'll make sure that others hear about it too."

Irene put down her cup and leaned forward. "Are you threatening me?" she asked gently.

"No," Jin Zhi said, a little too quickly. "Of course not. I wouldn't think of blackmailing you to persuade you to do something unethical. I'm not trying to involve you in this on *my* side. I'm simply suggesting that you even the playing ground. I want you to make sure that my opponent"—her voice seethed with anger for a moment—"doesn't get help. That sounds reasonable, doesn't it?"

She watched Irene from under lowered lids. Piano music filled the silence, with an underlying hiss of rain against the windows.

"I would need some proof of what you're saying," Irene said slowly. At the moment this was merely supposition, based on Jin Zhi's story. But if this *was* true . . . then a Librarian somewhere had just made a huge mistake and had put the whole Library in danger. This would undermine the Library's hard-fought neutrality, the work of centuries. The average Fae would not overly object to Irene having tea and sandwiches with a dragon, any more than the average dragon would object to her having tea with a Fae—though both of them might sneer at it. But trying to affect dragon court politics? Getting involved in a life-and-death competition for high office, with the possibility of influencing the winner? Taking sides on *that* level? That would turn the Fae as a whole against every single Librarian they came across. And that could destroy the Library.

"I can't give you *proof* that another Librarian's involved." Jin Zhi opened her handbag and took out some sheets of paper. "But these are details of the book we have been instructed to find, and its world of origin. What you do with this information is up to you. I wouldn't want to be accused of putting any sort of pressure on you. Though no doubt you'll bear in mind that, now that we've met, I'll be able to find you again." Her lips moved in a smile. "Even if you're far too professional to let that affect your choice of action."

"I am a professional," Irene said flatly. "I don't waste my time on empty threats."

But she reached out to take the sheets of paper.

CHAPTER 3

It was raining back in London as well. Water cascaded down the brickwork of the lodgings that Irene shared with Kai, slicking the pavement outside. The heavy clouds and driving rain laid an overcast shroud across London, and it was already dark enough that lights showed in the upper windows along the street.

There were no signs of forced entry on the door, and Irene turned the key with a feeling of reasonable security. She stepped inside, hauled in her suitcase, and began shedding rain-sodden outer garments as soon as the door was closed. Kai wouldn't be back yet, so her next step had to be contacting the Library—

Footsteps came from the upper floor. She froze, then relaxed as she saw Kai step into the halo of lamplight at the head of the stairs. He was in formal clothing for their current world and period, his coat unrumpled and his shoes so newly polished that they gleamed.

"Irene . . ." He hesitated, then his voice grew firmer. "I think we need to talk."

"Absolutely we do," Irene said. "Though I have something to say too, unless you already know more than I do. I don't suppose there are any hot drinks up there?"

"Because if you insist on—oh yes, I just made some tea." He frowned down at her. "Are you trying to distract me?"

"Kai." Irene unpinned her hat and veil and draped them on the hat stand. "In case you haven't noticed, it's raining outside, and there was a very long queue for cabs at the zeppelin port. I am soaked through. Please get me some hot tea before I catch a cold. And then we'll talk. Incidentally, what are you doing here? I thought you were away for at least another three days."

"I came back early," Kai said with a shrug. "And it's the best weather we've had in weeks." He retreated towards the lounge and Irene followed, thinking uncharitable thoughts about dragons and their love of rainy weather.

A few minutes later she was sitting in one of the armchairs in their scruffy, book-crowded lounge, with a cup of tea warming her hands. Kai was still on his feet, and was drifting round the room in short undirected tangents. He had every sign of a man choosing his words carefully before an argument got into full swing.

He was every bit as handsome as Jin Zhi was beautiful. All dragons were gifted in this way. The harsh white ether-light brought out the dark blue tinge to his black hair, giving it the shine of a raven's wing, and turned the lines of his face into an ink draw-ing, all perfect cheek bones and pale skin. His eyes were a shade of blue that was almost too dark to define as standard "blue," and he moved with the effortless grace of someone who'd been born with it and then trained for years on top of that. Next to him, Irene al-ways felt as if she should be fading into the background rather than spoil his artistic perfection. Fortunately she liked fading into the background, for it suited her work, but it could occasionally be demoralizing.

All right, often demoralizing. She tried not to brood about it.

He stopped pacing and glared at her. "We agreed you weren't going to go on solo missions."

"It wasn't intended as such," Irene said defensively. "It was supposed to be a straightforward book exchange. And why are you assuming that I've been on a mission—and ran into trouble—anyhow?"

"I don't know," Kai admitted. "I just suspect. Mostly because you came back early, by zeppelin rather than by train. And because you aren't denying it . . ."

"I left you a note," Irene said. "And you've been away for days. I can't simply let everything else slide while you're not here, Kai. I'm the full Librarian, and you're the apprentice." And as a Librarian, she needed to investigate Jin Zhi's claims as soon as possible. The fact that it would distract Kai was a convenient bonus. "Please sit down and stop looming. We have a serious problem and I need your advice."

That caught his attention. He flung himself down into the chair opposite. "So ask. You know I'm at your service."

"What can you tell me about the court of the Queen of the Southern Lands?"

"Well, it's . . ." he began, then paused. "Irene, why do you want to know?"

"Tell me what you know first; then I'll tell you. I don't want to bias your opinion until I have the information."

"You can't expect me just to sit back and give you information, after a lead-in like that," Kai complained. "Can't you at least tell me why?"

"Kai," Irene said firmly, and sipped her tea. "Talk."

Kai sighed. "Oh, very well. Her Majesty's personal name is Ya Yu, but neither of us is ever likely to have the opportunity to use it. The Queen of the Southern Lands has an excellent reputation for fairness and for a sympathetic attitude towards her subordinates. In practice, I think that means that she gives them plenty of rope if anything goes wrong, before expecting them to hang themselves with it. She's only ever had to move against the Fae herself twice, and each time she was very decisive."

"As in there was nothing left of those Fae?" Irene said, hoping against hope that this dragon queen wasn't as ruthless as some.

Kai avoided her eyes. "As in there was nothing left of those worlds afterwards. It was very conducive to peace and good order."

They make a wilderness and call it peace. Irene nodded, not wanting to get into a discussion of ends, means, omelettes, and broken eggs. "Go on."

"Her attitude mostly carries over to her court," Kai continued. "That is, the senior members of the court are quite lenient about original behaviour by their juniors, just so long as the job actually gets done, and done well. She tolerates members of both the war and the peace factions, though I think that herself she's more inclined to peace. She is on good terms with my uncle Ao Shun, the King of the Northern Ocean, and my father too. And she has companied with both of them in the past to bear children." He paused for a moment, hearing his own words. "At separate times, of course," he added hastily.

"Is she actually on bad terms with anyone?" Irene asked.

"Not as such," Kai said, considering the question. "But she gets on less well than most with my uncle Ao Ji—you haven't met him, he's the Dragon King of the Western Ocean. He is rigid in his opinions."

Irene could live without meeting any more dragon kings. One had been quite enough. "And are there any significant troubles in her court?"

Kai began to speak, then stopped. For half a minute he was silent. Finally he said, "Irene, we've always been good at navigating conversations that might compromise my family's interests. But that involves me not disclosing this sort of information. It helps us deal with . . ." He gestured vaguely.

"With the fact that I'm a Librarian and you're a dragon. And, ultimately, neither of us wants to compromise our family or our occupation?" Irene suggested.

Kai nodded. "I don't want to cross that line." But his tone suggested that he would very much like an excuse to share his thoughts on whatever it was.

Irene frowned. She considered the previous evening's events. "There's something going on that could seriously compromise the Library," she finally said. "But it could compromise one or more dragons too."

"If it's in those dragons' interests, I could at least give you the broad details," Kai said, relaxing. "Yes, then, there is significant news. One of Her Majesty's most senior ministers was assassinated a month ago. Ya Yu's court is in turmoil."

"Assassinated?" Irene said sharply. "Not retired?"

"No, definitely assassinated," Kai said. "It's a matter of high scandal. I don't know who's been accused. Unless it's the Fae, of course. They could easily be guilty of an action like that."

"And what are the implications of this assassination, besides the minister's death?"

"In terms of high politics?" Kai hesitated again. "You understand that I'm not likely to be told about that sort of thing. I may be of royal blood, but I am a youngest son, my mother was not of high rank, and I hold no current position. And even if I did know . . ."

"You'd be expected to keep your mouth shut about it?" Irene guessed.

Kai nodded. "Thank you for understanding. But I don't think it's unreasonable to tell you that Her Majesty is filling the minister's position with . . ." He looked for the right words. "Unexpected haste. Usually that sort of thing takes years, especially as it's such a key position. But this time the new appointment will be announced within five days."

"And who's taking the minister's place?"

"That's the interesting thing. There are two candidates, who have been set a number of highly challenging tests. The rumour is that the queen's set them a final private task to show their abilities."

"What happens to the loser?" Irene asked. Somehow she doubted there was a runners-up prize.

Kai stared over her shoulder, as he did when explaining something he found completely natural, but knew Irene was likely to have issues with. "Well, their family will be embarrassed, so naturally the loser will have to make amends. The most appropriate demonstration of apology would be to commit suicide . . . Of course, self-exile is an option, but I can't imagine anyone actually doing that." His tone made it clear that he thought suicide would be far less painful for any dragon than cutting himself off from court, family, and kindred. "But there will certainly be consequences."

"Damn," Irene said. She held her cup out for more tea. "I was really hoping I was being paranoid."

Then she stopped. "We need to get out of here right now."

Kai could have hesitated, or asked her what she meant, but instead he set down his cup and rose to his feet. "Do we need to take anything with us?"

"Just coats and money," Irene said, "and we go out the back way, in case the front is watched. I'll explain in a few minutes, but we can't risk staying here."

Five minutes later they were sitting in a small café down the street, from which they could watch the front door of their lodgings. Irene didn't let herself relax. If her guess was wrong, then they'd just wasted time and effort, but if she was *right* . . .

"You said you'd explain," Kai reminded her.

Irene ran through last night's events, from Jin Zhi's arrival onwards, and Kai's eyes narrowed as he listened.

"Sounds like the descriptions I've heard of Jin Zhi," he finally said. "And yes, she is one of the candidates for Minister Zhao's position. I've never actually met her. It's a pity I wasn't there."

"The whole thing was very carefully timed to make sure you weren't there," Irene said sourly. "Which is why we're sitting here now."

Kai raised an eyebrow.

"Jin Zhi let me walk away with the details of the book because she knew you were visiting your family," Irene said quietly. "And therefore she knew I couldn't discuss how explosive this situation really was. If her spies were watching you that closely, she would think—as I did—that you'd be there for a few days longer. Now, tell me, what's likely to happen if she finds that you came back early—and that we're having an informative little conversation like this?"

Kai's eyes narrowed. "She can't afford to take any further risks—the stakes of the competition are so high. You know too much, and you might be a threat. Which suggests there's more going on than she said."

Irene nodded. "I may be overreacting, but she probably knows our address, and I don't want to take any risks." She yawned.

Kai looked at her thoughtfully. "How much sleep did you get last night?"

"Not enough." After she'd left Jin Zhi, Irene had quietly slipped out of the hotel's back entrance and found somewhere else to spend the night. And she'd had to get up early to catch a zeppelin down to London; it was faster than the train, and she'd wanted to save time.

There had been nightmares too, about burning books and destroyed Libraries. Perfectly reasonable nightmares, based on the events of not long ago. But she wasn't going to discuss them.

"I dislike the fact that she treated you like a servant," Kai commented. His voice had an undertone to it that promised reprisals.

"Leave it for the moment," Irene said wearily. "I'm not going to waste my time feeling insulted. And don't you think we've got more serious problems to consider? Much more serious problems?"

"You're a Librarian-in-Residence," Kai said firmly. "And you're a Librarian, anyhow. That gives you a diplomatic ranking that any proper court would recognize. She behaved as if your honour was for sale. That sort of attitude is politically unwise. I don't like what it says about her."

"Let's get back to what Jin Zhi said, then," Irene said. "Assuming it was Jin Zhi and not just another gold dragon posing as her in order to confuse the issue. If she's telling the truth and her rival's enlisted another Librarian—who is her rival, by the way?"

"Qing Song," Kai said. "I only know the basics about both of them. Neither has any particular scandals to their name. I could try to find out more . . . if you don't mind it being known that I'm asking questions."

"When you say 'basics,' how far does that go?" Irene asked.

"The key word I kept on hearing about Jin Zhi was *gracious*," Kai said slowly. "Always courteous, always reasonable. Very much like the person you met, when she was being pleasant to you. Generous to her servants, amiable to her allies, polite even to her adversaries. Only loses her temper on rare occasions. Very good at playing the piano," he added as an afterthought. "But . . . unobjectionable. A convenient candidate. No real enemies."

"She sounds too good to be true."

Kai shrugged. "It can happen."

"Or just good at covering her tracks?" Irene asked.

Kai frowned. "That's a good point. Li Ming's cousin had said she's much less public than most of her rank about her activities and relationships. There might be something that she doesn't want people to know."

"Other than contacting Librarians on her own?"

"Yes, normally one would have a servant do that," Kai agreed. "Still, she's certainly competent. She passed all the other challenges the queen set. If she is doing something behind the scenes, that doesn't necessarily make her flawed."

Irene nodded. "And Qing Song?" Half of her attention was outside. Nobody had tried to approach their lodgings or do anything she could interpret as suspicious, but her instincts were still on the alert, from years of experience. She and Kai needed to stay out of sight.

"Oh, he has the experience," Kai said. "Three times now he and his servants have stopped Fae infiltration of worlds under his control. Though, to be technically accurate, one of those worlds was under a cousin's lordship. There was some criticism there. The cousin should have dealt with it himself, or should at least have *asked* for help before Qing Song stepped in." He thought about it. "A stern personality, Li Ming said, but not unjust. A firm hand in rulership and in punishment. Someone with strong expectations of the world around him, who might react badly if those expectations weren't met. A lord who expects other dragons to respect his territory and property."

Irene frowned. "Was that a warning from Li Ming? It sounds like one." If Ao Shun wanted a warning dropped unobtrusively in his nephew's ear, Li Ming would be the logical conduit.

"I didn't think so at the time." Kai paused, considering. "But why should it be? Why would he even think I'd go anywhere near Qing Song? He knows I'm with you at the moment."

"And he knows I'm a Librarian," Irene said. "I wonder how many other people have heard that Qing Song might be employing a Librarian?" Her stomach knotted in foreboding. If these rumours had already spread, then the situation might have passed the point where it could be disproved. And people were more than ready to believe gossip. There was no time to lose. She had to find out if this was true—and if it was, then she had to stop it. Or the Library was in grave danger.

"All right. Let's consider this," she finally said. "I've been approached by someone who was definitely a dragon, no doubt about that, and who *claimed* to be Jin Zhi, and who *claimed* that her rival—Qing Song, you say—was being helped by another Librarian to get this book. The approach was made at a time when you definitely wouldn't be there."

Kai nodded. "The timing's too exact for it to be an accident."

Irene considered the possible political fall-out. "Now, this could all be an attempt to slander Qing Song. Or it could be a bid to get Jin Zhi in trouble, by having someone posing as her. Or it could be someone else wanting to drag the Library into this. Or a Librarian could really be colluding with a dragon. In which case, it might only be a matter of time till the word gets out that Librarians are running errands for dragons and assisting with high-stakes political manoeuvres. At which point other dragons and Fae both start hunting us down—as tools or enemies. And that is a point I don't want to reach." Saying it made it all the more dreadfully plausible. She looked at Kai. "You know dragon court politics better than I do. Would you say any of these options are particularly likely? Or unlikely?"

"I don't know enough to say." Kai leaned forward, steepling his fingers in a gesture that Irene recognized as one that he'd borrowed from Vale. "Any of them are *possible*."

"And am I compromising you by discussing this with you?" Irene wanted to be absolutely clear on this. Dragging Kai in might make things even worse.

"No, I think it's fine—for the moment," Kai said slowly. "I don't have any personal ties to that court. I'm not telling you anything that isn't reasonably common knowledge. And my own father doesn't have a horse in the race himself."

Irene nodded. "Then we come back to the question of whether this collusion is real, and whether Qing Song does in fact have a Librarian helping him."

"It could be a personal friendship," Kai said. "Like ours."

"If that was so, then the Librarian shouldn't have let it go this far," Irene said quietly, "and they shouldn't have let themselves be found out. You and I have managed to get by, Kai, because technically *you're* helping *me*, and I'm not playing dragon politics. If Qing Song is in cahoots with this Librarian—call them X—and it becomes publicly known, that way danger lies. And if X gives Qing Song the book that lets him get Minister Zhao's position, then Librarians become *tools for hire*. They become *servants*. And they become generally known as allies of the dragons, which means they're automatically enemies of the Fae. Not to mention that if we support one dragon family or faction, then we make enemies of the others. The Library survives in the middle. We are not on anyone's side. If X exists and has done what Jin Zhi says they have, then X has just put Librarians in danger across all the alternate worlds."

And if I'm not careful, I might do the same. Because how long could she go on like this with Kai before someone accused them— wrongly—of exactly the same thing?

Kai reached across to take her hand. "You worry too much about possible implications," he said.

She looked up to see understanding in his eyes. He was getting to know her far too well. "It's part of my job to worry," she said, trying to make a joke of it. Trying to reassure herself as much as she was trying to reassure him. "I am supposed to be your mentor, after all. Management positions always come with ulcers attached. But this is serious. If it's real, then it's much more dangerous than just one Librarian doing a favour for one dragon."

He gave her hand a squeeze. "Let's not borrow trouble till it's actually here. What do you think we should do next?"

Irene pulled herself together. She had a metaphorical hand grenade in her lap, and she needed to work out what to do with it. "Do we have a time limit?" she asked. "You said earlier that the announcement of the new minister would be within five days. Does that mean they have five days left to find the book, or less than that?"

Kai pursed his lips, thinking. "Call it three days. Four at the maximum."

"And if neither of them brings the book to the queen?"

Kai shrugged. "I don't know, but the queen will be displeased, even if she awards the position to the one she considers less incompetent. Both of them will have disgraced their families. This sort of post won't be vacant again for centuries. Both the candidates have put their reputation and their families' good names at stake in order to compete for this position. I think you can expect both of them to be willing to try anything to avoid losing." His eyes darkened at the thought of what that *anything* might involve.

Irene was about to reply when one of the cabs rattling down the street outside drew to a stop outside their lodgings. "Well, damn," she said softly. "I'd been hoping I was wrong."

Kai followed her glance. "It might be someone else," he said.

"It might," Irene agreed. The two of them watched as the cab-driver swung down and held the cab-door open for the occupants to emerge. Jin Zhi was quite recognizable, even from across the street and through the café window, though the two men with her—the two large men—were strangers. "But it isn't."

"We could confront her," Kai suggested.

"She might take it badly. And there are so many breakable things around here." Like most of London, for a start. Irene had never witnessed a fight between dragons, and she didn't want to start now. "Right now I need a lot more information, and that means visiting the Library."

"And leaving through the café's backdoor before she sees us?"

"I like backdoors," Irene said.

CHAPTER 4

Kai was brooding as Irene led the way to a small local library. "Perhaps I should visit my contacts while you're checking inside the Library," he finally offered. "It'd save time. We could meet up afterwards and compare notes."

"It might take too long for us to reconnect," Irene said. "I did consider it, but what if you ended up being delayed for days, and I had no way of finding you? Or what if I was held up in the Library, since you can't access it without me?"

"I suppose you're right," Kai said reluctantly. "I wish I knew why it works that way."

"Why it works which way?" She showed her library card to the man at the front desk and was waved past. The main room was a comparatively tiny place with a very small selection of books, with a few doors off it leading to offices and storage. It had been built quite recently and it clearly showed it, with clock-work shelf extrusions and cheap wrought-iron girders, rather than the wood and stone of older libraries in London.

"Why I can go to other alternate worlds, assuming they aren't too high in chaos, and find people I know—but I can't reach the Library." Kai glanced around the room. "No witnesses," he added, in the same quiet tone of voice.

Irene couldn't help thinking that if some of the more powerful and less friendly dragons *could* reach the Library that way, it would have a much harder time maintaining its independence. "And something *I've* been wondering," she said, "is whether Jin Zhi will be able to find me in future, whatever world I'm in. She did hint at it, but she might have been bluffing."

"It's . . . unlikely," Kai said. "It's not usually the sort of thing we can do after a single meeting. Besides, she couldn't even sense you at the end of the street, drinking coffee."

Irene nodded. "So Jin Zhi couldn't get me looking for the book, so that she could drop in on me once I'd found it."

"She might regret it if she did," Kai said casually. "Interference with another dragon's, ah . . ." He gave Irene a sideways look, and she could almost see the words *property*, *possessions*, and *servants* being considered and discarded. "Interests. That sort of thing could even be a duelling offence."

Irene came to a stop in front of a side door to the building's cellars and focused her mind on the Language. **"Open to the Library,"** she said, grasping the handle.

On the other side there was now a spacious, well-lit room, floored and walled in steel, its shelves overfilled with irregular-looking books. She gestured Kai in, then shut the door behind her, feeling the portal close. Anyone trying to follow them from the alternate world they'd just left would only find the building's cellars. The Library could be reached solely by Librarians—and a very good thing too.

"Irish sagas," Kai said, checking a small sign that dangled from one shelf. "World designation A-529, copied from ogham script." He looked around at the handbound volumes, and at the stacks of computer printout and handwritten parchment piled on the floor. "That must have been a lot of transcription work for someone."

Irene shrugged. "Well, it's easier than bringing a pile of carved sticks or logs into the Library. When we're on a job for the Library, we only need a copy of the story in question, not the actual original. For which I'm deeply grateful. All right, next stage: find a computer. Preferably find two computers, so we can both do some research."

She led the way into the corridor outside. Paper lanterns hanging from the ceiling shrouded electric light bulbs, diffusing a soft light that caught sparks from the granite walls and floor. There were no windows in this corridor, only a long sequence of doors in either direction. Dust had gathered in the corners, and the air hung still and silent.

The next few minutes were spent peering into rooms piled with fascinating stacks of books, not finding any computers, and resisting the urge to stay and investigate anyway. This was the sort of thing that made Irene wish she had more free time—or, come to think of it, any free time at all to spend in the Library.

Since getting the job of Librarian-in-Residence to "her" alternate world, she'd been kept constantly on the go. Not only had there been a queue of missions to collect various books from that world, but she'd also needed to make certain arrangements. Setting up secondary identities, arranging places for visiting Librarians to stay, assembling handouts on current history, secret societies, etiquette, and so on. She'd avoided involving Vale, though a detective's connections with the underworld would have been invaluable. But as Vale was an ardent supporter of the law, explaining the need for her colleagues to come into his world to covertly "acquire" books would not have gone down well. She just hoped the two sides of her life wouldn't be in conflict anytime soon.

"Found one!" Kai called. "No, found *several*!"

"Coming!" Irene answered, and hurried to join him.

The room in question had a whole ring of computers around the central table, and was clearly the research nexus for the area. A pile of research notes in the middle was gathering dust. Irene commandeered some plain paper and a pen, passing it to Kai. "All right. Here's what we're going to do. Jin Zhi couldn't tell me the name of the world where the target book is located, in the terminology Librarians use. And I was hardly going to let her take me there. So she gave me as much information as she had about the world and the relevant version of *Journey to the West*. Now I'm going to drop Coppelia a quick email and warn her about the situation. You're going to research the book while I search for the world, and then we'll compare notes. We're looking to find a place that matches Jin Zhi's description, and which also contains the correct edition of the book. Right?"

"Right," Kai said, dropping down in one of the chairs. "So—the book is *Journey to the West*. And according to Jin Zhi, the plot contains higher-than-usual amounts of political satire, and a vastly increased plot for the dragon. And almost all copies were confiscated by the Chinese state at the time, due to this political satire. Anything else?"

"I wish there had been," Irene said, seating herself more carefully. "Go for it! Best of luck."

Her email to Coppelia was answered almost immediately. That in itself was worrying. Kai came round to read the response over her shoulder.

You do keep getting yourself into trouble, don't you, Irene?

Now, that was *totally* unwarranted.

I'm currently in the middle of something else extremely serious, I'm afraid. Other ongoing projects, and you're not the only fish in the sea. But you're right—this could be very bad indeed. So I want you to take this directly to Library Security—which is what I'd do anyway. I'll arrange a transfer shift from your current location to the central lifts in an hour's time, command word *unreliable*. Take a lift down. You'll need to speak to Melusine, and I'll let her know you're coming.

"I've never been down to Library Security before," Kai said. He sounded a little too enthusiastic about it.

"Nor have I," Irene admitted.

"Why not?"

"Because I've never done anything that warranted it, that's why not. You really don't *want* to get involved with Library Security, Kai."

Hopefully this will be a false alarm, but be very careful if it isn't.

Coppelia

Irene sighed. "Right. We have an hour's deadline. Back on the job."

She and Kai settled into their research. The Library files on alternate worlds varied in terms of how much information they contained, but they usually had at least basic history and socio-politics. She could rule out at least half the possible worlds. Jin Zhi had been clear that the book's world of origin didn't contain magic—or at least none that actually worked. (There would always be people who claimed to be able to use magic, whether it worked or not.)

Jin Zhi's notes had said America was the dominant power in the target world, driven by a huge surge in American exceptionalism and manifest destiny, and all that sort of stuff, in the early nineteenth century. It had broken away from Britain, but without civil wars before or after. China had been invaded by various powers and was a collection of warring states. Europe was barely hanging together, merged into a quivering mass, mostly controlled by a republic centred in France. (Previously on good terms with America, currently shifting to a who's-going-to-invade-first basis.) Africa and Australia were both off on their own and doing quite nicely for themselves, thank you very much. And nobody at all was on Antarctica, except possibly penguins. Some mass-communications technology, telephones, radio, and so on. Heavy criminal activity in America, Europe, and Britain, serious enough that Jin Zhi had thought it worth mentioning as a background detail. Electricity, but no nuclear power. Contraception. Lots of guns.

Irene rubbed her forehead as she noted down possible alternate worlds that would fit the description. She hated guns. They were so unreliable. A stray bullet could hit anyone.

After much data sifting, and with fifteen minutes to go, the Library records had revealed four potential alternate worlds. She raised her head from the computer screen to look across at Kai. "Any luck?"

"Still checking," Kai muttered.

Kai went back to his half of the research, and Irene pulled up the *Encyclopaedia* function on her own screen. This bit of the Library archives didn't relate to worlds or to books, but to Fae and dragons. It was a compendium of information contributed by Librarians in the field, heavily biased and full of personal opinion, so it wasn't necessarily reliable. On the other hand, it was better than nothing.

She wanted to be doing *something*. Time was limited, the stakes were high, and there was no knowing what Jin Zhi might do when she found out that Irene had slipped away. Irene tried not to think about what might happen if Jin Zhi held a grudge. She might have to retire her *Irene Winters, freelance translator, friend of Vale* identity permanently. That would be a shame. She *liked* being Irene Winters.

As it was, the upcoming meeting with Security loomed in her mind. They had a reputation of the scorched-earth type. If they were involved, then it was because a Librarian had done something bad enough to warrant extreme punitive action. Even though Irene had a relatively clear conscience at the moment, she didn't like the thought of willingly marching into their jaws.

Five minutes later she was tapping her pen on the notepaper and muttering to herself. Nothing on Jin Zhi, and nothing on Qing Song—or at least, not under those names. Nothing personal on the Queen of the Southern Lands, though there was a twenty-year-old listing of her ministers and various worlds where she had influence. Irene sent that document to the printer, frowning. Something Kai had said earlier was nagging at her . . . they were supported by their families, that was it. "Kai, can you tell me anything about the families of our two candidates?"

"Jin Zhi is of the Black Mountains family, and Qing Song is of the Winter Forest—" Kai started.

Irene held up a finger to pause him. "Kai, I meant to ask this earlier. All the references to oceans, lands, mountains, forests—is this a translation issue? Does it mean something different to dragons?"

"Yes," Kai said, drawing the word out slowly. "But it's not exactly a translation issue. I've carried you between worlds before now, so you know that dragons perceive the way the worlds are placed differently from humans."

Irene nodded, remembering an endless blue space with countless currents flowing through it in deeper shades: like a sea raised into the sky, or a sky as deep as the oceans. "Yes, that's true. All I could see was colour and emptiness. But you saw—no, you *perceived*—it differently?"

"Right. But I'm sorry, there *aren't* human words to express it." Kai spread his hands helplessly. "It's something we have to learn through experience. And we refer to some areas within and between worlds as oceans, or lands, or mountains or forests, or rivers, because those are the terms that we associate with our perceptions of those places. And that's why some families or some kingdoms have the names they do, because they refer to a particular world or group of worlds. Earth references are generally more orderly places, and water references are less orderly. Other than that, I can't give you convenient translations."

"Well, drat," Irene said. "So much for my hopes of learning a new language and expanding *my* perceptions."

That coaxed a faint smile from Kai. "I regret being the one to tell you this, but even languages can't do everything."

"Hush," Irene said, raising a finger to her lips. "That's heresy here. Anyhow, Black Mountains and Winter Forest families, right?"

"Precisely. And no, the two families don't get on well at all. They're not exactly enemies, but if they're involved in a political matter, then they'll be on opposite sides."

Irene tried a few searches on those terms. She did wonder, occasionally, if she should be grilling Kai for information on every dragon he knew and then putting it down in the database. But that would put Kai in an impossible position.

"There's something here about the Winter Forest family," she said in surprise, as it appeared on the screen in front of her.

Kai was on his feet and peering over her shoulder before she could even consider the protocol of his reading Librarians' comments on other dragons. "What does it say?" he asked.

"As you can see," she said drily, "the author approves of them."

Honourable, reliable, and consistent. Open to negotiation and willing to come to terms over the ownership of certain books, in return for information about Fae, the note said.

"Qing Song isn't usually described as open to negotiation," Kai said doubtfully.

"Perhaps they were dealing with a different family member," Irene suggested. She checked the author. "It was entered by someone called Julian, not anyone I've ever met . . ." She followed the link on his name. "And unfortunately he's unavailable to ask, due to having died a few weeks ago. Heart attack."

"The timing's . . . interesting," Kai said. His tone was very neutral, suggesting that he didn't want to be the first one to jump to paranoid conclusions. "Since that would have been about the time the search for the book began."

"I'll mark it as background," Irene said, noting it down. Let Security be paranoid: that was their job. "How's your research on the book going?"

"I have three possible worlds for the book," Kai said proudly. "A-15, A-395, A-658."

"And I've got four for the world." Irene checked her list and tapped her finger against the second. "And one of *mine* is A-658. We have a match!" For a moment the pure joy of successful research made her forget why they were investigating. Then the implications caught up with her. "So Jin Zhi's story could well be true."

She checked her watch. "And it's time to get that transfer shift. Come on."

Irene and Kai emerged from the transfer shift cabinet into the vaguely central area of the Library. This collection of rooms sprawled over several miles, and was widely believed to be expanding at moments when people weren't paying attention. It included vital areas such as the main classrooms for new trainees, the sets of rooms belonging to elder Librarians who couldn't walk far, and the main sorting points for incoming books collected from their native alternate worlds. As such, the area was moderately busy, and Irene and Kai nodded to various other Librarians or trainees as they passed.

"Over there," Irene said, nodding to the main lift-shafts. They ranged in size from heavy steel-walled lifts large enough to hold a lorry full of books, to little one-person lifts with brass fold-across lattice doors. "Pick a lift. Any lift. As far as I know, they all go down to Security, if necessary."

"If you've never been down there, how do you know?" Kai asked. He led the way to a moderately sized lift, one large enough to squeeze in half a dozen other people besides them.

"Well, that's what I was told," Irene admitted. She scrutinized the bank of buttons inside. They were labelled with a variety of floor names and numbers, but none actually read *Security*. After a moment she gave up and pressed the one labelled *Basement*.

The door slid shut, sealing the two of them inside the lift. The ceiling light flickered. Irene saw Kai twitch out of the corner of her eye, shifting his weight nervously from one foot to the other. A pointed jab of memory reminded her that it wasn't *that* long since he'd been locked in a prison cell, waiting to be auctioned. "I hope it's not too far down—" she began.

"State basement level," an automated voice intoned from the ceiling, with all the warmth and charm of a railway-station announcer.

Irene suppressed her own twitch. "Er, Security?" she said hopefully.

The light went out.

The lift began to fall.

CHAPTER 5

Irene's stomach dropped along with the lift as it fell down into darkness. There was absolutely no light, not even a fraction of a gleam on the lift metalwork or a glimmer in the overhead bulb. Her ears popped as the pressure changed. She reached out in sheer terror for something to hold on to, and caught hold of Kai.

He braced her, his body firm against her, the only thing she could be sure of in the pitch blackness. But he was shaking too, bone-deep shuddering that spoke of panic on the verge of breaking loose.

What went wrong? The thoughts shrieked in her head. *Did I say the wrong thing? Is this some sort of security measure? What happens when we hit the bottom?*

And then, abruptly, it all stopped. The lift came to a halt gently, as if it had been coasting down at a rate of mere inches per minute, rather than miles per second, and the light came on.

Sanity dribbled back into Irene's mind. She tentatively detached her fingers from Kai's shoulders. But it was harder to avoid looking at him, and she realized she was blushing. All her long-held principles about being in loco parentis were apparently much easier to crack than she'd thought. It simply took a dose of panic and here she was, clinging to him like the worst sort of romantic damsel, and wishing she could do more than just cling.

He was holding on to you too, the part of her mind that wasn't busy lecturing her pointed out. *You weren't the only one who was afraid.*

Kai was very nearly smirking. "First they assign us together," he said. "Then they put us in a dark box together and shut the door . . ."

Irene abruptly found it very easy to disregard her softer emotions, as she was now boiling over with embarrassment and longing to push Kai over the nearest convenient precipice. Unfortunately he'd probably turn into a dragon and fly away. "I'm sorry," she said stiffly. "That shouldn't have happened."

Kai released her, letting her step back. "Irene," he said carefully, choosing his words. "Just because you're my superior in the Library doesn't mean you have to be perfect. You've seen me at my weakest. I'm not going to say anything now—"

You are saying it, right here and now, Irene thought sourly. She could guess where this was going. He was always a perfect gentleman in his suggestions that she expand their relationship to include the bedroom, but that didn't stop him making them.

"—but I am an adult and I can make my own decisions, and if you don't believe that, then you shouldn't be letting me risk my life while we work together. Please bear this in mind next time I suggest we share a bed."

Irene felt the flush mounting on her cheeks again. "Your opinion is noted," she said as flatly as she could.

Did Kai think it was *easy* for her to keep on saying no to him? She was his friend. It would be so very straightforward to let it be more and simply say yes. Didn't he realize she was saying no for his own sake? She was in a position of authority. From the bits he'd let slip about dragon culture, she suspected that a dragon's liege-lord or liege-lady had pretty much any rights they cared to exercise over their servants. She wasn't going to take advantage of him like that.

She turned away and pushed the *Door Open* button hard enough that her finger hurt.

Irene stepped out into the foyer beyond. It was a large room, covered from floor to ceiling in smooth white tiles, with a heavy steel door at the far end. A couple of armchairs in daffodil-yellow upholstery sat next to the lift entrance. There was no way of knowing how far below ground-level they were. She looked around, then up towards a whirring noise near the ceiling. A camera focused on the two of them.

"Hello," she said, raising a hand in greeting. "I'm Irene, and this is Kai, my currently assigned student. I'm here to speak with Library Security."

Next to the steel door, one of the tiles at waist height slid to one side, revealing a flat metal pad. "Please place your right hand on the reader by the door," an anonymous voice intoned from the direction of the camera.

A little reluctantly, Irene walked across and put her palm against the metal pad. She'd had a number of bad experiences from touching things and then regretting it later, and the scars to go with them. Still, she should be safe in the Library . . .

A searing wave of electricity rippled across the pad, stinging her palm like a lash of nettles, and she yelped and jerked her hand back.

Kai looked down at his own hands and sighed. "My turn now?"

"Identity confirmed," the voice droned. The steel door in the wall slid back. Beyond it was a small airlock-sized room, with another steel door on the far side. "The Librarian is to step into the waiting area. The student will wait outside."

"But I—" Kai started, then stopped. "Security. Right. Okay." His glance up at the low ceiling was distinctly unhappy.

"I'm sorry," Irene said. "If I'd known, I'd have left you upstairs."

She realized half a second too late where *that* statement led to, and she could see the same thought going through Kai's head. Fortunately he didn't make any witty comments about not wanting to miss that lift. He simply nodded and dropped into one of the armchairs. "Be quick?" he said plaintively.

"I'll try," Irene reassured him.

Still shaking her hand to dispel the pins and needles, she stepped inside the airlock. The door slid shut behind her. She looked around for cameras but couldn't see any. In fact, there wasn't *anything* visible except the flat metal of the walls. It wasn't even clear where the dead white light was coming from.

Of course there had to be some sort of ventilation. Common sense demanded it. Or else anyone trapped inside would simply suffocate . . .

"Please show your Library brand," the disembodied voice said. It was more human now, and Irene was fairly sure it was a woman speaking.

"This is going to take a moment," she warned, starting to pull her coat off. She would have preferred a method of identification that didn't involve her stripping down to show her bare back.

"Oh, *I'm* in no hurry," the voice said. "Take your time."

Irene took a deep breath, reminded herself that Library Security presumably had reasons to be paranoid, and unbuttoned her dress at the back. She slipped it down to show the Library mark across her shoulders. "Should I turn any particular way so you can see it?" she asked politely.

"That'll do nicely." There was a flash, and Irene flinched. For a moment the Library brand seemed to vibrate, and her bones ached in response, like the thrumming of tracks when the train was a long distance away. "Thank you. You can cover yourself again now. State your name and Library position. In the Language."

Irene pulled her dress back up, doing up the buttons. **"I am Irene; I am a Librarian; I am a servant of the Library,"** she said. "And I did say earlier who I was."

The door in front of Irene slid open at last.

She picked up her coat and quickly stepped through. Then she stopped, looking around.

The primary word that came to mind was *cave*. It was spacious but low-ceilinged, and the shelving only went up to four feet high on the surrounding walls. Several computers and monitors were netted together with a web of cabling on the central table, amidst a sea of scribbled notes and highlighted sheets of paper. The walls were lined with books, heavy volumes in thick leather binding; they were too far away for Irene to read the titles or authors. Doors at the far end of the room suggested further recesses. The light came from various points in the ceiling, where wide pale lampshades glowed like insectoid eyes.

The woman sitting in a wheelchair next to the computers lifted her head to inspect Irene. "I like to confirm these things," she said, her gaze assessing and uncomfortable. "Welcome to my retreat." She had mouse-blonde hair trimmed close to her head, and was dressed for comfort in a plain checked shirt and jeans. Her wheelchair looked high-tech and modern, but the tartan rug thrown over her lap was battered and threadbare.

"Melusine." Irene recognized her from a previous encounter, during Alberich's attack on the Library. Melusine had been with the senior Librarians delivering the briefing.

"Correct. Kindly forgive the precautions." It was a demand rather than a request. "If anyone was trying to betray the Library, we'd be a primary target."

"That sounds reasonable," Irene said cautiously. *Paranoid, but reasonable.* "And I'm assuming Coppelia forwarded my email about our problem? It could be extremely serious."

"Indeed it could—if you have your facts straight." Melusine tapped on the keyboard and examined the computer screen. It was out of Irene's line of sight, so she couldn't see whether Melusine was viewing a message from Coppelia, checking related evidence, or looking up information on Irene.

After a moment Melusine said, "You have an interesting record."

Saying *I'm delighted that you think so* would be satisfying but rude. Irene shrugged. "I'm not sure I can claim that much credit. It mostly involved just responding to events as they happened."

"Child of two Librarians," Melusine said, apparently reading from the screen. "Raziel and Liu Xiang." She paused for a moment, just long enough for Irene to relax, then added, "Adopted."

Irene felt her mouth go dry. "What . . . Are you absolutely sure—about that last part?"

"Why?"

"Because *they* never said so." A few months ago Irene had been told that two Librarians couldn't have children. Which had left her whole parentage in doubt. But the person who'd told her had been Alberich, the Library's worst enemy. It had been easy, after the fact, to write it off as a lie meant to distract her. She'd avoided thinking about it. She hadn't even asked her parents.

And was that because, in the deepest part of her mind, she'd been afraid of what they would say?

Melusine shrugged. "What they may or may not have told you isn't my business. My job is Library security. Are you disputing what I've just said?"

Irene wanted to dispute it. She wanted to stamp out of the room and slam the door behind her. But most of all she wanted to find her parents and shout, *Why didn't you tell me?*

She wanted to cry. Her eyes were hot with unshed tears.

"Just go on," she said, hearing the strain in her own voice.

Melusine didn't change her tone. It remained light, uninflected, dispassionate. "Educated at boarding-school, owing to your parents having growing problems with your behaviour."

"It was nothing like that!" Irene protested.

Melusine gave her a pale-eyed stare. Her eyes were as cold and distant as the winter sky at dawn. "Who's reading this record, you or me?"

"Well, you are, but—"

"Put your complaint in writing." The older Librarian looked back at the screen. "The usual sort of apprenticeship. Mentored by Bradamant for a while, but that was dissolved at your request. Though you weren't the only junior to do so."

"No, I don't think I was," Irene agreed blandly. She was mostly over her tendency to twitch at any mention of Bradamant—a competent Librarian, but also manipulative, ambitious, and prone to blaming any failures on her students. It seemed that Library Security had noticed.

Melusine nodded. "Appointed as Librarian-in-Residence extremely early in your career, for good performance. Placed on probation after you abandoned your post without orders, in order to retrieve your apprentice, Kai. Yes, I do know what he is." She looked up from the screen. "And yes, I do realize that the whole probation business was political—despite his successful retrieval, we had to be seen to be taking steps."

"I didn't get into this job to play politics." Irene tried not to let too much resentment slip into her voice. "Is there a point to this career review?"

"I'm trying to get a better understanding of you." Melusine didn't smile. She inspected Irene as though she were a substandard essay. "You've associated with Fae and dragons. You survived *two* encounters with Alberich." Her tone shifted from bland to corrosive at the name *Alberich*, and Irene nearly flinched. "This isn't standard practice. At all. Most Librarians manage to get through their careers without anything half as dramatic. I was . . . curious."

"If the Library didn't want me to associate with dragons, then they shouldn't have assigned me to be Kai's mentor," Irene snapped. "And the Fae just happened to me. You know, like cockroaches. Have I answered all your questions?"

"Are you in a hurry?"

"Actually, yes." Irene thought of Kai, outside on his own, trapped in a small room fathoms underground. "We have a possible crisis on hand. And my student's waiting outside. As you know."

"Only authorized Librarians are allowed in here."

"It's less than a year since Kai was kidnapped and imprisoned by the Fae. He doesn't like being shut in small places, and I don't see why I should keep him waiting any longer than necessary."

"I can send him back up in the lift," Melusine offered.

"I'm not sure he'd go," Irene said reluctantly. "He's a bit protective."

"Then I suppose we should probably take his comfort into consideration." It wasn't clear whether Melusine was joking or serious. "Explain everything, as though I hadn't seen your email to Coppelia. I want the details."

Wishing there were a second chair in the room so that she could sit, Irene ran through the sequence of events again. She started with the conversation with Jin Zhi and continued to her own research in the Library, with Kai's comments included.

Melusine paused her from time to time to ask a question, but otherwise her reactions were hard to read. She folded her hands in her lap, leaving her computers alone, and didn't even twiddle her fingers. Irene would have been encouraged by some sort of response, rather than this stillness.

Finally Irene ran dry of information. "I don't want to sound as if I'm panicking," she finished, "but I think this could be very serious. Librarians in the field depend on the Library's neutrality to survive casual encounters with Fae and dragons. If that's gone, then we're all in danger individually—and it can only be a matter of time till the Library itself is under threat." She stood there, feet aching, waiting to be asked more questions.

Melusine nodded. "Yes," she said slowly. "I think we may have a problem here. A big one."

"You believe me, then?"

"Oh, I always believed you, but it was possible that you'd been deceived. But this is sounding uncomfortably plausible. The book is on A-658, you say." She tapped in a query on her computer and inspected the result. "No Librarian-in-Residence, and no authorized or requested activity there for fifteen years now, though the last Librarian who was sent there did leave a cache behind for emergencies. Current activity . . . hmm. Let's have a look." She turned her wheelchair and it glided across to one of the low shelves of books. Irene realized, a little belatedly, that everything in the room was set up to be reachable from Melusine's chair.

"Do you have anything on Qing Song or Jin Zhi?" Irene asked. "Anything that's not in the general records, that is."

"Only their names, families, and court affiliation," Melusine said. "Nothing more than what your apprentice told you. No—what's the right term?—'hot gossip.' I can and will make enquiries, but that'll take time." She tapped the edge of the shelf. "A-658, please."

The books began to slide smoothly along the shelf as if it were a conveyer belt, vanishing into the wall at each end of the room. After about twenty seconds they came to a stop, and Melusine pulled out the one next to her hand. It was bound in red leather, with *A-658* on the spine. Irene went to peer over Melusine's shoulder.

"This records all transit to and from that world," Melusine explained. She didn't command Irene to stand back or look away, to Irene's relief. "If a Librarian has been visiting the place, then it'll show on the records here."

Irene watched as Melusine flipped through the thin pages. The entries were somewhat like passport stamps, showing the names of the Librarians involved and the internal Library date when they used the Traverse. It was fascinating to have this highlight on Library history. While Irene had a reasonable grasp of the history of a number of alternate worlds—all right, a vague grasp—she knew very little about the Library itself. It had always been there, and presumably it always would, and nobody had more than speculation about how or why it was first created. And junior Librarians were not encouraged to ask questions.

Alberich might have known more, but Alberich was dead. Probably. Hopefully.

"Here." Melusine ran her finger down the list of names. "Evariste. Now that *is* interesting." But her tone suggested she'd just discovered a nest of bookworms in a favourite novel.

"He entered that world a month ago," Irene noted. The previous entry caught her eye and she frowned. "But . . ."

"Yes, precisely," Melusine said. "Evariste entered that world from the Library a month ago. That was two days after he *entered the Library from that world*, going in the reverse direction. But there's nothing in the record here about how he got into that world in the first place."

"Which means that he reached that world through either Fae or dragon transport," Irene said slowly, thinking it through. "So Jin Zhi might have told the truth and he was working for Qing Song. If so, Qing Song could have brought him to that world, but then Evariste would have needed to enter the Library through that world's Traverse—in order to work out what the world's designation was. Then he could research the book before going back there—"

"Yes, quite so," Melusine agreed, cutting off Irene's increasingly long string of speculation. She passed the book to Irene. "Put that back on the shelf. I'm about to look up Evariste's record, and this time you don't get to lean over my shoulder."

Irene re-shelved the book, feeling a frisson of excitement. She shouldn't feel pleased at the growing mass of evidence—quite the opposite—but at the same time there was a certain satisfaction that she hadn't been wasting her efforts.

Melusine grunted softly to herself. "Oh, did he, now . . . All right, Irene, we have some more information. Evariste is on compassionate leave. The Librarian who recruited him died last month of a heart attack, and Evariste was allowed some time off to sort out the man's affairs and so on. No record on where he was going to spend his leave, though one would assume it would be his recruiter's assigned world, G-14. No reason to assume anything odd there."

Something about the time factor was nagging at Irene. "Who was his recruiter?"

"Julian. Librarian-in-Residence to G-14."

And now the nagging was turning into a full-blown alarm bell. "Not the Julian who"—Irene pulled out her notes and checked them—"made a comment in the Library *Encyclopaedia* about the Winter Forest family of dragons, Qing Song's family—saying that they were reliable and consistent and open to negotiation?"

Melusine tapped some more keys and then stopped. "The very same," she said softly. "The very, very same. And now we have Minister Zhao assassinated, the Queen of the Southern Lands scrambling to fill her position, and the Fae testing their boundaries. And the Library may be about to be dragged into the middle of the whole conflict zone. While Julian's protégé has wandered off course, and is possibly playing very dangerous games with one of the Winter Forest's most aggressive scions."

"I thought you'd said you didn't know anything about him," Irene commented.

"Barely anything," Melusine said, brushing it off. "Your Kai already told you he was dangerous. I'm telling you that both Qing Song and Jin Zhi are dangerous. No dragon is safe. And Evariste doesn't even have *your* experience with dragons. He's an extremely good researcher, but he hasn't your level of exposure to practical field operations." She turned the computer screen so that Irene could see it. The dark-skinned young man in the photo had perhaps been photographed at a graduation, given the gown and hood he was wearing over a neat suit and tie. He had an air of dazzled disbelief and triumph, and was smiling at the camera. "He was due to be seconded to other Librarians for the next few years, for seasoning. I can easily believe that he's out of his depth."

The theoretical mouse that Irene had smelled earlier had become a full-blown rat. No, make that a plague rat. "What do we do?"

"You brought this one to my attention, which means that you're first in line to sort it out." Melusine swivelled round smoothly, and again Irene had the sense she was being inspected and assessed. "You're ideally qualified for the job. You're used to operating without backup or support, and you have a reputation as a rogue agent. If things go badly wrong, we may need to claim that you were acting on your own, and cut you off."

"Forgive me if I'm not exactly jumping at this chance," Irene said, with a growing feeling of dismay. "Phrases like *we may need to cut you off* sound rather final. I'd *like* some support. I'd *like* some backup. I'd like some guidance."

"That's part of the problem," Melusine said. "We have no idea what the situation is. As you suggested, it might even be a complicated lure meant to trap us into doing something that can be used against us later. I'm not trying to flatter you, but you *are* good at assessing a situation and deciding on the most appropriate course of action. It's possible—but highly unlikely—that this situation has an innocent explanation. We won't know until we've spoken to Evariste. But we need an agent on the scene who can determine whether or not we're compromised, and take action if we are. And with things being as possibly catastrophic as they are, it also needs to be an agent whom we can claim acted on their own initiative and cut loose. If necessary."

Irene swallowed. "This is not reassuring."

"The door's behind you," Melusine said with a shrug. "If you aren't prepared to take this risk, this mission, then I can't force you. I will just have to give the job to someone else. Probably someone not as well-qualified. Without your background knowledge. And with several hours' delay while I find them and brief them. It's entirely up to you."

Irene stared at her in combined admiration and disgust. "Have I told you that I hate emotional blackmail?"

"I'll add it to your record."

Irene reluctantly turned her mind back to the job. "Can you send Evariste a message the Library way?" she asked. It was possible for the Library to send a message to any Librarian, printing it out on all the written material surrounding them. While it was costly in terms of energy, surely a situation like this warranted the effort. "For all we know, he's a prisoner and being forced into this."

"We can, and we will, but he doesn't have to answer it. Which brings us to the next point on the agenda. How *you* find him."

"I'm really hoping you have some special secret way to do that," Irene said resignedly. "One that we regular Librarians don't get told about. Because otherwise, trying to find one man in a strange world is going to take time. Even if I look for the nearest draconic disturbance and assume he's involved."

"Fortunately for you, you're correct." Melusine picked up a sheet of blank paper from the desk, then steered her wheelchair across to the far wall and a shelf there, lined with cream-bound volumes. She tapped it in the same way she'd done to the previous one. "E, please."

The books cycled through as the world-access ones had done, but this time Melusine was forced to check several volumes. She finally settled on *EU-EW XIV*, opening it to a particular page and laying it in her lap. "Stand back," she advised.

Irene kept her distance but watched with interest.

Melusine laid the blank piece of paper across the open page of the book. "**Copy the name of Evariste,**" she said in the Language.

The blank paper literally sizzled, shuddering against the book as if someone were pressing a hot iron against it on the other side. Irene's own brand seemed to fizz for a moment in sympathy, and Melusine twitched her shoulders as if she was feeling the same thing.

"There," Melusine said. She removed the paper, and closed the book and re-shelved it. She offered Irene the paper, which was now marked with a full Library brand—Evariste's name in the centre, in the Language, surrounded by the usual Library cartouche.

Irene took the paper carefully, examining it. Rumour had it that if you examined the surrounding markings in a Library brand closely enough, such as with an incredibly high-powered microscope, you would find that they were composed of words from the Language in very small print. It was the sort of thing that might be true. "I can use this to find him?" she asked.

"The principle of similarity," Melusine said. "Use the Language with this to locate him—using the symbol to scry for him on a map, employing directional pointers, the usual sort of thing. He's been off our radar for nearly a month now, so he might be anywhere in that world."

Irene nodded. "I have another question while I'm here, if you don't mind."

"Oh, ask, ask," Melusine said. "Don't be so polite. I'm interested in getting the job done."

Irene was fairly sure that if she *stopped* being polite, Melusine would be significantly displeased. But that was one of the perks of being higher-ranking: you could tell your juniors to cut back on the courtesy, while simultaneously being offended if you felt they were being too rude. A win-win situation, for the people on top. "All right," she said. "As I understand it, dragons can trace people to a particular world. And if they follow them to that world, then they may end up emerging right on top of where they are in that world. Is there any way that I can *stop* dragons finding me that way? Jin Zhi could try following me, and I'd rather not have her in my general neighbourhood, let alone closer."

"Library wards," Melusine said briefly. On seeing Irene's blank look, she explained, "The usual Library wards that you'd put up if you were trying to avoid Fae interference—get inside a large collection of books and invoke the Library's presence. That'll keep dragons from tracking you as well, so long as you stay inside. And speaking of dragons finding you, try to avoid it. Ideally you'll be in and out without them knowing you're there. Keep Kai away from them too. If you get him involved in this political situation, and we have to explain it to his family—"

"You don't have to tell me," Irene said. "I'll need to take the blame."

Melusine nodded, a little reluctantly. "I'm afraid so. We can hide you, if you get back here safely. But you wouldn't be able to leave here for a few centuries, until they'd given up looking for you."

So it wouldn't be just Irene's career at stake, but her personal life too—her friends, Vale, Kai, the world she'd grown used to living in . . . "Then it's a good thing I'm planning not to get caught," she said, forcing optimism into her voice. "Or lying about my identity, if I do. Now, you said the previous Librarian who went to A-658 on official business left an emergency cache behind?"

"Yes, and I *was* going to give you the details." Melusine glanced at one screen, scrawled down an address and a number, and passed it to Irene. "Stop in at Wardrobe after you leave here, and pick up some appropriate clothing for Jazz Age America—suits, short skirts, guns, whatever. The Traverse to that world comes out in the Boston Public Library in America, so that's where you'll be arriving. It shifted there in 1875. Used to be to the Escorial Library in Spain. When Gassire was there, he left a stash of local money and identity papers at the Northern Bank in Boston. Here's the bank address, that's the safe-deposit box number, and I'm sure you won't have any problems getting access. Assuming that Evariste hasn't already emptied the safe-deposit box, I suppose, in which case you're on your own. You can track Evariste from there. The *Journey to the West* is a Chinese text, so I suppose he may be in China. Good thing that world has planes. We haven't time for you to take a slow boat. Any remaining questions? Your student will be waiting."

"Just one." Irene didn't want to ask it, but she couldn't avoid it any longer. "What do I do if Evariste *is* cooperating with the dragons?"

The faint traces of camaraderie, such as they were, drained out of Melusine's face. "That can't be permitted. You're to bring him back here to answer questions, by whatever means you find necessary. Unless there's a watertight explanation for his actions, he may be facing far worse than simply suspension or probation. You understand how serious this is?" She waited for Irene's nod. "We *can-*

not afford to look as if the Library is playing politics. We can't even let that rumour get started. You were right: this could be fatal to all the Librarians currently out working in their worlds, and to the Library itself. Evariste may be an innocent dupe, he may have been deceived or threatened into this, but ultimately that's not important. You need to pull him out of there now and close the situation down. Whatever it takes."

Irene nodded. "Understood."

And she knew that she might just have agreed to his death sentence.

CHAPTER 6

It was always difficult to decide where one should hide vitally important papers when going into dangerous situations. An outer pocket? Too easily lost—or too easily found by casual searches. An inner pocket? Better, though if you were being searched, it was still likely to be found, and in that case it was clear the document was important. Tucked into the cleavage or clipped inside a stocking-top? Much more uncomfortable than romance novels would have you think. Irene settled for the inner-pocket approach for the paper with Evariste's name on it, and hoped that nobody would be interested in it anyway.

"It was helpful of Melusine to arrange a transfer shift to the Wardrobe, and then to A-658's Traverse," she said. It had saved them half a day's walk through the Library. And they now had clothing roughly suitable for this nineteen-twenties America. Kai was embracing his sharp-fitting zoot suit and fedora with enthusiasm, while Irene was simply grateful for a knee-length skirt that she could run in.

"No, it was merely practical." Kai would be the first to deny that he was sulking, but his mood since having to wait in Melusine's antechamber was thoroughly contrary. Irene had yet to venture an opinion he agreed with. "A significant matter needs a quick response. She'd have been even more practical if she'd sent additional Librarians."

"Besides us?"

"Besides you. She made it clear that she didn't consider me a Librarian."

"She's paranoid," Irene said. "She made me strip down to show her my own Library mark before she'd allow me in. And I'm fairly sure she had a gun in her wheelchair underneath that blanket. And she knew you were a dragon. I'm surprised she didn't try to stop you coming along, given how the situation's shaping up . . . Note that I'm not on *her* side, Kai."

"There wasn't even anything to read," Kai muttered.

Irene rolled her eyes in exasperation. "If the worst that comes of this is you being stuck in a cellar for half an hour with nothing to read, then we've been lucky."

She looked round the room they were standing in one last time. It was stacked full of Westerns from A-658. The covers were festooned with lurid pictures of stern-jawed cowboys, rearing horses, and women falling out of their bodices. She hoped she never had to go anywhere like that. Horses weren't one of her enthusiasms. "Anyhow, let's get moving. It should be late afternoon or early evening by the time we get there. If we're lucky, the bank will still be open."

She walked over to the door and turned the handle, pushing at it. For a moment the door seemed to stick, as if hampered by something on the other side, and she frowned.

"Is something the matter?" Kai asked, dropping his moodiness.

"Maybe there's something leaning against it on the other side. Just a moment." Irene shoved at it, and this time it gave way; she stumbled through into the room beyond, and then stood absolutely still, horrified.

The place was a ruin. The noise of the city beyond the walls was like distant mockery, with the faint hum of traffic and voices a horrible contrast to the recent damage that had hit the building they stood in.

In the early-evening light, recently fallen timbers and collapsed brickwork were everywhere. The room they'd entered was typical of nineteenth-century American or European municipal buildings, but it was badly damaged on one side. The wall had fallen into the room, charred with scorch-marks. One timber had fallen against the door that they'd just come through—the blockage that Irene had pushed away. Tattered books lay everywhere, scorch-marks like stains on pages white as bone. There was dust in the air—from some recent explosion or fire—and it made Irene choke. She put her hands against her face, trying to breathe, trying to calm herself. Trying not to think of fire, burning pages, smoke, and ruin—and Alberich's voice above all of it.

"This conflagration, or blast, or whatever it was . . ." She looked around her. "This must be very recent. Look, the ceiling's gone." She could simply look up and see the twilight sky above, the clear blue of dusk. Her voice sounded strange to her own ears. She had to pull herself together, she thought remotely. The situation was too dangerous for her to have some sort of flashback here. She felt herself digging her nails into the palms of her hands and forced herself to be calm, composed, rational. It didn't help—not deep down, not where it really mattered. She still remembered fire and books burning. "But none of the books are wet yet. So they can't have been rained on. We need to find out what's happened. And when. And how."

Irene began to pick her way across the fallen stones that covered the floor, then looked up in surprise as Kai caught her wrist. "What is it?"

"Are you all right?"

"Of course I am." Her momentary weakness had passed as the memories faded. She was entirely in control of herself again. She *had* to be. "I'm just *furious*. That's all. How someone could *do* a thing like this, destroy a place like this . . . Even if it isn't involved with our investigation, I want someone to *pay* for this."

She shook Kai off angrily and walked across to kick the door open. The corridor beyond was blocked to the right by fallen masonry and shattered windows. They had to turn left and then half climb down past the stairway to reach the ground-floor. Every movement disturbed stone-dust from the explosion damage and set trapped pages fluttering as if reaching for assistance.

"How much longer will this place stay linked to the Library?" Kai asked as he followed her.

"I don't know," Irene had to admit. "I'm grateful it allowed us to get through—but who knows how long the gateway will hold? We don't go round destroying libraries just to test theories about what would happen if we did . . ."

Kai fell silent. Outside, beyond the broken walls of this shattered building, Irene could hear the hooting of car horns, the bells of trolley-buses, occasional yells and shouts. But in here there was nothing but the destruction all around her, and all the fallen books, with nobody even trying to save them. It was like walking through a personal hell, with a layer of glass between her and the

rest of the world. She wasn't even conscious of Kai a few steps behind her any more. And she wondered, *Should I have come earlier?
Would that have made a difference? If I'd come straightaway, or per-
suaded Melusine or Coppelia faster, or . . .*

Kai grabbed her again, and she realized they were approaching
one of the building's outer walls. "Irene, do we have a plan?"

She forced herself to focus. She would have tried breathing
deeply, but there was still too much dust in the air. It burned her
eyes. "Nothing's changed. We're going to the bank first. Money.
Documents. Accommodation."

"You got my attention at the word *money,*" a strange voice said.

Irene and Kai both turned. A man was watching them, standing
in a crevice between two fallen walls that gave him a commanding
view of the area. His suit was pin-striped and sharply cut, and his
hat was tilted to half conceal his eyes. Stone-dust had settled on his
shoulders and sleeves, suggesting that he'd been waiting there for a
while.

Of course, the thing that *really* caught Irene's attention was the
gun that he was holding, pointed directly at the two of them. It
was about a yard long, and he was supporting it with one hand
while keeping the other on the trigger. She didn't know very much
about guns, but it looked large and unpleasant. "Is that a Thomp-
son submachine gun?" she said.

"I see you're an educated type, lady. We call it a tommy gun.
Don't give me no reason to fire and we'll do just fine." He pursed
his lips and whistled. An answering whistle came from their right,
followed by approaching steps.

"But why are you pointing a gun at us?" Irene hoped that
sounded like an innocent question, rather than just a completely
stupid one. But then pointing guns at people frequently resulted in

stupid comments. She'd been on both sides of the barrel, so she should know.

"That's how it goes," the man said unhelpfully. "Rob, you think he's going to want to talk with them?"

Another man emerged from the shadows. He was holding a tommy gun too, and like the first one, he was pointing it right at them. This was a significant problem. Irene knew a number of ways to disable a gun by using the Language, but words took time. And if either of those men so much as twitched a finger on the trigger, Irene and Kai could end up dead.

"He said he wanted to interview anyone caught wandering around here," the presumed Rob said. "I reckon that's a yes."

"Right. Don't try anything stupid, you hear me? Or you'll both regret it." The first man gave a quick jerk with his gun towards their left, down a shattered stretch of colonnade. "Walk along there nice and easy, and stop when we tell you. There's a gentleman who'd like a word."

Irene didn't have to look behind her to know that Kai was tense. She reached out to touch his sleeve. "Let's do what the gentleman tells us," she said, putting a quiver in her voice.

Weighing the alternatives, she decided to run first and answer questions later. They had a job to do. As the men had relaxed at her apparent capitulation, she focused her words. **"Dust, rise."**

As she spoke, she dropped to the ground and rolled sideways, pulling Kai down as well. Dust billowed upwards from the ground, from every nook and crevice, swelling into a choking, eye-burning cloud around them.

A quick spray of bullets ripped through the air above their heads, and then one of the men yelled, "Stay where you are! Or we'll shoot!"

Without needing to exchange a word, Irene and Kai rose and quickly edged sideways. Irene caught Kai's sleeve so they weren't separated. A few more seconds and they'd be out of these thugs' immediate zone of fire.

It was an absolutely *textbook* escape, and in an ideal world it wouldn't have been spoilt by Irene turning her ankle on a loose stone and going down with an audible thud, losing her grip on Kai.

She tried to pull herself to her feet, but Rob was abruptly on top of her, pointing the gun directly at her. There were no ifs or buts in his reddened eyes. If she tried anything at all, she could tell he'd pull the trigger.

Irene raised her hands meekly. "You got me," she said. "My friend's already out of here."

She knew Kai would obey her implicit instruction to make a break for it, no matter how unhappy he felt about leaving. To be fair, Irene wasn't that happy about it herself.

The other man loomed out of the dust. "On your feet," he ordered.

Irene pulled herself upright, wincing. "I've sprained my ankle," she said pitifully.

"Hop," Rob advised. "We'll walk slow."

Irene limped along, exaggerating her difficulty in walking, with the two men a few paces behind her—close enough that she didn't have a chance of dodging and running for it, but far enough away that she couldn't try to grab at them. On the whole, she had to rate these two as professionals. She tried to convince herself this was a positive sign. Less chance of being shot by accident.

She was escorted to a boarded-up side door, where a third gunman was stationed. His eyes widened as he saw her, but he nodded to the other two mobsters.

"You call the boss, Pete," Rob said. "We've got someone here he's going to want to talk to."

"He might not be around," Pete whined. "You know he's been out of town these last couple of days."

"Yeah, well, this dame had better hope he *is* around, or she's going to be standing on that busted ankle of hers a lot longer. Now get to it before the cops take an interest."

Pete muttered, but put down his gun—out of Irene's reach—and left through the side door. The boards pulled aside easily, taped in place rather than nailed down, more of a visible deterrent than an actual barrier.

Irene mentally debated whether to signal for Kai, or wait to see if she could get anything out of this boss. The need for information won. "Mind if I sit down?" she asked.

"No problem, but keep your hands clear and where I can see them," Rob said. "You want a cigarette?"

"Not for me, thanks." Irene eased herself to the ground, rubbing her ankle. The more helpless they thought she was, the better.

"Suit yourself."

She tried to start a conversation a couple of times, with no luck. Finally she gave up, and hoped that Kai was less bored than she was. And *neither* of them had anything to read this time.

After about fifteen minutes the barrier swung open again, and Pete poked his head around it. "He's here," he said. "The usual car."

Rob put down his tommy gun but pulled a revolver from an inner holster. He kept Irene covered while his friend did the same. "We're going to walk out onto the sidewalk and to the car that's parked there," he informed her. "You just keep on behaving yourself."

"I just wish you'd tell me what's going on," Irene tried.

"Sorry," Rob said. "That ain't what they're paying me for."

Rob took Irene's arm, pressing the revolver unobtrusively into her side, and walked her onto the street, towards a car parked by the curb. The other man was just a few paces behind.

The street was busy, with yellow cabs shooting by and people walking past. It was almost strange to see so many people without the scarves or veils that Irene had grown used to in Vale's world—a combination of local fashion and local pollution. Instead hats were worn jauntily, both male fedoras and female cloche hats. Clothing blazed out in vigorous colours, with all the advantages of cheap machine-made dyes. The whole street scene buzzed with an energy completely different from the quiet drive of Vale's world, with people hailing each other or talking loudly as they strolled past, rather than moving through the fogs and murmuring politely so as not to disturb other pedestrians. But nobody looked twice at Irene and her escorts. If anything, they were rather obviously *not* looking at them, which gave Irene a good idea of how freely organized crime was operating in this city.

The windows of the car were darkened glass. She couldn't see inside. If she was going to make a run for it, she needed to do it now.

Then she realized the car wasn't idling at the curb: the engine was dead. She'd have at least a few seconds of warning before being driven away anywhere, long enough to do *something*. She'd play along.

"Get in," Rob ordered. The other man was already opening the rear car door, muttering something to whoever was inside. Still exaggerating her limp, Irene stepped up on the running-board, ducking her head to enter the car.

There was another man sitting inside. It took a moment for

Irene's eyes to grow accustomed to the darkness and see him clearly, but one thing was very evident from her first glimpse. He was a dragon.

He was wearing the same basic type of three-piece suit as the two men who'd escorted her to the car, but it was more expensive by an order of magnitude. No surprise there; Irene had yet to meet a dragon (admittedly she'd only met five so far, that she knew of) who didn't prefer high-quality clothing. His skin was pale enough to be almost luminescent in the enclosed darkness of the car. He was handsome, with the sort of profile that begged to be sculpted in marble. But he didn't possess quite the same *dangerous* degree of perfection as Kai or Li Ming. Irene wondered if she'd managed to walk into Qing Song during her first hour on this world. That would be remarkably unhelpful.

"Would you mind identifying yourself?" he said gently. "It must be a shock to see a library in ruins." Perhaps he thought he was dealing with a novice, or a Librarian who'd never interacted with dragons before.

That settled it. This *wasn't* Qing Song. A dragon with the same rank as Jin Zhi would have felt more powerful to Irene's senses, and would never have been this polite to a total stranger. But in that case, Irene had even less idea who this was, and no choice but to go with the flow and appear harmless. He'd clearly been waiting for incoming Librarians. If this *wasn't* connected with the whole Evariste business, then she would eat her hat without mustard.

"Oh, thank goodness," she gushed. "I was afraid this was some sort of Fae kidnapping. I can't tell you how relieved I am."

He raised an eyebrow. "Relieved?" But Irene thought she could sense a slight relaxation of tension on his side. She was being stupid, obvious, and predictable, and it was what he wanted to hear.

"To meet a dragon, of course. I mean, not that I've really met many dragons before, to be honest . . ." She put her fingers to her lips, like a nervous teenager confronted with a pop idol. "I'm so sorry, I think I'm babbling. My name's Marguerite. And you are?"

"Hu," he said. Now that she was more accustomed to the light, she could see that his hair was light copper. His suit was a pale reddish brown, but his tie and cuff links were dark green. "And you're a Librarian, I take it."

One of the few fragments of cultural information that Irene had dragged out of Kai concerned the colours that dragons wore. Most dragons preferred to wear clothing in the same shades as their natural colouration, where the local culture allowed it, but accented with the colours of their direct superior. The dragon for whom Hu worked was probably dark green—as a dragon, not a human, of course. She filed that information away for later.

But for the moment she was supposed to be a total innocent, and a nitwit on top of that. She nodded. "I should have said I was a Librarian, but you seemed to know already. Did your men say that I behaved strangely?"

"They said that you dropped a smoke-bomb, actually. And two oddly dressed strangers came out of a library, when no one went in . . ." He spread his hands. "A reasonable guess."

Irene nodded. "Oh, that makes sense. And ordinary people wouldn't have known you were a dragon. I hope it isn't awfully rude of me to say so."

Was she overdoing the cute inexperience? She leaned forward. "But why did you have your men bring me over here with a gun in my ribs? The Library and dragons are on good terms."

"This world is disputed," Hu said, drawing back a little. "We're on the alert for any signs of Fae intrusion."

Yes, which totally fails to explain why you have armed guards watching a ruined library. You don't do that because you're worried about Fae—you do that because you're worried about Librarians.

But Irene nodded, putting as much sincerity into her eyes as she could manage. She pointed in the direction of the library. "You think they did that, then?"

"Exactly. We were hoping to find some trace of them. I'll be reporting to my own lord later. I'm sorry that you walked into the wrong end of my investigation, but under the circumstances . . ." He shrugged elegantly.

"No, please don't apologize! I've learned so much because I ran into you." That was absolutely sincere. Irene wasn't sure what Hu was up to, but she was sure it was worth pursuing. "So if it was the local Fae, do you know where they're based, or if they have any particular leaders?"

"My men are investigating," Hu said. "This . . ." He gestured towards the ruins of the library. "It only happened a couple of days ago. I'm still trying to get the full details. The police are patrolling regularly, so we'd better not stay here too long. By the way, my men also said that you were accompanied—another Librarian?"

Irene nodded. "He's my supervisor on this mission. Of course we both took cover when your men tried to capture us, but he managed to get away. I'll meet up with him later . . ."

"And the mission?" Hu said, a little too casually.

At this point, Irene decided, even an overwhelmed novice Librarian would be starting to worry that she was saying too much. "I—that is . . ." she faltered. "Of course, it doesn't involve the *dragons* at all, quite the opposite. And now that you've confirmed the Fae were behind blowing up the library, we know what to watch for. So we won't need to bother you any further."

For a long moment he was silent.

Irene's heart was in her mouth as she waited to see if he'd swallow it.

And then he smiled. "Of course we'll do our best to help you," he said, reaching across to touch her wrist reassuringly. "We've worked with the Library before, after all. You might know some of the Librarians we've collaborated with? Petronia, Julian, Evariste . . ."

Irene was reasonably sure that her face didn't give anything away as he dropped those names, but she couldn't be sure about her pulse. *If you can't hide a reaction, then cover it up with something else,* she thought. She dropped her gaze to his hand, and worked on recalling every single moment of holding on to Kai in the lift. She could feel a blush coming to her cheeks. "Ah, no, I don't think so," she whispered.

He patted her hand and released it. It wasn't the sort of *I'll seduce you later, I'm just too busy right now* gesture that Lord Silver (the most notorious Fae rake in Vale's London) would have bestowed. It conveyed more of a *There, there, you poor humans simply can't help yourselves* attitude. Which was what Irene had been hoping for. She kept her expression timid and awed. And she wondered if he realized that he'd just betrayed *himself* by mentioning those names.

"I should go and meet my colleague before he gets too worried," Irene suggested. She considered clasping her wrist where Hu had touched it, but decided that would be overkill. "Is there some way we could contact you again?"

He reached into a pocket, flipped out a card-case, and offered her a card. It had only a phone number on it. "Ring this and leave a message for me. I'll be glad to talk to you and your supervisor. With any luck, we'll be able to dispose of the Fae who did this. Can I drop you anywhere?"

"No, thank you, it's within walking distance," Irene said, tucking the card into a pocket. "I'm so very grateful. Thank you again." She'd have liked to ask more questions—who *his* superior was, for a start. She regretfully decided that she'd settle for getting out of this car alive and with a little more information.

"Think nothing of it," Hu said. "It's the least I can do."

If you had anything to do with this library being blown up, then it's definitely the very least you can do, Irene thought venomously. She murmured further thanks and let Hu wave her out of the car. The mobster Rob, who'd been standing next to the car door in a position of casual readiness, nodded to her as she walked away.

There was no immediate sign of Kai, but Irene was sure he'd be in a position where he could watch the car and could see her. She spread her right hand casually in one of their pre-arranged signals—*five minutes*—and began walking down the street.

A part of her unwillingly fizzed with the buzz of excitement that any Librarian had on entering a new alternate world. Even though they had a mission to complete, she could still appreciate the thrill of new surroundings and different—well, different *everything*. The wide streets, broader and straighter than most of London's, were well lit by street lamps and glaring shop windows. Rather than the plain black or navy or grey of many of London's inhabitants, bright colours surrounded Irene as she jostled through the early-evening crowds—fur collars, silk and rayon jackets, wide-shouldered suits on the men. Tight cloche hats clung to female heads, ornamented with ribbons in particular styles as if to convey the wearer's intentions, while male fedoras were tilted in such a wide variety of angles that Irene was surprised they didn't fall off. Even the perfumes were different. Artificial violet and rose odours warred with cigarette-smoke from all the smokers—both men and women. Semaphore signals flapped on a traffic light at the intersection nearby, and long-bodied cars prowled down the street like wolves amidst the urban jungle, overshadowed by the tall buildings rearing a dozen storeys above her head.

She pulled herself back to focus on the job. There was a lot to do: get to the bank for cash and documents, obtain some new clothing to blend better into this world, and, most important, work on locating Evariste. But the first item on her list was losing her pursuers. Even if she'd managed to convince Hu that she was an utter novice, he would certainly be having her followed.

And right now Hu was the last person she wanted to know about her whereabouts. She had too many unanswered questions about *him*.

CHAPTER 7

It was past midnight before Irene and Kai could stop running. They'd met up outside the Northern Bank just before it closed. Irene had been aware of the men following her: they'd been getting closer and taking an interest anytime she stopped to talk to someone, even if it was just to ask for directions. It was becoming increasingly obvious that Hu hadn't so much let her go as let her run on a long leash with the intention of picking up her contact—the presumed other Librarian—as well. She did her best to make it look as if she and Kai just happened to be entering the Northern Bank at the same time, but she wasn't sure the watchers were fooled.

On the positive side, requesting a private interview with a bank clerk did mean that she and Kai were escorted into a private room, out of public view. And after using the Language to convince the poor clerk that she'd showed full identification, Irene now had an extremely large amount of local currency. She also secured the unfortunately out-of-date identity papers that the previous Librarian had left in the cache. They'd left through a backdoor, after some lies about avoiding newspaper reporters, and hadn't stopped since.

Admittedly the men following them hadn't been overtly flashing guns, or making suggestions such as "Stop or we'll shoot you." But they were the same breed as those who'd captured her earlier—calm, professional, and definitely armed. Other people saw them coming and moved out of the way, or answered questions (such as "Did you see where that man and woman just went?") with respectful terror. Irene would have bet money that in the event of a police line-up, nobody would have admitted to recognizing these men, even if they were standing in a row of potato sacks. It wouldn't be good for the health.

So after a busy evening full of banks, shops, and nightclubs—frequented only to try to lose their pursuers—they'd finally paused. Right now they were holed up in a department store that was closed for the night. The security guard was far more interested in a quiet life than in catching burglars. He made his rounds noisily, flashing his torch in a way that could be seen from the other end of the building. That gave Irene and Kai time to sit down and plan their next step.

"Fetch me down the biggest atlas that you can," Irene directed. They were in the section that sold books and stationery. She'd stopped off on the way up through women's clothing and jewellery to shoplift a large locket, decorated with rhinestones and in appallingly bad taste. She was going to have to collect some new clothing as well. Irene's usual instinct in clothing—to go for the plain and unobtrusive—had steered her absolutely wrong in this time and place. Even if she'd chosen the right skirt length, at just below the knee, her clothing was far too drab. She wasn't wearing any jewellery, and she was in muted dark colours, not bright ones. And the fashionable cloche hat just looked wrong on her. It was no wonder they'd been easy to follow.

"Let me find one . . ." Kai trailed along the shelves of books, having to lean in closely to read their titles in the dim light. They couldn't risk putting the actual shop lights on. He had to make do with moonlight and the glare of street lamps through the windows. "Street or country?"

"Global," Irene said. She removed the page with Evariste's name on it from its concealment, and began folding it up as tightly as possible. "Our next stop's probably China, given the book, but let's try to find out *where* before we hit the airport."

"That's reasonable," Kai said. "Now how about an explanation of why a department store, rather than a hotel or somewhere we could actually get some sleep?" He pulled out one of the largest books and carried it across to where Irene was sitting on the floor. "And what do I do with this now?"

Irene nodded towards the floor in front of her. She squashed the small folded piece of paper into the locket and forced it shut. "Sorry, Kai. I've been so busy running these last few hours that there hasn't been the chance for us to talk properly about our plans. I'm going to try to scry for Evariste. And then we're going to do some shopping."

"I thought you didn't practise magic." Kai put the heavy volume down with a thud, then pulled it forward a few inches so that it lay in a beam of moonlight. "There, that should be enough light to read by. And shopping? This place is *plebeian*."

Irene dangled the locket by its chain. "This isn't magic, it's the Language. I've a clear link to Evariste here, through his name in the Language. I'm hoping—note the word *hope*—that I'll be able to find out where he is on these maps. Then our next step is to go after him and pull the plug on this whole situation—or at least remove the Library from the equation." She ignored Kai's attack on off-the-peg shopping with the ease of practice.

Kai was silent for a moment as Irene opened the atlas and held the locket above it. "Don't you think we should be investigating the damage to the library here in Boston?" he finally said. "If that *was* a Fae strike against the Library itself . . ."

Irene looked up at him and raised an eyebrow.

"Just because Hu may have lied to you about some things doesn't mean he was lying to you about *everything*."

"It's not only the fact that someone—Fae, or whoever—blew up the library that happens to contain the Traverse from our Library to this world," Irene said. The earlier anger was still seething within her. "They blew up a library. A *library*, Kai. They haven't just offended me, they have attacked and insulted every single citizen of this place who used that library, who contributed to it, who even so much as might have used it someday in the future." She saw the locket trembling with her fury and took a deep breath, controlling herself. "I do want to know who damaged the library here in Boston. But it's not my priority. It can't be, until we've found Evariste and we know what's going on with him. But I sincerely hope that whoever *is* responsible ends up being dragged to the police station and torn limb from limb by the mob."

"Irene . . ." Kai said in a tone that suggested *You don't really mean that, do you?* He did have these misconceptions about her being a fundamentally nice person. After the last year, she wasn't sure why.

"All right. Cancel the vivid daydream about them being torn limb from limb." She looked away from him. "But don't expect me to be lenient towards someone destroying books, Kai. Whoever it is."

Even if it's me, the thought ran through her head, as she swung the locket over the open atlas. **"Pages of the atlas in front of me, turn; locket, indicate the place where the Librarian whose name you contain is to be found."**

The pages shifted as if touched by a wind, then began to ripple and move, one after another flipping over to show the next country, then the next—as the locket swung in Irene's hand like a dowsing pendulum. Irene breathed deeply as she watched, bracing herself against the light drain of energy as the Language took its toll. It wasn't a significant strain—not as bad, for instance, as having to bemuse half a dozen onlookers or freeze a canal—but it had been a long day, and she was tired.

"If Hu isn't someone you know," she said, her eyes still on the swinging locket, "who could he be? You knew Qing Song and Jin Zhi, after all—or at least you knew who they were, even if you hadn't met them."

"His manners and bearing sound as if he's at least minor nobility," Kai said. "But I don't know anyone by that name of royal blood, or of the major nobility. I wonder if he might be someone's servant."

"With the someone in question being one of our two book-hunters?"

"Or another faction who wants to influence the situation. It's a pity I couldn't get close enough to see him . . . but yes, I do realize the problem with that is that *he'd* see *me.*"

Irene nodded. Kai didn't want to interfere in other dragons' business—or at least, he didn't want to get caught. She agreed with that. But from her rather more selfish point of view, the longer Kai's presence here went unknown, the more help he could be in finding Evariste.

And there was another factor. Did dragons gossip about her and Kai? If anyone here recognized Kai, would they deduce who Irene was—a librarian on a mission that might involve them? And in the longer term, could she really keep working with Kai? Might she inadvertently cause the very same problems to the Library, concerning forbidden dragon alliances, which she was currently trying to avoid? Irene had steered them well clear of dragon politics, so they should be above reproach. But if wholesale collusion between a dragon and the Library was proven—or even suspected—then rumour could label Irene and Kai as another piece of evidence.

The pages stopped turning. The locket jerked downwards. Irene frowned as she recognized the country on the page. "Wait a moment. That's America. That's *here!*"

"Are you sure it's working properly?" Kai asked.

Irene rubbed her forehead and wished for sleep. "Well, if it isn't, then we're metaphorically already ten miles down and sinking . . . with all due apologies to any dragons who like to live in oceanic trenches."

"The company down there's very dull," Kai said, with such a straight face that he had to be joking. Probably. She thought. "But America makes no sense. The book's Chinese."

Irene nodded, considering. "Let's assume that it's working and that there's some reason for Evariste to be here." She leaned in to peer at the chunk of North America that the locket was indicating, but the fine print on the map was too small and the cities were all close together. "You'd better get me an atlas of North America. Or America, at least. And grab any city-by-city guidebooks, if there are any."

A minute later Kai was back with another atlas, and an apology for the lack of local guidebooks. Irene repeated her earlier use of the Language, and watched the turning pages and the swinging locket. The result was unmistakeable. "New York," she said. "It's pointing to New York."

"Well . . ." Kai finally shrugged, as much at a loss as she was. "It's closer than China," he offered.

Irene checked the map in front of her. "It's about, um, two hundred miles away."

"A plane might be fastest," Kai said thoughtfully. "But I'm not sure how frequent the flights are—and I have no idea what the security would be like. There should be a train route between Boston and New York, or would a car be faster?"

"Hiring a car means leaving a paper trail," Irene said.

Kai folded himself down to join Irene on the floor. "But if Hu suspects we're going to flee the city, then it would make sense for him to watch the major exit points. He could expect to catch us there. Whatever his intentions are. We've avoided his men enough times this evening already to know that he wants us."

Irene chewed her lower lip. "Yes," she said slowly. "But Hu would have to spread his resources thin to watch air, road, rail, maybe even sea . . . which gives us more of a chance to slip through. Especially after we've changed our appearance."

"Ah, so that's what you meant by shopping," Kai said. He looked around at the shadowed shelves and racks gloomily. "Couldn't we at least break into somewhere more expensive?"

"We're trying to go unnoticed," Irene reminded him.

"There is something else . . ." he said before she could mock his vanity. "Your hair."

"Is it loose?" Irene's hands went up to touch it, to see if her bun had started to unravel.

"No, it's long. You have *noticed* that women of your apparent age wear it short in this time and place, haven't you? With those little hats?"

"But it's taken me years to grow it out . . ." Irene stopped, took a deep breath, and resigned herself to short hair. All the women they'd seen so far, from twenty to forty, had their hair cut and styled short. "Oh, all right, but it would be a great deal easier if you weren't smirking at me. Let me guess: all young royal dragons get trained in hair-styling, along with everything else."

"No, but I'm always ready to learn," Kai replied.

They ended up in the haberdashery section on the fifth floor, dodging the security guard on the way. Irene sat down in a section of street-lamp glare while Kai fussed with the scissors. With a regretful sigh she pulled the pins and combs out of her hair and made a little pile of them on the floor. "Tell me," she said softly, trying to distract herself. "Dragons and royalty, major nobility, minor nobility, servants, whatever . . . I'm trying to work out what we're dealing with here. If Hu is working for Qing Song or Jin Zhi, then how many other agents might be lurking in the shadows—"

"Dragons do not lurk in the shadows," Kai interrupted firmly.

"Even those dragons who are temporarily experimenting with a criminal lifestyle?"

"You're never going to let me forget that, are you?" He moved behind her, gathering her loose hair into his hand. "One of these days I'm going to find out something embarrassing about your past and I'll spend the next few decades reminding you about it."

Irene tried not to dwell on the warm feelings conjured by *the next few decades*. Planning that far in the future was asking for disappointment. She'd always found it best to concentrate on what was directly ahead—the next book, the next lesson, the next job. It was Kai's fault that he made the idea of decades of friendship sound so *possible*.

Then he began to saw at her hair and she bit back a yelp as he tugged at the roots. "Ow," she said, softly but with feeling.

"This always looks so easy when they do it in the barber's," Kai said, his tone perplexed. "Can you keep your head still?"

Having her ears accidentally cut off hadn't been on Irene's list of Possible Mission Hazards. Truly the life of a Librarian was full of rich learning experiences. "If either Jin Zhi or Qing Song has brought agents in to search for the book, what sort of numbers might we be looking at?" she asked through gritted teeth.

"Well, you remember when I said that someone like myself—a very young dragon of the royal blood—could carry one or two people?"

"I do."

"Normally someone of royal blood wouldn't *personally* carry things or people," Kai explained. "So the servants do that, and follow in our wake. We'd only make an exception for personal favourites." His finger brushed the side of her neck for a moment, but the gesture was affectionate rather than seductive. Even if it succeeded quite well at both.

"All right," Irene said, doing her best to ignore the touch of his skin against hers. "So correct me if I'm wrong. Jin Zhi and Qing Song aren't of royal blood, but they are major nobility. They're powerful enough to travel between worlds themselves, but are they strong enough to bring some servants behind them?"

"Probably," Kai admitted. The pressure on her head eased. Cold air breathed across the back of her neck. "Perhaps half-a-dozen at most? Though more likely just two or three, if that. Someone of high birth couldn't manage without their servants."

"Well, yes," Irene said. "Who else would arrange the hotel rooms, bribe the mobsters, do the research . . ." She wanted to turn and look up at him, but he was busy with the scissors again. "Though you've never suggested that you wanted servants."

"I'm too young," Kai said calmly. The cold metal of the shears touched her skin. "If I were older, I'd be expected to be involved in more important matters. I'd have an aide or a bodyguard, or someone like that, just as my honoured uncle has Li Ming."

"*That's* who Hu reminded me of." Irene remembered those moments with him in the car.

"Li Ming?"

"It was the way Hu handled me." Irene tried to gesture in explanation without moving her head. "He had the same sort of bearing and authority, and he mentioned his lord. He's not just a casual minion, he's someone's trusted assistant."

"Unfortunately that still doesn't mean I know who he is. Turn your head a little to the left . . . yes, thank you." The shears brushed her skin again. "There are more dragons than there are Librarians, and it's not as if *you* know every Librarian."

Irene had admittedly been thinking it was a nuisance that Kai didn't know every single dragon, but she tried to look innocent.

"Could a dragon change his or her status?" she asked. "If they were spectacularly good at their job, perhaps?"

There was a long silence from behind her. She had the impression that Kai was picking and choosing between several possible answers. Maybe the intricacies of dragon rankings weren't for Librarian ears. "Well, there are standards," he finally said. "Blood does count. You can't expect it to be as it is with Librarians. Some dragons are simply born superior to others. Most human cultures accept that sort of thing too. Nature and abilities do make a difference, though good service would naturally be recognized. The situation in the Library is different, of course . . ."

Kai's apologetic tone was only because he knew Irene had strong opinions about hereditary superiority. He didn't actually think she was right, but he was generously making allowances for human sensibilities. Dragon courtesy towards lesser beings.

And who was she to judge? Irene wondered with a vast weariness. She was someone who stole books for a living. Even if it was theoretically to protect the balance of the universe, it was still stealing books. What gave her any sort of greater moral perspective or superiority?

"There." Kai smoothed her hair, and for a moment it felt as if he was stroking it. She suppressed a shiver. He stood back. "What do you think?"

Irene pulled herself to her feet and walked over to the nearest mirror. To her surprise, her hair actually looked quite elegant. "Good job," she said.

Kai shrugged, but he looked pleased. "So, what are our next steps?"

"Burn my hair, in case anyone can use it to track me. Take some clothing. Pack a suitcase." She saw his mulish look and reluctantly added, "Leave a suitable payment in the tills, of course. Then reach the railway station and catch a train to New York." She thought for a moment. "And don't forget to stop off in the book department of this store while we're packing. We don't want to be stuck on the train with nothing to read."

CHAPTER 8

The train came rattling into New York as dawn spread across the sky and began to colour the surrounding world. Irene gazed out the window, trying to come to terms with the fact that it was morning and she needed to wake up. The countryside had been left behind, as had the out-of-town residences of the wealthy and famous, with their surrounding greenery and walls. Now the train was sliding along a complicated diagram of parallel tracks, through a landscape of warehouses and industry, brown brick and grey brick and concrete. Looking ahead, she could see the city itself: the morning light caught on the high buildings and skyscrapers, making them gleam like silver and ivory. Their dozens of windows stared back at her like dark eyes. The sky was clear—unnaturally clear, after her time in Vale's fog-shrouded London—and the city unfolded in front of her like a treasure-box full of possibilities.

Kai was still asleep next to her, his hat tilted over his face and his breathing steady. Around them, other people in the carriage were waking up and rubbing their eyes. A few women had pulled out compacts and were making repairs to their make-up, repainting the curves of their lips and patting powder onto their faces. Two elderly white-bearded men packed away the miniature set of draughts that they'd been playing on through most of the night. They spoke softly to each other in a Slavic dialect that Irene couldn't quite catch. The noise level in the carriage rose as other groups of travellers began to chatter, and three young men in cheap sharp suits lit cigarettes almost in unison as they sneered at the world around them. The train was moving through the city now, alongside apartment buildings and tenements, close enough that she could glance through the windows as they passed and catch fragmentary scenes of life. A mother corralling her family for breakfast. A boy leaning out of the window with a boxy camera.

They'd reached North Union Station in Boston without being caught by their pursuers. Unfortunately there hadn't been many people catching a train at that hour of the morning, so there was no way to get lost in the crowds. On the positive side, Irene thought determinedly, it also meant that if someone *had* been following them, she or Kai should have spotted him. So with any luck, Hu would have lost their trail for the moment—whatever he wanted with them.

A few hours of sleep had dramatically improved her mood. Admittedly she wasn't properly awake yet, and she needed coffee, breakfast, and a bathroom. And she still didn't know what was going on, only that it might be immeasurably bad. And yet . . .

Tunnels loomed ahead of the train, dipping down under the city of New York. The train rattled into them with a whoosh and a deep chuckle of wheels, and abruptly the carriage was darker, lit only by the electrical lamps along the ceiling. It was a setting that invited paranoia. There was no way to get off now. Irene found her perspective shifting: previously she'd been journeying into a city of possibility, but now it felt as if she was being delivered into the darkness to an inescapable destination.

Irene took a deep breath. The situation would not be improved by mental nail-biting. Instead she nudged Kai gently in the ribs. "We're coming into Grand Central Terminal," she murmured. "Time to wake up."

Kai raised his hand to tilt his hat and inspect the world around him. "Not for another few minutes yet, surely," he said hopefully.

"We're closer than that, I think." Irene edged her own powder compact out of her handbag and checked her face in the mirror. She looked passable. Certainly not worth anyone's interest. Which was exactly what she wanted. "Hopefully we can get our business out of the way and be heading home as soon as possible."

The train finally jolted into the station, bursting out from the darkness of the tunnel to come to a stop next to a platform walled in white tiles, with GRAND CENTRAL inset mosaic-style. Kai got to his feet and reached their suitcase down from the overhead rack, then offered Irene a hand to help her rise. "Any priorities?" he asked.

"Breakfast and coffee."

Kai nodded. They let a few of the carriage's other occupants go ahead of them—Irene didn't intend to be the first person onto an empty platform—and then stepped off the train and headed for the stairs.

With a nasty shock of surprise, Irene saw that there were police waiting. A dozen or so blue-uniformed men were checking passengers as they filed past, and behind them crowded an entourage of men waving cameras and brandishing notebooks. "I have a bad feeling about this," she muttered.

"It could be coincidence." Kai sounded as if he was trying to convince himself, and failing. Irene would have been worried that their sudden low-voiced conversation might look suspicious, but fortunately—if that was the word for it—other passengers were suddenly slowing and eyeing the waiting cops. It was a Horatius-at-the-bridge situation, with those at the back trying to push forward, and quite a few of those at the front doing their best to move back.

Irene's own good mood was dropping like a barometer faced with an oncoming storm. But there was nowhere to *go*, except back on the train. And retreating down the platform would be useless: they'd run out of platform. "If we get closer, perhaps we can hear who they're waiting for—"

"That's her!" one of the cops yelled.

He was pointing at Irene.

Irene's first impulse was to shrink back into the crowd or hide behind something. Unfortunately the crowd (apart from Kai) was shrinking back from *her*, and hiding behind Kai wasn't a viable long-term strategy. She tried to look as falsely accused as possible.

The police came driving towards her and Kai in a flying wedge through the crowd, trailed by the newspaper reporters in a sea of fedora hats and cheap sharp suits. A couple of them were already snapping photographs, the flash-bulbs on their cameras flaring brightly. Irene raised a hand to shield her eyes, and cursed the fact that she couldn't use the Language to break all their damned cameras. But it would attract more trouble than it was worth.

The leader of the group of policemen—an overweight man with thick glasses, displaying noticeable extra braid on his cap and jacket—held up one hand as he approached. "Excuse me, ma'am.

NYPD, Captain Venner. Would you be Miss Jeanette Smith from England?" His accent was pure New York.

A chill made its way down Irene's spine and settled in her stomach. Somehow she didn't think this would end with *And as our millionth visitor, you've won a thousand dollars!* She and Kai had just walked into trouble.

"Well, I am English," she said. She knew that her American accent wasn't very convincing. "But my name is Rosalie Jones." So said her identity papers, at least.

The cop turned to a colleague. "Make a note—the accused denied being Miss Jeanette Smith." In the background, reporters scribbled. More cameras flashed.

"And who is Jeanette Smith, anyhow?" Irene demanded.

"In a moment, ma'am," the cop said. "In a moment. Would you mind if I see your identity papers? And your friend's papers too?"

Irene cursed mentally. Kai wasn't going to be able to slip away. She fished in her handbag, rather unnerved when all the cops tensed as she pulled out the papers. She'd retrieved them from the bank and "updated" them later, so she hoped they'd pass muster.

The cop gave them a professional once-over. "According to these, ma'am, you're thirty-eight."

Irene smiled sweetly. "Is that a crime?"

That evoked a laugh from the crowd. Though not from the police. The lead cop folded the papers and tucked them into his jacket, pointedly not returning them. "And you claim that you're not Jeanette Smith?"

"I've never heard of her."

The cop turned slightly, presenting his best profile to the newspaper cameras. "Since you're claiming ignorance, ma'am, Jeanette

Smith is one of England's most notorious mobsters. Which makes us all kind of curious what you're doing in New York."

Irene stared at him in shock. "I am not a mobster!"

"The biggest protection-racket woman in Great Britain!" one of the reporters yelled.

"Smuggles brandy from the Continent!" another called.

"The Girl with a Gun in her Garter!" a third chimed in.

Suddenly they were all taking photos again. Irene backed against Kai, barely able to see through the hurricane of flashes.

"This could have gone better," Kai murmured, barely audible through the noise of the crowd. He'd pulled his hat down to shield his face.

"Think of something," Irene said, a little desperately. She'd been accused of a lot of things, but being a mob boss was a new low. And while she'd certainly *committed* crimes in the Library's service, she'd generally avoided arrest. And she hadn't even had her coffee. "You're the one with the dubious past. What do you do in this sort of situation?"

"Deny everything, keep your mouth shut, and demand a lawyer," Kai said with the quick certainty of experience.

Their exchange had gone unheard under the noise of the crowd, but the cops had certainly noticed it. "Something to tell us, ma'am?"

"I don't know anything," Irene said firmly. "I've only just got here. If you're going to be accusing me, then I want a lawyer."

"We can arrange that for you just fine, ma'am." The cop gestured, and the other policemen moved to surround Irene and Kai. "You and your friend here will be coming down to the precinct with us."

Irene would have been willing to agree to almost anything if it would get her away from the mob of reporters. "Will you be able to sort this out once we get there? There's been some sort of mistake, and we simply want to get on with our holiday."

"It's exactly as she says," Kai said, backing her up. "I don't know what sort of police system you have here, but this *certainly* wouldn't happen in England." He did *outraged* well, Irene thought.

Captain Venner snorted. "Yeah, sure, whatever. Let's move it—unless you really want to stand around and give interviews."

Irene and Kai were hustled through the mob. She vaguely regretted not seeing more of Grand Central Terminal as they were rushed through it. One of the cops took custody of their luggage, and Irene suspected it would shortly be inspected for hidden . . . well, hidden whatever was carried by the biggest protection-racket woman in Great Britain. Guns? Brandy? Money for bribes? It was going to be awkward if she had to explain the large roll of high-value bills in her handbag. She resisted the urge to touch the heavy locket around her throat. The paper with Evariste's name on it was the only thing she couldn't afford to lose.

"I understand that you call these paddy wagons Black Marias in England," one of the cops said helpfully, as he assisted Irene into the back of a police vehicle. A heavy metal partition separated the cell area from the front seats, and the walls were reinforced with thick steel plates. He clambered in to join her, and when Kai followed, he also had his very own attendant cop.

"We do," Irene agreed. "But I've never been in one before." She looked around nervously, shrinking closer to Kai on the plank seat.

He put an arm round her shoulders on cue, glowering at the cops. "I won't have any of you bullying my girl like this," he said arrogantly.

"Seems to me your girl was doing just fine sticking up for herself back there," the other cop said. "Now, don't you give us no trouble and we'll have a nice quiet trip."

The police van jolted into motion. There were no windows, but the regular bursts of high speed followed by jarring stops gave Irene some idea of their progression through traffic, and the sound of offended car horns provided the rest. Prisoner transport vehicles were similar, whatever the culture or time period.

She patted Kai's hand. "I'm sure that we can get this sorted out once we get to the police station, dear."

"Station house, ma'am," the first cop said. "That's what we call them over here. Don't worry, you'll get the hang of it in no time."

"Thank you," Irene said. "Will they have a lawyer at the station house?"

"Not unless you're planning to call one in," the second cop said. "But I suppose a lady like yourself has the numbers of all the local law firms, mm?"

Irene was forced to accept that Hu's frame-up job on her must have been *really* good. These two cops weren't even considering that she might be an innocent victim of circumstances. "I'm just here on vacation," she said helplessly. "With my boyfriend. I'm just a secretary."

"Sure you are, ma'am," the cop agreed. "And you can have a nice long chat with the captain about it, real soon now."

Irene and Kai exchanged glances. She could read her own impatience and frustration in his eyes. They couldn't afford to be delayed. The contest would be over in a few days, and if Evariste was up to something, then he had to be stopped before that deadline. But running would just confirm any police suspicions, and being hunted by the police would hamper their attempts to locate Evariste.

All too soon the police van screeched to a stop. They were hustled out of the vehicle and into a heavy building that had clearly been built for security. It tried to look impressive but merely succeeded in looking monolithic and forbidding. It was faced with sandstone and—to Irene's hasty glance—marked with recent bullet scars. "Has someone been *shooting* at this place?" she asked her escort.

He followed her gaze. "Oh yeah, that was last year. Don't you worry about it, ma'am. The gangs have been quiet lately. And we're all hoping they stay that way."

Captain Venner caught up with their group in the main entrance-hall. The gaggle of reporters who'd followed from the station eddied and flowed round the edge of the group, notebooks at the ready. The place was clearly warming up to the day's work. Cops strode briskly from place to place, their voices echoing under the high ceiling. Hard-bitten men and women seated behind heavy desks listened to visitors—lawyers, reporters, relatives, or arrestees waiting to be booked in—with the air of cops who'd heard it all before. A janitor pushed her mop across the floor, leaving a streak of clean tiles behind her. The place smelled of sweat, dust, and coffee.

"I'll be talking to Miss Smith in my office," the captain said. "Barnes, why don't you have a little chat with her friend here. What's your name?"

"Robert Pearce," Kai said helpfully. "Shouldn't you be reading us our rights?"

"Oh, we've got a smart one here. For your information, Mr. Pearce, that only happens when we're arresting you, and we haven't arrested you . . . yet."

Irene and Kai exchanged a loaded glance. It certainly *felt* like an arrest. Sadly, while insulting the police captain in front of all his men would be extremely satisfying, it would bias any future conversation. But a genuinely innocent person would be saying *something* at this point . . .

"Your uncle's going to be furious if he hears about this," she said to Kai, letting a wobble enter her voice. "Do you suppose he'll think it's one of those slice-of-life moments? Visitors to New York getting mistaken for famous mobsters and hauled off by the police . . ."

"I hope he doesn't hear about it in the first place." Kai took her hand and squeezed it. "Chin up, Rosalie. Stiff upper lip. We'll be out of here in no time."

"And the sooner we have that talk, the sooner it might be," Captain Venner said. He stalked off down a side corridor, his belly swaying under his uniform.

Irene didn't bother hiding a last, lingering look at Kai as the two of them were led away in opposite directions. After all, it fitted the part she was playing.

In the captain's office the smell of cigarettes was overlaid with one of more expensive pipe tobacco. Captain Venner sat down behind his desk with a grunt of relief, adjusting his glasses. He noticeably didn't offer Irene a chair.

Irene took the opportunity to look around while she waited. The window had a view overlooking the street below, and it was already full of morning traffic. Iron bars across the window provided an incongruous note—precautions against theft, or against more direct assault? She remembered the bullet-marks on the building's exterior. Photos of the captain shaking hands with various expensively dressed people hung on the walls. The filing cabinets were heavy steel, and looked proof against anything up to dynamite. The captain's own desk was good-quality wood, with the sheen that came from regular polishing. *Political connections, expensive office furniture, and a private interview . . . he's looking for a pay-off,* Irene suspected.

The room held only her, the captain, and another cop on guard at the door. And she was willing to bet the cop at the door would have a very selective memory about this interview. Her odds had just improved.

Captain Venner finally fixed his gaze on her. "For a woman who's supposed to be innocent, Miss Smith, you're taking all this very calmly."

"I trust the police," Irene said. "We went along with you because of all those reporters, but surely now that you can check up on things here, you can see there's been some sort of mistake. And I'm not Miss Smith," she added stubbornly.

The captain leaned over and extracted a folder from one of the desk drawers. He slapped it on the desk in front of him. "Some sort of mistake, you say."

"Yes." Irene spread her hands. "I mean, really, do I look like a woman who runs a protection racket?"

"And how would you know what a woman who runs a protection racket would look like, ma'am?"

"Well, I'm sure she'd be better dressed than I am," Irene snapped. "I demand to know what sort of evidence you have against me!"

Captain Venner tapped the folder. "This morning, ma'am, the New York Police Department received an urgent message from the Boston police. They'd received evidence that Miss Jeanette Smith had come over from England, and they confirmed she'd been in their vicinity and talking business with some of the local gangs.

However, they'd also tracked her to the railway station, and they knew that she'd gotten a ticket to New York. I think you can probably see where I'm coming from."

Irene folded her arms. "That's all well and good, but it still doesn't label me as this Jeanette Smith woman. If she was on the train, she probably escaped while you were wasting your time with me."

He flipped open the folder. "That's a curious thing, ma'am. Because from where I'm standing..." He extracted a piece of paper and turned it so that Irene could see it. "She surely looks a lot like you."

It was a pen-and-ink drawing of Irene, head and shoulders. While it showed her with her previous long hair, it was quite definitely her.

Irene mentally sorted through appropriate reactions and settled on *horrified disbelief*, which wasn't that far from her current emotional state in any case. "That's—how—where did you get that?"

"By fast car from Boston this morning." He settled back in his chair again. "So, Miss Smith, perhaps you'd like to explain a few things. Or would you rather sit in the cells while you think about it? I'll tell you flat out that I'm more interested in local individuals than foreign imports. So if you're willing to talk, then I'm willing to listen."

Denying everything wasn't working. Admitting everything would be even worse.

Waiting in the cells wasn't acceptable. And what if Hu's plans to detain them turned into something more lethal?

"May I get something out of my handbag?" she said, priming the captain for a bribe. "And is the gentleman behind me . . . reliable?"

Captain Venner relaxed. "Surely you can, ma'am," he said. "And surely he is. I'm glad to see we're on the same page now."

Irene fished in her handbag and found a leaflet from the Boston railway station. She stepped forward and offered it to Captain Venner. As he blinked at it suspiciously, she said in the Language, "**You perceive that this is my authorization from the FBI and my identification as an employee of Scotland Yard.** Congratulations on catching me, Captain, but I'm afraid this is a sting operation."

CHAPTER 9

"Let's have a look at that," Captain Venner said, his voice suddenly rough and uncertain. He snatched the leaflet from Irene's hands, holding it up to squint at it. "Could be forged."

"But you know it isn't," Irene said. She shifted her stance, no longer folding her arms defensively, and stepped forward to lean on the captain's desk. "Don't you?"

The Language had told him what to perceive, and at this precise moment he could be looking at dead leaves and he'd believe he was seeing valid documentation. The only problem was that the effect wouldn't last very long. And when the captain realized he'd been conned . . .

Irene snapped her fingers and reached out to take the leaflet back from him. "If you please, Captain."

"What the hell's going on here?" he snarled. "I didn't receive any notification of this."

"Of course not," Irene agreed. "That's because the system leaks. Unfortunate, but true. If Scotland Yard had notified your city hall about my mission, then half the gangs in New York would know about it too. That's why my identity's strictly on an eyes-only basis."

"Captain, what's going on?" the cop at the door said. Irene could hear the unspoken *Should I do something about this woman?* tone in his voice, and the back of her neck itched nervously. But she didn't turn round. It wouldn't have been in character for an undercover Scotland Yard agent.

"Looks like it's some sort of op the feds are running." Captain Venner's tone made it quite clear how much he disliked the feds. "And Scotland Yard's in bed with them too."

"It's a long story," Irene said. She tucked the leaflet back into her handbag. "But it works because people over here don't know what Jeanette Smith looks like. Your FBI thought Scotland Yard could send someone over from England posing as her. Then if she liaised with your major gangs, they could trace how alcohol was coming into the States from overseas." She hastily searched her memory for relevant facts from yesterday's newspapers. "We want to track the booze from when it leaves England, to when it arrives here. Then your FBI—sorry, your feds—can roll up the whole network. I didn't need to contact the police in Boston, so they won't know the truth. Someone there must have thought I was the real thing. At least my cover's not blown yet."

"You'd be dead if it was," Captain Venner said bluntly. "And any witnesses would have a bad case of what the doctors call 'Chicago amnesia'—meaning they wouldn't remember a thing about you, least of all who gunned you down. You've got guts, lady—I'll give you that."

Irene shrugged. "It's my job."

"Why did they get a woman to do it?"

"It had to be a known criminal making this trip," Irene said. "A big enough name to talk with your gangs on equal terms. And the male English crime bosses are better known over here." She just hoped he wouldn't ask for any of their names . . .

He nodded slowly. "And the guy with you, he's in on this too?"

"He's one of Scotland Yard's top men," Irene said. "Could you have him brought in here too? I'll need to brief him without your men hearing." And it would lower the risk of Kai blowing their new cover.

Captain Venner grunted and waved a hand at the cop by the door. "Dorrins, you go fetch Miss Smith's friend. And get this straight: *nobody* outside this room hears anything about this for the moment. Tell Barnes I want to check his story with something she's said. Tell him . . ." He hesitated. "Tell him I'm sweating her and I think she's about to crack."

"Oh, it'd take more than ten minutes' sweating to crack me," Irene said helpfully.

"Lady, I've cracked better men than you in half that time." He pointed a pudgy finger at the door. "Go fetch him, Dorrins. And make it clear we're taking this seriously."

Dorrins shut the door behind him with a click, and Captain Venner turned back to Irene. "All right, lady. How do you want to play this?"

Irene had noticed his slippage from the carefully polite *ma'am* to the more casual *lady*. She hoped it was a good sign. "Well, it's a positive that the Boston Police Department warned you I was coming. It shows that police communications across America are functioning properly. It's just inconvenient for me. It's going to be difficult for me to do my job as Jeanette Smith, if everyone in this city knows where I am and that the cops are keeping a close eye on me. Nobody from the mobs is going to want to talk to me—"

Captain Venner brought his hand down on the table. "Lady, hold it right there. You've got it wrong. You're in more danger than you realize."

"Why?"

"You're a hot property now," he said. "Any gang that doesn't make a deal with you is going to want you out of the way so that the opposition doesn't profit. Hell, some of the boys may be thinking about taking you off the board right now, just to keep things simple. The moment you walk out the door, you'll have them on your tail."

"Damn." Irene hadn't thought of that. This must be the other half of the trap: slow her down by tagging her as "Jeanette Smith," and give most of the gangs in New York a reason to want her dead. She had to admire the plot's efficiency, from an academic standpoint.

"Yeah." The captain sighed. "Tell you what, I could have a couple of the boys drive you back to the station and put you on the next train out of New York. You wouldn't talk to your targets, but at least you and your friend would be alive."

"That's certainly a possibility," Irene agreed. She could see that it would suit Captain Venner. It would get her off his hands, and he wouldn't have to take any blame for letting the reporters publicize her arrival. A win-win situation for him. Less useful for her. "But my superiors will still want me to get the job done."

"Do they want you to get shot?" the captain asked. "Because that's what's going to happen, if you walk out of here."

Irene shrugged. "One thing I suspect we've got in common, Captain, is that our superiors can be a bit unrealistic about what they think we can do."

"You got that one right." He took off his glasses and polished them thoughtfully. "Still, if you'll take my advice, you'll find a good excuse and get the hell out of town. This isn't Atlantic City and it's not conference season." He saw her blank look. "You know, when the big boys meet up to talk terms and make deals. But the boys aren't playing nice with each other right now, and you're going to be in the middle."

"I'm no happier about it than you are, Captain," Irene said feelingly. "This wasn't what I had in mind at all."

There was a knock at the door. "Come in!" the captain called.

Dorrins entered and waved Kai in before firmly shutting the door. "Captain, some of the reporters downstairs are asking questions," he said. "They're wanting interviews."

"With *me*?" Irene said.

Dorrins shrugged. "With anyone, ma'am. But it's going to make it harder to get you out of here."

Irene nodded and turned to Kai. "It's all right, Robert," she said. "These gentlemen are in on the mission now." She turned back to Captain Venner. "Please allow me to introduce Detective Inspector Murchison of Scotland Yard."

Captain Venner leaned across the desk and offered his hand for Kai to shake. "Good to meet you, Inspector. Your colleague here's been giving me the real story. I hope the boys downstairs didn't give you too rough a time."

Over the last year or two, Kai had become adept at remaining impassive while being introduced under various unexpected aliases. This one didn't even rate a blink. He returned the hand-shake easily. "Not a problem, Captain. They were just doing their jobs."

"What we need from Captain Venner, right now, is a way to get out of this police station and lose anyone following us," Irene said.

She was aware that time was slipping past. Every minute made it more likely that Captain Venner's Language-induced misperception would wear off and he'd remember that she'd just flashed a random advertising leaflet at him.

"You got any thoughts on the matter, Murchison?" the captain asked, turning to Kai.

"The same as her, to be honest." Kai gestured to Irene. "We need to get out of here, and we need to do it without being seen."

"The easiest way for you to lose your tails might be at a sub-way station," the captain said thoughtfully. "All right. Here's how we'll play it. Dorrins, you'll get a couple of the boys who know how to keep their mouths shut and tell them to bring a car round to the back of the station. Make it one of the ones with tinted windows. Then you'll take our guests here down the backstairs. They'll hop out and into the car before the reporters can catch up with them. Then the boys will run them down to, oh, say East Penn Station, and they'll jump on a subway car. Change lines a few times, and you should be able to lose any tails. That work for you, Murchison, lady?"

"An excellent plan," Irene said warmly. "Thank you, Captain. I do realize that we've placed you in a very awkward position, and I appreciate your help."

Captain Venner looked mollified by her prompt agreement and Kai's nod. "Set it up, Dorrins," he directed. "You got any more questions, either of you?"

Irene glanced at Kai. He shrugged. She was about to shrug as well when a thought struck her. Dragons were skilled at many things, but avoiding attention wasn't generally one of them. "Have there been any unusual new arrivals in town over the last month?"

The captain snorted. "This *is* New York. Everyone comes here. Even Scotland Yard agents."

"They'd probably have been claiming to be foreign nobility or royalty," Irene persisted. "And they'd have had a lot of money to throw around."

He frowned, thinking it over. "Now that you mention it . . ." He counted on his fingers. "There's a guy at the Plaza Hotel, says he's Prince Ludwig of Bavaria, but he's not. He's running a scam, claiming that he just needs some money to go retrieve his art treasures. We'll be pulling him in next week, or sooner. And there's this guy staying at the St. Regis Hotel on Fifty-fifth Street. Been here in New York the last couple of weeks. It's not so much him making claims about being royalty; it's the fact that he has pet wolves and likes to take them for walks down Broadway and around town. It ain't exactly illegal, but we had some concerned citizens making representations about it."

Irene saw Kai's eyes narrow. "So, did he have to keep the wolves at home after that?" she asked casually.

Captain Venner rubbed his thumb against his fingers, in the universal shorthand for cash. "Money talked, and a whole lot of people decided they could live with wolves on Broadway. Course, they're the well-behaved sort of wolves. But when you ask about visiting nobs with more money than sense, that's who comes to mind."

Irene nodded. "Thanks for the information. But I'm more concerned about anyone who might know the real Jeanette Smith."

"I still think you'd be safer out of town. But it's your decision. At least once we get the two of you on the subway, you'll be . . ."

"Out of your hair?" Irene suggested. "Someone else's problem?"

"I've got enough problems without you giving me any more of them, lady." He fished in a desk drawer. "Here, these are subway tokens. Make sure you're both carrying a few of them. That way you can walk right through the turnstiles and onto the train."

The captain made desultory conversation with Kai while they waited for Dorrins to return, fishing for details about Scotland Yard and clearly happier to be dealing with a male cop than a female one. Kai did his best to respond, while Irene retreated into the background with relief. She leafed through a newspaper, trying to get a sense of current affairs. The news was highly coloured, even if the print was black and white—scandals, mob crimes, movie news, temperance marches, and other entertaining flashes of life in the big city.

Suddenly, mid-anecdote, the captain snapped his fingers. "Hell, I forgot something. They're still turning your suitcase over downstairs. If I tell them to bring it up here, someone's going to smell a rat. Anything you needed in there?"

Irene shook her head. "Nothing important." The only vital things were the money in her handbag and Kai's wallet, and Evariste's name in the locket round her neck.

"Not even a piece?" The captain remembered he was speaking to a non-American. "You know, a gun? Aren't you travelling tooled up? And what about your clothing?" There was a tinge of uncertainty to his voice, as if he was struggling with something in the back of his mind that hadn't quite surfaced yet, but was sending out early warning tremors.

Irene swallowed, her throat suddenly dry. The Language's effect was beginning to fade. "The whole point was to go unobserved," she said calmly. "We weren't planning on getting into any shoot-outs, even if the police did catch up with us. **You perceive that this is reasonable and makes sense, and explains any inconsistencies.**"

The captain swayed in his chair. "Right," he said vaguely. "Of course. That makes sense."

Irene felt a pang of guilt through the haze of an incipient headache. She hadn't previously tried using the Language multiple times on the same person like this. She hoped she hadn't somehow damaged the captain. He'd only been doing his job.

Fortunately Dorrins knocked on the door. "Captain?" he called. "It's all ready to go."

"Thanks for all your help," Kai said. He gave Captain Venner's hand a quick shake. "We'll be in touch."

"Just stay out of trouble," Captain Venner said, pulling himself together. Irene suspected he'd have liked to add *And stay out of my city,* but he shut his mouth on that and simply waved them towards the door.

Dorrins led them at a fast trot down the backstairs. "Once we're at the bottom," he puffed, "we go straight out the door and you get into the car that's waiting there."

"Right," Irene agreed. The sooner they were out of this police station and off the radar, the better.

A few minutes later they were in the back of a police car again, but this time as passengers rather than as prisoners. The city outside the car's tinted glass windows was in full swing, bright and cheerful, humming with activity. Even though only about thirty years' development (and a lack of airships) separated this city from Vale's London, it was deeply, profoundly different—the clothing, the attitudes, the mix of people outside the window, even the way they moved. New York had its own pace: the brisk thrusting stride of the pedestrians, the jarring snarls of the traffic, and the busy throb of the place.

Tyres ground against the pavement, horns squealed, and people shouted. While the car might theoretically be heading for the subway station as fast as possible, in practice it was having to contend with the traffic. A lot of traffic. This gave Irene a chance to catch up with Kai on the current situation.

The two cops in the front had clearly been ordered not to ask inconvenient questions, meaning that Kai and Irene could talk undisturbed in the back. In order to avoid eavesdropping, they were talking in Chinese. Of course this in itself would be reported back to Captain Venner as suspicious behaviour, but by the point it *did* get reported back to him, they'd be out of reach. Hopefully.

"So, what was it about the wolves?" Irene asked.

"It slipped my mind earlier," Kai admitted. "But Qing Song *is* reputed to keep them as pets."

Irene sighed. "I take it these are more likely to be slavering man-eaters than the well-trained type who might fawn on him in public."

"A dragon lord who keeps wolves does so because he wants wolves, not lap-dogs," Kai pointed out. "If he'd been known for keeping chihuahuas, then that would be entirely different."

Irene allowed herself to entertain fantasies where the worst-case scenario would be having her ankles nibbled on. She dragged herself back to reality. They were apparently at ground zero with one of the two participants in this contest. This meant that she and

Kai might be getting closer to finding out what was going on, which was fantastic—especially as time was running out like sand through her fingers—but it also raised the prospective danger level. "But if it is Qing Song, why is he prowling the streets with his pack of wolves?"

"You're being a little dramatic there," Kai said. "That sounds like the sort of thing a Fae would do."

"Wolves." Irene held up a finger. "Public streets." She held up another. "The two don't go well together. If all he's doing is taking them for a walk so they can get some exercise, fair enough, but that seems implausible. And even if that *is* the case, what's he doing in New York at the same time as Evariste? That does not look good *at all*."

"It doesn't," Kai agreed uncomfortably. "But it could be . . ."

"It could be what?"

"It could be a friendship. Like you and me." His hand touched hers. "I know the Library can't afford the appearance of a full alliance, but surely what's done between friends is a different matter? And if that is the case, perhaps we could even sympathize?"

Irene wanted *so much* to simply agree with him.

But she couldn't. "If it is simply friendship," she said, "and notice that I'm saying *if* here, then he has messed up big-time. I can and will feel sympathetic, but that won't change what I need to do. We've been through this. The stakes are too high. If he's acted improperly, even out of friendship, then he should have known better." She knew her words were harsh, and she saw the anger in Kai's eyes, but she felt no need to retract them. "Kai, Evariste and I are Librarians. We buy our privileges at the cost of responsibility. He should understand that."

"And if he disagrees?"

"Then I'll listen to what he has to say and make my decision based on that." She spread her hands. "We don't know. We're speculating. All that we do know is that he's not here on Library orders. This is a matter of internal dragon politics at the highest level, and if Evariste has involved the Library, then he has to answer for it."

And if I mess up, the thought ran through her head coldly, *then I'll be answering for that too, and taking as much blame as is necessary to keep the Library safe. Evariste's not the only one who's gambling with high stakes.*

"Just a moment," Kai said suddenly, turning to peer out of the window. He switched to English. "Officer! Is that car following us? The green one, back and to our left?"

Irene turned to follow his gaze, but it took her a moment to pick out the car. She hadn't noticed it before—it had been lost in the sea of long-bodied cars and heavy taxis, or shielded by one of the passing buses packed with people on both floors. She wasn't used to judging this place's rhythms yet, or spotting what was unnatural.

The cop in the right front seat swore and stepped on the gas. "Those damn reporters must have gotten on our tail after all. Sorry about that, ma'am, sir. You'll just have to run for it, the moment we get to the subway."

"How far is it now?" Irene asked.

"Just around the corner, ma'am. You all ready to go?"

"Ready and waiting," Irene said. She reached into her handbag and pulled out a few ten-dollar bills, passing them forward into the hand that was already extended to accept the bribe. "Thanks for the assistance."

The car pitched around the corner and screeched to a stop against the curb. Kai scrambled out almost before the car had finished braking, pulling the door open for Irene. As she jumped out, she saw the green car weaving through the traffic to pull in behind them.

Its windows were rolled down and something metallic glinted in the sun.

Kai swept her legs from under her and dropped her to the sidewalk, throwing himself protectively across her as the first few shots rang out.

CHAPTER 10

Irene plastered herself against the pavement as bullets whined through the air above her head. They chewed holes in the car they'd just left and scythed into the crowd at the station entrance. Screams mingled with shrieking car wheels as every bit of traffic in the vicinity attempted to get out of the vicinity.

Including, she suddenly realized, the police car that had brought them here. And it was the only thing between them and whoever was firing the tommy guns.

"**Car wheels, lock!**" she shouted with the speed of panic.

Every single car within the range of her voice squealed to a stop. The air was thick with dust and exhaust fumes. The two cops abandoned the car, scrambling out to run for cover. But the bullets didn't stop.

"Jam the guns?" Kai suggested. He wriggled sideways, trying to get farther out of the line of fire.

"Yes, I was getting to that!" Irene snapped. She should have done that first, rather than clog up the entire area with stopped cars. Panicked decisions were rarely good decisions. "And then we run."

"We should deal with those gunmen."

"No guns, no gunman problem. If we get away, that'll defuse the situation." A bullet whined just above her head as she prepared to move. "Get ready. **Guns, jam!**"

Kai pulled her to her feet, and they were running before anyone realized the shooting had stopped.

Irene had assumed people would take cover in the subway station entrance. But she hadn't considered the impact of two men with tommy guns, indiscriminately hosing the street with lead. Now that she could see the bodies, she forced herself to carry on, ignoring the copper stench of fresh blood in the air. She didn't have time for it if she wanted to get out alive.

The turnstiles inside the subway station were deserted, apart from the guard hiding in his booth. Everyone had, quite sensibly, chosen to run away rather than wait to see what was going on. It drew a very clear picture of this America—or at least this New York—when it came to guns and violence. Irene had to admit that Captain Venner had been justified when he told her to leave town.

A flood of people were streaming down the tiled stairs beyond the turnstiles, hurrying down corridors and piling into any trains that were leaving the station. Men and women jostled shoulder-to-shoulder, abandoning any semblance of politeness in their urgency to get away from the gun-fire. Women in narrow knee-length skirts and thin draping jackets were pushed up against men in wide-shouldered suits, staggering to keep their feet in the mob. The wide entrance-hall was full of voices screaming and re-echoing, curses cut short, and pleas to let someone through. A group of sailors in blue and white formed a flying wedge, punching their way through like an arrowhead. Kai swerved to one side to grab something from a magazine stand, and Irene had to struggle against the crowd to catch up with him.

"Which train?" he shouted, catching her wrist and pulling her closer.

"Any!" she called back. "But we want the end carriage."

He didn't ask why, but instead forced his way through the crowd, dragging her behind him. The New York subway was no place for weaklings under normal conditions, and the shooting outside had pushed it towards a new level of pandemonium. Unlike the normal semi-civility of the London Underground, this was a morass of screaming, elbows, and trampling feet.

Still, she thought grimly, it would make it very difficult for anyone to follow them.

The two of them staggered onto the next subway train that came along, then—before it left the station—scrambled through the door at the far end, and exited onto the track, carefully avoiding stepping on any rails. Irene wasn't sure which rails were electrified and didn't want to find out the hard way.

A quarter of an hour later, they were hiding in a maintenance room. A single light bulb dangled from the ceiling, casting a dim light over the cans of paint, mops and buckets, and other dust-shrouded impedimenta that filled the place. There was barely enough room for the two of them. But it was the first time in hours that Irene had been sure they were safe and unobserved.

And hopefully there weren't any werewolves in *this* underground railway system.

"This wasn't what I planned at all," she said. She raised a hand to brush dust and soot from her face, and noticed that her fingers were smeared with blood. That must have happened outside the station. When she'd been crawling on the ground as the bullets whipped by above her. Irene wasn't a stranger to violence: she'd been shot at before. But this casual level of overkill, with absolutely no regard for civilian casualties, was disturbing. "I knew we should expect trouble from dragons, but I hadn't planned on being shot at by organized crime, or chased by the police."

"The level of surveillance is worrying," Kai agreed. "And it seems to be intensifying. I don't think we can afford to stay in any one place for long."

"Then let's get this over as fast as possible, before anyone *else* gets shot," Irene said. "I've had enough of being reactive. Time to get proactive. We need a map."

"Done," Kai said, pulling a folded street map out of his jacket.

Irene blinked. "How on earth did you get hold of that?"

"When we were coming into the station. I saw some maps on that bookstall." He frowned. "I regret not being able to leave any money for it, but under the circumstances . . ."

"We were in a hurry," Irene agreed, taking the map eagerly. She upturned a couple of buckets to make a makeshift table. "Very good job, Kai. Seeing as we're in New York, have a cookie."

"I'd settle for cocktails and a dance," Kai said hopefully.

"They'd probably recognize me as 'Jeanette Smith' the minute I walked into a nightclub by now." Irene unclasped the locket with Evariste's name in it and dangled it over the map. "You too. As an imported English mobster, that is. You were standing right behind me when the reporters were taking photographs."

"I managed to hide my face more than you did. Which is probably a good thing." Kai frowned. "If Qing Song is here, and if he or Hu recognizes me . . ."

"That would be inconvenient," Irene agreed. She focused her thoughts and held the pendant over the map, as she'd done before. **"Locket, indicate the place where the Librarian whose name you contain is to be found . . ."**

A couple of hours later, Kai was assisting Irene off a streetcar in the middle of Brooklyn. Brown-stone buildings three or four storeys high walled the streets and turned them into canyons, rising high enough to block off most of the sunlight. The entrance doorways were higher than street level, and little flights of steps ran down from each one to the sidewalk. Ranks of windows looked down at the people hurrying below, blank eyes in shadowed faces watching the crowds of New Yorkers going about their business.

Nobody had spotted them yet—or at least nobody had pointed at them and yelled, "Hey, aren't you Jeanette Smith, the famous English mobster?"—and Irene was tentatively starting to relax.

The brown-stone on the street corner they'd located on the map looked like any of the other brown-stones in the area. It had been a single building once, before being converted into apartments: Irene could just make out the row of door-bells inside the porch. There was a convenient corner shop opposite, giving Irene and Kai an excuse to look in the window while they pondered their next move.

"The front door would be too obvious," Kai said quietly. "If anyone's watching it, they couldn't miss us."

Irene nodded. "But the back's suspicious to any watchers." Their route had taken them all round the block while they scouted the place. There was a fire escape visible up the back of the building, but that approach had its own risks. "Better to walk up to the front door, as if we're regular inhabitants."

"As long as you let me do the talking," Kai said. "Your American accent is . . ." He looked for a tactful way of phrasing it. "Unconvincing."

Irene glared at him in the shop window, and adjusted a wrinkle in her stocking rather than look at him directly. "Oh, very well," she agreed.

Kai tilted his fedora, inspected his reflection, re-tilted it, then led the way to the brown-stone. He mimed fumbling in his pocket and finding a key, then unlocking the door. Irene stood behind him and, just loudly enough to be audible, said, **"Door-lock, open."**

The door swung open and Kai held it for Irene before closing it behind them. The hallway inside was sparsely furnished, with only a numbered set of letter boxes to break the entrance corridor's monotony. It was floored in battered linoleum, and the old wood that panelled the walls was scarred and dented by years of casual punishment. There were two doors on the left-hand wall, and a flight of stairs at the end of the corridor. Irene glanced at the letter boxes, but none of them had names next to them, just apartment numbers. A pity: it would have made things easier.

The second door on the left swung open and a woman poked her head out. She was in her mid-fifties, her hair a brassy orange and her shawl-collared dress a battered purple. "Have you got the— Oh, sorry." She looked over Kai and Irene. "I figured it was someone else."

"Sorry," Kai said, managing a rather convincing New York accent. "Hope we didn't bother you."

"Nah, not a bit. I was waiting for my Tom to get back from the store. You new here?" Her eyes were bright with curiosity.

"Just here to see an acquaintance," Kai said. "I think he's on one of the upper floors. He gave me his key but not his apartment number."

"What's his name?" the woman asked.

"Evariste," Kai said. They couldn't be sure he'd be using his real name, but one had to say *something*. "He won't have been here long; a month at most."

"Oh, him." The woman pursed her lips in disapproval. "I don't know his name, but there's this new fellow who's been here only a couple of weeks. And everyone else has been living here for years. He's on the fourth floor, left-hand side. I have got to say, while I'm not *prejudiced*, a boy like him would have done better taking rooms in Harlem. I mean, it's only natural, isn't it?"

Irene was sharply reminded of the prejudices of 1920s America. But if they wanted information, unfortunately they'd have to play along. "That's what we told him, wasn't it?" she said to Kai, struggling to match his accent. "We said he should have taken rooms there."

Kai nodded soberly. A glint in his eye showed that he'd caught Irene's direction. "I hope he hasn't done anything to disturb you while he's been here," he said to the woman.

"Well, no, not so much," she admitted, in a tone of voice suggesting that she wished she had something to complain about. "It's not as if he even leaves his apartment that much. Just sits there all day and does I don't know what, and only goes out to get some food and a glass of something from around the corner. What does he do for work? It looks real shifty—know what I mean? I've heard about that sort of thing on the radio."

This was interesting. It sounded more like hiding than active cooperation with a dragon partner. Irene filed it away thoughtfully and nodded. "I'm sorry to have disturbed you," she said to the woman.

"Not a problem," she said reluctantly. Clearly she'd been hoping for a longer gossip about their new tenant. "Have a nice day."

As the door shut behind her, Irene and Kai trotted up the stairs.

They paused on the third floor. Irene unclasped the pendant from her neck and looped it round her left wrist. **"Point to the Librarian whose name you share,"** she instructed it softly.

The pendant jerked and pulled at her wrist like an impatient puppy, pointing upwards and to the left. She and Kai quietly began ascending the stairs.

On the fourth floor the pendant's pull became horizontal, tugging towards the left-hand apartment. Just as the woman had said. There was no obvious sign of anything out of the ordinary. No swarms of flies, no smell of corpses, no suspicious noises . . . Irene forcibly jerked her mind away from trashy detective-novel tropes, and glanced at Kai to see if he had any thoughts.

Kai mimed knocking and raised an eyebrow.

Irene considered it. If Evariste was guilty of something, then even knocking at the door might panic him into trying to escape. Perhaps she should have had Kai wait outside, beneath the fire escape.

Oh well, hindsight always had all the best ideas. *Be ready to open the door,* she mouthed at Kai.

He nodded.

"Door, unlock," she said softly.

The lock clicked audibly. Kai kicked the door open: it swung back to crash against the wall, giving them a clear view of the apartment lounge.

The room was full of books. Volumes had been piled up against the walls in gaudy slices of colour, and bags and boxes of yet more books turned the floor into an obstacle course. There were no pictures hanging on the walls, no furniture other than a table and a couple of chairs, no rugs, no decorations—nothing except the books.

It reminded Irene of her own rooms back at the Library.

The man sitting at the dining-table jerked his head up from his arms, looking at them in bleary-eyed shock. He was in his shirt-sleeves: his tie hung unfastened round his neck, and stubble made his dark skin even darker. He looked at Irene, his attention skipping over her as unimportant, and then at Kai, and his eyes widened with shock. **"Books, hit that dragon!"** he shouted, pushing his chair back and shoving himself away from the table.

Kai threw himself back from the doorway with a curse as books came tumbling from their piles and rising from the floor, slicing through the air towards him.

"Books, down on the floor!" Irene shouted, abandoning all hope of silence. She couldn't see past the books, but: **"Trousers, hobble Evariste!"**

The crash of books hitting the floor—and a few of them hitting Kai—echoed through the building. Another crash from inside the apartment suggested that Evariste had gone from vertical to horizontal. **"Clothing, release me!"** he ordered. **"Door, close!"**

Irene dived into the room, rolling across the floor, just as the door slammed shut behind her. That was the problem with duelling in the Language: the longer you spent talking, the more opportunity you gave your opponent to take action. Evariste shouldn't have wasted time disentangling his legs. **"Tie, choke Evariste,"** she said quickly. It was cruel, but it was the quickest way she could think of to silence him. **"Table, pin Evariste to the wall."**

The table slid across the floor, catching Evariste between it and the wall behind, and his tie rose to circle his throat and twist round his windpipe. He struggled with it, his fingers clawing at the fabric, but he didn't have the breath to say anything in the Language.

Irene rose from her crouch and walked across to him. "Stop fighting me and we'll talk," she said. "Nod if you agree."

Evariste jerked a tiny nod. It wasn't a gesture of surrender, just a temporary accommodation.

"Tie, release Evariste's throat," Irene said. She felt a twinge of guilt as she saw the red mark it had left behind. "Sorry. But we need to talk. I'm from the Library."

"That much is obvious," Evariste snapped. "And I see that you've sold out *too*."

"I beg your pardon?"

"Him." Evariste pointed at Kai, who'd entered the room and was kicking aside the fallen books that littered the floor as he stalked towards them. A trail of blood streaked Kai's temple where one of the missiles had connected. "So much for the Library's neutrality!"

"He isn't my ally, he's my student," Irene said, conscious that this might look like splitting hairs. "And *I* am a full Librarian, sent by the Library to find out what you're up to. It will make things a great deal easier for us both if you tell me, here and now. I think we both know just how dangerous the current situation is."

Evariste flinched. Guilt and desperation fought visibly across his face. He took a deep breath, attempting to calm himself. "All right. If you let me go, then we can talk about this."

He might have been a good researcher, Irene decided, but he

wasn't a good liar. Perhaps it was because he was exhausted. He looked as if he hadn't slept properly for days. But the way his eyes flickered around the room, looking for options, indicated that he was going to try something the moment she ordered the table to release him.

She hoped she was a more convincing liar than he was. It would be *embarrassing* to be that obvious.

"Very well," she said with an inner sigh. Best to give him the chance to behave, even if she suspected he wasn't going to take it. This was not going to be tidy. "**Table—**"

A sound from outside made her break off mid-sentence, and all three of them turned towards the window.

It was the howling of wolves.

CHAPTER 11

S heer panic filled Evariste's face. "**Floor—**" he began in the Language.

Kai's fist caught Evariste in the jaw, cracking his head back against the wall. Evariste sagged across the table.

"That was a bit hasty," Irene said, picking her way across the book-strewn floor to the window. She was feeling conflicted. Normally she'd be absolutely against the idea of Kai punching other Librarians. But the next word out of Evariste's mouth would have been something like *collapse*, to facilitate his escape.

Kai shrugged. "You're the one who's always saying an operative needs to know when to take decisive action."

"My life would be easier if you didn't have such a good memory," Irene muttered. "Or at least it wouldn't involve you using the word *hypocrisy* quite so much. Or giving me meaningful looks." She peered out the side of the window, to avoid being spotted from the street below.

The wolves were just turning the corner at the intersection a block away. There were half a dozen of them—large, vigorous-looking creatures, their glossy dark coats gleaming in the shadows as they stalked along the sidewalk. They weren't running. They moved with a slow deliberate pace that nevertheless ate up the yards.

A burst of cold atavistic fear told Irene they'd be reaching this building within a minute or so.

Behind them walked a couple of men, their pace making it clear they were following the wolves, not guiding them. It was difficult to see them clearly from this distance, but the one in the lead was obviously in charge.

"Is that Qing Song?" Irene asked.

"I don't know what he looks like," Kai replied. "But if it is . . ."

They both turned to look at Evariste.

"Right," Irene said briskly. There was no time to waste. "You take him down the fire escape—no, wait, go up the fire escape, not down, and along the roof if possible, and see if you can break the trail. Then get a cab. Tell them he's sick. Get a hotel room somewhere. And give me the map." She held out her hand for it. "I'll catch up with you later—I'll track Evariste and find you both. You'll need to make sure he doesn't escape."

Kai handed her the map reflexively, then stared at her. "What do you mean, *I'm* doing this? What are you going to do?"

"I'm going to slow down pursuit." She tucked the map under her arm and quickly unwound the locket from round her wrist, fastening it around her neck again and hiding it beneath her blouse. "I'm going to delay them while you get Evariste out of here. We need answers from him."

"But what if he wakes up?"

"Gag him, tie him up, whatever; tell him it's all my fault. You know what I can do—assume he'd be able to do the same. Don't tell me you've never thought of tying me up to keep me in one place." The way he avoided her eyes confirmed her suspicions. "Come *on*, Kai, we're running out of time here."

"And what if Qing Song takes offence at something you say? He does have wolves, after all . . ." But he was already dragging the table away from the wall and bundling the unconscious Evariste over his shoulder.

"I'll make it clear that the Library knows exactly where I am. Right now you're my big ace in the hole." Irene tried the room's other door. It gave onto a small hallway leading to a little kitchen and an even smaller bedroom. The window looked out onto the back of the building. "As long as they don't know you're here, or who you are, I want to keep it that way. Come *on*!"

She wasn't surprised to find that the window giving onto the fire escape had been well-oiled, and the furniture had been arranged to make it easy to climb out. Irene held the window open while Kai dragged the other Librarian through it and gave them a cheerful wave. "Be careful!" she said.

"Oh, certainly, I'll just follow your excellent example," Kai said drily. He closed the window behind him with a thump.

Irene quickly moved to check Evariste's bedroom. It was small, dingy, and packed with books. She checked the underside of the mattress, the bedside chest of drawers, the washstand, and everywhere else that came to mind. But there were no convenient caches of secret documents or diaries, hidden stashes of gems, or anything else that might explain Evariste's behaviour. She left the room as it was, with the drawers open and the covers pulled back. It would support the story she was going to tell.

A glance out the front window showed that the wolves had gathered at the door of the building. The street had, unsurprisingly, emptied of bystanders.

A number of things were coming together now in her mind. The books scattered around this apartment were a jumbled assortment of fiction, ranging from cheap dime novels to second-hand hardbacks going mouldy at the edges. There was only one reason why a Librarian would have gathered such a haphazard assortment of low-cost texts and then not even *tried* to put them in order. Evariste hadn't been collecting them to read: he'd been using them to create a Library ward. By creating a metaphysical link between this apartment and the Library, he'd been trying to hide from someone or something. And, given his reaction to Kai—and to the wolves outside—it was a reasonable deduction that he'd been hiding from dragons in general, and from Qing Song in particular. Though she didn't yet know how Hu and Jin Zhi were involved in this picture.

She'd told Kai that he was her ace in the hole—that she wanted to keep him a secret. But there was more to it than that. The moment Kai came into conflict with other dragons here, he would have to decide which side he was on. Whether he was going to help the Library, or whether that would be a betrayal of his family and his own kind. And for both her own sake and Kai's, Irene intended to put off that moment for as long as possible.

Outside, the wolves set up a clamour. Irene took a deep breath, mentally crossed her fingers for Kai and Evariste, and walked out of the apartment. She began to descend the stairs.

There was a crash. Probably someone kicking the building door open. The growling of wolves echoed up the stairwell.

Irene reminded herself forcibly that if the wolves were randomly attacking anyone who came near them, Captain Venner would have known about it. She kept on walking.

Unless they completely devoured the victims and disposed of the skeletons, her imagination inconveniently suggested.

Don't be stupid, wolves can't dispose of skeletons, she told herself firmly. *Even unnaturally intelligent wolves that are the personal pets of dragons. That's the sort of thing a dragon has human minions for . . .*

She turned the last corner on the stairs and looked down at the ground-floor below. Although there were only half a dozen wolves, they managed to fill the corridor with a sea of dark fur and gleaming eyes, weaving back and forth and around each other. Their breathing was loud and heavy on the air, a raw edge against her nerves. But even when compared to the pack of predators, it was the two men behind them who drew her attention.

She paused in her descent, trying to slow her suddenly rapid heartbeat. If she didn't get them on the defensive immediately, she'd already lost.

"I *beg* your pardon," she said, raising a disdainful eyebrow. "What are *you* doing here?"

The frozen pause at the other end of the corridor gave her a better chance to assess the men—one clearly a dragon, the other not—as they stood there. The one in the lead was obviously in charge, from his poise, his manner, and the fact that his suit looked about twice as expensive as the other's. His skin and hair were both black, though his hair had a very slight tinge of dark green to it, like the sheen of a starling's wing. He was broader in the shoulder than Kai. He looked up at Irene, with an air that suggested he'd rather have been looking down. He had the same powerful presence as Jin Zhi. He stood like a statue formed from the living earth, a more-than-human entity that had temporarily taken on the form of a human.

The second man was instantly classifiable as a professional— the sort who fixed problems for his employer, permanently. He was dapper and smooth-looking, but his eyes were thin and careful, and he didn't stop scanning the room. But he held back, waiting for the first man to speak. *Bodyguard,* Irene decided, though he might not know his employer's true nature.

Finally the first man spoke. His voice was bass, clear, and definitely not local. "I don't believe we've been introduced."

Irene stamped down her inner flame of relief that she hadn't been eaten already. "My name is Marguerite," she said coolly, "and I work for the Library. I assume you know of us?"

Now was that a flash of *guilt* she saw flicker across his face? How very interesting. "Of course," he said. "And I assume you know who and what I am."

Time to roll the dice some more and hope they came up as a winning combination. "Naturally. Lord Qing Song, I believe?"

He didn't visibly react. But the wolves did. They retreated to surround him, pressing against his legs and raising their heads to rub against his hands.

Lord Qing Song, Irene reflected, *if you want to remain unfathomable, you shouldn't surround yourself with pets who respond to your moods.*

When he replied, she detected a note of caution. "I didn't realize the Library knew me well enough to recognize me on sight."

Irene shrugged. She began to walk towards him. Of course this meant approaching the wolves too, but no plan was perfect. "Well, we do try to keep records of prominent members of the dragon courts. But I have no idea what you're doing here."

She wanted to keep him off balance. Her words were technically polite, but her tone was so casual, by dragon standards, as to be verging on an insult. And the longer they baited each other, the more chance Kai had to make a clean getaway.

One wolf padded forward to sniff at Irene's hand as she reached the bottom of the stairs. She desperately tried to remember whether she'd touched Evariste. She didn't think she had: she'd only gone through his belongings. She held her hand out for the wolf to inspect, and mentally crossed her fingers that she wouldn't be drawing back a bloody stump. "How charming," she said, listening to it growl deep in its throat.

"My own personal breeding," Qing Song said. "Dire wolves, of course."

"They certainly look it," Irene said drily.

"A very early form of wolf, that is," Qing Song explained. He rubbed behind the ears of the largest of the six. "Every man needs a hobby."

"Unfortunately I spend so much time chasing books that I have very little opportunity to do anything else."

"And are you here to 'chase' a book?" Qing Song slid the question in quickly, like a knife between armour plates.

Irene had been planning her answer to that question. Now she just needed to make it look natural. "No. To be honest with you— should it be Prince or Lord, by the way?"

"Lord will do," Qing Song said. "For the moment." He seemed more comfortable, now that they were standing on the same level and Irene no longer had the advantage of height.

She nodded. "I'm here because we've misplaced one of our own."

Qing Song frowned. "Another Librarian? Has something happened to him?"

Now, it could be that Qing Song habitually defaulted to male exemplars, as in his comment that every *man* needed a hobby. Or maybe he knew it was a male Librarian. Vale would have said they didn't have enough data. Vale would have been right.

"We don't know," she said, with a slight shrug. "That's part of the problem. He was on record as coming to this world, but he's dropped out of contact. I was quite astonished to see you in the vicinity when I came downstairs. I mean, what are the odds that we two should meet up, in such a large city?"

Qing Song hesitated. "I will explain," he finally said. "I would not normally share these matters with an outsider, but possibly you can help." He paused, as if expecting her to express her gratitude for the opportunity to be of service. When she didn't react, he continued. "I am hunting down a thief. The trail led me here."

Irene took an angry step forward, even though all her reflexes would have vastly preferred backwards. "Are you suggesting a Librarian has *stolen* from you?"

"Certainly not!" Qing Song said quickly. "It occurred to me that the thief might have stolen from your colleague as well. That would explain why his trail led me here."

It would have been easy for Qing Song to claim that this Librarian had stolen from *him*. It might even be true. So why should Qing Song emphatically deny that? Unless he wanted to keep Irene on his side for some reason.

Irene nodded slowly. "I must admit that, from his apartment upstairs, it looks as if my colleague was kidnapped."

Qing Song turned to the bodyguard. "Lucci. You know something of these things."

"Have to look the place over first, boss," the man said, touching his hat.

"On the fourth floor," Irene said helpfully. "The door is open. I'm not an expert, but it looks as if there was a struggle."

Lucci glanced to Qing Song for permission, received a nod, and padded up the stairs to investigate, as silent as the wolves.

Irene wondered how long she could keep him here. Kai would be going as fast as he could, but an unconscious body was an inconvenient deadweight to carry. If she could just keep Qing Song's attention on her for a little longer . . .

She sighed. "This is so irritating. I was in the middle of quite an interesting piece of research about Gnostic imagery in the literature of post-revolutionary France, and I was called away to come and look for a very junior Librarian who'd simply overstayed his holiday. And now it looks as if he's got into trouble. Why would someone be kidnapped in this place?"

"Have you considered the possibility of Fae action?" Qing Song suggested.

"They're here *too*? Our records are badly out of date. I'd been told this world was comparatively untouched by interference."

"Did that come from other dragons?" Qing Song enquired. "We might have acquaintances in common."

Irene's composure vanished like ice in a kettle. She couldn't risk compromising Kai. She didn't even want to risk compromising his uncle Ao Shun, or Li Ming. But claiming that she'd never met any dragons would lower her importance in Qing Song's eyes. "None that I am at liberty to discuss," she said, in a tone that implied he should understand her position.

His slow nod suggested that he did. "I will shortly be taking up high office in the court of the Queen of the Southern Lands. Possibly we may assist each other in future . . ."

"Congratulations on your future elevation," she answered neutrally. "I'm sure you'll do an excellent job." But if he was that certain of the role, did he have the book? And if so, what was he still doing here, hunting down Evariste? The awareness of her current ignorance chilled her with the thought of all the things that might already have gone wrong.

One of the wolves whined, and a trickle of panic wormed its way down Irene's spine as she wondered if it had smelled out a lie. Then a moment later she saw Lucci coming down the stairs.

"Report," Qing Song ordered. "You may speak freely in front of this woman."

"He's gone," Lucci said. The wolves cleared a path for him as he walked across to Qing Song. "This dame's right—there was a struggle. Books all over the place. Someone went out the back window: it wasn't locked. There were scuff marks. I figure it was one, maybe two people, and they were carrying someone with them. They turned the place over before they left. Pulled out the drawers, checked under the mattress—all the usual tricks. Sorry, boss, but we're too late here."

"How long ago was it?" Irene demanded, cutting across Qing Song before he could ask any questions. "And was there any sign of who they were?"

"Not more than an hour ago," Lucci said, after a glance at Qing Song for approval. "And no, lady, they weren't the obliging sort who'd leave a ransom note behind. But I can tell you that whoever it was, he opened the door for them."

Irene frowned. "How can you tell that?"

"No scratches from picklocks, the lock wasn't forced, and the door wasn't kicked in." Lucci's eyes slid to the building door, which still hung open. "Speaking of which, boss, we might want to consider taking a walk before the cops get here. The neighbours might get nosy and call it in."

"I will inspect the place first . . . for signs of my property." Qing Song tagged on the second sentence a little hastily, as if realizing he'd need an explanation for his interest. "If we find news of your colleague, we will inform you. What is his name? And where will you be staying?"

Irene cast her mind back to the hotels Captain Venner had mentioned, and picked the one *without* a visitor with a wolf pack. "I'll be taking rooms at the Plaza Hotel until this is sorted out," she said. "And my colleague's name is Evariste. If I run across your property while I'm looking for him—what is it, by the way?"

"A jade statue of a wolf," Qing Song said. "You couldn't possibly mistake it."

"I see." Irene almost wished she was wearing glasses so that she could adjust them disdainfully. She decided her persona needed one more little push, just to confirm herself in Qing Song's eyes as a powerful, arrogant, but conveniently ignorant idiot. "I trust that your investigation won't get in the way of mine. Which I shall start to commence now. Good day." *A powerful, arrogant idiot with bad grammar,* she amended her own thought.

Qing Song's eyes narrowed in anger at being so casually dismissed, but he didn't speak. However, his wolves growled as they backed away from the door, leaving Irene clear passage, and the note of rising fury in their voices told her that she had managed to prick his temper. The air was close and heavy with leashed power; even Lucci had removed his hat to swipe a handkerchief across his forehead and was standing well clear of his boss.

Irene strolled to the door, keeping her pace even, and left the building. She'd need at least one trip by subway, just to make absolutely sure that no wolves could track her scent.

And she had a lot of questions for Evariste.

CHAPTER 12

"Congratulations," Irene said when Kai opened the door. "I believe you have managed single-handedly to find the most dubious hotel in New York."

Kai waved her into the room and closed the door behind her, then sat down with a thump in the battered armchair. He rested his elbows on his knees and put his head in his hands. "This has been very stressful," he said in muffled tones.

Irene looked from him to Evariste. Evariste was lying on the room's only bed, thoroughly gagged with the remains of a torn-up pillowcase, with his wrists tied to the far corners. He glared back at her. "For all of us, I think," she said drily.

"I had to assume that he might be as resourceful as you are." Kai paused. "Which *is* meant as a compliment. But then I had nothing to do except sit here and wait."

Irene imagined it. Sitting here in this windowless room in a seedy New York hotel, with nothing to do except look at the wall and listen to Evariste's breathing. And no way for him to know what she was doing, or how much danger she was in. She laid a hand on Kai's shoulder. "I know," she said. "I wish I'd been able to think of a better option."

"Did you manage to deal with Qing Song?" Kai asked, sounding slightly mollified.

"The answer would be yes, obviously, since I'm still alive and talking to you."

Kai snorted. "Seriously."

Irene noticed that Evariste, at Qing Song's name, had gone very still and tense on the bed and that he was giving her his full attention. "Seriously," she said to both men. "I accused him of interfering with my investigation, before he could suspect *me* of interfering with *his* investigation. Then I acted like an arrogant, over-privileged idiot until he was only too pleased to see me go. I've broken my trail enough times between there and here that his wolves won't be able to follow me. But he left me with a number of very interesting questions."

She walked across to the bed where Evariste lay. Like everything else in this dump, from the lampshade to the carpet to the washstand in the corner, it was old and battered. But it was solid enough, and the bindings round his wrists held him firmly in place.

He looked up at her, struggling for self-control. His throat jerked as he swallowed. His skin was a washed-out greyish brown against the off-white of the pillowcase, as though he'd been indoors for weeks on end without the chance to see the sun and he'd been living in fear for all that time.

Irene felt a twinge of guilt but suppressed it. Evariste wasn't an innocent; he was a sworn Librarian, like her, and as such he had responsibilities. Right now the best thing she could do for both him and the Library was to establish the truth. "Evariste, we need answers," she said. "If I take the gag off, will you help us?"

He jerked a nod.

"All right. Hold still . . ." Irene fumbled with the knot. "Kai, please can you get a glass of water? I imagine Evariste's mouth will be dry, after he's been gagged."

"That sounds like personal experience," Kai said, splashing water into a glass.

"My exploits aren't *always* brilliantly successful." Irene managed to tease the knot open and dropped the strip of fabric on the pillow, then helped Evariste work the remaining wad of fabric out of his mouth. She sat down on the bed next to him and wished that she'd had some actual training in interrogation. As opposed to practical experience of being on the other end. "All right, Evariste. I realize that we haven't met under the best of circumstances. Would it help if I said I'm sorry about that?"

"No," Evariste croaked.

Perhaps that had been a bit too much to expect. She took the glass of water from Kai and held it to Evariste's lips, letting him sip from it. "I'll introduce myself. I'm from the Library. My name is Irene."

Evariste choked on the water, and Irene hastily pulled the glass away. "Are you all right?"

He stared up at her. "You're her? *The* Irene? The one who stopped Alberich?"

"Most of our teachers would be getting migraines at such an imprecise sentence," Irene said, wondering about her reputation. "My name is Irene, and yes, I recently left Alberich abandoned in a burning library, which I can only hope *did* stop him. Permanently." She left out the part that she'd started the fire. She was, after all, trying to get Evariste to trust her.

He hesitated for a moment. Then he said, "Prove it. Let me see your Library brand."

Irene suppressed a sigh. It would have been nice if the one person in this world to whom she'd actually told the *truth* had believed her. "Very well. Just a moment."

After a few contortions, she was able to bare enough of her back for Evariste to see it. She was conscious of Kai's eyes on her as well, and for a moment she wished Evariste wasn't there. She forced herself back to the task in hand. "Satisfied?"

"I'm satisfied that you're a Librarian and that you're called Irene." Evariste's voice was stiff with disbelief and stubbornness, as if he was building his barricades before the rest of the world had the chance to betray him. "I still don't know why you're associating with a *dragon* or why you kidnapped me."

"That's exactly the same tactic I was using earlier today," Irene said approvingly, covering herself up again. "Challenge the other person to explain what they're up to, in order to hide the weaknesses in your own position. I'll give you a good mark for that when we get back to the Library. But I need to know what's going on first."

Evariste jerked his head in Kai's direction. "I want to know what's going on with him before I tell you *anything*."

"For the moment I am studying under Irene here," Kai said coldly. "I am her apprentice. My father and uncle are aware of the situation. I don't yet know if I will take permanent vows to the Library. But my presence doesn't imply that the Library and the dragons are allied." He paused. "Even if maybe they should be."

"You aren't helping, Kai," Irene muttered. "You aren't helping at all."

"I concede that the Library shouldn't be dragged into disputes like this one," Kai said, "but you and I have far more in common than the Library does with the Fae."

Irene passed him the empty glass. "More water, please. Look, Evariste, getting back to my questions—"

"Is this where the threats come in?" Evariste asked. "Are you going to offer to go out of the room while he works me over?"

Irene took a deep breath. "We are not here to play good cop, bad cop. Or even bad cop, worse cop. Evariste—we're on your side."

Evariste just looked towards Kai.

"I'm on Irene's side," Kai said. "Don't give me an excuse to be otherwise." His voice was neutral, even mild, but it still managed to have an undertone like the edge of a razor.

Irene strongly considered running her hands through her hair. "Evariste . . ." Perhaps he'd be more helpful if she could convince him that she was speaking the truth. She switched to the Language. **"I have been sent here by the Library to find you and to establish what's going on. Rumours that a Librarian is meddling in dragon court politics are a great danger to the Library and to Librarians. The Library is *not* allied with the dragons, and I am *not* working for either Qing Song or Jin Zhi, and nor is Kai. I can't promise that you won't be in trouble from the Library . . ."** And she couldn't promise that she was here to save him either. Not if he'd betrayed the Library. She chose her words very carefully. **"But I will do my best to help you escape from Qing Song, if you will explain the current state of affairs."** The words seemed to hang in the air as Irene spoke them, like distant organ notes in a far larger space: a guarantee of truth, and a promise that would bind her.

Evariste still hesitated. "You swear you'll help me?"

"I won't help you get away from the Library," Irene said, "but I can and will help you get away from Qing Song. Evariste, you need to understand how bad this is. We have two major dragon factions competing for power, and one of them's claiming that the Library's been helping the other. Do you realize how much danger that puts Librarians in if the Fae hear about this? Or if other dragon factions get involved and take sides against us?"

She saw Evariste's face twitch, and with a sick feeling she recognized guilt in his eyes. *He has done something, and he knows it . . .*

She put every ounce of sincerity she could muster into her voice. "I've been sent by Library Security to make sure that the Library doesn't get dragged any further into this. And let's be honest, I'm here to bury the evidence if it has been. We are neutral: we *cannot* afford to be otherwise. We're past the point of covering up minor breaches of regulations. I need to know what you've done and what's going on here. I'm not trying to railroad you or blame you, but I *have to know*."

Evariste shut his eyes for a moment. "All right," he finally said. He swallowed. "I'm not stupid. I understand what you're saying. I know this looks bad—no, I know this *is* bad—but I had my reasons. And I didn't realize how serious it was until I was too deep to get out. I'll tell you. But will you untie me first? Please?"

Irene started to unknot the torn sheets that leashed his wrists to the bed-posts. "Where would you like to start?" she asked.

"It started with Julian." Evariste watched the ceiling as Irene untied him. "He was my mentor, you know. He recruited me into the Library."

"Was he your mentor while you were training too?" Irene freed his right wrist and walked round the bed to undo his left wrist.

"No, that was Neith." Evariste flexed the fingers of his right hand, working out the stiffness. "Julian was Librarian-in-Residence on the world I came from. I knew him when I was growing up. He helped me get a scholarship to the local university, you know? Got me trained and everything. I hadn't found out about the Library then, and sometimes I thought there was something a bit weird about him—about the people who came to see him. But it wasn't that important. He was an okay guy."

"Where did he live?"

"Chicago. On G-14. There were a lot of wizards around there; it was a high-magic world. That let him hide in plain sight. People just assumed he was one of the crowd." Evariste's words came spilling out as if he'd been waiting for the chance to tell someone about it. "Things went wrong for me—I couldn't get a job, I didn't have the credentials for big-time research, I'd broken up with my girl. Then Julian recruited me for the Library. It was my big chance. My way to something better."

Irene nodded, trying to assess his age. He was younger than she was, but it was difficult to judge by how much. He looked as if he was in his mid-twenties, but he wouldn't have aged during his years of study in the Library. "You had the standard apprenticeship?"

"Yeah. He sent me letters from time to time. I was apprentice, then journeyman, and I got my brand. And so finally I thought I'd go and see him. I'd been holding off, you know." His voice slowed. "I guess I wanted to show him all of it at once—to show how far I'd come, what I'd become, to tell him I was grateful . . ."

"To go back as an adult," Irene suggested quietly. "As an equal colleague, rather than just his student."

"Yeah, that was it. I'd sent him a letter. He knew I was coming…" Evariste took a deep breath. "Can I have some more water?"

Irene handed him the glass and waited while he drank.

"Thanks," Evariste said, putting the glass down on the bedside table. "That gag. It does dry your mouth out." He glared at Kai.

Kai shrugged. "If you want me to try to think of some other way to stop a Librarian talking, then by all means encourage me to experiment."

Evariste didn't quite flinch, but he drew in on himself, retreating behind that personal barricade again. "Yeah, there are ways, and your sort know *all* about them."

Irene held up a hand to stop Kai before he could escalate things. "What happened when you went to see Julian?" she asked, keeping her tone as encouraging as possible, though nervousness was a tight ball in her stomach. The suggestion that the dragons had ways to *inconvenience* Librarians—to use a mild, non-terrifying word—was unnerving. But it was more important to keep Evariste on track and telling his story. And they had limited time before someone tracked them down, whether it was dragons, police, criminals, or all three.

Evariste looked down at his hands. "He was dead," he said quietly. "He'd been dead a few days. It was a heart attack. The local cops had done a post-mortem. There wasn't anything suspicious about it. He'd left his property to me in his will. But it was too late. I was too late."

"I'm sorry," Irene said quietly.

"I didn't know, okay?" Evariste looked up at her, and she dismissed thoughts that he'd been trying to hide his expression in order to tell a more convincing lie. The grief in his face was too raw to be anything other than genuine. "I mean, I knew he had a bad heart, I'd seen him take pills, he'd been to the hospital and all that,

I knew that he didn't do active missions because of it, but I didn't, you know, I didn't figure he would . . . die." He took a deep sobbing breath. "I didn't know. I wasn't in time."

Irene reached across to put an arm round his shoulders comfortingly. "You couldn't have known," she said. "There was no way you could have known." But underneath she was conscious of a colder self saying, *Yes, get his confidence, you need the information.*

There were parts of herself that she didn't particularly like.

Evariste swallowed after a moment and his back straightened. "I'm okay," he said, shrugging her off.

Irene nodded. "So what happened next?"

"It was that night. I'd gone to his house to start cataloguing his books—and to make sure there wasn't anything that might give away stuff about the Library. Diaries, whatever. I didn't think he kept any, but . . ."

"But you had to check," Irene agreed.

"And then *they* turned up." Evariste's eyes moved to Kai again, and his body tensed. "Two dragons. Qing Song and his liegeman."

"Hu?" Irene asked.

"Yeah, that's him. The wolf and the fox. I was polite at first, asked them in, figured that I didn't want to insult anyone. They said they'd known Julian and . . . well, I knew he'd known some dragons, so what was the harm? But then he started making demands."

"'He' being Qing Song?"

Evariste nodded jerkily. "He said that Julian and he had had an arrangement, and Julian owed him a few debts. And since I was Julian's protégé, I had to pay what Julian owed. The way he said it, it sounded like I should be *grateful* for the opportunity."

Irene could see Kai was biting back a comment so as not to interrupt Evariste's flow. She suspected he would have agreed with Qing Song. "How did they react when you weren't enthusiastic?"

"Yeah. Yeah, that's one way of putting it." Evariste's laugh was bitter, grating in his throat. "First Qing Song just stares at me, and then Hu tries to sweet-talk me, and both of them saying that it's simply a matter of finding a book for them. Then Qing Song admits it's something to do with dragon politics—and shit, I *know* we stay out of dragon politics. So I'm saying not only no but hell no, as politely as I can. And finally Hu takes out this envelope and shoves it across the table and suggests I read it."

He shut his eyes, his energy draining from him again. "It was a letter from Julian. Remember I said my girl broke up with me before I joined the Library? Well, turns out it hadn't been as neat and tidy as I'd thought. She'd been pregnant. She'd had a daughter. And Julian never told me."

Irene tried to think of something helpful to say, something that would bridge the gap to him and convince him that she understood, but absolutely nothing came to mind.

"Anita died a couple of years after I went to the Library," Evariste said. His voice was numb now, as if he were reading the lines of a play but had no idea how to put the right emotion behind the words. "It was a car accident. Her family looked after her daughter. Miranda Sofia, that's her name. Julian had kept track of it all. He wrote in his letter that he hadn't wanted me to be distracted. *Distracted,* he called it. He wrote that he wanted me to get experience as a Librarian without having to worry about a daughter. That he'd kept tabs on Miranda. That he was sort of an occasional uncle. That he was looking forward to when he could get us together . . ." Evariste's hands clenched in his lap. "He had no right, he had no fucking *right* to do that to me, to never even *tell* me about her!"

One part of Irene was all horrified sympathy. But as she nodded and agreed, the other part of her, the colder part, could guess what was coming next. *This is why it's dangerous for Librarians to have families. It makes us vulnerable. It leaves us open to pressure.*

"That's what Qing Song's holding over you, isn't it?" she asked. "He has your daughter."

CHAPTER 13

"Yeah." Evariste glared at Irene now, his shoulders hunched defiantly. "That's what it comes down to. He has my daughter. He and his men came to talk to Julian—like I said, they'd done deals with him before. Qing Song figured Julian would help him out again. But when they arrived, they found he'd died."

"The timing on that is rather coincidental," Irene said. Had Julian tried to refuse Qing Song's request? An old Librarian, threatened and alone, who already had a heart condition . . . could Qing Song's pressure have prompted that final heart attack?

But Evariste just shrugged, apparently less suspicious than Irene. "Qing Song must have really been cursing his luck on that one. But they went through his papers, saw my letters, and knew I was going to visit. And they found this letter too, the one about my daughter. Qing Song admitted he'd read it. One of his people had gone to Anita's family, pretended to be Miranda's father, and taken her away. I don't know how he did it, but he convinced them. But he's holding Miranda now, and I don't even know where he's keeping her. I've spoken to the family, I've seen a photo of her—Miranda's real, it's not some sort of hoax. He has my daughter. And if I don't find the book, he will have her killed. I had to play along till I knew where to find the book—so I had something to bargain with. What choice did I *have*?"

"He wouldn't hurt her," Kai said firmly. "Not an innocent child." But his face was troubled.

"It's his future at stake," Evariste countered, his voice acid with bitterness. "He might regret it, but that's not going to stop him. It's a matter of the greater good, as he sees it: for him, for his family, for his court. And what's one human being's life against *that*?"

Irene nodded. She felt very cold. It was easy to imagine someone trying to put that sort of pressure on her own parents, to get to her. Even if she was adopted, even if they'd been lying about that throughout her life . . . They'd have tried to save her too.

She held up a hand to stop Kai from protesting. "It's Qing Song's life at stake as well," she said to Evariste. "He wouldn't have told you the full details, but there's a competition going on for a high-ranking post between him and another dragon. The loser isn't going to survive. And even if you did what he wanted and he returned Miranda, that sort of arrangement would come back to haunt you. You'd never be free of him."

"Yeah, I worked that out." Evariste stared at the wall as though he was visualizing possible futures, and all of them bad. "It'd just be the first small favour of a long, long list. And Miranda would never be safe outside the Library, because anyone who wanted to put pressure on me . . ."

He turned back to Irene and Kai, his hands extended as if he wanted them to understand.

"So anyhow. I said yes. I figured I'd work out how to fix things later. I thought that if I could get the book, then I could set my own terms. And I'll be honest with you, I was kind of panicking. I was afraid if the Library knew about it, they'd put me under house arrest right away, even if it meant Miranda—" Evariste broke off. When he spoke again, his head was bowed as though he'd already given up. "I reported in. I said Julian had had a heart attack. I asked for compassionate leave to tidy things up. Qing Song said this would be over in a few weeks, so I figured that was long enough. I went back to G-14, and Qing Song and Hu took me between worlds to here. That was freaky."

"So he just left you here to do the research?" Kai asked.

"Kind of." Evariste shrugged. "I've had people watching me most of the time. Qing Song, or Hu, or one of his human goons. The only time I left was to visit the Library for research. The Traverse from this world, it's in Boston . . . But I guess you'd know that, since you're here now."

"It's been blown up." Irene could hear the flatness in her own voice as she struggled for control. It was still hard to remember the utter ruin of that library. "I'm fairly sure Hu was behind it, though I'm not entirely sure why."

Evariste lowered his head into his hands. "That's my fault," he said, his voice muffled. "Oh shit, that's my fault too."

"Why?"

"Because I told them that was where the Library could access this world. I thought that if I told them that, it'd keep their attention there and it'd give me a better chance of escaping. And maybe they wouldn't watch other libraries so closely. When I went on the run, they must have thought that'd stop me leaving this world—"

"Tell me one thing," Kai interrupted. "Why are we here in America? Why aren't you looking for the book in China?"

"I lied." Evariste didn't look up. "I know America—even if it's not *this* America. I don't know China. I had a plan. But I needed to make sure I'd have the chance to run when the right moment came. So I found a reference to a copy of the book right here, and I fed them that. They'd already run into problems trying to find the book in China. Plus Qing Song said that someone else was looking for the book there too. That must be the other dragon who's competing, right? I'd send them flowers and good-luck wishes, if I had the chance. So Qing Song was only too glad to go somewhere else to find a copy. I said I just needed a little longer to locate exactly where it was. Then a few days ago I skipped out on my guard. I figured if I got hold of the book myself, I could bargain from a position of power. Get Miranda back, get them to promise never to come anywhere near me again. But they were on my tail before I had the chance to grab the book. They've been searching the city. And I was afraid that the moment I stepped out of my rooms for more than a few minutes, they'd grab me. But I can't stop thinking about Miranda. I didn't know whether to give myself up or run for the Library and beg for help—or what to do. And then *you* show up." He made it sound as if Irene and Kai weren't much of an improvement on Qing Song.

"We arrived about ten minutes before Qing Song did," Irene pointed out. "Even if you'd gone out the back window the moment you heard his wolves, how do you think things would have turned out?"

Evariste's shoulders slumped. He looked sick. "So what happens now?" he asked bluntly.

And that was the million-dollar question.

"We need to think," Irene said firmly. "And we don't have much time before someone catches us. Kai, would you mind stepping downstairs to see if you can spot any watchers? And Jeanette Smith might still be in the news—so pick up a newspaper while you're out."

Kai frowned but nodded, coming smoothly to his feet. "Don't go anywhere," he said, closing the door behind him.

"Did you really send him out for a paper?" Evariste demanded.

"Kai's not a sworn Librarian—at least, not yet—and I am. And I don't have any second loyalties. So if there's something you want to tell me that you didn't want Kai to hear, this is the time to do it."

"Actually, yeah," Evariste said slowly. "There is something."

Irene nodded. "I'm listening."

He moved without warning, and his fist took her squarely in the stomach. As she folded over, gasping for breath, he made a break for the door.

But while Irene was surprised by his speed, she'd been expecting his bid for freedom. It didn't take an FBI agent to realise that Evariste might want to handle things himself.

She tumbled to the floor, sweeping her leg round in a wide kick, which took him at the ankles. He went down with a thud, face-first, and she threw herself on top of him. She hooked her arm round his throat and dragged his head back, bracing her knee in the small of his back as she choked him. "Tap the ground if you surrender," she grunted, her own breath still coming with difficulty.

Evariste struggled underneath her, clawing at her arm across his neck. His breathing rattled harshly in his throat as he fought for air, unable to form words, let alone the Language.

Irene gritted her teeth and held on. "Tap the floor. Surrender. Or I swear I'll choke you unconscious and have Kai carry you back to the Library here and now. But if you work *with* me, then I'll try to help you."

Common sense urged her to tighten her grip until Evariste was unconscious. He was compromised, and the choices he'd made had put the Library in danger. The safest thing to do would be to take him back to the Library via the nearest big collection of books.

The safest thing, perhaps, but not the right thing. What about the very real threat to his daughter's life? She could imagine the Library taking Evariste in, protecting him, but leaving his daughter to take her chances. One child's life, against the Library's safety? Older Librarians might consider it a regrettable but necessary sacrifice. And Evariste had been victimized, betrayed, and used. He was another Librarian—in many ways her brother, by choice and by oath. She could take the safe option. Or she could take a risk.

She'd been ordered to bring Evariste in. She'd be risking her place in the Library if she defied those orders. Melusine had outright warned her that she'd take the blame if the Library needed a scapegoat. She'd be putting the Library itself in danger—all for the sake of one little human girl who might already be dead. This was not the sort of thing that a sensible, competent, loyal agent did.

She didn't want to have to make this decision. She couldn't endanger the Library. But she wasn't sure she could live with herself if she left Miranda to die.

And yet . . . family ties might be the key to this whole business.

Qing Song had a family too, and that might be the lever that could reverse the whole situation.

Irene had to make a decision, and she had to do it now.

She thought for a moment that Evariste was going to fight to the end. But then his fingers weakened, losing their grip on her arm. His right hand slapped against the cheap carpet.

Irene slackened her grip a little, enough that he could breathe. "Give me a pledge in the Language that I can trust you," she said coldly. "I won't give you another chance."

Evariste's breath came in rough, hissing gasps as he filled his lungs. He was silent, and Irene wondered what he was thinking: whether he was willing to accept her terms, or whether he was trying to think of some way round them, another method of escape. Finally he said, **"If you will swear not to give me to the dragons and to help me get my daughter back safely, then I will cooperate with you in this place freely and fully, to the best of my abilities."**

Irene considered his words. The *freely and fully, to the best of my abilities* were probably as good as she was going to get. Now she had to give a counter-pledge and not compromise herself too far. **"I swear to do my best to help you remain free from the dragons and save your daughter's life, but with the understanding that my duty to the Library comes above all other oaths.** Will that suffice?"

"I accept," Evariste said with a sigh, his voice barely audible. "There. You can let me up now."

"We'd better tidy up before Kai gets back," Irene said, releasing her grip on his neck and rising to her feet. "We'll need to move, once he returns."

"What *is* it with you and him?" Evariste demanded. He sat up, prodding his throat uncomfortably. "You do know you can't trust them, don't you?"

"I notice you're not saying that while he's in the room."

"That's because I'm not stupid."

"Glad to hear it." Irene straightened her clothing. "Every now and again a young dragon is apprenticed to the Library. None of them ever take the final vows . . ." Her throat tightened, and she forced herself to continue the sentence, to say out loud what she'd been suspecting for a while now. "And I don't think that Kai will either. He isn't going to leave his family behind."

It's only a matter of time before I lose him, she thought. *And I'm compromised too, just like you, because I care about him. But family blood rules dragons—and that might be the key we need.*

"But why does the Library allow it?"

"I don't know," Irene admitted. "I can make a few guesses. Even if we don't have a formal alliance with the dragons, we are generally on better terms with them than with the Fae. Or more cynically, maybe it's to keep the dragons thinking they know what we're up to, by letting a few in at a very shallow level." She turned to look at Evariste. "But if you want proof of Kai in particular, then believe me when I say that he helped me stop Alberich, at great personal risk to himself."

"Yeah, I can see he's the hands-on type." Evariste sighed and sat down on the edge of the bed. "All right, I'll give him the benefit of the doubt. Just don't go thinking they're all like him, okay? Qing Song's bad news. And even if Hu's more friendly about it, he's still dangerous."

"Oh, I believe that," Irene said drily. "But getting back to business, *is* there anything you want to tell me before Kai gets back? Librarian to Librarian?"

Evariste shook his head. "It wasn't easy, but I've told you everything."

They both jumped as the door's handle turned. Before panic could set in, Kai entered, a folded newspaper tucked under his arm. "There's no immediate threat, but it's time to get moving. And here's part of the reason why." He offered Irene the paper. It was already folded open to a particular article, and her jaw dropped as she read it.

"What is it?" Evariste asked.

"It has to do with how we arrived in New York." Kai was clearly enjoying himself. "Irene used the Language to convince the police chief she was really an FBI agent, but it wore off shortly after we left. And Captain Venner ended up giving an interview to a newspaper reporter, where he had to explain why he let us go."

"You can now add 'master hypnotist' to my list of titles," Irene muttered. "To go with 'mob boss.' I had no idea Captain Venner was such a gifted raconteur."

"I liked the bit about how you fixed him with your glittering eyes and he found himself helpless to move in his chair."

"Did you memorize this whole article?" Irene said with some annoyance.

"Only the good bits." Kai leaned against the door. "He had to rationalize things somehow, Irene. Try to be sympathetic to the poor man. How else could he explain what he saw?"

"You aren't the one being described as having a brow like Shakespeare and a deep serpentine gaze like Satan . . ." Irene pulled herself together. This was getting off track. "Very well. Add one more item to the list of problems I'll have if the police catch up with me."

"Right," Kai said, "and that's the other part of why we need to move now. I think this place is being watched. A couple of men in plainclothes out front. We need to clear out before they can bring in reinforcements."

Irene nodded. "Let's move this elsewhere. Evariste, you've been in town longer than us—where can we continue this conversation?"

The closest "where" turned out to be a deli nearby, patronized by students, the less well-off, and people who wanted to drink coffee rather than alcohol. The high student concentration meant that the racial mix of Irene, Evariste, and Kai was less obvious than it might have been elsewhere. And the lack of alcohol probably meant fewer gangsters. They annexed a corner table with a good view of the door and sat down to plan.

Irene had been thinking. "Several thoughts," she said, "in no particular order. Evariste, Qing Song is in just as deep trouble as you are. Possibly even deeper."

She turned to Kai. "Kai, if someone in your father's court was found trying to force Librarians to help him, by kidnapping their dependents . . . what would happen to that person?"

"Public disgrace and loss of office," Kai said without hesitation. "Possibly even death or banishment, depending on his or her rank. Even if we don't have a formal alliance, that's unsanctioned behaviour. My father and his ministers wouldn't endorse such conduct. It'd be a declaration of hostilities in itself."

"Yes, but Qing Song said—" Evariste started. Then he stopped, as if realizing how far he'd been duped. "You mean he's just as incriminated as I am," he said slowly.

"Exactly," Irene said. "Whatever Julian's relationship with him or his family was, Qing Song badly overstepped the line in taking your daughter hostage. And now that he's lost track of you, not only has he lost his big chance to get hold of the book, but there's a witness on the loose who can make things politically dangerous for him. Possibly fatally so. The Queen of the Southern Lands isn't going to want a subordinate who causes this sort of mess. Most of all, by acting like this, Qing Song's endangered his family."

"You mean other dragons would actually *care* what he's done?" Evariste said cynically.

But Kai had sat back in his chair at her final words, as though she'd gut-punched him. "They'd care," he said quietly. "They'd care very much indeed. This isn't some kind of petty gamble between two individuals. This is a challenge where both participants have been supported by their clans. If Qing Song has done what he did—unprovoked, against the servant of a neutral power—and his clan is incriminated, then *all* of them risk disgrace. The queen would enforce it. He was a fool to do it."

Irene nodded. "Qing Song's overplayed his hand. He might be prepared to risk death, but he won't risk *his* family. And that's how we're going to retrieve your daughter."

Evariste nodded slowly—not quite convinced yet, but wanting to believe. "But we're going to get spotted sooner or later, and Qing Song will track us down," he said. "I don't know whether he can trace me directly. That's why I had the wards up. But even if he can't find me that way, then he has—or rather, Hu has—contacts with the mobs. Not the main man round here, Lucky George, but some of the smaller contractors."

"'Lucky' George?" Kai asked.

"It was Giorgio Rossi originally, but these days he's George Ross if you know what's good for you," Evariste explained. "He started with the Mafia and branched off on his own, and he took a lot of his Mafia associates along with him too. These days he's very all-American. Land of the free, home of the brave. And on the not-so-legal side, importer of alcohol from across the world. Anyhow, Hu's hired gangsters will be out watching for us. And even if you can blackmail Qing Song to make him give my daughter back, he's not going to want to let us go. We'll know way, way too much. Especially if he realizes we're a threat to his family, from what you're saying. So what are we going to *do*?"

Irene glanced at Kai. Her heart sank as she realized that he was looking at her as if she'd be able to sort things out. He wasn't even *trying* to make a contribution. He shouldn't just be depending on her to come up with answers. As his teacher . . . she'd failed him.

This was something she needed to correct. And at the back of her mind, an idea was beginning to come together that might fill several objectives at once.

"Where is the book?" she asked. "I'm assuming you tracked it down."

"It's in the archives at the Metropolitan Museum of Art," Evariste said promptly, his syntax shifting as if he were reporting to his Library supervisor. "It was in a collection donated by Judge Richard Pemberton in 1899. He inherited it from his father, Colonel Matthew Pemberton, who brought it back after the invasion of China. Professor Jamison's currently curating the collection."

"Good work," Irene said. "Next question: have you made sure it's there, or is this an assumption based on research?"

"I didn't dare go find out," Evariste admitted. "I hid the research on it in all the rest of the documents I was pulling. And I took them when I escaped."

A horrible thought seared through Irene's mind. "You didn't

leave them in your apartment, did you? If Qing Song's searched it by now—"

"Yeah, that would have been bad, wouldn't it?" Evariste said coldly. "What with you knocking me out and dragging me away, and all that." Clearly certain things weren't quite forgiven and forgotten yet. "But we're safe so far. I burned those papers once I was safely away. I didn't need them to remember the important facts."

Irene relaxed. "That's a relief."

"Was there anything else in the apartment that we should have brought?" Kai asked. "I suppose I should apologize if we dragged you out of there and left your favourite books behind."

Evariste looked as if he would have liked to list any number of things, but after a moment he shook his head. "Yeah, there were some books there that I'd have liked to keep. But most of them were for a Library ward. I figured it might slow Qing Song down, if he had some . . ." He waved a hand vaguely. "Some sort of dragon way of trying to find me. But I guess I can live without the books. And I was almost out of dollars anyhow."

"He probably can't pinpoint you directly," Kai said comfortingly. "If he was arriving in this world, then Qing Song could locate your general vicinity, but he wouldn't be able to arrive right on top of the house where you were staying. He hasn't taken any tokens from you? Blood, breath, whatever?"

"Hell no," Evariste said. "He was having enough trouble getting me to cooperate without that sort of weird dragon stuff. Er, no offence."

"I suppose Qing Song funded your research," Irene said before Kai could take offence.

"Right. But I didn't want to risk drawing on the bank account he gave me, after I'd skipped out on him. If the bank got in touch with him . . ."

"All right. The main priority here is Miranda. Is Qing Song holding her in this world or somewhere else? Or don't you know?"

Evariste frowned. "I don't know," he said. "I think he's keeping her at his home base, wherever that is. He hasn't let me see her." His shoulders sagged.

"Right." Irene's voice hardened. "So first of all, we're going to get our hands on that book, in order to make Qing Song listen to us. We'll need to promise some sort of bribe to get him to negotiate— even if we don't plan to deliver on it. And besides, if he does find the book himself, he'd leave this world behind and the Library would be left smeared by rumour. So we need to get hold of it, whatever happens. And then, Evariste, we are going to make it absolutely clear to him that he will hand over your daughter and he will leave you and the Library alone in future. Because if not, his whole family will be going down in disgrace, once we reveal what he's done. I'm not going to give him the book. I'm not going to give *either* of them the book. I'm going to get your daughter back, and then you and she will be returning to the Library."

Anger was giving focus to her thoughts—but this felt right. Even if her plan was successful, losing her position as Librarian-in-Residence could be just the start of the price she'd have to pay. But when she looked at the personal consequences to *her*, balanced against the life or death of Evariste's daughter . . .

It was no choice at all.

"Are you both in agreement with that?" she asked. "Because if so, I have a plan."

Evariste clenched his fists on the edge of the table. "Will it work?" he asked. He turned to Kai. "You're the dragon. You'd know how Qing Song thinks. Will this actually work?"

Kai's eyes glittered red for a moment, a flash of crimson deep in the pupil. "Oh yes," he said softly. "Qing Song will have no other options. And I cannot bring myself to feel sorry for him."

CHAPTER 14

The Plaza Hotel was a great square building, as pale and ornate as a wedding-cake and as big as some castles. It overlooked an elegant plaza with tastefully arranged statues, trees, and fountains. And despite its urban location, it sat alone and impressive amidst carefully manicured lawns and gravel paths. The pillared main entrance was flanked by a whole rank of waiting taxicabs, mirrored by a set of horse-drawn carriages on the other side of the street.

Irene walked through the main door without a moment's hesitation and headed directly across to the front desk. Her heels clicked confidently on the mosaic tiles that covered the floor.

The desk clerk was a polished young woman whose sleek blonde hair gleamed under the light of the overhead chandelier. She sat behind a desk whose top was a single piece of marble, and the wall behind her had a six-foot array of inset buttons and speaking tubes. Two presumably lesser clerks sat on either side of her, murmuring into telephone mouthpieces and taking notes.

"Yes, madam?" she enquired politely.

"I wish to take a suite for the night," Irene said, letting her English accent show. She needed to be as visible as possible now. "Possibly for several nights. I can't be sure how long I'll be staying in New York."

"Of course, madam," the desk clerk agreed obsequiously. "Do you have any preferences?"

Irene waved a hand vaguely. "Oh, just something that's suitable for human habitation. I've been told that this is *the* place to stay in New York. I trust you not to disappoint me."

"Our rates, madam—" the woman began.

Irene looked down at her and raised an eyebrow. "Do not concern me," she cut in. "You may rest assured that money is not an issue. My comfort is."

"If I might have your name, madam?" the desk clerk asked.

"Jeanette Smith," Irene said. And she smiled.

The desk clerk's eyes widened. She swallowed. "Yes, ma'am," she said quickly. "Certainly we can arrange a suite for you. Will there be anyone else in your party?"

"Some friends may be joining me later," Irene said carelessly. "Now, if you don't mind, I would like that suite so that I can freshen up. Then have someone call a cab for me. I need to go shopping."

She turned and leaned against the hotel desk, scanning the lobby. The pale floor-tiles and cream walls made the room seem even larger than it already was. Hotel staff in brass-buttoned uniforms trotted back and forth, criss-crossing the room on constant silent errands, like electrical current—or was it voltage?—whizzing around a circuit. (Physics had never been Irene's strong point. In fact, it was on her list of weak points, along with visual art, human anatomy, and the ability to maintain a convincing American accent.) Hotel guests drifted in and out, few of them paying attention to her. For the moment, at least.

The desk clerk murmured into one of her speaking tubes, then turned back to Irene as a hotel porter came trotting up to grab her bags. "We have a suite on the twelfth floor, ma'am, which I hope will be acceptable. About the question of payment—"

Irene reached into her handbag, took out a roll of bills, and dropped it on the hotel desk. "You will understand that discretion is paramount," she said. "Also, it is possible that certain friends of mine may be trying to reach me here. They will be asking for someone by the name of Marguerite. I imagine you can handle that?"

"It will be our pleasure, madam," the desk clerk said, her hand sweeping out as quickly as a hungry crab's pincer to secure the money, making it vanish under the desk.

Irene smiled again. But the smile didn't reach her eyes.

Irene sat down on her very elegant bed after the hotel porter had left the equally elegant suite, and spent a minute just breathing deeply and allowing herself to relax. Tension had knotted itself permanently into her spine and her shoulders, and coiled around her throat with the thought of the plan ahead. Everything had to go just right.

She reminded herself that she was a professional and opened her suitcase. Inside was the rather battered tourist map of New York. She arranged the map on the quilted counterpane and repeated her now-practised manoeuvre with the Language and the locket. It indicated an area in the Bronx. Good. That was where they'd agreed Kai and Evariste would spend a few hours lying low.

This all felt deeply wrong. Normally Irene's policy was to work undercover. But this time she was about to go out on the town and see just how much attention she could attract while Kai and Evariste accomplished the actual book theft behind the scenes.

It was a calculated risk, based on the fact that *she* was the person everyone had seen so far, while Kai had remained mostly in the background. Qing Song would hope that she could lead him to Evariste, or that he could use her to find the book. With any luck he'd go for her as the easy target, taking the pressure off the other two. As for the local gangsters on the one hand, and Captain Venner on the other, Irene would just have to avoid being assassinated or arrested. But she was used to that.

Time to go ahead with the next step of the plan and focus on drawing attention without getting killed.

Time to *shop*.

When Irene left the hotel, she noticed a second taxicab following hers. She was pleased. If she wasn't directing attention from Kai and Evariste, she wasn't doing her job.

She'd spent half an hour in her suite, freshening up and having a quick meal. It was mid-afternoon by now, and she was hungry. That had been quite long enough for hotel staff to make discreet phone calls about her identity. She'd been on edge walking out through the lobby to the waiting cab, just in case someone was going to try another assassination, but nothing had happened. Every instinct in her body was screaming at her to dress more unobtrusively and sneak out of the hotel via the staff entrance. It was hard to fight the habits of a lifetime.

"Somewhere that I can buy some decent clothing," she ordered the driver. "My own luggage was held up. And then a good bookshop. And then I need to visit the New York Public Library."

That should put the cat among the pigeons. Qing Song's watchers would see her doing *something*, but they wouldn't know what. Would Qing Song think she was going to collect the *Journey to the West*? Or that she was going to report in to the Library?

As it turned out, she didn't even reach the library before trouble came calling.

She'd made her first stop a very expensive clothing shop. Jeanette Smith would not wear off-the-rack clothing. Jeanette Smith was more in the silk-dress and fur-coat line—and, most important, shoes that fitted perfectly and wouldn't give Irene blisters.

She came out of the shop in a little cream cocktail dress that waved around her knees, cut up to her neck in front and down to her shoulder-blades at the back, only just avoiding showing her Library brand. It was patterned diagonally with scarab beetles in shades of ultramarine, to go with her turquoise necklace and bracelets. Her coat was wide-sleeved black velvet, collared and cuffed with chinchilla fur, and her hat matched it perfectly. And even though she didn't like to admit it, the whole experience of being fussed over and properly dressed had improved her mood. She felt more integrated into this New York now. More in character.

Her second stop was the area known as "Book Row" on Fourth Avenue. It covered six blocks and housed at least forty bookshops. Possibly more. Irene could happily have spent days there, but the plan was for her to keep moving around New York, keeping the watchers busy.

She noticed the men closing in on her as she walked back towards her cab. She wasn't surprised when they crowded in around her and two of them hustled her into the backseat, squashing her between them, while the third jumped into the front with the cabbie and murmured instructions.

She could feel the men's holsters through their suits. "Are we going somewhere?" she asked.

"Ain't nothing the matter, lady," the man on her left grunted. "You just sit quiet and we'll be there in a few minutes."

Her driver's forehead was beaded with sweat. He stamped on the accelerator, and Irene was knocked back in her seat by the car's sudden jump forward.

"I can pay, you know," Irene offered. She was trying to work out who these men were working for. Were they Qing Song's minions, random gangsters, specific gangsters, or undercover police? So many enemies, so little time.

"Now, there ain't no need to get worried," the man on her left went on, as if he were reading from a pre-prepared script. "There's just some people as want to talk to you—"

"Pay *quite a lot*," Irene said meaningfully. She glanced out the window. The geography of the city told her nothing. Curbside trees and tables, and lower buildings with shops and delicatessens, gave way to colder skyscrapers and more anonymous streets. She could wait and see where she was being taken. But she might be on her way to her very own gangland execution.

The driver stood on the brakes as the car made a right-angle turn, its wheels screeching on the roadway. In the back of the car they all slid sideways, the man on Irene's right crushing her against the one on her left and grunting an apology. They both smelled of tobacco and cheap aftershave. Irene could hear the angry shouts of other drivers as they braked in response.

"Lady, the sort of money you could offer ain't enough to cross the boss." Her kidnapper tried to sound reassuring, pulling himself back to vertical and straightening his lapels. "Look, they just want to talk. It's not like you're gonna turn up in a sack. It's just business."

"How reassuring," Irene muttered. She directed her next words at the driver. "If they're going to shoot me, they'll probably get rid of you, to make sure there aren't any witnesses."

Clearly this had occurred to the driver. He chewed nervously on the ends of his moustache. But he didn't slow down or stop. "Lady, I don't like doing this," he muttered. "My mother's brother Josef, he always said, you get a job as a cab-driver, boy, you're going to end up working day and night for all sorts, no way to call your soul your own, driving your cab all the hours God sends just to pay the rent . . ."

"Shut it," the man in the front seat directed him. "You didn't see nothing. Just drop us off, then go find some new fares. And you, lady. You oughta know how these things work. There's no call to get the help nervous. If he don't squeal, he's got nothing to worry about."

The car came to a sudden jolting stop, which nearly threw Irene and her guards into the partition. Irene could have lifted one of their guns during the confusion, and the thought reassured her. They weren't that competent; they were just average thugs doing their jobs.

"Right," the man in the front said. "Lady, you go through the brown door there and down the stairs, and you do it fast before the cops catch up with us. There's someone down there who wants to talk."

Irene scrambled into a deeply shadowed back alley. The buildings on either side rose high enough to block out direct sunlight at this hour in the afternoon. Crumbling mortar filled the gaps between decrepit bricks, and trash cans were spaced irregularly along the sidewalk, odours leaking out of them to fill the air. The doorways along the alley were all in shades of grey, brown, and black, as if they were trying to find the most unobtrusive shade possible. If New York was a piece of music, then this was the ominous pause leading up to an intense climax.

The specific brown door that her kidnapper had pointed out was noticeably different from the others. Vale would probably only have needed a single glance to mark it as worth investigation. Someone had taken care to sweep its door-step clean, and there were no Dumpsters nearby.

The cab remained idling at the curb. Presumably the men inside were waiting to be sure she actually went through the door and didn't make a run for it.

It could be an ambush in waiting. It could be a death-trap. But if it had been, Irene reasoned, then she'd be dead by now.

There was a wide range of reasons why she should walk through that brown door and down the stairs. They ranged from keeping her cover (as Jeanette Smith, mob boss, Girl with the Gun in Her Garter) to avoiding the police who might have been trailing them. She also needed to keep Qing Song and his mob minions convinced by her diversionary tactics. But ultimately there was an even better reason why Irene headed for the door.

It was simple curiosity.

Irene hoped that none of her enemies ever realized how much she was driven by an urge to find out how, what, where, when, and, in this case, who.

Nobody answered the door. She hadn't really expected them to. She opened it and stepped into a narrow hallway lit by a swaying bulb, with a stairway entrance opening like a dark mouth on her left. The hallway's whitewashed walls were dirty, but its tiled floor was scrubbed clean, still wet from recent work with a mop. She didn't need to be a great detective to deduce that. The mop was propped beside the doorway in a bucket of brown-tinged water, like some sort of sentry.

She started to make her way down the unlit staircase, one hand on the battered rail. The wooden stairs creaked under her new shoes in spite of her attempts to move quietly, and she knew that whoever was waiting down there could hear her coming.

The door at the bottom of the stairs stood a few inches ajar, outlined by light on the other side. Irene hesitated for a moment, considering knocking, but then simply pushed it open.

Bright lights glared at her. A hand grabbed her wrist and dragged her into the room, twisting her arm up behind her back. The cold metal of a gun-barrel nestled into the back of her neck.

"How nice of you to join us," a voice drawled from beyond the lights.

CHAPTER 15

"I had to do some shopping first," Irene answered, her mouth on autopilot.

As her eyes became used to the bright lights, she could pick out more of the room. It was larger than she'd expected, emphasized by the whitewashed walls and ceiling, which went past bland whiteness and all the way to stark sterility. Dark gleaming objects hung on the walls. On closer inspection, these were guns of all shapes and sizes, hardly any of which she recognized. A few armchairs were dotted around the room, upholstered in black leather. Two of them were occupied by seated men, expensively dressed and holding cocktail glasses. At the far end of the room was a weather-beaten table and half a dozen low banks of drawers, the sort that craftsmen would have in their workshop.

The whole room smelled of metal and gun-oil, right down to the person—it was a woman, Irene realized—who was holding Irene's arm locked behind her back. Her gun was pressed into the nape of Irene's neck, and the cold metal focused Irene's mind wonderfully. It was the sort of wake-up call that was usually bottled with caffeine and sold to college students or van-drivers who'd been up all night. It reminded Irene that curiosity sometimes came at too high a price.

The man who'd spoken before chuckled, and took a sip from his glass. His heavy Southern accent—a little too heavy?—dripped like thick honey. "Well, I'd say that women always make that excuse, but it'd be mighty impolite to my little Lily there. She's the lady who's got one of her favourite guns pointed right at you."

And as he spoke, a surge of fear swept across Irene like an ocean wave. It clenched her throat and chest, then dragged back through her body in a freezing undertow that put ice in her veins. The smell of cold steel seemed to sear her nostrils and the back of her throat. It was the fear of death and everything that went with it in this place: the fear of guns, the fear of violence, the fear of casual murder. The Library tattoo on her back ached in response like an old burn.

The woman behind Irene pushed her sideways, turning her so that she faced the wall, and casually ran her hand down Irene's body. Through the terror that was trying to impose itself on her, Irene realized the woman was checking for weapons, patting her down professionally and checking her handbag. She'd released her grip on Irene's wrist, but her other hand kept the gun at Irene's neck.

When she spoke, her voice was clear and uninflected, with the faintest of local New York accents. "She's not carrying."

"Now, that's a surprise. Turn her around, Lily. Let's have another look at Miss Jeanette's face. She's come all this way here to visit us. It strikes me that it's the least we can do."

The woman turned Irene again, spinning her round to face the men. Again that rush of fear beat against Irene, as threatening as a gun against her lips.

But this time she swallowed it down. It wasn't her own fear. Someone in this room—a *Fae* in this room—was trying to enforce it on her. Knowing that the fear was an external force made it easier for Irene to strangle it into compliance.

She brushed a stray hair back into place. "The least you can do is offer me a drink," she said calmly. "God knows I've come far enough to get one."

There was a pause, almost a stunned silence, and then the man burst out laughing. But his laughter was a little forced, as though he was using it as a stopgap while he decided what to do next. "You've got just the cutest accent, Miss Jeanette. I should hire you to read the phone book to me all day long. Sure, have a seat. Dave, you fetch the little lady here a drink. What'd you care for?"

"I'll have a Black Russian," Irene said as she walked forward to the indicated armchair. She could hear Lily's footsteps behind her, high heels ticking on the tiled floor like a countdown.

The second man, who'd risen to his feet, halted. "What's that?" he asked.

Oh, wonderful, Irene thought. *Yet again a Librarian engages in cross-cultural contamination.* She couldn't remember when a Black Russian had first been mixed, but she did at least know the recipe. "Five parts vodka to two parts coffee liqueur, if you have it," she said. "Or I'll take a gin sling—however you make them here."

"Maybe England's got more to teach us than I realized," the first man mused. "Go see what you can do about it, Dave. And make yourself comfortable, Miss Jeanette. We've got a few things to discuss. I don't suppose you know who I am?"

"I'm guessing that you're the gentleman they call Lucky George," Irene said. She sat down in the armchair and allowed herself to look him over as obviously as he was considering her.

He was a small man with sharply cut and oiled dark hair, a flabby nose, and the sort of manly unshavenness that needed careful effort to maintain. His double-breasted suit was styled to minimise his waist and improve his shoulders, but it couldn't disguise the lines of a holster underneath his jacket. His tie was either a masterpiece designed by an abstract artist or the result of someone throwing blobs of paint at silk. And his shoes were so highly polished that mere contact with the air should have dulled their shine.

He swirled his drink in its glass and smiled at her, displaying tobacco-stained teeth. "And who told you that, Miss Jeanette? Anyone I should know about?" *So I can have them killed,* his tone suggested.

Irene shrugged. "Your name's hardly a secret," she said. Unobtrusively she scanned Lily, the woman who'd been holding a gun to her neck. She had wandered round to perch on the arm of George's armchair. Lily had the sort of looks that should have been described as *pretty as a picture.* But there was something a little off balance about her whole presentation, like the foundations of a building in a Lovecraftian horror story. Her blonde hair was cut like a cap and fell to hide her left eye, but the visible right eye assessed Irene as though she were measuring her for a coffin. Her skin had the perfect pallor of someone who didn't go out in the sun, and her violet satin dress clung to her as tightly as her stockings.

George took in the direction of Irene's glance and chuckled. "I see that you're admiring my Lily here. I'm a modern up-to-date man, Miss Jeanette. I don't care if it's a man or a woman—I employ whoever can do the job. And my little Lily . . ." He patted her thigh just above the knee, with a proprietorial air. "She's the best with a gun in the whole Big Apple."

"It's nice to meet a man with an open mind," Irene said cheerfully. The Library itself might be a gender-neutral organization—after all, books didn't mind whether they were read or stolen by men or women—but some Librarians needed time to shed the attitudes of their worlds of origin. And while Irene might be able to manipulate other people's prejudices during assignments, that didn't mean she *enjoyed* them. "And it's a good start to possible working relationships."

"So you're going to be straightforward about this?" George demanded.

"There comes a point when it's a waste of time and effort to keep on lying," Irene said. "I think, in poker, you'd call it knowing when to fold. So." She leaned forward in her armchair. "You've got my attention. What do you want?"

"You're more blatant than I expected, Miss Jeanette," George said. He leaned back in his chair and took another sip of his drink.

"May I be frank?" Irene asked.

"Sure, sure." He pointed two fingers at her in a miniature gun-barrel. "Just as long as I'm the only person you're frank to, honey. We don't like squealers around here."

"We don't like them back home either," Irene agreed. He'd accepted her as a crime boss. It was time to play on that fact. "That's partly why I'm annoyed."

"Annoyed?" George said. Lily didn't move her head, and her face remained expressionless, but her gaze shifted to focus on Irene.

"As I said, I'll be frank. This was not supposed to be a public visit. Someone has been talking a bit too loudly. I don't know if the leak came from my organization or from Boston, but either way, people now know I'm here. This is not a tenable situation."

"Tenable situation. I just *love* your accent." George emptied his glass. "So what are you thinking of doing about it, Miss Jeanette?"

"I need to go home sooner than planned. The police may take a few pay-offs, but if you get too obvious about it, the prices go up and the security goes down. The situation here's not working, and I have too many people gunning for me. This game's not worth the risk." Irene shrugged again. "Is that man of yours going to be all day fetching my drink?"

"Lily, you go see where Dave's gotten to," George said. He didn't look away from Irene as the woman slid off his chair and moved to the door at the back of the room, as smoothly as a snake. "So you're just dropping everything here in America, Miss Jeanette? Calling it a day and heading back home with your tail between your legs?"

"Oh, I'm not saying *that*," Irene disagreed. "I've already made a couple of deals, and I'd like to make a few more. I hate wasting my time. That's why I'm suggesting we drop the formalities and cut to the deal."

She hoped George would lay out his proposal. Then all she'd have to do would be to go along with it, with a bit of bargaining to cement the part of gin-running mobster. It was so much less work than making up her own tissue of lies. And it would get her out of here safely so that she could get back to laying false trails for Qing Song to chase.

Irene actually found herself relaxing into her part. Here, in the middle of the territory of the biggest crime boss in New York, she was actually—temporarily—*safe* from all the other people who were chasing her. She had a character to play, and her lies were holding up to casual examination. This was as good as it got.

And to be honest, she was having fun being Jeanette Smith, Crime Boss. It was much less nerve-racking than being Irene Winters, Librarian.

The door at the far end of the room swung open and Lily swayed back in—her shoes clicking on the tiles, hard as a skeleton's vertebrae. Dave was right behind her, Irene's glass in his hand.

Lily settled herself on the arm of George's chair, in a position that would have looked kittenish if she'd seemed at all vulnerable. Once again the fear of death stroked its way up Irene's spine, urging panic and obedience. It was like sitting in a machine gun's sights.

Now Irene was certain. That first feeling of terror might have come from anyone in the room. But it had left the room with Lily, and returned when she did. Whatever the truth of the Boston situation, there was clearly at least one Fae in the New York mobs, and she was sitting right here.

The situation had just become rather more complicated.

Irene sipped her Black Russian. She knew it might be poisoned, or drugged. But really, if they'd *wanted* her dead, then they would already have shot her. (Kai was going to disapprove when she updated him. Maybe she'd censor the story, just a little.) "Not bad," she judged. "Thanks."

George took a long swallow from his own glass. "Okay," he said. "This is how it seems to me, Miss Jeanette. You're here to find trading partners. Well, I'm looking to import. If we can agree on that, then the rest is just details for our accountants."

Irene nodded. "Right. We don't need to have some sort of high-powered conference for that. The percentage points either way are important, but . . ." She shrugged. "Not as important as us agreeing to work together in the first place. Besides, you know where I'm staying. I'm not trying to hide. Not from you, at least."

He slowly pointed a finger at her, understanding dawning on his face. "*That's* why you've been strolling around the city like some kind of tourist. You were waiting for someone to get in contact."

"Guilty as charged," Irene said, and watched him chuckle at the metaphor. "I figured someone professional like yourself would get in touch before I had to leave town."

"Yeah," he agreed. "The cops may not have anything definite on you yet, but the longer you're around, the more chance there is that they'll make something up, just to hang a charge on you. Even if it's just the Sullivan Act."

Irene raised an eyebrow.

"Being caught carrying without a licence," he clarified. "Something that a good half the guys and a quarter of the dolls in the speakeasy next door might have a problem explaining. An awful lot of people in this town are afraid of catching a cold if they go out of doors without a bit of pre-emptive self-defence."

"I'm English," Irene said. "We handle it a little differently."

"So how are you going to handle it when you find out who talked?" George asked, a little too casually.

"The English way." Irene lifted her glass and swirled the liquid in it, watching it catch the light. "Whoever it is will vanish and never be heard of again. Except for the part where somehow everyone knows what happened to them, and why."

She took another sip of her Black Russian, savouring the jolt of caffeine and vodka, but enjoying the look of approval in George's eyes just as much. It occurred to her that she might be getting a little *too* far into character. She ignored the thought. She didn't often get to play mob boss.

"All right. Now that we've got an understanding, I'd better not detain you. Don't want the cops sniffing around." George jerked a thumb towards the door at the back of the room. "That goes through to the private establishment under Armstrong's, and you can have yourself a drink before calling a cab. I'll be in contact with you at your hotel this evening and we can work out the details. And I'll put out the word on the street that you're in good with me, and nobody is to try anything. That okay with you?"

"Sounds good," Irene said. *Especially the bit about no more random assassination attempts.* "But there is one thing I'd like before I go. I'd like a private word with Lily here. Woman to woman."

George glanced up at Lily, then shrugged. "Sure, no problem. Mind if I ask why?"

"I want to talk about guns," Irene said.

George nodded, satisfied. "Fit our guest up with something in her size, Lily, darling. Dave, come along with me—I need another drink."

Lily stayed sitting on the arm of the chair as the two men left, considering Irene as thoughtfully as a raven would consider a tasty-looking snail. "Well?" she said as the door clicked shut.

"Are we being listened to?" Irene asked bluntly.

"No," Lily said. "George knows I'm as loyal as it gets. So what do you really want to talk about? And who are you?"

"I have a question first," Irene said carefully. She wanted some answers, but not at the price of being shot.

"Sure," Lily said, without a moment's hesitation.

"And I'd like you to give your word—by your name and power— that the answer's true."

Lily's visible eye narrowed. If she had been a raven, she would have been looking for a nice edged stone to smash the metaphorical snail against. "If you can ask me that, then you know too much."

"Or not enough," Irene said regretfully. "But if you will answer my question truthfully, then I can be more honest. I think that just this once, we might have no reason to be enemies."

"Who are you?" Lily asked. Then more carefully, she said, "*What* are you? You're no dragon."

"My question gets answered first," Irene said. She leaned back in her chair, as casually as she could manage, and sipped her drink.

Lily hesitated, then sighed. "What a fuss. All right, it's a deal. I give you my word, by my name and my power, that I'll answer your question truthfully."

"I accept your word," Irene said. The Fae were punctilious about keeping their oaths, even if they were prone to sticking to the letter and not the spirit. "Now tell me: were you, or any other Fae, involved in bombing the Boston Public Library?"

Lily stared at Irene blankly. "No, and no again. What would be the point?"

"That was pretty much my thinking too," Irene admitted. "And in answer to *your* question, I'm a Librarian."

"Oh, interesting." Lily rolled the word out, savouring it. "I've heard about your kind before, but I've never met one. You're the book thieves, right? The hoarders?"

"We don't like to put it that way," Irene said, "but yes. For a higher purpose, of course."

"You just keep on telling yourself that," Lily said sympathetically. "So what's your name?"

"I have many names but a single nature," Irene quoted. "And if my real name did get to certain people's ears, then I'd be in deep trouble."

"What makes you think you aren't?"

"We're talking like rational people, aren't we?"

"Rational's an arbitrary sort of concept," Lily said. She might as well have been discussing drinks, or stockings, or a game of cards. "Some would say I wasn't at all reasonable by nature."

"Then they don't know Fae," Irene said, from experience. "You choose a story to model yourself upon—and then you become it. You're what you've made yourself."

"Now you're saying something interesting." Lily swung herself off the arm of her chair and paced towards Irene. Irene couldn't help wondering how many guns the other woman was carrying, and how she managed to fit them under her tight knee-length dress. The smell of gun-oil and metal cut through the woman's sweet floral perfume as she stood in front of Irene. Fae might have an aversion to cold iron, but apparently they had no problems with steel. "Why don't you tell me what you think I am?"

"I've met seducers and libertines," Irene said. One of them, Lord Silver, was a frequent irritation back on Vale's world. "You're neither."

"True enough," Lily murmured. "Guess again."

"I've met Machiavellian plotters." And killed one. But that was in another country, and in another story, and hopefully Irene would never have to face the results. "I've met storytellers and snake-tenders, lords and ladies and minstrels."

"None of which is me." Lily held herself like a drawn weapon. "If this was a story, you'd be on your third guess."

Irene took a deep breath. If she guessed wrong, then she might have overstepped for the final time. Once Fae locked themselves into story patterns and narrative tropes, they didn't want to leave them. And if characters in a story guessed incorrectly three times, they often ended up as cautionary examples to the next protagonist.

But she thought she knew what archetype Lily was choosing to embody. It all fitted.

"You're the faithful assassin," she said. "You're the cold killer who only cares about following the boss's orders. If he says kill, you kill. If he says let them live, then you let them live. You don't care. Your only concern is being the very best at your job." She deliberately forced herself to look away from Lily and around the room, at all the guns hanging from the walls. "You're an assassin. You're a gun-moll. You're his executioner."

Lily bent forward and picked up Irene's free hand from the arm of the chair. She brushed her lips against it, in a mockery of a courtier's salute. "You've got a real gift for words, Librarian."

"I read a lot," Irene admitted. "It's an addiction."

"And you're used to working with your hands." Her fingers traced across the old scars that laced Irene's palm. "Perhaps you're right, and we don't have to be enemies for the moment. I can respect another professional who's prepared to get her hands dirty."

"Unless your boss says differently," Irene said.

"Well, yeah, of course." Lily made it sound like the most reasonable thing possible, and to her, Irene reflected, it would be. "A servant like me doesn't disobey orders."

"Why a human boss, though?" Irene asked. "Why not a Fae one?"

Lily made a rude noise as she released Irene's hand. "Have you met some of the guys who'd like to take that sort of role? They'd be more interested in their own career than in mine. I need to be stronger before being the servant of anyone who really *matters*. A powerful patron needs a powerful servant. A weak patron just uses up servants like chewed lemon-peels."

"And a human boss is willing to take suggestions about the right orders to give?" Irene guessed.

"George is a good boss," Lily said. She spoke with an affectionate tolerance, as though discussing a well-trained dog. It was the sort of tone that went with statements such as *And he knows to go outside before doing his business.* "I've taught him exactly how to use me. And he takes a hint when I want him to. I've spent a while cultivating him, and I don't want it messed up. So what exactly are you doing here in my neighbourhood?"

Lily had slipped the question in casually, but there was no doubt she wanted an answer. Irene turned her glass in her hand while she considered the best response. "I'm looking for something that's been stolen," she finally said.

"A book?" Lily asked.

Irene was tempted to say *No, a child* and ask for Lily's help in retrieving Evariste's daughter. But that wouldn't help. Quite the opposite. The risk of ending up in Lily's debt, and compromising the Library *that* way, paled in comparison to the risk of telling the Fae the full story. If the Fae caught wind of a dragon contest going on in their midst, there'd be no end to the trouble they'd cause. They'd see a weakness and move to exploit it—just as the dragons would do to them, if the positions were reversed. The situation would degenerate faster than the eye could follow. And if the dragons traced the leak back to the Library via Irene . . .

She'd thought the situation couldn't get much worse. She'd been wrong. The situation could *always* get worse.

"Sorry," she said. "I can't tell you. But it doesn't involve you or your kind."

"I'm glad to hear it," Lily said. "There are too many dragons in town lately, and they're messing with me and mine. I'm concerned that they're moving in on my territory. And I wouldn't want to think you're working with them." She levelled her gaze at Irene again, like the barrel of a gun.

The implied threat echoed in the room.

"I might *talk* to dragons," Irene said with a smile. But fear crawled its way down her spine and nestled in her stomach like a block of ice. She forced herself to keep on speaking. "But that's not an excuse to shoot me on sight. Or them."

"Are you sure?" Suddenly Lily was holding a gun in her hand— a small sleek piece of metal that gleamed under the room's lights like silver. It seemed to have its own gravity, drawing Irene's eyes to it like a black hole. Lily had moved so fast that Irene hadn't been able to track the movement.

"I'm sure you aren't going to shoot me without an order from your boss," Irene answered, her throat dry.

Lily actually smiled. "Just so long as you understand that I would put a bullet through you without the least little bit of hesitation. If he gave me an order."

The gun vanished into its holster. "Now, do you want me to fit you out with something before we go outside?"

"That might not be the best idea," Irene admitted. "I don't want to risk the police taking me in on the Sullivan Act."

"Well, if you do change your mind, come back to me," Lily said. "But we should go join the boys before they wonder why we're taking so long. The drinks are on me, with no obligation to you. You okay with that?"

"It's a deal," Irene agreed. She followed Lily towards the door at the far end of the room.

It had insulating felt lining on the other side, and gave onto a short, deeply carpeted corridor, which led to another felt-lined door. Irene could hear the faint sounds of music on the other side.

"Welcome to the Underground," Lily said, swinging open the door. A wave of noise, music, and cigar-smoke swept into the corridor. "Come and sit over at George's table so he can say bye-bye politely."

"And so I can be seen with him, of course," Irene said with resignation.

"That's how it works," Lily agreed. She kicked the door closed and led the way into the large room.

Irene was very conscious of people staring at her and Lily—some obviously so, while others pretended to hide their interest. This was a speakeasy that served people who had money to spend or to waste. Everyone was well-dressed—even the waiters were outfitted in smooth black-and-white suits, and the fawning hostesses were clad in expensive, barely-there confections of fringe. A few couples drifted around on the small dance floor, but most people were clustered at their tables.

The room buzzed with a febrile sense of tension. The laughter was too loud, too self-indulgent. Women in their cocktail dresses with bared shoulders and arms posed like marionettes' in the dim lighting, exposing flashes of knee or thigh as they sipped drinks and played with long cigarette-holders. The men in their tailored suits, all wide lapels, big shoulders, and silk ties, were posturing as much as the women. And they all knew that at any moment the police might arrive. Irene could smell the nervousness in the air just as much as the alcohol or smoke.

Electric light-fixtures hung from the ceiling above, but they were deliberately dim. The light picked out the glitter of necklaces, cuff links, and tie pins, and sparkled on full and empty glasses. The only well-lit spot in the whole room was the bar: the bottles behind it gleamed like a distant promise of heaven from the outskirts of hell.

"Over here," Lily said, leading the way through the scattered tables. Irene noticed that even though many of the female guests and the hostesses were tolerating wandering hands from male companions, nobody so much as tried to swat Lily's passing rear. Irene wasn't surprised.

Then Lily stopped. The table ahead was obviously the best one in the bar, with a commanding view of the entire room. And, unless Irene was very much mistaken, there was a concealed door hidden in the wall mouldings behind it. George and Dave were both sitting at it, nursing their drinks.

So was Hu.

CHAPTER 16

"Come and have a seat, Lily," George said, beckoning her forward. "You too, Miss Jeanette. This gentleman's like you. An entrepreneur from out of town."

Dave pulled out chairs for Lily and Irene. Lily took the chair on the other side of her boss, watching Hu and Irene as if she expected to see the dragon and the Librarian exchange secret codewords and meaningful handshakes. Which meant that Irene had to sit with Lily on one side and Hu on her other.

"This gentleman here's Mr. Hu," George explained. "He's come from Hong Kong, looking for business opportunities. And this lady here's Miss Jeanette Smith from England, who's doing similar." He smiled at the two of them. "All I can say is, if either of you is thinking of an exclusive contract with me, well, business is business."

"Delighted to meet you, Miss Jeanette Smith," Hu said. He offered his hand to be shaken.

Oh, so that's how we're going to play it. Irene shook his hand politely, conscious of everyone at the table—and quite a few at other tables—watching them. "Charmed," she said. "What a pleasant surprise."

"For me as well," Hu said. His eyes glittered with vicious amusement.

"I'd love a drink," Irene said, turning to George. "Straight whiskey, if you don't mind. I'd be interested to test the house quality."

George snapped his fingers and a waiter was at his side a moment later. "Straight whiskey for the lady. Gin for my Lily. Gin and tonic for Mr. Hu here, and what was it you said before? The best ice in the house."

Hu casually lit a cigarette. "Do you intend to be here in New York for long, Miss Smith?" he asked. "Or should I call you Jeanette . . . or something else?"

Irene shrugged. Across the room, the piano music changed to something with a faster beat. "As George here knows, I just want to finish my business and get out of town."

"Yes, I hear you've been interviewed by the chief of police." Hu gestured with his cigarette to where a folded newspaper lay on the table. "Very dramatic. Do you really go round hypnotizing people?"

Irene could sense Lily's tension on her other side, like a coiled spring. Having a dragon at the table must be grating. "I suppose he had to give the papers some sort of excuse for why he let me go," she said pleasantly. "Clearly the man's wasting his time as a policeman. He should be writing cheap novels featuring sinister masterminds."

George and Hu both laughed, and Dave joined in a moment later in quick sycophantic agreement. Lily didn't laugh. Her gaze shifted from Hu to Irene like a gun's sights.

"So why *did* he let you go?" George asked.

"Why do you think?" Irene tapped her handbag.

"A policeman's bank account is limited," Hu agreed. "Like most professionals, really. Doctors, policemen, even librarians . . ."

"Not my problem, fortunately," Irene said.

"Come now, Miss Jeanette," George said as the waiter set drinks in front of them. "Money's everyone's problem. A sensible businessman doesn't turn down a good deal. Nor does a sensible businesswoman."

Irene felt a shift in the atmosphere at the table. She picked up her glass and took a sip to buy herself time. The whiskey was adequate—or at least it wasn't *obviously* brewed in a backstairs still. "Am I missing something?" she asked lightly.

"Just trying to be helpful," George said. "I've got one new partner sitting here." He tilted his cigar towards Hu. "And another new one sitting right there." This time the glowing tip of the cigar pointed at Irene. "Mr. Hu's saying that his boss would like to do some business with England. I figure it would be doing a good turn to get you two people heading up the aisle together, so to speak."

Hu's smile looked a little pained. "It's true that my superior is looking for a suitable contact. We did have someone in mind, but he seems to have vanished . . ." He shook his head sadly. "My superior was very unhappy. It's going to take a lot to clear *that* slate."

"Yeah," George commented. "It's a false economy wasting your time on second-raters."

"Such as the 'contact' that Mr. Hu here was using previously?" Irene suggested.

"But it's not who a man buys first that counts," George said. "It's who stays bought. Right?"

"Exactly," Hu agreed. "And errors of ignorance are pardonable. It's when you have continuous, knowing disobedience that one has to . . . bring the whip down. So to speak." His cigarette snapped sharply down between his fingers, the point making a brief arc of brightness.

Irene shrugged. "If your boss—sorry, your *superior*—can't control his own people, that's his problem. Not mine."

"But if you make a deal with my boss, then it becomes your problem . . . though such a deal could be to your advantage too," Hu said pleasantly.

"This is going far too fast," Irene said sharply. She took another sip of her whiskey. "I've already made one arrangement today. I'm not going to be rushed into another."

"Perhaps we could discuss it while we dance?" Hu suggested, nodding towards the dance floor.

"Perhaps not," Irene disagreed. "I've got two left feet. You don't want either of them treading on yours." It wasn't strictly true, but something deeply rooted in her brain, sited between the part that handled primal terror and the part that handled rational threat assessment, was very strongly against the idea.

"I'm sure we could manage," Hu said, a smile coating his voice.

"I'd rather not try," Irene said. She wished throwing her glass of whiskey in his face was a viable option. It would be so satisfying.

"Are you sure you two don't know each other?" George asked. "You're certainly talking like a couple with prior acquaintance."

"Our organizations have been in contact previously," Hu said. "There's disputed territory between us. You know the sort of thing."

"Don't I just. Well, I need to circulate, so I'll leave the two of you to talk it out." George favoured both of them with a toothy smile. "Dave, you're with me. Lily, darling, you just stay here to make sure nobody actually kills anyone else."

"Not unless you say so, boss," Lily said. Her visible eye watched Irene and Hu mockingly as George rose to his feet and strolled off, Dave a shadow at his shoulder.

"And are you going to get involved?" Hu asked Lily, as soon as George was plausibly out of earshot.

"Not unless I get told to." Lily licked a drop from the brim of her glass. "I mean, it's all one to me what you play at, as long as you don't mess with my business. I know what you are, and I'd just *love* to put a bullet in your skull. But unless and until my boss tells me to, I guess I'll behave myself. Frankly it's amusing as hell to watch the two of you fence."

"We don't have to fence," Irene said bluntly. "We could just stop. I'm not making a deal with your superior."

"Make it with me, then," Hu suggested. "An understanding between the people who actually get the work done."

"How do you mean?" Irene asked.

Hu leaned across the table towards her. His body language was open, almost vulnerable, she realized. This wasn't Kai's casual arrogance or armoured pride. Hu was reaching out for understanding. It was almost as if he had a personal stake in the situation. "I believe we're the people who do the work, while our superiors take the rewards. Which is reasonable enough. I'm no prince, and you're no—well, whatever your Library has to fill such roles. Even the third party at the table understands that, I think." His glance towards Lily wasn't exactly courteous, but it was—just barely— polite. "What's ordered at the highest level isn't necessarily what's done at ground-level. And it's often easier to get a job finished first, and then make a report later when everything's under control."

Lily didn't answer, but she did incline her head very slightly.

Irene considered the offer. If Hu could bypass Qing Song and get Evariste's daughter back, then maybe she should at least hear him out. "I admit life's different for us working-class types," she said. "But I'm neutral. And you *both* know that. I haven't made a deal with Lily, and I can't make one with you."

"You should do," Hu said, and his voice darkened. "You really should. It'd be better for you, and for anyone you're hiding."

Irene raised her eyebrows and sipped her drink. "Threats? Again? And so quickly?"

Hu took a long drag on his cigarette. "No. It's a friendly warning—as you put it, between us working-class types. My lord is not the sort who appreciates being deceived, mocked, or betrayed. If he finds out that you've done any of those things, Jeanette or Marguerite or whatever your name is, I will not be able to protect you."

"Your lord seems to think that he has carte blanche to do whatever he wants," Irene said, anger igniting inside her. "Since when have his rights and privileges included commandeering Librarians to work for him? Does he realize quite how dangerous his own position is?"

"Don't blame me for the world being the way it is," Hu said. "If you don't want to play politics, then don't. All my lord wants is the book."

"Which book?" Lily asked curiously.

Hu flicked a glance at her. "It's bad enough that I have to sit with you. I'm not sharing information."

"Not even if I could help you find it?" Lily asked.

"Based on the way they're treating *me*—a theoretical neutral—how well do you think they'd treat *you*?" Irene pointed out. She wanted to stamp out this avenue of enquiry before it went any further. Especially as Hu would blame any leaks on her. "Besides, I thought that your job was shooting people, not stealing books."

"That would depend on whether George told me to steal it," Lily retorted. "And think how much less fuss a book would make than a person, when you put it in a sack."

Irene forced aside a number of distressing mental images. "Fine. Far be it from me to get between you. I can only say *I'm* not interested—and no thanks."

Hu's lips tightened. In the dim light his eyes gleamed like emeralds. "Fool of a woman! I'm trying to save your life here. You can call it whatever you like when you're back at your Library. I'm not trying to *win*. I'm trying to find a solution that doesn't involve either of us losing."

Irene *liked* compromises where both sides won. But Hu's offer would involve *her* making a private deal to influence dragon politics—with all that entailed. This didn't solve anything: instead it involved *two* Librarians transgressing rather than just *one*. With twice the potential for the Library to be dragged down with them.

And even if Qing Song was the iron hand and Hu was the velvet glove, they were both asking for exactly the same thing. Besides, just because Hu might make promises didn't necessarily mean he'd be able to keep them. Qing Song was the one in command.

"No," she said. "I can't and won't take your offer. And for the record, yes, the Library *does* know I'm here and why. Making me vanish without a trace isn't an option."

Hu leaned back in his seat. "I never thought it was," he said. "But I wish you weren't ruling out other possibilities."

"Don't try to put the blame for this on me," Irene said calmly.

She was keeping her voice down—Lily might be a lost cause, but she didn't want anyone at other tables hearing this. But her anger and frustration sharpened her tone to a razor-edge, and she saw Hu draw back a little in response. "*We* have been drawn into this because of *your* power games. I am not going to make an agreement with you, and I will not be liable for any consequences."

"Sometimes you can only play the hand you're dealt," Hu said. "And if you're following orders—well, then so am I."

His eyes flicked to the door, then to his watch. The movement was casual enough, but Lily tensed. "What are you playing at?" she demanded, her voice low and dangerous.

Hu raised a thin eyebrow, his copper hair dark in the dim lighting. His hand moved to rest against an inner pocket. "Why do you assume I'm playing at anything?"

"Because I'm not stupid." Her gaze flickered across to where George was still glad-handing his way around the other tables, slapping shoulders and accepting gestures of respect. "Jeanette, or whatever your name is, you're on your own. My responsibility's to my boss." She was out of her chair as smoothly as a lizard, her blonde hair catching the light as she headed towards George.

Yet before Lily could reach him, a harsh alarm ripped through the piano music and quiet conversation. Irene looked round, but she couldn't tell where it was coming from. Suddenly the waiters were all moving at once, removing any evidence of alcohol. They scuttled through the room, scooping up glasses and bottles before retreating behind the bar. One waiter snatched up the drinks from Irene's own table, moving with practised speed.

More of the servers vanished behind the bar than was physically possible. Irene could hear the distant sound of feet rattling down steps underneath the growing turmoil, and realized there must be a concealed trapdoor and stairs. The bartenders were hastily dragging metal shutters in front of their ranks of bottles, and fitting veneered panels of wood in place to cover them up. Other waiters were hurrying with bottles of water and fruit juice, distributing them together with fresh glasses.

Irene pushed her chair back to rise. "You knew about the raid . . ."

"I wouldn't move," Hu said. He was holding a gun in his hand, concealing it from the rest of the room, and it was pointed directly at her. "I really wouldn't."

"You'll be in real trouble if you shoot me." Irene knew she could use the Language to blow up the gun—but could she do it before he pulled the trigger? "Besides, you don't want me dead."

"No, but injured is a perfectly valid option." Hu tilted his head as though listening. "We can both be arrested together, if you like."

He's playing for time, Irene suddenly realized. *He just has to make me hesitate for long enough for the police to stop me escaping . . .*

Then the door by the dance floor slammed open and cops came pouring through, jostling each other in the narrow space. The piano music abruptly stopped, and the dancers on the floor stuttered to a halt, exclaiming in overdone annoyance.

"What's going on here?" George demanded loudly. He still held his cigar in one hand, and paused to take an arrogant puff. "Who's responsible for this gross invasion of a private club?"

The ranks of the policemen broke, and Captain Venner stalked through. "We've received notice that there's alcohol being sold in this establishment," he said. "Contrary to the Volstead Act, Mr. Ross."

"My name is on the ownership papers," George said graciously.

"But I'm entirely shocked at your accusation. All the gentlemen and ladies here are good, law-abiding citizens. Isn't that so, people?"

Amidst the raucous yells and raising of water-filled glasses, Irene counted exits and discounted them just as quickly. Which left the possible hidden exit behind this table, perhaps George's own private way out. But she could be wrong. And even if she was right, how could she get through it without being noticed?

Hu had slipped his gun back inside his jacket and was watching her in a way that made the back of her neck prickle.

"My men are going to be looking into just how law-abiding you all are," Captain Venner announced. "Boys, spread out. We're going to be stripping this place down to see if there's anything here that shouldn't be."

"You're taking a hell of a step, Venner," George said. "You know your bosses are going to be hearing about it if you make a mistake."

Venner pointed a meaty finger at him, unconsciously echoing George's own play with his cigar. "Yeah. Bosses. And some of us still think that the best way to deal with a boss of *your* sort is to put 'im behind bars. Whether they're American or English." His gaze slid across the guests and came to rest on Irene.

Irene suppressed her instinct to hide, which at the moment was screaming for her to crawl under the table. This wasn't the sort of situation where that would help. To be honest, very few situations were. Instead she raised her glass of water to Captain Venner in an ironic toast, aware that she'd only keep George as an ally if she played the part. "I'm fairly sure that's what we call slander, over my side of the Atlantic," she said. "Harsh words for a woman who only came to New York to do some shopping."

"Book shopping?" Hu murmured, and Irene almost laughed.

Captain Venner stamped towards her table. "You! Jeanette Smith. You're under arrest, lady, and you'll be coming with us."

Irene rose to her feet. Hu didn't try to stop her this time, but then he didn't need to. This was just what he'd wanted. She could hardly help Evariste from behind bars. Several of the cops lowered their hands to their holsters, but she raised her hands, showing they were empty. "This is really unnecessary. And what's the charge, anyway?"

"Trust me, we'll have a whole lot of them before we're done." Captain Venner came to a stop a few feet away. More quietly he said, "And don't think you'll pull that hypnotism trick on me again."

Genuine anger twisted his jowls into a frown. Irene realized, with a pang of guilt, that his fury wasn't just because she'd twisted his will. She'd offended his professional pride as a cop. From his perspective, she was a master criminal who'd posed as an FBI agent, hypnotized him, and was now sitting in the speakeasy run by one of New York's biggest crime bosses. Perhaps it was unrealistic to expect him to go easy on her.

"All right," she said, playing for time herself and taking a step back. She looked across to George. "Mr. Ross, please excuse me for a little while. And perhaps you can recommend a lawyer?"

Captain Venner took a step towards her. "You can call one from the station," he snapped.

"Don't be like that, Venner," George called. "Let's not be harsh to a poor helpless English visitor on her own in New York. She's got the cutest accent, hasn't she?" he confided to the crowd, who laughed on cue. "I'll be hospitable and send one of my lawyers to advise her."

"Sure you will," Venner said in tones of deep bitterness. "We all know that you've got every mouthpiece in town on a contract, Ross. You don't need to tell us." He turned towards George, allowing Irene to back a few steps farther towards the wall.

"You know a lot about me, Venner," George said. "And you know we could help each other . . . Life could be a hell of a lot easier for you that way."

"Save your money for the cops on your payroll," Venner growled. "Right now I'm the one in charge. Boys! Let's get this place turned over. Guns and booze, you know the drill. And you, Miss Smith—"

Irene could feel the wall at her back. "I'll come quietly," she said. "I mean, what do you expect me to do? Snap my fingers and say"— she switched to the Language and raised her voice—**"lights out!"**

And there was total darkness.

CHAPTER 17

I rene dropped to the floor and started crawling sideways the
moment the lights went down. It wasn't one of those situations
where everyone remained quietly in their seats, waiting for the
lights to go back on. The room was full of screaming, as if caged
animals were turning on each other in the darkness. Glass hit the
floor and smashed. She made out Captain Venner's voice through
the hubbub, yelling for his men to restore order. Irene hoped he'd
find someone else here to arrest besides her. It would be a shame
to have completely wasted his time.

She traced her fingertips along the wall as she crawled. Suddenly she felt a breath of cooler air through a crack in the mould-
ing. Biting back a sigh of relief, she followed the crack up and
round, rising to her feet as she worked out the rough dimensions
of the door.

Standing to one side of it, she said softly in the Language,
"Door, open."

The door swung back into the wall, but unfortunately the corridor behind was illuminated. Light came spilling out into the dark room, falling across the struggling mob.

Irene flung herself through the door, hunching to make herself as small a target as possible. There was a crack as a bullet hit the wall next to her, and she heard Venner shout, "Get after her!"

With panicked haste she pelted along the corridor, turning a corner to find a flight of stairs blessedly leading upwards. The door at the top was locked, but the Language opened it, and another few words closed it behind her.

She'd emerged into a garage. It was large and well lit, with several expensive-looking cars, and several more hefty-looking mechanics. They were looking at her in surprise, and she raised her hands again to demonstrate that she wasn't holding a gun.

"Who're you?" one demanded.

If this *was* George's private escape route, these would be his men. "I'm with George—we've just done a deal. But the club's being raided. Would you mind if I left before they come through?"

"They won't be coming through," the speaker grunted. "Jim, Luigi, you know the drill. Lady, you'd better be telling the truth."

"George knows where I'm staying. That's a major incentive not to tell him any lies." Irene watched two of the men drag heavy crates in front of the door she'd just come through. "And I need to catch a cab?"

"That way." He pointed to an unobtrusive door.

"Thanks," Irene said, and dipped into her handbag to pass him a few bills. He took them with a nod of acceptance, clearly reassured by this normal gesture of everyday sanity.

Irene hurried through the door, out into a side alley, and from there onto the main street. It was late afternoon by now, on the cusp of early evening: the skyscrapers above filled the street with shadows. Traffic was chugging past in both directions, clogging the street with a stream of cars and buses. People just released from work hurried along, turning the pavement into a solid block of crowd—a mingled assortment of ages and races, accents and languages, well-off and poor, all seething together in a loud and cheerful stream. Irene lost herself gratefully in the mob for a couple of blocks.

This would be the ideal moment to *really* lose her pursuers and shake them off for good—then locate Evariste and Kai. And perhaps she should acknowledge that she was out of her depth, running just to stay a step ahead of her enemies. Police, mobsters, and dragons. Oh, and Fae too. Morbid humour made her wonder if she ought to collect anyone else, to have a complete set.

But standing around feeling guilty about her own recklessness wouldn't get her anywhere. She forced her way through the crowd and hailed a cab.

"Where to, lady?" the driver asked as she clambered in.

"New York Public Library," she answered automatically. "As fast as you can, please."

The cab peeled away from the curb and into the traffic, with the driver honking on his horn as though sheer sonic power would help clear a path. Irene gripped the edge of her seat and pondered her next tactics. There would probably be someone watching the entrance to the New York Public Library. All she had to do to continue her diversion was let herself be seen . . .

"Why are we slowing down?" she asked.

"Police check-point ahead," the driver replied. He pointed to where a couple of black vans were half blocking the road at the next junction. Irene recognized the same model that had transported her and Kai to the police station. Was it only this morning? It felt like longer ago. "Seems like they're looking for someone."

Irene felt her stomach clench. They *could* be looking for any number of criminals, but she had a feeling her name was high on the list.

Of course there was a standard method of dealing with this— and it would be the perfect way to keep the hounds on her tail.

Two cars to go. Then one. Then it was her cab.

The cop checking the driver didn't see her immediately, but the one peering into the car grinned as he caught sight of her, with the delight of a man who's pulled the winning lottery ticket. "Hey, aren't you—"

"**Policemen, you perceive that I'm not the person you're looking for,**" Irene said very quickly. That turn of phrase had caught on extremely fast among Librarians, once it entered popular fiction. She decided to up the stakes. "**In fact, you perceive I am a pregnant woman about to give birth and I need to get to the hospital.**"

The driver frowned at her in the mirror in bewilderment, but both cops reacted as the Language adjusted their perceptions. "Right you are, lady," the one who'd been looking at her said. He stood back and blew on his whistle, waving other cars to a halt as the other cop gestured them forward.

Fortunately the driver didn't hesitate. He stamped on the accelerator and the cab jolted forward to the sound of more aggrieved horns, before burning rubber down the street. It was a good couple of minutes before he said, "What the hell—"

"Just keep on driving and I'll double your fee," Irene said.

"Right." A turning later, he spoke again. "You're her, aren't you? That English boss?"

"If I was, would I tell you?" Irene was listening for the sound of police sirens behind them.

"Sure you would," the driver said cheerfully. "I mean, hey, this is New York—people like you are famous here! Look, if you are, can I have your autograph?"

He tossed her back a notepad and pencil-stub while managing the cab one-handed. Irene gritted her teeth and scribbled *Jeanette Smith.* "For anyone in particular?" she asked.

"It's for my daughter. See, I'm always telling her that women can get ahead in this world—"

"Hold it a moment," Irene directed. She could hear sirens in the distance. She fished out several bills from her now-depleted handbag and passed them over with the autograph. "I'll jump out; then you keep on going—and keep the cops following you for as long as possible. Tell them whatever you want when they catch up. Okay?"

"You got it. I'll drop you at the next corner; the library's two blocks straight from there."

"Good man." Irene braced herself to move.

Ten seconds later she was on the sidewalk and blending in behind some office workers while the cab raced on. The police followed about half a minute later, snarling up the traffic as they claimed the right of way, forcing other cars to the sides of the street.

Irene took a moment to catch her breath. The streets here weren't as busy as the ones she'd left, which meant less potential cover to reach the New York Public Library. And the streets were wider. On either side the buildings reared up like cliff faces, as smooth as fractured mica. At street level there were shop signs, restaurant signs, people going in and out, lights, noise, action— but above her, the whole of New York seemed to be watching.

There wasn't time for a complete costume change—the police, the mobs, and Hu's men were too close behind her. She needed some way to hide. She needed divine inspiration. She needed a miracle.

The raucous noise of a brass band and stamping feet became audible even through the squealing of tyres and blaring of car horns. On the opposite side of the street a group was marching, banners raised and heads held high. The slogans on their signs declared VOTE DRY, ALCOHOL IS POISON, LIPS THAT TOUCH LIQUOR SHALL NEVER TOUCH MINE, and similar sentiments.

For a moment Irene wondered if this was just a little *too* convenient. Coincidences like this might occur in a high-chaos world, but were less likely elsewhere. But the papers had warned of temperance marches across the city today. It was ideal.

She made her way across the street and folded herself into the rear of the column. She bowed her head, trying for an expression of sincere devotion to the Cause. Other pedestrians were either pausing to mock the group or avoiding even looking at them. And at this moment, that was precisely what Irene wanted. She opened and closed her mouth in time to the hymn the marchers were singing and hummed along with the chorus.

The sun was setting in the distance in a triumphant glow of reds and oranges as the march drew to a stuttering halt in front of one large building—not too far from her destination. Several of the more muscular-looking women quickly assembled a makeshift podium from planks and boxes that they'd been carrying. There were clear class divisions among the protesters: the upper-class ones stood back and gave the orders, while the lower-class ones did the actual work. Some things didn't change, no matter how many worlds you visited.

A couple of police cars rattled by, but to Irene's relief they didn't stop.

But before she could make a break for the library, a hand tapped her shoulder. "Haven't seen you here before," the woman next to her said.

"I don't recognize you either," Irene answered, smiling pleasantly as she assessed the other woman. She was neatly and smartly dressed, but not expensively, and she was wearing glossily buckled high heels rather than something that would have been comfortable to walk in. "Do you work near here?" she guessed.

"I'm a legal secretary at Sallust and Floddens," the woman said, offering Irene her hand to shake. "Lina Johnson. Pleased to meet you. Love the coat. You're English?"

"I can't really hide it," Irene admitted. She ran through her mental list of aliases. If the name "Rosalie" had made it into the newspapers, it would be unsafe to use it. "Clarice Backson," she said, falling back on an earlier pseudonym. At least she should be safe from any dragons recognizing it. "On holiday from England. When I saw the march, I felt I had to join in. I hope you don't mind."

"Mind? I should think not!" another woman chimed in. "If more women were willing to stand up for their beliefs, we'd have a better America. We need more citizens like you."

There were approving nods around her. Irene was just congratulating herself on her blending skills when she recognized a couple of George the Dude's men approaching. And they were looking at the women.

"Perhaps you'd tell me about how you're operating here," she said to her questioners, turning her back to the mobsters. "Give me some suggestions I can take back home."

The ensuing surge of comments meant that she could keep silent, hiding her telltale English accent as the mobsters passed. But her throat was dry with nerves. The worst thing was being so *close* to the New York Public Library. Having her goal within sight made it that much harder to hold her position. She hoped Kai and Evariste were having an easier time.

"You ought to be one of the speakers," Lina Johnson suggested. "You could tell us how our British sisters are fighting the good fight!"

"Oh no," Irene said quickly. "I'm not a good public speaker."

But the idea had unfortunately caught on. "You just need to speak from the heart, Miss Backson," another woman said firmly. "Stand up there and tell them God's own truth."

"No, really, I couldn't possibly . . ." Irene said. It wasn't working. She was being shoved through the crowd by her admirers, towards the podium. Strong-minded women with a cause accepted even fewer excuses than the average gangster when it came to getting what they wanted, and what they wanted right now was Irene making a speech. "I don't think . . ."

Then she saw the gangsters coming back towards the group of marchers. And Hu was with them.

Irene rapidly reassessed her possible options: she was out of time and out of luck. Her best option now was stalling for any delay she could gain.

". . . but if you say so, I suppose I could try," she said, and let herself be pushed forward.

Irene took a deep breath and stepped up as the previous speaker stepped down. She was only a couple of feet off the ground, but the sea of faces looking up at her in the sunset light made her stomach swim with vertigo. Or perhaps that was just stage-fright. Now that she had a better point of view, she could see more of George's men—looking dangerously alert.

They hadn't noticed her yet. Oh well, Irene decided, she might as well make this last for as long as possible.

"Brothers and sisters," she began, and saw Hu's head jerk round in her direction. "We are marching to fight a demon, and that demon is alcohol." She took a deep breath, raising her voice. "Some of you may never have visited England. Some of you may think of it as a distant homeland, an old motherland that can do no wrong. But my country—the land of my birth—is cursed by alcohol."

She turned from side to side, making eye contact with members of the audience. "You may laugh. But you haven't seen English gin palaces! Gilded constructions of glass and iron, where the bartenders dole out glasses of ruinously strong pure gin to all comers! I've been there. I've seen it. And then I've walked outside and seen the drunks slumped in the gutters, *begging* for one more glass of the vicious liquid! From the highest to the lowest, the richest to the poorest, alcohol is stamped on the face of England like a festering sore. The Members of Parliament are served fine wines in the very House where they debate the law!" She paused, and to her surprise received a few cheers. "The poor mother in her garret watches her husband go out to drink away their savings! When he comes back late at night, staggering and blind-drunk, he responds to her pitiful pleas for household money with blows and curses!"

The gangsters were spreading out in a rough circle now, loosely spaced around the podium to block any escape. Hu nodded at her in a friendly manner, then raised his watch and tapped at it, in the traditional gesture for *Hurry up and finish*.

Which was the last thing that Irene intended to do. "Let me tell you about the depravity, the debauchery, of the rich and famous of

England," she declared into a sudden interested silence. Even a couple of the gangsters were listening. "Why, only last year . . ."

It was half an hour before she ran out of words. Hu was waiting to shake her hand.

"Are you going to make a scene?" he asked softly.

Irene sighed. "I'll come quietly. I don't suppose there's any chance of a drink?"

CHAPTER 18

"What we need is a really good way of disguising you," Kai said. "Qing Song's watchers will be everywhere." He walked around Evariste, inspecting him thoughtfully. The man was of average height, with dark skin marred by an underlying pallor. His black hair was plainly and unflatteringly styled, and his face had good solid lines, with a firm jaw and strong brow. His clothing was well-made and cut to fit him, but showed the traces of too much recent wear and not enough recent washing.

They were in another seedy hotel room, with only a limited amount of time until someone—criminals, police, or gangsters—caught up with them.

"You're talking as if I haven't thought about this already," Evariste said sourly. He sat on the edge of the bed, propping his unshaven chin on his hands. "There's only so many ways I can change how I look. Especially when some of them have seen me face-to-face."

"Bandages, maybe? You could be a wounded war veteran—"

"No recent wars in this world," Evariste said. "Or at least none that America's been in."

"I'm *trying* to be constructive here," Kai said. He throttled down a flare of irritation. Evariste had been living off his nerves for weeks now. Kai would simply have to be tolerant. "We can't change your skin colour, and your hair's too short to restyle. We can't disguise you as a woman . . ."

"Wait. Hold up." Evariste stared at him. "Were you seriously considering that, even for one moment?"

"I'm just going through the options," Kai pointed out. "Besides, Irene's disguised herself as a man once or twice. Though it wasn't very convincing."

"Stop trying to get me to trust you," Evariste said. "It's not going to work."

"Irene thought we could work together. Are you going to argue with her?"

"She's not here to be argued with." Evariste glanced at his watch. "She's left us to do the actual work while she goes shopping."

Kai was about to snarl at him for such casual disrespect, but he sensed the undertones of fear in the other Librarian's voice. Instead he said, "You're deluding yourself if you think that."

"She's got you as cover, hasn't she? If Qing Song gets too close, he'll back off, because he won't want to mess with another dragon's *property*." Evariste rolled the final word in his mouth as though he meant to spit it out.

"That's wrong in so many ways that I can't even start to explain how many," Kai said.

"Is it? Hu said other dragons would know that I was under Qing Song's authority—"

"How? Because you told them? It's not as if I can just smell him on you."

Evariste flinched away, then tried to make the movement look deliberate rather than nervous. "Don't you even try it."

"Try what?"

"Sniffing me."

Kai folded his arms and looked down at Evariste. Memories of days spent in a street gang seeped into his diction. "Lose the attitude. I'm not asking you to like me. I'm telling you to work with me. You're a professional, aren't you?"

"Okay," Evariste said. "Fine. Give your word—on whatever dragons believe in—that no dragon you know and trust would ever, *ever* take a hostage and blackmail someone in order to get what he wanted. Or she wanted. Let's not be gender-specific here. And hey, let's suppose they think they're doing it for a really good reason. Can you promise me that none of your *nice* dragons would do a thing like that?"

Every sinew in Kai's body wanted to back-hand the insolent human across the room. He was not accustomed to being criticized like this. But instead he said, "Do you want your daughter back or don't you?"

Evariste looked at him for a long moment. Then he slumped back onto the bed. "Screw you and the horse you rode in on," he said. "You know I do."

"Then get your head out of your—" Kai remembered that he was royalty. "Then pull yourself together and help me. You must have had a plan to get into the Metropolitan Museum."

"I had a plan, yes! But that was before *someone* seeded Museum Mile with a load of thugs who know what I look like. He may not know *which* museum it's in, but he saw the early research, and he can be sure it's in one of them."

Kai ignored the attitude. He couldn't understand why Evariste was so hostile to planning the operation. "You must have done jobs like this before," he said encouragingly.

There was a pause. Then Evariste said grudgingly, "Not many. That is, nothing like *this*. The way you're behaving, I get the impression you've actually done more than I have."

"But you've got the Library brand." Kai had checked that while Evariste was still unconscious. He preferred to be certain. "You're a full Librarian, like Irene."

"Some of us are better at research," Evariste said through gritted teeth. "Disguise is not my thing. I'm not good with disguise."

Kai sat down on the chair. "You know, it would have helped if you'd said that earlier. Such as when we were planning this."

"Define 'we.' Irene was planning this. You were agreeing with everything she said. I just . . ." Evariste's indignation trailed off. His voice cracked. "I didn't have any better ideas. I just want my daughter back. I didn't even know she existed, I spent years working at the Library without being there for her . . ."

Kai breathed in, then out again, controlling his frustration. "Right. Let's consider this as a military operation. Enemy forces consist of gunmen working for the local gangs, who may know what you look like." He raised one finger. "And possibly the police, if they've been paid off." Another finger. "And Qing Song and Hu—who will certainly recognize me as a dragon if they see me." And if they thought he was after the book in order to influence the contest, then . . . well, accidents could happen. They shouldn't. But they did.

Evariste nodded. Fortunately he couldn't hear Kai's thoughts.

"Yeah. Assume they've got a couple dozen men scattered up and down the Mile, maybe more."

"There aren't any secret police round here in this time and place that we could pose as, are there?" Kai asked hopefully.

"Nah," Evariste said. "There's the FBI, and the anti-drink task forces, but those aren't quite the same thing. And if we try showing up at the door, claiming that we're there to raid a secret distillery underneath the Metropolitan Museum of Art, not only are we going to get noticed; we're going to get laughed out of town."

"That wasn't what I had in mind," Kai said with dignity, reluctantly putting the idea aside. "We're going to have to get in there unnoticed . . . We could bribe our way into one of the cleaning crews and get in that way, but we haven't the time."

Kai paused and looked Evariste up and down measuringly. An idea had just alighted in his head, fully formed and arrestingly plausible.

"I'm not sure I like the way you're looking at me," Evariste said.

"There may be dozens of thugs watching for you," Kai said, "but they won't be able to see through solid wood. I'm going to have us crated up and shipped in there as a work of art."

Evariste stared at him. "That's crazy."

"But would it work?"

There was a long pause. Then Evariste said, "You know, it just might."

CHAPTER 19

The early-evening sounds of Fifth Avenue—and Fifty-fifth Street—drifted in through the open full-length balcony windows. The sky outside was that perfect shade of clear dusky blue that came after sunset but before true nightfall. Twilight lay like a curtain over New York, waiting to be drawn back for the evening's entertainment. And up here, at this level above New York, one *could* see the sky without the buildings getting in the way.

Qing Song was sitting in one of the suite's large armchairs, a book open in his lap. Two of his wolves lay on either side of his chair, their heads cocked as though they'd been listening to him reading to them. The others were sprawled around the room like unusually three-dimensional rugs. "I see you found her," he remarked to Hu.

"Not without some difficulty, my lord," Hu said. "One would think she was trying to take in as many landmarks as possible."

A thread of unease ran down Irene's back. For Kai's sake, she couldn't afford for them to suspect she'd been leading them on a false trail. "Well, I'm here now," she said coldly. "And I would appreciate it if this gentleman"—she jerked her head at the thug behind her—"would kindly point his gun somewhere else."

Qing Song gestured, and Irene felt the pressure of the gun leave her ribs. "Of course," he said. "I'm glad there was no need for anything more excessive. Humans are such fragile creatures. Even Librarians."

Irene would have had to be deaf to miss Qing Song's switch from courtesy to barely veiled threats. Maybe he'd decided there was no further need to hide. "We manage to get by," she said. "Has there been any news about your stolen jade statue?"

Qing Song closed his book. "It might surprise you to know that I was not entirely honest with you earlier."

He considered her thoughtfully. The wolves beside him raised their heads to look at her, their eyes utterly impassive, as if they were assessing her weight in pounds of steak. "I am about to make a request. It will be to your advantage to listen. It will be even more to your advantage to accept."

"You have my full attention," Irene said politely. Over his shoulder, in the open windowpane, she could see the reflection of the room. The two thugs who'd been sitting on either side of her on the car ride here were still a couple of paces behind her. Hu had walked across to the sideboard and was filling a glass with water. And the wolves, of course, were all over the place. Making a break for it looked impossible.

But if Qing Song was about to come clean on what he'd been up to, then the next few minutes were going to be very interesting.

"I am looking for a particular book," Qing Song said. "I require it as a matter of urgency. My previous researcher was kidnapped, but I still have his materials. If you can find it for me, within the next couple of days, then you will have my gratitude. I and my family will remember your conduct."

Irene had to admire the way he'd explained Evariste's absence. "Kidnapped?" she asked.

"Fae interference." Qing Song's face was set like stone. "They foul all they touch."

"So when we met this morning . . ."

"I was tracking them," he admitted. "Their trail led me to your fellow Librarian's door. He may be another victim of their schemes. But for now, my priority is locating that book. I trust I can count on your service."

"But I may not be able to find your book within the 'next couple of days,'" she temporized. "I'm a Librarian, not a miracle-worker."

"I will be satisfied only by your very best efforts," Qing Song said. His voice was inflexible. "You will remain here. Hu will provide everything you may require."

"You're assuming that I'm going to say yes." Irene tried to gauge his mood, but the wolves weren't providing any clues this time.

"I don't think you can afford to say no. And if you value the health and safety of other servants of the Library, then you will obey me."

"You're asking me to break the Library's principle of neutrality," Irene said. Anger coloured her voice. "Why is one book *so* important that you'd set yourself against the whole Library—breaking a truce that has existed for longer than either of us has been alive—if I don't help you find it?"

"You don't need to know," Qing Song replied. He was address-ing her as a subordinate now, as if she'd already given in. "And it will be up to you what you tell your Library, once you've found the book."

He watched her and waited.

But before Irene could decide exactly how she was going to say no, there was a knock at the door.

Qing Song raised a hand and glanced at Hu. "Investigate," he ordered.

Hu moved to open the door, then fell back a step, startled, as the person on the other side strolled into the room. The two thugs both reached into their jackets, but dropped their hands again when they saw it was a woman. Qing Song rose to his feet.

It was Jin Zhi.

She casually kicked the door shut behind her. Her golden hair was pinned up in a loose coil around her head, and her evening coat was a wide-sleeved golden velvet wrap that draped like a court robe. She simply walked in, confident that the rest of the world would catch up, get its act together, and be ready to take orders. "Good evening, Qing Song," she said. "I'm sure you don't mind me joining you."

It was only training that kept Irene's expression of mild con-fusion pinned to her face: her stomach was dropping like the ex-press lift down to Security in the Library. Jin Zhi *knew who Irene was.* If she shared that information with Qing Song, and he real-ized that Irene had been lying to him from the very beginning, then . . .

"Be welcome to my lodgings, small as they are," Qing Song said. His voice was emotionless, but his wolves were all awake, watching Jin Zhi with burning eyes. "I had thought you were in

China. Might I ask what brings you to this place, alone and without attendants?"

"Servants aren't always reliable," Jin Zhi said. "And China didn't reveal what I sought. You must feel the same way, or you wouldn't be here." She shrugged off her coat and allowed Hu to take it, which he did without a word. Her trailing dress beneath it was in a harmonizing shade of gold, sculpted to bare her shoulders. Even without her heels she stood an inch or two taller than Hu—with them, she easily overtopped him, dominating the room like an open flame. Her eyes flickered from Qing Song to Irene and narrowed. "You're keeping curious company."

"An offer of employment," Qing Song said flatly. "A minor matter. Your visit takes priority, of course."

"A minor matter?" Jin Zhi moved across to take a chair while Qing Song resumed his seat. "Given our circumstances, I'm not sure I'd call hiring a servant of the Library a *minor* matter. I seem to recall that we were absolutely forbidden to ask for help from the Library."

Irene felt her stomach tie itself slowly in knots. The dragons had been *ordered* not to get Librarian help? Then Qing Song hadn't only gone against custom—he'd outright broken the rules of their competition. He couldn't allow the slightest chance of that information getting out. Evariste would never have survived handing the book over. And as for Irene's own survival . . .

And Jin Zhi had just revealed that she knew Irene was a Librarian, even if Qing Song hadn't realized it. How fortunate Qing Song had so much on his mind, Irene thought gratefully. If he'd spotted Jin Zhi's slip, and assumed that the two of them were in collusion, then the situation would have lost whatever traces of civility it had left.

"I am not asking for help," Qing Song said dismissively. He signalled to Hu, who moved noiselessly to pour him some water and offer a second glass to Jin Zhi. "I am commanding it. There is a difference."

Jin Zhi flicked a finger towards Irene. "Has she accepted your service, then?"

Qing Song's mouth tightened very slightly. "The Librarian Marguerite was about to give me her pledge," he said.

Jin Zhi's lips slowly parted in a smile. She took the glass from Hu and turned to Irene. "How very interesting. Perhaps I should bid for her service too. I could offer good terms."

She's figured out that Qing Song doesn't know who I am. Irene felt a metaphorical precipice yawn in front of her. *And she's going to use that.*

"It is discourteous in the extreme to attempt to steal my servants," Qing Song said coldly. But this was something he clearly hadn't considered.

Jin Zhi laughed. "Qing Song, I would pity you if I didn't know you so well. I'll make what offers I please to her. Or do you want to throw me out?"

The fingers of Qing Song's free hand tightened on the arm of the chair, but he didn't reply. Apparently the rules of engagement between high-ranking dragons prevented that sort of action. He flicked a quick glance at Hu, who twitched a shoulder very slightly in response: very much a question-and-answer, a query of *Can you think of anything* and a response of *There's no help for it.* Hu might be the servant here, but it seemed Qing Song trusted his opinion a great deal.

"Very well, then." Jin Zhi turned to Irene. "Marguerite." She pronounced the name as if it were a dollop of honey, drawing out the syllables. "I'm not sure what Qing Song has offered you, but I imagine that I can offer you more. In addition to my personal gratitude, and my guarantee of your safety."

"My safety?" Irene said, breaking her silence.

"From the rest of this room, for a start." The curl of her smile was, as Kai had commented a day ago, extremely gracious. "You must be aware that you are in a dangerous position."

"Believe me, madam," Irene said, "I am very much aware of that fact."

"Then why hesitate?"

"Perhaps because she is not the sort to be cowed by threats," Qing Song said.

"I'm not the one threatening her," Jin Zhi answered. This time there was a note of venom underneath the honey. "She is in danger, but I'm not the one who put her there."

"A rational man keeps his temper within bounds," Qing Song said. "Even if she might offend me by refusing, I am hardly going to behave like some sort of *child*."

For some reason that made Jin Zhi twitch, her whole body going rigid as her glass splintered in her hand. Water trickled down over her briefly scale-patterned fingers. "Apparently you have nothing better to do than recall past insults."

"And apparently *you* have nothing better to do than repeat them." Qing Song's tone was vicious.

Irene looked back at the reflection in the windowpane. The men behind her were both still in the same position, but their attention was on Qing Song and Jin Zhi rather than on her. For the moment, the bickering pair weren't looking at her either.

Unfortunately it was probably only a matter of time until the dragons turned back to her and demanded an answer.

She should have been afraid. She should have been *terrified*.

But a swell of anger was rising inside her. If Jin Zhi wanted to play Use the Librarian just like Qing Song, then Jin Zhi would get exactly the same treatment. They were the ones who were breaking their own competition's precious rules. If they'd left themselves open to blackmail by doing so, then that was their own fault. It was time to get out of here.

She took a step forward, and both of the dragons turned to look at her. "Madam. Sir. Before going any further, I would like to make it absolutely clear that the Library knows I'm here and what I'm investigating. You can't just snap your fingers and make me disappear. However great your powers, and however noble your families."

"Must I repeat myself?" Qing Song asked. "I am not making that sort of threat."

"Let's at least agree that everyone in this room is threatening me in some way," Irene said. And this was where she tore up her cover story and danced on the fragments. "And my name is not Marguerite."

Jin Zhi leaned back in her chair in surprise. Clearly she hadn't expected Irene to deliberately blow her own cover. For a moment her eyes showed confusion, not calculation.

Qing Song, on the other hand, leaned forward. His fingers dug into the arm of his chair, and around the room the wolves stirred, their heads rising and their eyes focusing on Irene. "You lied to me?" he demanded. There was an undertone to his voice like the wind in heavy forests.

"I was not entirely honest with you," Irene said. She saw his lips tighten as she threw his earlier words back at him. "Nor was I honest with Hu. I came to this world to investigate what had happened to one of our own Librarians. Evariste. I believe you know the name?"

Qing Song was silent.

Irene could feel the coldness entering her voice. "We're aware of your arrangement with him." She saw the brief flash of confirmed suspicion in Jin Zhi's face, and wondered briefly how she'd known about that in the first place. "He is out of the picture—for now."

"Out of the picture?" Qing Song said slowly.

"Under investigation." Irene looked down at him. "Such an investigation can stretch to great length. All the way to his family, for instance. It would be a shame if it should spread to *yours* as well. Since I understand that you have broken any number of rules."

Qing Song hadn't expected that. The arm of the chair actually creaked as his hand dug into it, and his nails pierced the leather. Irene could see the scale-patterns flicker across the skin of his face and hands, deep emerald as dark as holly leaves. His anger was palpable in the air, as thick as the tension before an earthquake. "You—how *dare* you threaten my family—"

"You will return your hostage," Irene said, cutting him off. "And in return we will keep silent about your actions. You will make no attempt to take vengeance on him." She took a step forward, her Library brand burning across her shoulders in the face of his power, her anger a deeper and hotter fire within her. "That is the only deal I'm offering. I suggest that you take it."

"I would know your true name," Qing Song growled. A red light flickered in the depths of his eyes. "I will be remembering it for a long time."

"Irene," she said. She saw his eyes widen. "Some people call me Irene Winters."

Hu's left arm came round her throat from behind, tight enough that she couldn't breathe. He caught her right wrist with his free hand, twisting it up behind her as she struggled for air, trying to speak—to use the Language—and failing.

"My lord," he said, "she's lying."

CHAPTER 20

"Careful, now," the man in charge of the group said. He patted the side of the crate that held Evariste and Kai. "That's expensive stuff in there. Worth more than your salary."

Kai heard the other men carrying the crate grunt in agreement. For a moment he anticipated a smoother ride for the two of them.

It didn't happen.

The last few hours had been a frustrating sequence of steps, each of them with the deadline burning down like the lit fuse of a bomb. The first step had been to find a speakeasy where there would be men for hire. The second step had been to convince them that, as part of a joke, Kai wanted himself and a friend carried into the Museum of Metropolitan Art, crated up as a new exhibit. The bribe helped. But it had all taken time, too much time, and it was getting near to sunset already.

"Whatcha got there?" someone demanded. One of the museum's security guards, Kai assumed.

A pause as the leader of the crate-carriers fumbled in his pocket. "It's a set of Ming Dynasty sculptures," he said, reading from the note Kai had prepared. "To be delivered to Professor Jamison's rooms. Got this letter for the professor too."

Another pause. Kai resisted the urge to push the crate lid off and ask whether this was going to take all day.

"I guess if it's arranged," the guard finally said, after far too long a delay. "You'd better take them up. Professor Jamison's on the third floor, along from the Asian art section there. Peters here will go up with you, show you the way. The professor's out at lunch right now, but he should be back soon."

Five minutes later the crate had been deposited inside Professor Jamison's office. Kai listened to the door slam shut, and to the sound of feet retreating down the corridor. He gave it another five minutes before he nudged the bowstring-tense Evariste. "Now," he whispered.

"Thank God," Evariste muttered. "**Crate fastenings, come undone. Crate lid, open.**"

Kai straightened with a sigh of relief, shoving the crate lid the rest of the way off. He looked round the office. It was part of a small set of rooms—one actual office, and two store-rooms that had once been dignified little anterooms. They were now piled high with disorderly stacks of notes. Miniature skyscrapers of books rose towards the ceiling as though they would blot out the light. The faint odour of rotting cheese suggested that sandwiches had been lost in the trackless wastes of paper and never found again.

Evariste rubbed the small of his back and surveyed the area.

"Shit," he said succinctly. "We don't have time to search through all this. The book could be anywhere."

"Then I suggest we get started," Kai said firmly. He checked that the door was locked. "Before Professor Jamison comes back from lunch."

"Assuming he's coming back at all." Evariste glanced at his watch. "It's nearly five o'clock already."

"The longer he's out, the better for us," Kai said.

They'd powered through the room, by the expedient of checking everything they came across and dumping everything that wasn't their target in a big heap, and were just about to try the store-rooms. Then Kai heard footsteps, and a key grating in the lock. He gestured Evariste to silence, and stepped to one side of the doorway.

The door swung open and an elderly man stepped inside. He'd already shut the door and was removing his hat before he noticed the state of the office. "What—" he began.

Kai clapped one hand over the man's mouth, grabbing his wrist with the other. "Don't say a word," he warned.

The man stayed silent, allowing Kai and Evariste to hustle him across to one of the chairs and bind him there with his own tie. Kai locked the door again. "Now," he said, feeling a bit guilty, "I understand that you may be worried—you are Professor Jamison, aren't you?"

"I am," the man said. He was looking at them with fascination. His grey hair was receding, leaving most of his head bald, and the redness of his nose and the stains on his jacket suggested that his lunch had been largely alcoholic. "Tell me, are you the Tongs?"

"No," Kai said, a bit confused.

"Triads?"

"No."

"Yakuza?" He looked at Evariste. "Leopard Society?"

"Absolutely not," Kai said. "Are you expecting them?"

"I've been predicting it for a while now," the professor said gloomily. "It's the logical consequence of removing valuable arte-facts from native cultures. This sort of pandering to American greed, at the expense of the dignity and self-determination of the cultures concerned, is certain to cause long-term results—"

"If you really believe that," Evariste broke in, "then why are you working here?"

Professor Jamison shrugged. "A man must eat, my dear boy, and there are remarkably few jobs on the market unless you're in the alcohol trade."

"All right," Kai said slowly. "Now if you'll just stay quiet, we'll be out of here as soon as we've found what we're looking for . . ."

"Tell me what it is?" the professor suggested. "I might be able to help."

It was a little too easy. Kai glanced at Evariste and received a brief shake of the head in return. Clearly Evariste didn't trust the man either. "I think we can manage," he said.

"Fair enough," the professor said with a shrug. "I don't suppose I could ask you to dust a bit while you're moving the books around? It's been a while since the cleaners came in."

"No," Kai said firmly. Dusting was for servants.

Kai waved Evariste on to the first store-room. He wanted to attack the second one, but something was nagging at his sense of caution. The professor had given in too fast. It might have been because he was a coward, or drunk, or . . . because he was expect-ing someone else to turn up at any moment.

"Sorry about this," Kai said. He pulled the professor's handkerchief from his vest-pocket and stuffed it into the man's mouth. "I'll apologize later if this is really unwarranted . . ."

Footsteps outside. The door-handle jiggled. A female voice called, "Professor Jamison?"

Evariste appeared in the store-room doorway, an expression of horror on his face.

Kai opened the door a few inches. Fortunately the professor wasn't in the line of vision. "Can I help you?" he asked politely.

The thin young woman on the other side of the door had a white cotton smock over her neat royal-blue suit and was carrying a pair of white cotton gloves. "I'm here to see Professor Jamison," she said. "It's about the archival work he wanted done."

"I'm afraid the professor's indisposed," Kai said.

"Indisposed?" the woman echoed. "I hadn't been told he was ill."

"He had a long lunch. A *very* long lunch." Kai wondered how far he could go in conveying *alcoholic stupor*. "He felt he needed a little nap."

There was a snorting noise from inside the room—probably the professor trying to make himself heard through the gag.

"There, you see?" Kai said hopefully. "Indigestion too."

The woman rolled her eyes skywards. "Now, you listen to me here, I don't care if the old sot is awake, asleep, or so drunk he can't stand. I'm here to collect his copy of Melchett's *Commentaries on the Romance of the Three Kingdoms*. So if you'll kindly step aside—"

She peered into the room, and her eyes went wide.

With a silent curse, Kai grabbed her shoulder and dragged her into the room, spinning round to kick the door shut behind them. He put his hand firmly over her mouth. "Evariste," he said. "Get another chair."

"We can't keep on doing this," Evariste protested. "We're going to run out of chairs."

"Hopefully there won't be any more callers." The woman was squirming in Kai's arms. "Look," he said, trying to sound calming, "don't make a disturbance and we won't gag you. We're just here to collect a book. We're not here to hurt anyone."

The woman relaxed a bit. As Evariste tied her hands behind her back in the chair (with *his* tie this time), she asked, "Are you with Lucky George?"

"Possibly," Kai said. "If we were, we couldn't admit to it. You know how that works."

"Right." She nodded at the professor, who was fighting his gag. "Let me guess. He's been playing the horses again, and you've come to collect on his debts."

"It'll all be over very soon," Kai said reassuringly, hiding his own growing nervousness. How many other people were going to walk in here while they were searching the place? Or might come checking to see what had happened to this woman? "Just a moment."

He walked across to the professor and removed his gag. "Look," he said, going down on one knee next to the chair. "We want to get this over with just as much as you do. You might as well cooperate. Where's the Pemberton Collection?"

"The what?" Professor Jamison said, failing to sound convincing.

"The collection donated by Judge Richard Pemberton in 1899," Evariste said. "The one you're supposed to be responsible for."

"Oh, that collection." The professor looked vague. "Now that you mention it, I think it's being held in the Cloisters—you know, out at Fort Tryon Park . . . ?"

It was a brave attempt. Kai respected it. He didn't want to hurt either of their two prisoners. Neither of them deserved it. And every part of him revolted against the idea of torturing a pair of helpless innocents for information. But what was he supposed to *do*?

Then the woman's earlier words gave him an idea. He walked over to the desk, where the telephone was half-buried under a mound of discarded papers. "It's a pity I have to do this," he said to Evariste.

"Yeah, it sure is," Evariste said, an uncertain note to his voice. "Look, we don't need to hurt these people . . ."

Qing Song or Hu might have done so, Kai realised, and Evariste was judging him by their standards. It felt surprisingly galling. "You're right," he said. "We need to ring up the boss and find out how *he* wants us to play things, since our friends here aren't willing to talk."

"Yeah, that sure is a pity," Evariste said, with growing assurance. "You know how the boss is, when he doesn't get what he wants. Still, no skin off *our* backs, right?"

Both the professor and the woman had gone pale. The woman was the first to find her voice. "You just want the Pemberton Collection? That's all?"

"That's all," Kai reassured her. "We can take it from there."

"Downstairs, in the basement," she said very quickly. "Past the reception desk there, second right, signposted 'Asian art section,' third room on the left, check the cupboards on the right at the entrance to the section and they'll have the full index there."

"Maria!" the professor protested. But the guilty note to his voice suggested to Kai that he'd been about to crack.

"That's good," Kai said. "Now we'll just leave you here. They'll probably let you out when security does their final rounds."

"But the museum doesn't close till nine o'clock tonight!" the woman protested.

"Trust me," Kai said, walking round behind her to insert a gag in her mouth. "It could be worse."

It was coming up to six o'clock as they headed downstairs to the basement, having left a DO NOT DISTURB sign on the professor's door. The crowds of visitors were thinning out, and the light coming through the windows was shaded with sunset colours, painting the exhibits in red and orange tones.

"I'm surprised they haven't already put the *Journey to the West* out on display, given all the other classics here," he said quietly to Evariste, keeping his tone of voice conversational.

"From the description in the catalogue, I don't think the copy's in the best condition," Evariste answered. "It'll be a low priority for exhibition."

"At least we're not having to bring back the provenance as well." Kai tipped his hat to a young lady who was smiling at him.

Evariste gave him a look of mild horror. "You're just enjoying coming up with ways to make this worse, aren't you? How do we prove that it's the correct book, without waving the provenance under Qing Song's nose?"

"Irene will think of something," Kai said confidently. "She's very persuasive."

"Yeah," Evariste muttered. "She talked us into this, after all."

Loyalty demanded some sort of response. Unfortunately nothing convincing came to mind.

The elevators down to the basement were half-hidden behind

grand displays of medieval and Byzantine art, which filled several rooms. The elevators' polished brass and wooden doors almost seemed artworks in themselves. But the basement below had been designed for efficient and clean storage, with white-tiled walls and floors.

At this time of day the only person around was the entry clerk sitting behind the reception desk. Kai stepped back, allowing Evariste to take the lead.

"Good afternoon," Evariste said politely. "We've been sent down by Professor Jamison to collect some texts from the Asian art section."

The clerk sniffed. He was a thin fellow, his chin jutting out like a promontory, with suspicious bloodshot eyes. Unfortunately there was an alarm button on his desk, within easy reach of his hand. "Entrance desk is up on the ground-floor," he said flatly. "Only graduates and above get access to these archives. If you want to look something up, you need full proof of your identity, and letters from at least a few of your professors. This here isn't some sort of public library."

"But I am a graduate," Evariste said persuasively. "I took my degree in—"

"Harlem?" the clerk snorted. "Don't give me that, boy. I've seen your sort before."

Evariste's mouth tightened, and there was a very nasty glint in his eyes. **"You perceive that I'm currently showing you full documentation of everything that you should need to give me access to the archives,"** he said firmly in the Language.

The clerk frowned. "You can show me all the documents you like, boy, but you're not going to walk through those doors till I've had a word with my boss. He knows how to handle people like you." He reached for the phone. Apparently the Language could bypass his perceptions, but that wouldn't alter his prejudices.

Evariste glanced back at Kai, and the expression on his face was a clear invitation to violence.

Kai stepped forward and caught the clerk's wrist, dragging him forward over the desk. As the clerk gasped for breath, Kai brought the edge of his free hand down on the nape of the man's neck. He went limp with barely a sound, flopping across the desk.

"Sorry," Evariste said with a shrug. His tone made it more of a pro forma apology than a genuine expression of regret. "I guess this is where we tie him up and hide him till later."

Kai considered. "If we do that, they'll raise an alarm when they find he's missing. He should be unconscious for at least half an hour . . ." He tipped the clerk back into his chair and arranged the man with his hands folded over his belly, chin resting on his chest as though he'd fallen asleep. He also reached under the desk and ripped out the wire leading to the alarm bell. "There. That will buy us a little more time."

When they entered the archive section, it became clear that they were going to *need* every bit of that time. Kai was grateful for the woman's directions, but even so, the place was large. He approved of large collections in principle, but they were a nuisance when you had to trek through them to steal something.

"I'd rather have been doing this at night," Evariste said quietly as they hurried through the corridors. "We wouldn't have been so likely to run into people."

Kai nodded. "Yes. But there wasn't time." He imagined the fervid hum of the city above them, the constant buzz and surge of business and activity, and Irene drifting through it like a single butterfly with a pack of wolves on her tail. The image lacked poetic balance, and he frowned. "What chases butterflies?" he asked.

Evariste glanced at him sidelong. "What the hell does that have to do with anything?" he asked.

Kai looked back in disdain. "Poetic metaphor," he said.

A few minutes later they were finally opening a small corner cupboard.

The books inside had been carefully organized, much like one of those puzzles where one had to fit a set of blocks into a limited space. The person who'd filed them had been extremely careful not to squeeze them in or cram them together, but had clearly found it necessary to use every last fraction of space.

"Careful now," Evariste said, abruptly taking charge. He began to lift the books out from the cupboard, placing them one by one on the room's table. "No, not this, nor the other . . . wait, *here* they are. Six-volume set. All there."

The volumes that he drew out from the depths of the cupboard were not in ideal condition. Kai could see why the museum might have preferred to put other, more obviously striking books on display. But when he opened one volume and began to leaf through it, he was relieved to see that the interior condition was sound. The pages were firmly attached, the yellowed paper was solid and untouched by damp or insects, and the ink was clear. He opened his mouth to congratulate Evariste.

And then an electric bell broke into wild shrieking peals, ripping through the silence of the archives like a chain saw.

CHAPTER 21

Hu's arm was an iron bar across Irene's throat, cutting off both breath and speech. It brought back unwelcome memories of her doing the same thing to Evariste. Unhelpful thoughts about poetic justice pinwheeled dizzily through her head. She tried to get the fingers of her free hand underneath Hu's arm and pry it loose from her throat. She stamped on his feet, throwing her weight into it, then kicked back at his knee-caps.

All she managed was the satisfaction, through the buzzing in her ears, of hearing him grunt in pain. "My lord," he said, through what sounded like gritted teeth, "I know you reserved the dose for the other Librarian, but under the circumstances . . ."

"Very true." Qing Song rose from his chair and reached into his jacket.

Whatever it was, it couldn't be good. Panic worked almost as well as oxygen in giving Irene a burst of fresh strength. She tried to get her balance and hook a foot behind Hu's ankle, but he simply shifted his weight. He yanked her arm farther up behind her back, dragging her onto her toes.

Irene's vision was muzzy, veined with flashes of light. Qing Song was standing next to her now, holding something cold against her lips. *As if he were dosing one of his pet wolves . . .*

With the last of her consciousness she tried to keep her mouth shut, but Hu's hold on her throat loosened, making her gasp for air, breathing in huge racking swallows of it. A cool liquid ran down her throat. She choked on it, barely conscious of anything except her struggle for breath.

When the room stabilised, she became aware that Hu had let go of her throat. He was saying something to one of the two gangsters. The more she heard, the less helpful it sounded. ". . . handcuffs?"

"We generally kinda leave those to the cops, Mr. Hu," the gangster answered.

"Very well. Just hold her for the moment, then. I don't think she'll give any trouble." Her free arm was twisted behind her back, to join the one that was already pinioned, and a stranger's hands took a firm hold of her. Qing Song was scrutinizing her critically, and Hu stepped in front of her again. "You won't cause any further problems, will you, Miss Winters?"

Irene opened her mouth to speak.

Nothing came out.

Something in her throat was numb. She tried to form the words, but she couldn't make a sound. She realized with despair that the Language was out of her reach. Sheer panic made her struggle in the grip of the man holding her, until common sense made her stop. But her fear didn't go away. She was helpless in a way that she had never been before.

"Where did you get any of that stuff?" Jin Zhi indicated the flask that Qing Song was sliding back into an inner pocket. "I'd thought it was being reserved for . . . special cases."

Such as for really important Librarians? Irene wondered. She supposed she shouldn't be *too* surprised that the dragon courts had something specifically adapted to deal with Librarians, though it was a worrying discovery. But at the moment she was more concerned with how fast it would wear off. She could still *write* in the Language, but not while restrained like this.

Qing Song ignored both the question and Irene. "The urgent matter is what to do next. Hu, you said that you thought she was lying about the Library knowing what's happening here."

"My lord, she's been under observation for most of the day." Hu absently neatened his jacket. "If she had known everything when she came to Boston, or even to New York, she wouldn't have acted the way she did. If all she'd wanted to do was tell you to leave the other Librarian alone, then she'd have come here directly—rather than having to be dragged into your presence. But we've seen that she's a shameless liar: she'll tell you anything that would persuade you to release her. We can't trust a word she says."

Show me a single person in this room who's actually been telling the truth today, Irene thought venomously. *Apart from the wolves. And the gangsters.*

"Yes, but what about Ao Guang's son?" put in Jin Zhi. "She's been known to share his company. He might be involved. And what about the other Librarian?"

Qing Song rounded on her. "You appear to know far too much about my affairs."

"Don't be ridiculous," Jin Zhi said, a little too fast. "I *have* been listening for the last five minutes, after all. I heard what she said. You had a Librarian in your hand. She took him from you. And now we have another Librarian, but she's not ready to cooperate—yet. Or worse still, she could be cooperating with someone else."

Except that's not quite right, Irene thought. *Even if Qing Song didn't spot it. How has Jin Zhi been finding these things out? And how did she know about Qing Song's employing a Librarian, but not about Evariste's escape till just now . . . ?*

But Jin Zhi's words made Qing Song hesitate. "You cannot be serious," he finally said.

"What if Ao Guang wants to influence which of us gets the position? If he offered one of us the book on terms of obligation or alliance, could we afford to refuse? It would be the perfect opportunity for the King of the Eastern Ocean to get a foothold in the Queen of the Southern Lands' affairs. And here we see the boy's pet Librarian meddling in our business, hunting down the book for her own ends. Am I wrong?"

Irene almost admired the way Jin Zhi glossed over the fact that *she'd* asked Irene to get involved—even if only to prevent Qing Song receiving Librarian help. But she felt a growing panic at the way this was implicating both Kai and herself. And Kai's father, Ao Guang, the King of the Eastern Ocean. The idea of him being involved in this mess—and blaming the Library for it—was a horrible new way in which things could go wrong.

She struggled frantically for speech again, but nothing came out: she shaped words in the Language but couldn't give them voice.

Qing Song considered. "You may be right," he said grudgingly. "If she's been acting as his servant throughout, that would explain a great deal. Hu, can you confirm this?"

Hu seemed reluctant to take the limelight. "The Librarian was in company with another man earlier, my lord. The photographers didn't manage to get a picture of him. The best description they could give of him was that he was dark-haired and handsome. She'd said at the time that he was another Librarian—"

"It's quite clear that she lies a great deal," Jin Zhi said, cutting him off. "I don't know how they keep their little thefts straight. But has it occurred to you that if she's here and he's not, then he's busy doing something else?"

Irene glanced at the reflection of the gunmen in the mirror. They were both doing a good job of looking blank, but she was certain they were paying attention. The professional part of her mind noted that expert conspirators didn't discuss this sort of thing in front of the hired help.

Or at least, not in front of hired help who were going to survive the next few hours.

Qing Song surveyed Irene sidelong, as if pricing up a piece of second-hand furniture. "You think that the son would exchange the book for her?" he asked.

Irene forced all telltale emotion from her face. Because yes, Kai probably *would* hand over the text—which would leave Qing Song holding Evariste's daughter, Irene and Kai compromised, and the situation even closer to the edge. She twitched a shoulder in a silent shrug, attempting to convey that Kai wouldn't exchange a piece of cold toast for her.

"It would help if she could speak," Jin Zhi said. "But she'd probably lie again. How long till the drug wears off?"

"It should last for at least a few hours," Qing Song said. "It's hardly been tested on these people. Only on . . ." He paused, his eyes flicking to the guards, and let the sentence drop with a meaningful shrug.

Jin Zhi walked towards him. "Qing Song, much as I regret doing this, I'm going to suggest an alliance."

Qing Song looked as unenthusiastic as Jin Zhi sounded. "Really," he said. "An alliance. With you."

"I know it's unconventional," Jin Zhi said. "But Her Majesty has been known to reward results and ignore tradition. I will be honest with you. My searches in China have been unprofitable. We have three days left: there is no time to waste. If we can bring Her Majesty the text together, then perhaps she'll set us some other challenge, one that will allow us to compete *fairly*." She studied Qing Song carefully. "My lord of the Winter Forests, has it occurred to you that *both* of us may die over this? And what will that achieve? Will our families thank us if we both fail and shame their reputations? There's more to be gained by looking at the situation from a new angle." Her tone turned sour. "Such as using a Librarian."

"As always, you make an appealing argument," Qing Song said. His tone was neutral, but the wolves were raising their hackles and stretching, their heavy muzzles dropping open briefly to show long white rows of teeth. Hu made a small gesture of contradiction—negation, even—but Qing Song ignored it. "So. We keep the Librarian as a hostage. If Ao Guang's son contacts us, we are prepared to exchange her for the book. If my men locate the other Librarian, then he may have the book too. But if neither option plays out in our favour, what then? What do we do with her?"

"It would be wasteful to kill her," Jin Zhi said. She didn't even bother to look at Irene. "But it's too risky to keep her here. Place her in one of our private territories. Even if Ao Guang's son can track her, he can't intrude there without violating our territory and making it a political matter. Keep her away from books—use drugs and shackles, of course—and she should be safe enough."

For a moment Hu caught Irene's eye, and the expression on his face was one of sympathetic regret. *I did try to warn you,* his eyes seemed to say.

Panic and fury chased each other round Irene's brain like angry cats. She knew what the Library would do if this played out: they'd disclaim all knowledge of her actions, claim that she'd been working on her own—just as Melusine had warned her. But even that might not be enough to save the Library from the political fall-out. And it certainly wouldn't save Irene. *Drugs and shackles.* The words whispered in the back of her mind like a little musical-box tinkle from the depths of nightmare, and wouldn't go away.

"And which of us keeps her?" Qing Song demanded.

"I do." Jin Zhi raised a hand to cut off his objections before he could make them. "One of us has to. Why not me?"

Qing Song didn't mince his words. "Because I don't trust you."

"And I'm supposed to trust you if *you* keep her?" Jin Zhi asked. "Given your recent behaviour?"

"You have a habit of using what other people give you. How else would you have found me here, except by tracing my token?" An undertone of bitterness ran through Qing Song's voice like a vein of ore in stone. "We did once exchange tokens and vows, but *you* were the one who told me that time was past. But now you seek me out and propose a new alliance. How can I trust *you*?"

Irene shifted her weight and took the opportunity to check her guard's grip on her arms. His hold was still firm, but less so than earlier. If she could only manufacture a distraction . . . Qing Song and Jin Zhi seemed absorbed, rehashing what sounded like an old love affair and break-up. But she could also hear the desperation in their voices. They were almost as trapped as she was, with no way out except to get hold of the book. To them, Irene, Evariste, and his daughter—and the whole of this world, and the Library itself— were acceptable collateral damage.

If pure anger had somehow made her able to use the Language at that moment, then Irene would have burned down the entire room, with them in it.

Hu refrained from comment, as a subordinate. But the hint of sourness in his expression suggested that he wasn't enjoying the discussion. His eyes were distant with thought, as if he was trying to formulate an effective objection to the plan.

Faint music drifted in through the open windows, an accompaniment to Jin Zhi and Qing Song's debate on how they were going to avoid mutual betrayal, who took custody of the Librarian, whose fault it was anyhow, and whose fault it had been fifteen years ago.

The ringing of the telephone cut through the room like a knife, cutting all talk dead. Qing Song and Jin Zhi both turned to look at the device as if it should be executed for improper behaviour.

Hu picked up the receiver. "Hello?" he said.

A pause.

He turned to Qing Song. "My lord, 'Lucky' George Ross requests an audience."

"He has my permission," Qing Song said without hesitation. "Bid him approach."

"Are you sure this is a good idea?" Jin Zhi asked, as Hu murmured into the phone. She nodded, very slightly, towards Irene and the two guards.

"These men are in my service. I trust their discretion—and George could be useful." Qing Song didn't move, but the wolves rose simultaneously to their feet and padded towards the men—and Irene. "And my pets have their scent, should it prove necessary. They can, and will, find them."

Irene heard the man holding her catch his breath, and felt his hands tighten sweatily on her wrists. She wasn't entirely sure how long the two men would remain loyal, but she had no doubt that for the next few minutes they were going to be very loyal indeed.

One of the wolves sat down at Irene's feet. Its eyes were deep amber, as clear and rich as thick honey. It was odd, Irene decided with the calmness of terror, that a simple wolf should be so much more frightening than all the werewolves she'd stared down in the past. Perhaps it was because Irene had been able to use the Language then: she hadn't been weaponless. Or perhaps it was because werewolves were ultimately people, and Irene could deal with people. But she couldn't lie to an animal—only run from it or kill it. And right at this precise moment, she couldn't do either.

"And her?" Jin Zhi indicated Irene.

"She can say nothing. Besides, I'd rather have her under my eye than in another room, even if she is guarded. The woman is slippery."

Irene decided to rate that as a compliment.

Hu put the phone down. "George Ross will be joining us in a moment, my lord. He will have attendants with him."

"You think he'll know something useful?" Jin Zhi queried, directing the question to Qing Song. She barely looked at Hu; he was apparently beneath her notice.

"If he does, then it might remove the need for an alliance," Qing Song said smugly. He settled back in his chair.

"Assuming that *you're* the one he makes any deal with," Jin Zhi said with a smile.

Qing Song's expression froze.

There was a knock on the suite door.

Hu nodded to one of the two gangsters, who went to open the door. The wolves parted in front of him before settling back onto the floor. Their eyes showed in thin yellow slits under their half-closed eyelids.

George strolled in, with Lily one step behind him, swathed in pale furs that could conceal half a dozen pistols. Her visible eye was narrowed and dangerous. Behind them, like a royal train, came two more gunmen. The place was getting crowded.

This was a possible distraction, and Irene considered how she could use it. But she could also feel the level of danger in the room rising like a thermometer in boiling water. If guns were fired, a bullet could hit anyone. Including her. She *really* didn't want a posthumous report finishing with *Was shot by mistake and died.*

"Good of you to see me," George said. He sat down in an armchair and crossed his legs. "I appreciate the prompt invite up here."

Both Jin Zhi and Qing Song were staring at Lily, their faces frozen masks of distaste. It took a moment before Qing Song turned his attention to George. "How may I assist you?" he asked coldly.

"I think it's more a question of how I can assist you," George said. He reached into his jacket. "Mind if I smoke?"

Qing Song flicked his hand. "As you wish."

George extended the ritual of lighting his cigar, clearly using this bit of incivility to assert his status. Finally he gestured with the cigar towards Irene. "I see you've got Miss Jeanette here with you. If you'd like her to be out of the room first . . ."

"I guarantee that she will say nothing of the matter," Qing Song replied. The twitch of his lips was as close to a smile as Irene had ever yet seen him give. "I am more interested in why you are here."

"Well . . ." George drew the word out luxuriously. "I know that you've been looking for something these last few weeks. Or should I say someone?"

"Either is possible," Qing Song agreed.

George nodded, and puffed on his cigar. "You see, Mr. Qing— I can call you that, right?—just because you weren't hiring *my* men didn't mean that I didn't hear about your little manhunt. A lot of people out there are real eager to do me a favour and get on my good side. So when your man Hu came by this afternoon, I already had some idea of what you were searching for and where to start looking."

"And your point is?" Qing Song asked. One of the wolves opened its mouth and ran its tongue delicately over its teeth.

"Not long ago one of my people got a phone call," George said. "A lot of foreigners are real ignorant about how the Teamsters Union works here in New York. They think that just anyone can handle museum deliveries. They don't seem to understand that it needs an expert to handle that sort of delicate stuff, and that experts don't like amateurs getting in the way. It's the sort of thing that leads to those amateurs having accidents." He waved his cigar sadly. "And it means that I hear about that sort of thing."

Inwardly Irene was putting two and two together and getting a horrifying four. What had Kai and Evariste tried? And were they already prisoners? She'd taken all these risks to keep them safe . . .

Hu stepped forward and murmured in Qing Song's ear, and Qing Song nodded. "So, your people know the whereabouts of the man I'm looking for. Where is he?"

"At the moment he's tagged," George said, "and real soon now he'll be bagged as well. Which is why I'm here. I thought you might like to talk price."

"Price?" Qing Song said. "I thought we already had an arrangement."

"Arrangements go out the window when one person has what everyone wants. It's supply and demand." He pointed at Irene again. "Miss Jeanette there, she knows when to fold and make a deal. I'm hoping you'll think the same way."

"Are you open to offers from other people as well?" Jin Zhi asked smoothly, her tone like silk.

"I'm prepared to listen, if you can show me the money," George said generously. "I know Mr. Qing here's good for plenty of dough, but I like to be sure that my customers can cover their purchases. Unless Mr. Qing here wants to vouch for you?"

Jin Zhi's face went still. Clearly she hadn't expected this. She'd assumed that her word would be enough.

The expression of pure delighted spite that flashed through Qing Song's eyes was almost too fast for Irene to catch. "Reluctantly I must decline," he said. "I am not sure that the lady is a safe risk."

"There you have it," George said with a shrug. "So, Mr. Qing, I guess it's just you and me now."

Jin Zhi's eyes glittered like rubies, and patterns of scales fleetingly marked her bare arms like lace, momentarily enough that one might have imagined it was simply a trick of the light. "I am not accustomed to being dismissed in this way," she said, her voice hissing like water on molten metal.

"I'm a businessman, sweetheart. I don't have time for people who can't pay their bills." George turned back to Qing Song. "Shall we talk price?"

In three steps Jin Zhi was standing in front of him. Her right hand closed around his neck and she lifted him out of his seat. The muscles in her arm stood out like polished metal as she held him there, dangling him in mid-air, his feet kicking a foot above the floor. "We will start with an apology," she murmured, "and then—"

"You'll put him down." Lily had stepped forward, her fur coat swinging open, and she had a pistol in each hand. She shifted the gun in her right hand to cover the room, and forced the gun in her left hand into Jin Zhi's ribs. "Or we see how large a hole I can make in your spine."

Jin Zhi's free hand came up to catch Lily's left wrist, forcing the gun away from her body.

The room was abruptly full of shouting men and snarling wolves.

Irene brought her heel down on the foot of the man who was restraining her, cracked her head back against his nose, and wrenched her arms free. He grabbed at her, but she danced away.

She'd never be able to reach the door. But there was another way out, and she was desperate enough to try it.

The next moment she was out through the windows and swinging herself over the edge of the balcony.

CHAPTER 22

Evariste nearly dropped the book he was holding.

Kai had more control. To be honest, he had been wait-ing for something to go wrong—well, *more* wrong—so it was a relief for it actually to happen. Things could be worse, he reminded himself. They weren't yet being beaten to their knees by scores of minions while being collared by evil Fae overlords. The situation was still under control.

"Worst-case scenario, they're clearing the museum before com-ing down on us in force," he said. "Can you open a door to the Li-brary from here?"

Evariste frowned, looking round at their surroundings with an assessing eye. "Probably. There are enough books. You're saying we should run for it?"

"No, that's not it," Kai said. "We—that is, *you*—open a door to the Library, take the books through, and leave them there; then you come back and close the door. The books are safe, we retrieve them when we have the opportunity, and in the meantime we've still got them and they haven't." He could hear running feet and slamming doors as the few remaining people evacuated the archive section. "Then we get out of here and contact Irene." *And Irene can decide how we handle the next step*, he thought with relief.

Evariste nodded. He gathered the stack of half a dozen volumes into his arms, staggering slightly from the weight, and kicked the nearest door shut. His forehead drew into lines as he focused. **"Open to the Library,"** he said, his voice taking on a sharp tone of authority, deep with the harmonics of the Language.

He reached out to open the door, struggling to keep the books balanced. The door opened to reveal a different room beyond, high and arched, shelved and walled in pale wood. Electric candelabra filled the chamber with light. The smell of graciously old books drifted through to mingle with the archive's odours of dust and chemical preservation.

"Hold the door open," Evariste ordered. He staggered into the Library with the books and across to the nearest table, putting them down with a gasp of relief, then grabbed paper and pen to scribble a quick note.

Kai took hold of the door's handle and inserted his foot in the gap, just in case. He could feel the wood of the door trembling under his hands, shuddering with the tension of being forced to hold open a gap between worlds. He'd seen Irene keep a door like this open before for a couple of minutes. But Kai wasn't sure Evariste had the same deep-rooted strength that Irene did. And maybe it would be better if he stayed in the Library . . .

Evariste was an uncertain factor. He was unreliable. If Kai just shut the door and broke the temporary link between this world and the Library, it could take hours for Evariste to find his way back again. It would be easier to handle things without him.

And would you prevent him from trying to save his daughter? a voice as cold and firm as Kai's own father's said at the back of his mind. *Would you deny him the right to make amends for his mistakes?*

Then Evariste came barrelling back through the door, pushed Kai out of the way, and slammed it shut. "Library designation B-349, French nineteenth-century science fiction," he reported. "In case you need to tell Irene. Now can we get out of here?"

The fire alarm was still whooping in the background, but Kai spared a moment to look over the other books that Judge Pemberton had included in his bequest. "Here," he said, selecting a few of them. "You carry these. I may need my hands free."

"Why the hell are we taking *The Dream of the Red Chamber?*" Evariste asked. "Light reading, if we get stuck on the subway?"

"No, in case we get stopped by some of Qing Song's minions who can't read Chinese," Kai said cheerfully.

"Oh. Right. Hey, that's not a bad thought." Evariste paused. "Though if we're going to be throwing them away anyhow, why not take *The Investiture of the Gods* . . . ?"

"Because I like *The Investiture of the Gods*," Kai said firmly, "and I don't like *The Dream of the Red Chamber*."

"Typical dragon idealisation of heroes and divinities in order to justify divine mandate," Evariste muttered under his breath. "Let's try to find a bag on our way out of here, okay? Rather than carrying these around like little babies in my arms for the rest of the day."

"Right," Kai agreed.

The place was already deserted as they made their way out through the blank white twisting corridors, past cupboards groaning with the weight of their contents, and crates as yet unsorted. Kai turned his head from side to side, listening, but the constant shriek of the fire alarm drowned out any lesser sounds. In the distance, with a sense other than hearing, he could feel the slow pulse of the rivers that cut through the city of New York. But they were too far away to be of any use.

He and Evariste passed the desk where the clerk had been sitting—he must have been the one who sounded the alarm—and came to the elevator just as the alarm cut off.

The elevator wasn't working.

Kai eyed the stairwell next to it. It would make too convenient an ambush.

"Damn safety regulations and turning off the elevators during fire alarms," Evariste muttered. "What do we do if they're waiting at the top of the stairs?"

Kai considered. "There are multiple stairs up to the ground-level from the basement, right?" When Evariste nodded, he went on. "So they can't have people waiting at the top of all of them."

"Want to bet?" Evariste asked sourly.

"Pull yourself together!" Kai tried to will backbone into Evariste. "We got in here, we secured the target book—we can *do* this. If we can just get up to the ground-floor, we don't have to worry about the main entrance. There are plenty of windows."

"I thought you were supposed to have military training," Evariste snapped back. "We can't fight our way upstairs past opponents with guns when we aren't even armed. It's just stupid. We'll get shot! The Language doesn't stop bullets!"

"Who told you I'd had military training?" Kai asked, diverted.

"Don't all dragons? Qing Song was all about this battle and that battle—"

"Hey there," a voice called down to them from higher up the stairs.

Kai turned to look, stepping between Evariste and the stairwell. There were two men on a landing, where the stairs bent back on themselves to ascend to the ground-floor. Both of them were openly carrying tommy guns. But the guns weren't actually pointed at Kai and Evariste—yet. That was something.

"That's right," the man who'd spoken earlier said. "Now put your hands on your heads, boys, and come up the stairs in single file. Don't give us any trouble, and we won't give you any."

"What about these books?" Evariste asked, jerking his chin towards the four volumes in his arms.

The first speaker paused, frowning, trying to work out how to handle this breach in what was clearly a Standard Speech to Kidnap Victims.

His fellow sighed. "You don't put your hands on your head. You hang on to your books. Your friend does put his hands on his head. Now can we get the hell on with this before the boss loses his temper?"

Kai raised his hands slowly, turning to Evariste. "Are you sure we're the people these men are looking for?" he said meaningfully.

"I was about to say that," Evariste muttered. More loudly, he said in the Language, **"You men with the guns perceive that we are not the people you're looking for, and that we're just terrified bystanders who should be allowed to leave."**

The gangsters both frowned; then the second one waved them up the stairs with his gun. "Just keep on going and don't hang around," he instructed them in a friendly but casually menacing way. "What's going on here ain't none of your business."

"Absolutely," Kai agreed. He caught Evariste's elbow, surreptitiously supporting the other man as they headed up the stairs. "Can't you go any faster?" he hissed.

"Maybe if I wasn't carrying several large, heavy books . . ." Evariste muttered back.

They passed the two gangsters and hurried up to the ground floor.

"This is bad. I don't know how they tracked us here." Evariste looked round, orienting himself, then nodded to the left. "Through that way, to the Great Hall, and the exit. Try to act natural—"

"Stop!" came a yell from behind them.

Footsteps came running from the direction of the Great Hall, loud on the marble. Kai and Evariste made a hasty diversion to their right, past Egyptian sarcophagi and clay models of tomb entrances, followed by the echoing yells of their pursuers.

"How many—people—has he got hunting me?" Evariste panted.

"Too many," Kai grunted. They swung into a wide room whose north wall was covered with slanting windows. What looked like a genuine sandstone Egyptian temple entrance was erected in the middle. Unfortunately the gunmen in front of the window were of a much more recent vintage. Their tommy guns gleamed under the strong museum lights.

"Let's not do anything too hasty," one of them said. He shifted his gun so that it was pointing at the floor in front of Kai and Evariste. "Now, you boys have had a good run. I can respect that. But I only need one of you. So in the interests of both of you staying alive, how about we have a little agreement of no more funny business?"

"When you say you only need one of us," Kai asked in a tone of academic interest, "do you mean that either of us would do, or is it a case of you only want a specific one of us, and the other is unfortunately expendable?"

"You've got it," the gangster said. "I only need Mr. Evariste Jones over there. So if Jones wants *you* to stay alive . . ." He shrugged meaningfully at Kai.

"Be careful what Jones says, boss," someone called from behind them. It sounded like the man they'd passed on the stairs. "He can do some sort of hoodoo with his voice."

That provoked stirring and mumbles among the assembled gunmen, but unfortunately it didn't convince any of them to point their guns elsewhere.

Kai scanned the room. Their position wasn't good. They were too far away from the sandstone edifice to take cover behind it. While the windowed north wall offered certain possibilities, the glass looked too thick for a man to break through it easily. And Evariste couldn't deploy the Language faster than a speeding bullet.

Fortunately he had a plan.

"Mind if I smoke?" he asked.

"As long as you're real careful with your hands and don't try anything stupid," the leader said.

Kai ignored the way Evariste was looking at him—somewhere between desperate hope that Kai could sort this out and disbelief that Kai would choose this moment to have a cigarette—and reached carefully into an inner pocket of his suit. While he didn't normally smoke, he'd collected a cigarette-case and lighter while he and Irene were equipping themselves last night at the department store. One never knew when such things might be useful.

"Thanks," he said. "My nerves are a bit on edge. And would you mind if my friend here puts his books down before we go along with you? No need to crowd the car."

The leader cocked his head to one side. "That's not the way we're playing it, fellow. The way I was told it, we're to bring in Jones and his books. Half the city's been looking for them, so I don't think we'll be letting him take a rain check with them now." It sounded as if Kai was much more expendable than the books.

"The city's full of readers," Kai said to Evariste. He flicked the lighter open and touched the flame to the cigarette. "Who'd have thought so many people would want a copy of"—and he switched to Chinese—*"be ready to break the glass window when I tell you."*

Evariste kept a straight face, but his eyes lightened. "It's the New York education system," he said. "I hear it's the finest in the world."

Kai nodded. Then he dropped the cigarette to the floor, caught Evariste's shoulder to pull the armful of books within reach, and held the lighter flame to them, a fraction of an inch from setting fire to the volumes. "Lower the guns," he said calmly. "Everyone. Or the books go up in smoke. And then you have to explain that to your boss."

A dozen gun-barrels pointed directly at him. "Try it and you're dead," the leader snapped.

"What are you doing?" Evariste struggled in Kai's grip, trying to pull away from the naked flame. "You can't *do* that!"

"Can and will." Kai put all the command that he'd learned at his father's court into his voice, all the firmness and certainty of royal blood. "Back away. All of you. Or you'll have the man but not the book, and Qing Song will have all your heads."

"We're not working for him," the leader sneered. "You might want to check the facts before raising on a hand like that."

Kai blinked. "Jin Zhi, then." He kept the lighter flame steady.

The leader shrugged. "Never heard of him. *We* work for Lucky George."

Kai wasted a moment wondering exactly why the local crime boss had joined the hunt. "Nevertheless," he said, "if you don't want the books going up in smoke, you'll stand back." He took a pace sideways himself, dragging Evariste with him, moving towards the shelter of one of the sandstone arches.

"You can't get out of here." The leader made a surreptitious signal in the direction of the men behind Kai and Evariste, and they started to close in. "The boss ain't going to be happy about this. And when George ain't happy, nobody's happy."

"Then we've all got a problem, because if we don't walk out of here, then *my* boss is going to be unhappy," Kai said. Another couple of sideways steps. They were almost under the curve of the arch now. "Bosses. Go figure." A final step. "But you've got a point."

"So you're going to stop being a wise guy?" the leader said suspiciously.

"Now," Kai said out of the side of his mouth to Evariste.

Evariste had been waiting for the word. **"Glass, break!"** he shouted.

At the same moment Kai dropped the lighter and swept them both to the floor, rolling on top of Evariste. Dragons were less vulnerable than humans were. He could only hope it was enough.

He had a moment to tense in anticipation of incoming bullets. Then the wall of floor-to-ceiling windows shattered, with so huge a noise of fracturing panes and crashing shards that it drowned out all attempts at conscious thought. Kai flung his arms over his head, trying to block out the sound. Fragments of glass fell around him or ricocheted off the floor, bouncing like lethal raindrops. A few pieces sliced across his clothing and skin, drawing blood from his hands and neck. He felt Evariste shuddering underneath him, trapped and helpless—and, a few seconds later, he heard the screaming of the gangsters who had survived.

When Kai raised his head, he saw that a number of them hadn't.

But if human thieves were stupid enough to endanger his life, then a clean straightforward death was a moderate, reasonable response. Every dragon he knew would agree. Even Irene would be practical about it. Probably.

Though he had to admit, looking around, that the sheer scale of this was somewhat . . . excessive.

"Up, now," he said, pulling Evariste to his feet and scooping up a volume that had gone astray. "Come on!"

Evariste pressed his knuckles to his mouth hard as he looked around the room—the broken glass everywhere, the fallen bodies, the blood, the men struggling to stand and failing—and the colour drained from his face. "I didn't . . ." he began, and then stopped, as if uncertain what he wanted to deny.

There wasn't time for this. But Kai couldn't bring himself to ignore the pain that was so evident in the other man's face. "You didn't cause this," he said. "You didn't *escalate* this. Our job is to stop it, here and now, and to save your daughter. You want me to blame the other dragons? Fine. Qing Song has touched things off that he can't control. Help me stop them from getting *worse*. Help me to keep your Library safe." He met Evariste's eyes. "Please."

Evariste took a deep breath and nodded.

The two of them stumbled out through the empty lattice of

window frames, into the evening shadows of Central Park beyond. "We need a cab," Kai said. "Then we need to contact Irene . . ."

"If we can." Evariste had pulled himself together. "What if George has got her too?"

Kai showed his teeth. "Then that is going to be very unfortunate for George."

CHAPTER 23

The balcony was solid stone, faced with the same marble as the rest of the hotel. And it had heavy wrought-iron interlaced railings, to stop any theoretical suicides from stepping over the edge.

On the whole, Irene felt that climbing down the exterior of the hotel was slightly preferable to staying inside. Exactly how much ~~. ~~ was arguable.

~~...~~ she peered over the edge, she could see there was an-
~~...tly~~ beneath this one. It was just a question of
~~...~~ No worse, on a theoretical level, than
~~...~~ at school, involving vectors,
~~...~~ level, there was the issue of

~~...~~ ing capacity for self-deception
~~...~~ had to be useful *somewhere*.
~~...~~ nd leaned over the edge to toss

them onto the balcony below. Then she clambered over the iron railing.

The sound of Fifth Avenue below her came throbbing upwards, threatening to break her concentration. The honking of car horns and the screeching of tyres, the buzz of voices, even distant threads of music from clubs or radios, as far away as birdsong . . .

Inside the suite, a wolf's howl was cut short by two quick gunshots.

Irene swallowed, her throat very dry. *First floor. Visualize this as the first floor.* She lowered herself to a crouch against the outside of the railings, working her hands down as close as possible to the edge of the balcony. Then she took a deep breath and slid her feet loose, letting her body drop free, to dangle by her hands above Fifth Avenue.

The floor of the next balcony down was about three yards away, at a rough terrified guess. And of course she was hanging *outside* its scope, rather than it being a straight drop down. This was the sort of thing Kai was so much better at than she was.

A yell came from the balcony she'd just vacated. "She's not here! She must have jumped!"

"No, wait," came another voice, unhelpfully observant. "I see her hands, she's hanging on—"

No time left. Irene swung her body forward, fear massing in her stomach, then back again as if she were exercising on the apparatus in a gym—she never could remember all the gadgets, was it ropes or rings or parallel bars?—then forward again. And before anyone above her could grab her hands, she let go and dropped.

It was one of those falls that lasted long enough for Irene to envisage everything going wrong, and at the same time had her hitting the balcony before she could think twice. She hit the floor with a jolt and let herself roll forward, bringing her arms up to cover her head. Then she smashed through the apartment's full-length windows with a crash of breaking glass, loud enough to have been heard on the balcony above.

The room she'd just invaded had the lights on and blazing, but there was nobody actually in it. A shriek came from the bathroom. "Help! Help! Thieves!"

Irene would have shouted back something reassuring, but she couldn't speak. And in any case, she had trouble thinking of anything that would be reassuring under these circumstances. She staggered to her feet, shook broken glass off her dress and coat, and retrieved her shoes. Time to run and keep on running.

There was nobody in the corridor outside, and for a moment Irene thought that she'd made it free and clear. Then she heard the howling of wolves.

Elevator or stairs? It was a gamble. The sight of the elevator door opening ahead of her made her decision clear. She ran for it, pushing past the hotel guests emerging from it, and shouldered her way in. There was nobody in there except a thin young hotel page, barely out of his teens, all cap and buttons and Adam's apple, who gave her a hopeful smile. "Can I help you, ma'am?"

Down, Irene gestured. In case it wasn't quite clear enough, she pointed urgently at the big lever next to where the page was standing.

"No need to worry, ma'am," the young man said helpfully as he reached for one of the two levers next to him. Irene dredged her memory for the current state of elevator technology—one lever for the doors, the other for up or down. "We have some of the best elevators in all New York here—" He broke off at the sound of screams and howls. "Holy Mother of God, the wolves are loose!"

Four of the dire wolves were approaching the elevator at a run. Hotel guests were throwing themselves out of the way and hammering on the doors of the nearest rooms. And the page was just standing there, slack-jawed and in shock.

Irene cursed mentally and grabbed for the lever the page had been going for, yanking it with all her strength. The door slid smoothly across, slamming itself in front of the wolves' oncoming muzzles. Their baulked howling shuddered through the closed door.

The page had turned white. "We've got to call the cops," he stuttered.

Irene was more concerned with her immediate safety. She had to assume that what the wolves knew, Qing Song knew. Which meant that he knew she was in the elevator. Qing Song wouldn't turn the wolves loose on random civilians. But she didn't want to find out exactly how a pack of wolves would stop her from getting away. She suspected that, depending on Qing Song's mood, hamstringing might be the least of it.

"Don't you worry, ma'am," the hotel page said, managing to pull himself together. He pulled the other big lever next to him and the elevator began to glide slowly downwards. Above the door, a wide indicator like a clock-hand with a hole in the middle slid across an arc of floor numbers. "Too frightened to speak? Well, there's only one way to go. Once we've got you down to the ground-floor, we'll get the police in. My granny, she's from the old country, and she said that once wolves get a taste for flesh, the only answer is a bullet . . ."

Irene nodded silently as she watched the indicator overhead slide across the floor numbers one by one. *Ten. Nine. Eight. Seven.*

And then the elevator stopped dead and the lights went out.

Panic clutched at Irene's throat in the sudden silence. The darkness seemed to close around her. She reached out to the wall, stupidly relieved to find it was still there, and forced herself to think through the fear. The elevator wasn't going to drop out from under her. Really it wasn't. Well, probably not.

She thrust her hand into her coat-pocket. The one thing she'd managed to hide while the gangsters were searching her had been an eyebrow pencil—a woman's make-up tool, beneath their notice— but it gave her something to write with. If only she could see to write.

There was a scuffling noise from where the page was standing, and a click. Then the light of a torch cut through the darkness. The circle of luminescence lifted to the arc of floor numbers, and Irene could see that the indicator was stuck between six and seven.

What's going on? she scribbled on the elevator wall, and pulled the page round to see the words.

"There . . . there must be some sort of problem with the mechanics, ma'am," he stammered. "But don't worry, I'm sure the management will have someone sort it out in no time, and then they'll be lowering us to the next floor down and letting us out . . ."

Irene found herself almost as annoyed by the repetitions that she shouldn't worry as by the situation. She made herself focus. If she assumed the worst—which she did—then one of her pursuers on the higher floor had stopped the elevator between floors. Then all they'd have to do would be to wait for the elevator to be opened, to collect her.

Which meant that she had to leave the elevator first. *Where's the emergency exit?* she scribbled on the wall.

The page's eyes flickered betrayingly up to the ceiling. "That really isn't necessary, ma'am. It's much safer for us to stay here. Really it is. You needn't worry about it crashing or anything."

That was the *last* thing she was worried about. Although it might provide certain people with a very convenient way out. Dead Librarians tell no tales. She'd have died in a tragic elevator accident. Such a pity, but accidents do happen . . .

The mob is after me, she wrote on the wall. *If they catch me, they'll kill me.* Assessing the page's morals, she tried a word that was supposed to have its own sort of magic. *Please.*

The page's reluctance was visible in his face, but he nodded slowly. "All right, ma'am. There's a hatch up there in the ceiling; we're supposed to be able to climb through it, but I'm not sure how either of us can reach it—"

Irene didn't stop to ask for permission. She stepped forward, got a firm grip round the page's waist as he squeaked and tried to back away, and hoisted him up towards the hatch. Fortunately he caught on fast, and in a moment she could hear him undoing catches.

"It's real heavy, ma'am . . ."

Irene heard him panting, then a thud. She looked up to see that he'd worked the panel loose and had pushed it up. There was now a dark hole in the elegant panelled roof, haloed by the shaking light of the torch. Dust drifted through it, and the smell of oil thickened the air.

The page dragged himself up as she supported him, his feet scraping Irene's shoulders and leaving smears on her coat. He took the torch with him, of course. "I'm not sure that I'll be able to pull you up, ma'am . . ." he babbled.

She jumped for the edge of the hole in the ceiling, grabbing hold of it, and, with some gasping and straining, she pulled herself up and through. Her old gymnastics coach might give her a few marks for effort but would take several thousand off for lack of elegance. But she was through.

The dark lift-shaft was full of oily cables and dust. Six feet above where they were standing, the torch-light faintly illuminated the elevator doors. It must be the seventh floor, the one they'd just passed.

She pointed up at it meaningfully.

"We're not supposed to open the elevator doors if there isn't an elevator there," the page whispered. He looked miserable.

Irene patted him on the shoulder. Then she began to climb. There were enough handholds in the twisted cables for her to pull herself level with the closed doors in the wall. She had time for a quick prayer to any deities that might be listening and at all interested, as she reached towards the doors, eyebrow pencil in one hand, hanging on to the cables with the other. *Please let my pursuers be on the floor below this . . .*

Door, open, she scrawled in the near darkness.

With an agonized noise of metal against metal, the door obeyed. There was nobody on the other side.

"Holy Mother of God and all his angels," the elevator page muttered. But he didn't complain, and he scrambled up the cables and through the open door after Irene. "Ma'am, I don't wish to seem ungrateful, but . . ."

Irene nodded. She gave him a quick thumbs-up, then ran for the stairs.

The ground-floor was a seething mob of people running in all directions and demanding answers. Irene used her elbows to get through it. She could hear the wolves upstairs. It was only a matter of time until they picked up her scent. If she could just get a cab or steal a car, she could break her trail. But were Kai and Evariste prisoners? And exactly how much of New York would she need to take apart if they were?

The wolves were getting louder. Irene staggered onto the sidewalk and looked for a taxi.

There weren't any.

But there were police cars.

A small posse of policemen, or whatever the current collective noun was—troop? squad?—were organizing themselves into a flying wedge, with Captain Venner at their head. Some malign coincidence prompted him to look up just as Irene came into view, and he pointed a finger at her. She could hear his yell of, "Grab that woman!" quite clearly.

Irene weighed re-entering the hotel against being dragged off to the police station. The police station won, hands down. She raised her hands.

"Anything to say for yourself?" Captain Venner demanded sourly.

Irene shrugged.

"Well, lady, we're keeping you in one of our hurry-up wagons here until we've sorted out this little trouble with the wolves, and then you'll be going along to the station with us. And this time you're going to be answering *all* my questions."

Irene backed away. She wasn't keen on being locked in a police car and kept within range of the wolves, or their master.

"Cat got your tongue?" Captain Venner asked. "You've not been shy about talking before."

Irene touched her throat, and tried to make gestures suggesting that she was suffering from temporary but severe laryngitis. She looked as pathetic as she could possibly manage.

Unfortunately it didn't seem to be working. Captain Venner had clearly already been fooled too many times in one day. "Bitters, Johns, you handcuff her and sit with her—" he started.

Then the wolves burst out of the hotel. People scattered in all directions, screaming. There were only four of them now, but their muzzles and coats were marked with blood.

Captain Venner was a good enough cop to recognize that incoming wolves were the more significant threat. "Open fire!" he shouted.

Irene took advantage of his distraction and ran down Fifth Avenue.

The wolves parted around the police like the sea around a breakwater—following her.

Traffic streamed down the street in a rush of metal and rubber and fumes. Others ahead of her, fleeing the rampaging wolves, were cramming themselves through the nearest open doors. The buildings of this New York rose above her like distant mountains, leaving her deep in their shadow. She cast around desperately for a way out. The traffic was an impassable barrier down the centre of Fifth Avenue, and all the doors she'd passed had been closed.

Irene was heading towards Museum Mile and the Metropolitan Museum of Art, and she knew she might be leading the wolves right towards Kai and Evariste. She needed a place to hide. But shop doors were slamming in front of her as the wolves howled, and no taxis answered her desperate waves.

The wolves howled again. The noise seemed just behind her. Irene fought against the temptation to turn round and see how close they were.

Then something slammed into her from behind. She went crashing down, and only her training made her roll with the fall and bring her elbow round in a counter-blow. It hit something—probably wolf—but then a pair of jaws had her forearm in a firm grip. It wasn't enough to pierce the skin, but it let her know that option was definitely on the table.

One of the wolves was half on top of her, eyes watching her with an inhuman intelligence, its jaws clenched on her arm. The others were grouped around, waiting.

Irene fought for the ability to speak. Even normal language would have been sufficient. She could have tried to argue, to lie, to promise, to cajole, to beg—she might even have tried saying *please*. But nothing came.

Traffic flowed past. None of it stopped.

Irene looked up at the night sky above and let herself relax. A certain morbid curiosity made her wonder if the wolves would drag her all the way back to the St. Regis Hotel and, if so, whether they'd do it by the legs, the arms, or the scruff of the neck. Or perhaps they'd expect her to walk. In that case, they were going to have quite a wait.

"There they are!" someone yelled from the direction of the St. Regis Hotel. Question answered. If the wolves couldn't drag her, then human servants could, and nobody was going to interfere . . .

There was a screech of brakes as a car came to a stop, and a wild hooting of horns as every other vehicle objected. Evariste's voice cut through the noise. "**Wolves, get off her!**"

The wolf that had Irene's arm in its jaws released her, drawing back from her with a growl and shaking its head in frustration. The others withdrew a pace or two, moving with the slowness of creatures fighting against their orders. Irene scrambled to her feet, looking around with sudden wild hope.

Evariste and Kai were scrambling out of a taxi. Evariste was in his shirtsleeves, and had several large rectangular objects bundled in his arms, wrapped in his coat. Kai was striding towards her, wrath in every line of his body, and at the sight of him the wolves all put back their ears and snarled.

"Down," Kai said. He snapped his fingers and pointed at the ground.

The wolves ignored his command and moved to circle Irene again, growls throbbing deep in their throats.

"Are you threatening what is mine?" Kai's eyes glinted like rubies under the street lamps. Patterns of scales ran like frosty ferns along the blue-tinged skin of his hands and face, and his nails caught the light and gleamed like jewels. "Are you challenging me?"

And that was it. Kai had publicly involved himself in the situation. Irene was grateful for the rescue—there were no words to say *how* grateful—but this was one of the things she'd most wanted to prevent.

"Your Highness!" Irene turned. That was Hu, together with two henchmen. Both gangsters had guns drawn. "This need not come to hostilities. You have meddled in my lord Qing Song's private business, but he is willing to ignore that and return your property—if you will hand over the man with you."

"He is under my protection," Kai replied without a moment's hesitation. "Your master will withdraw his wolves and return *my* colleague at once, or I will have his head for it."

"That will do very little good if she is dead," Hu replied. "And whether you would best him in a fight is open to dispute. I suggest that we negotiate, Your Highness. Otherwise both sides are likely to lose something to their advantage."

Kai shot a glance at Irene. "Well?" he demanded.

By now Irene had a good estimate of how sharp Hu was: he

wouldn't be suggesting that they all sit down and talk unless he expected to get the upper hand. Unless he was buying time for Qing Song and Jin Zhi to arrive. And she was powerless to warn Kai.

But she wasn't entirely helpless.

And equally important was the fact that the dragons were watching each other, like Siamese fighting fish, considering each other as their main adversaries. Even Qing Song's wolves were watching Kai now, rather than Irene.

Irene touched her throat and did her best to mime *I can't speak.*

"What have you done to her?" Kai demanded.

"What do you think?" Hu answered. "She's healthy enough, as you can see. But if you want her returned to you as you left her, Your Highness, we need to discuss terms."

Irene caught Evariste's glance. He was a few paces behind Kai, still clutching his package. He returned Irene's gaze, then raised an eyebrow. It said, as clearly as words, *What do we do now?*

If they removed the wolf threat, Hu couldn't hold Irene—and couldn't manipulate Kai. As Kai and Hu continued to exchange words, Irene pointed at the sidewalk, then indicated the wolves around her. Then she upturned her hand and brought her fingers together in a grasping motion.

Evariste nodded very slightly. As Kai was opening his mouth to speak again, Evariste said in a conversational tone, **"Sidewalk, hold the wolves."**

The concrete flowed upwards as silently and smoothly as oil, rising to several inches high around the wolves' legs and locking them in position. Irene was already moving, throwing herself between the animals with desperate haste as they whined in shock, before their jaws could get a grip on her.

She stumbled forward as the wolves howled in fury, and Kai stepped forward to catch her. He swung her behind him and turned to sneer triumphantly at Hu. "No terms."

"No terms?" Hu said. "Can you stop bullets now, Your Highness? Because I think your Librarians are still vulnerable."

"And I think you're out of luck." Evariste clung to his bundle of books so tightly that his hands were shaking, but he stepped forward to stand beside Kai. "You want to know what I can do to those guns? What I can do to *you*?"

And then the night split open with a sudden flare of light that tore through the sky. Street lamps flickered and went out. The top of the St. Regis Hotel broke open, stonework and balconies cracking like egg-shells, as two tangled dragons rose through it into the night sky: one burning gold, the other dark emerald, both tearing furiously at each other.

Their mingled roaring ripped through the sky, shuddering through New York, and reality trembled.

CHAPTER 24

Irene had thought New York was noisy by night. Now she had an entirely new standard for comparison. People screamed and ran as the dragons clashed in the darkness above, with no idea of what to do or where to go, except to somehow get away: the ants' nest that was New York had been stirred into panic. The stream of traffic down Fifth Avenue dissolved into a dozen flows and counter-flows as drivers leaned out to see what was going on. Brakes shrieked and metal crumpled as cars collided.

In a way the noise was almost too huge to be understood. Here at street level, their small group seemed to be surrounded by an egg-shell of temporary calm, one that might be broken by violence at any second.

Hu needed only a moment to pull himself together. He took a step forward. "Your Highness. You have to stop them."

Kai looked at him in blank disbelief, his arm locked around Irene's waist in a clasp that felt more possessive than protective.

"What business is it of mine if they should want to kill each other? I'd say they both show excellent judgement."

"Sounds about right to me," Evariste said harshly. "Not my circus, not my monkeys. If they want to tear each other to bits, they can get on with it, and good luck to them."

Hu ignored Evariste. His face was a stark white in the glow of the street lamps. "This may well draw the queen's attention, and might even affect the balance of this world. Surely Your Highness doesn't want to be reported as the instigator of this . . . situation."

Irene knew his only concern was the battle between the dragons. All of this—all the gangs, the shooting, and now the growing confusion and damage, the city ripping itself apart—all of it was just a *situation*, insignificant when compared to the private politics of dragons. The thought burned inside her with a new anger. But fear mingled with it: Hu's threat had teeth.

Kai looked around at the confusion and the troubled night sky, his face as distant as if he had been reading an account of it in the newspaper. "I wouldn't want to intrude on your lord's territory or in his business," he said coldly. "Besides, what do you expect me to do? Throw myself between the two of them and hope that they halt in time? Even if I raised the river against them, it might not be enough to stop them both."

Irene needed her voice back, right this minute, in order to contribute to the discussion. She coughed loudly.

Kai met her eyes, and his expression lightened at the realization that she had something to say. "Of course," he added, "if you have the antidote to whatever's been done to Irene, that would affect my decision."

Hu shrugged. "I'm sorry, Your Highness. My lord has that."

He glanced at the ruined top of the St. Regis Hotel. "Well, had that. It might take a little while to fetch it. If you were to reason with my lord and with the lady Jin Zhi, while I take Miss Winters in charge . . ."

Irene made her opinion on that clear with a healthy sniff. She pried Kai's arm from around her waist, pointed at her throat, then mimed drinking something, looking at Kai and Evariste hopefully. If Kai knew what it was, he might also know some way of fixing it.

Kai shook his head. "I'm sorry, Irene. I don't know what he's given you."

"And if I don't know the words for it . . ." Evariste trailed off, his forehead furrowed in thought. It was all very well for a Librarian to have the Language, but if they didn't have the words, their power was useless.

In between her panic and fury, Irene wondered: what *was* the drug she'd been given? Ordinary magic, if one could use that term, wouldn't have worked on a Librarian. And a paralytic drug would have affected her mouth and throat too, not just her vocal cords.

Which meant it was dragon magic of some sort. She'd seen Fae magic powerful enough to bind dragons—Kai had been collared to stop him using his powers. So why couldn't dragons create something that could block a Librarian's abilities?

She held up one hand to Kai—*wait*—and then stepped over to Evariste, pulling out her battered eyebrow pencil and looking for something to write on.

Perhaps more than anyone else present, Evariste must have understood exactly how frustrated she was feeling. He pulled his coat back from the books he was carrying, offering her a cover to scribble on.

Irene looked at the cover of the topmost book. Her eyes widened before she could stop her reaction. It *wasn't* the *Journey to the West.* It was *The Dream of the Red Chamber.*

Evariste gave a very slight nod at her reaction. "It's under control," he muttered. "As much as anything is at the moment."

Irene pulled herself together. *Symbolic cleansing,* she scribbled on the cover. *Get water, as pure as possible. You use the Language— say it's washing my throat clean of dragon influence as I drink it.*

Hu saw what she was doing, and his horrified intake of breath was almost audible despite the noise going on around them. "Don't write on the books!" he nearly shrieked, in a manner worthy of a Librarian.

Kai stepped between Hu and Irene and Evariste before Hu could launch any one-dragon assaults to drag the books out of their hands. "Are you sure you can't get hold of that antidote? Before we end up defacing the queen's personal reading matter even further?"

Hu's face was tight with frustration. "My lord kept it on his person. I don't have it. Your Highness, there isn't much time—"

The two dragons clashed in the sky again, curling around each other like the links of a chain, before breaking free. Their roaring rippled across the city. The street lights flickered in a crazy chiaroscuro as their posts shook and trembled. People abandoned their cars, fleeing on foot.

Irene knew roughly how large Kai was as a dragon. Both of those dragons were bigger than he was. No doubt in time— possibly lots of time—his royal blood would have him outgrowing them both, but at the moment he was young. Purely on grounds of size, he'd be outweighed and outmatched in an open fight against either of those dragons. If they joined forces against him, he might even be risking crippling injury or death. She *couldn't* just send him up there and tell him to stop them.

But this *couldn't* be allowed to go on. Not for the sake of the dragons—but for the sake of this New York, and the whole of this world. Having two dragons fight might mean more than simply physical damage. It might mean that the world itself was somehow destabilized.

Evariste had been frowning at Irene's written instructions, but finally he nodded. "We need water!" he called to Kai.

Hu's backup thugs were looking rather overtaken by events, but they had been listening to the conversation. Before Hu could tell them to keep quiet, one of them spoke up, pointing at a side street. "There's a joint there," he suggested. "Brown door, third on the right, you knock three times and ask for Louie . . ."

"Right." Kai strode towards it, with Irene and Evariste hurrying to keep up. Hu followed, still protesting, his thugs trailing behind and looking increasingly confused.

There was indeed a speakeasy there, and it was doing a thriving trade. Many were reacting to the crisis by getting drunk, and Irene couldn't blame them. It was a perfectly reasonable response to the situation, and it was supporting local businesses. A win-win situation.

"Water," Kai said, forcing his way to the bar and getting to the point. "A large glass of the purest water you have."

The man behind the bar stared at him, then shrugged. "You want ice with that?"

"Wasting time on this is a bad idea," Hu said. The wolves had been left trapped in the concrete. Evariste had been extremely deaf to Hu's hints that it would be a good idea to free them, that it would give Qing Song a reason to show him favour, et cetera, et cetera. A small part of Irene hoped that nobody killed the wolves while they were helpless, but on her scale of priorities it rated rather low.

"On the contrary, I think it's an extremely good idea," Kai replied. "I think releasing Irene is a much better idea than me throwing myself into the fight and making matters worse."

"Well, if Miss Winters must contribute to the discussion, can't she simply write it down?" Hu offered. "Just gargling with water isn't going to restore her voice."

The barman pushed the glass of water across the counter, clinking with ice cubes. Kai caught it and slid it towards Evariste. "Will that do?" he asked.

"Give me a moment." Evariste put his bundle of books on the floor, glanced sideways at Hu, then rested a foot firmly on top.

Hu winced. "You won't improve your bargaining position by destroying them in front of me," he said.

"After all this shit, I'm not letting go of them." Evariste turned his attention to the glass, picking his words. **"Water in the glass in front of me, let your impurities enter the cubes of ice until you are pure."**

Just because most of the people in the speakeasy were busy getting drunk didn't mean that they were going to ignore free entertainment. When the ice cubes began to grow murky and dull, there were yells of laughter and comments of disbelief.

"Always knew your gin was bath-tub quality," one man commented to the bartender, "but looks like your water's even worse."

"Ready?" Evariste asked Irene. He flipped the cloudy ice cubes out of the glass and passed it to her.

Irene nodded.

She tipped her head back and took a long swig of water, then another. It was absolutely tasteless and oddly unappealing. If only she'd been able to think of a symbolic cure involving brandy.

"The water that Irene is drinking is washing her throat clean of all other influences," Evariste said, **"dragon, Fae, or anything else, so that she can once again speak freely."** He frowned, his mouth tight with concentration, and visibly swayed, putting out a hand to brace himself against the bar.

Irene buckled to her knees, dropping the glass and clutching her throat and her stomach. The water slid down her throat like broken glass, as if someone were scouring her gullet with a wire brush. Her breath sawed painfully in her lungs, and she would have screamed, but she couldn't get the sound out. She could hear her stomach gurgling, and her brain supplied violently disturbing images of fluids at war inside her. She was vaguely aware that she was curled up on the floor, with Kai supporting her. The speakeasy crowd had moved back to give her space, some of them even having the kindness to call for doctors. But nothing mattered besides the claws that seized her throat from inside and dug into her . . .

And then, like ice dissolving in rain, they were gone.

Irene took a breath that was mercifully free from pain, then another, and tried to speak. "I think I need a brandy," she croaked.

That was when Hu and his men moved. One of the thugs bowled into Evariste. He punched him hard in the stomach, grabbed him by the tie, then cracked his head against the bar. The other kept his gun on Kai and Irene as Hu stepped forward and picked up the bundle of books.

"I think I'll take these, Your Highness," he said smugly. "My lord will be able to make his explanations much more easily with these in his possession." Almost as a formality, he flipped back the fold of Evariste's coat to inspect his prize.

He stared.

Irene had read the phrase *He froze as if turned to stone*, but she'd never seen it happen. For a moment the only living thing in Hu's face was his eyes, filled with horror as his position collapsed like a house of cards. Not only did he not have what he wanted, but he'd just put a large hole in his chances of ever getting it.

Before Hu could think what to try next, Irene said, **"Every gun within range of my voice, open and eject your bullets."**

The resulting confusion gave Kai the opportunity to take Hu's thugs down. Irene checked on the groaning Evariste, helping him upright. "Can I have a brandy?" she asked the bartender. "Two brandies, in fact?"

He was staring at her as if she were a specimen in a zoo. "Lady, what the hell did you just do?"

"Look at her," another man said, pointing. "She's *her*. She's Jeanette Smith!"

"Yes. Right. Fine." Irene took a deep breath in the sudden silence. "I'm also a trained mesmerist and I can control the wills of everyone around me. And right now"—she looked the bartender straight in the eye—"I really, *really* need a couple of brandies."

"You want to stop for a drink now?" Kai demanded.

"We need to work out what we're going to do next—and I might as well have a drink while I'm doing it."

It wasn't just one of the fundamental principles of the Library; it was one of the fundamental principles of humanity, and it was found in all places and cultures. It wasn't altruism, or ethics, or sympathy for people in trouble. It was a case of clearing up the mess they had made.

The crowded room buzzed as some newcomers pushed their way through the door. The mob of drinkers parted to make way for them, and Irene recognized George, with a couple of his henchmen. Lily was one step behind, an attaché case in her hand, her face murderous as she caught sight of Kai.

"You." George pointed a diamond-ringed finger at Irene. "And you." He pointed at Hu. "I can't say I know what you're all up to in my town, but I am—what's that thing you Brits say?—I'm not amused. I am not one bit amused. And as for you." His finger shifted to Kai and Evariste, and his tone of voice slipped from furious to lethal. "The moment you get out of here, you'd best start running. And after what you did to my men, however fast you run, it's not going to be fast enough—"

"Stop it." Irene was surprised to realize that she'd interrupted. The room went even quieter, shifting to horrified anticipation. "Mr. Ross. George. Right now we just want to leave town and get out of your way. But there's a bigger problem than *us*, and that's the dragons."

The bartender had been quietly making up a drink, which he slid down the bar. George took a slug of it. "Lady, if you think I haven't noticed that we've got two honest-to-life giant flying dinosaurs out there, then you've had too much to drink. We can't just wait for the army to send some planes to shoot them down. But luckily my Lily here's got an answer to that one."

Kai had twitched at the phrase *giant flying dinosaurs*, but when he saw the curl of Lily's smile he stiffened. "What do you mean?" he demanded.

"I mean that I can shoot rifles just as well as handguns," Lily said, her eye on Kai as if she was sizing him up as another target, "and I haven't met a shot I can't make."

"Mere bullets won't hurt them," Kai said.

"I didn't say I'd be firing plain human bullets." Lily glanced to

Irene. "How about you? Should I be getting one with your name on it too?"

Irene put her glass down with a click on the bar. "No," she said firmly. There had to be a way round this, one where everyone got out alive. She could almost see it. She just needed time to think.

"I suppose that makes my life easier," Lily said. Though there was a disappointed note to her voice.

Kai lowered his voice. "Irene, if there's the chance that she *could* hurt them, then we can't just let her—"

"I know," Irene agreed.

They couldn't let Lily do this. Though no doubt Lily would say, how did they propose to stop her? If Lily could infuse her bullets with Fae power, it might indeed be enough to wound or kill a dragon. And if Lily shot down two dragons of noble birth, this world would become a Fae-versus-dragon battleground.

Which meant that Irene had to stop it here and now.

She had Kai, who could rouse the river. She had Hu, who was retreating towards the door. Though Hu only wanted the fight stopped on his own terms. But he was practical: he might help persuade Qing Song to negotiate, once they were all out of here. She had Evariste, with his Librarian skills. She had a Fae gun-moll, who might listen to her if she could offer a better alternative. She had the local crime boss of New York. And she had the resources of this bar, such as it was.

The tang of brandy still burned her throat and, as she swallowed, Irene saw a plan that just might work. But since half the people in the room wouldn't even consider going along with it, she also needed a plausible lie.

"Mr. Ross," she said. "George. What if I could offer you another solution?"

"I don't know," George said. "What've you got?"

"Lily," Irene said, "do you have something that would shoot tranquillizer bullets?"

Lily shrugged. "I have guns that'll shoot anything you like. But if you think I'm going to waste my time drugging those two, when I could be shooting them in the head, then you're dreaming."

Kai was also frowning. "Irene," he started, "there isn't a drug strong enough to affect those two—at least, not in a bullet-sized dose."

Irene unobtrusively spread her fingers in the *five minutes* sign that she'd given him earlier, back in Boston. "Just a moment," she said. She drew Lily to one side and lowered her voice, murmuring into the woman's ear. "I've got a plan. And it'll get those dragons out of here without wrecking New York or bringing their families after you. But I need your help. You and George."

"Lily?" George said suspiciously.

"Just a moment, boss," Lily replied. Her visible eye was as cold as frozen steel. "You'll give me your word on that?" she whispered to Irene.

Irene swallowed. This was a serious pledge for her to be giving, based on a plan she hadn't even fully formulated yet. But if she wanted Lily to cooperate, and George with her, then she had to convince her now. "I swear by my name and power that I intend to stop the dragons fighting and remove them from this world as fast as possible," she muttered. "But I need you to fetch your tranquillizer gun, I need you to act as if you think this'll work, and I need George to have a couple of lorries of high-proof alcohol waiting by the river at the location we agree upon. The lorries need to look inconspicuous so that nobody gets suspicious. Agreed?"

Lily hesitated. Then finally she said, loud enough to be heard, "Agreed."

The door slammed open again, blocking Hu, who'd almost managed to reach it. Captain Venner stood there, several cops filling the space behind him. "I don't know what the hell's going on, but I know you're behind it," he began, "and you're all—"

"Perfect." Irene stepped forward, conscious of all the eyes on her. "You can be useful too. Gentlemen, Lily—we can stop those dragons. But I'm going to need your help."

There was a silence that ranged from faith and trust (Kai) through horrified disbelief (Evariste) to a sort of harmony between high-grade suspicion (both Hu and Captain Venner) and consideration (George and Lily). Everyone else contributed slack-jawed incomprehension.

Finally George said, "Tell us what you've got in mind, Miss Smith. I'm interested."

CHAPTER 25

"Kai." Irene turned to him, trying to sound confident. If a single person here stopped trusting her, she might lose all of them. "You think that if you tried to stop the dragons fighting, they'd both turn on you?"

Kai winced, but nodded. "I don't have the authority to command them. I am technically of higher rank, but I can't back it up. If it came to a fight, my power over the elements is greater than theirs, but they both outweigh me physically. And there's nobody here to witness them," he added sourly, "at least, nobody who's not in their service. So they wouldn't have to answer for it."

"Right." Irene pointed a finger at him. "You're the bait."

"A few more details, please?" Kai said plaintively.

"In just a moment . . . George." She pinned her best smile on her face. "You've seen that I can do some unusual things."

"I've seen you turn the lights out," George agreed, "and I still haven't figured out how the hell you managed that one."

Captain Venner snorted. "The woman's a hypnotist. She gave one of your waiters a post-hypnotic order to turn out all the lights when she gave the signal."

That was a beautiful excuse, and Irene resolved to remember it. "We're in a hurry. I can do some parlour tricks to impress you, or I can get on with explaining the plan."

George nodded and made a *Go on* gesture.

"Kai here will lure the dragons to a pre-arranged spot above the river. Lily will be waiting with her tranquillizer gun. Evariste and I will guide the bullets to hit the dragons. The dragons will be knocked out and will crash into the river. Problem sorted."

She could see the uncertainty in Kai's face out of the corner of her eye. She ignored it for the moment. He knew how implausible her suggestion was, but for the moment he was trusting her and not dis-agreeing with her publicly. She'd explain to him—and Evariste—what she had in mind the moment that they were out of Hu's hearing. Because what she actually had in mind was far, far more destructive.

"I still think we should just shoot them," Lily said. Her visible eye was hungry. "Why are you so interested in saving them, Jeanette? Whose side are you really on?"

"See, that's one of the reasons I employ Lily here," George commented to Captain Venner. "She asks all the right questions."

"I'm on the side that wants to stop this fight before any more of New York gets damaged," Irene snapped. "You saw I was a prisoner in Qing Song's suite—do you really think I'm on his side? When he had his wolves chasing me down the street? And I believe you could shoot *one* of them without us helping. But could you hit the second one as well? Before it turned on *you*?"

"I could try," Lily said, as calm as ice. But there was a note of uncertainty in her voice, and Irene was relieved to hear it. Lily *wasn't* certain she could get them both. And Lily didn't want to get herself killed. She'd stick with their deal.

"You're not Jeanette Smith," Captain Venner accused. "You're not an FBI agent either. So who the hell *are* you, and what's going on?"

A smile flickered over Lily's face. She turned to George. "There isn't time for this, boss. I think she can do what she's saying, but we need to do it now."

"Then it looks like this is one of the few times you and I are going to be on the level," George said to Captain Venner. He tossed back his drink. "It sounds like we're going to need some space to work in. I don't want any of my paying customers getting injured when the lizards crash. Are you and the other cops going to play ball and clear the target area?"

Captain Venner bit back a growl. "Fine. If this is the only way to stop them. Where are we doing this?"

Irene relaxed for a moment. That was everyone in agreement. She could *do* this . . .

Then she caught sight of Hu, about to leave the room.

Lily saw the direction of Irene's gaze and, without a moment's hesitation, levelled a gun at Hu's head. Her finger was tightening on the trigger as Irene lunged for her wrist.

The shot slapped into the door-frame just above Hu's head. He froze.

"Nobody gets killed," Irene said through gritted teeth. "That's *my* price."

"They just walk away?" Lily demanded. Her gun was aimed at Hu's head again. "After all this?"

Irene looked Lily in the eye. "Hu is not the biggest threat at the moment."

"Oh, if we're making threats . . ." Kai put in, his own tone underscored with anger.

"Hu. Come back into this room and shut the door." Irene waited for Hu to close the door and step safely back from it before she looked at Kai. "I appreciate your feelings. But we're quite clear on who the offending parties are. And Lily is not the person who touched off this disaster."

George stepped forward, pushing Lily's gun arm down with one hand as he did so. She let him. "Miss Smith—seeing as we haven't anything better to call you—you say you want to do this somewhere alongside the Hudson?"

"The river," Evariste explained, as Irene blinked in momentary confusion.

"Right, the river. We have a map here." George tapped the map, which had been spread across the bar. The crowd was being held back by a combination of George's enforcers and Captain Venner's cops. "Where do you want your ambush?"

Irene beckoned Kai over. "Where would work best?" she asked. "If they thought you were running from them and heading to the river, where could you lead them?"

Kai frowned at the map. "Would there do?" he said, pointing. "About half a mile up from those piers, so that we don't have to deal with the shipping?"

"Sure," George said. "Plenty of good spots there for Lily to take her shot from. Lily, you tell one of the boys which of your specials you want from your collection, and they'll bring it right there to meet you. Can you get the area cleared, Venner?"

Captain Venner jerked a nod. "I'll get moving. See you there."

Irene found herself being hustled outside, together with Kai, Evariste, and Hu. It gave her the chance to murmur her real plan into Kai's ear. His hand tightened on hers, and he nodded in agreement. They were urged into a waiting car, with one of George's men as a driver and another as a guard. It seemed that George didn't want to risk them wandering off.

The night was as hot as an August evening, and dusty winds stroked through the air. The sidewalks were full of panicking people, stampeding in a dozen directions at once, a hair's breadth away from full riot. It didn't embody Irene's worst fears *yet*—the falling buildings, collapsing skyscrapers, earthquakes, and thunder and ruin that she'd been imagining—but the threat of future destruction hung in the air like a promise. The earth seemed to pulse beneath her in warning. Everyone in the city could feel the dragons and the power they controlled. It was like being an insect under the magnifying glass. You were safe only for as long as the focus didn't tighten upon you. New York wouldn't need to be physically destroyed at this rate—it would simply tear itself apart.

A roar cut through the night, louder than the colliding traffic or yelling mobs, and Irene felt the earth shudder in response.

"Why are the dragons doing that?" Evariste demanded. "They're only fighting *each other*, they don't need to—to . . ." He waved his hands, trying to illustrate the shaking ground beneath them. "To do *that* sort of crap!"

The car jolted as it took a corner hard, and all of them had to hang on. The traffic still on the streets had abandoned such minor suggestions as speed limits or traffic laws and was going as fast as possible. They hadn't hit anything—yet.

"Neither of them is going to turn down an advantage now, with them both so closely matched," Kai said tensely. He was in the backseat on one side of Irene, with Evariste on the other, and Hu was sharing the front seat with George's thugs. "Though Jin Zhi has the edge, if she can stay in the air. It'll make it more difficult for Qing Song to call the earth against her."

Irene shivered in spite of the rising temperature. She could guess what Jin Zhi's own metaphorical elemental affinity was now: heat. All the dragons she'd met so far had some sort of affinity to a natural or symbolic element, even if it didn't match classical Western or Chinese patterns. Kai's was to water, his uncle Ao Shun's to rain or storms, Li Ming's to cold and ice . . . she wondered what Hu's was.

Hu was staring out the window in a brooding silence. He was as tense as Kai, and Irene thought he was genuinely worried about his lord and master. "Are you going to cooperate?" she asked him.

"You're not leaving me much choice," Hu said in clipped tones. "I only hope, for your sake, that you can make this work."

"Speaking of which," Irene said, then shifted to Chinese, *"we need to consider the aftermath."* She knew Kai could speak Chinese, and if Evariste had been able to trace *Journey to the West*, then he understood it too. More to the point, the two thugs in the front of the car probably *couldn't* understand it.

"What do you mean?" Kai asked in the same language. His choice of words was polite student-to-teacher, and it brought a frown to Hu's face.

"I mean that we may need a fast getaway. So be prepared. Please be ready to use the river against George's gunmen if I give you a signal." She shifted back to English again, just as the gangster in the front seat turned round to stare at them. "Evariste, we're going to need to agree on our wording and speak in unison. It'll magnify the Language's effect. Have you done this before?"

"No," Evariste said, giving her a sideways glance. "Have you?"

"Me neither," Irene said. She felt a manic cheerfulness descending on her. It was the far-too-familiar sensation of being so neck-deep in trouble that it couldn't get any worse—hoping your feet would hit the bottom before your nostrils went under the surface. She recalled the good old Macbeth lines of *I am in blood stepped in so far*, and so on. Except that it always *could* get worse.

Be positive, she counselled herself. Kai knew what he had to do.

Two gleaming bodies collided in the night sky above with a crash that shattered the glass in street lamps and building windows up and down the street. Their car rocked on its wheels, and the driver swore as he jerked the steering wheel to the right, dragging the car out of the way of an oncoming vehicle that had veered off course.

Irene braced herself and slid back the window on her side, leaning out to get a better look. She saw the two coiling figures falling through the sky together, wrapped around each other in twists of gold and dark green like intricate embroidery. Then the two dragons broke apart, spiralling out into a wide circle that was clearly a preparation for another attack. Irene pulled her head back into the car. "How much longer?" she demanded of the driver.

"Ten minutes, lady. Five if we're lucky."

Irene took a deep breath. To distract herself, she asked Hu, "Out of curiosity, what touched off this particular fight?"

"They were already at cross-purposes," Hu said. "Then my lord saw, through the eyes of his pets, that the prince had arrived and taken you under his protection. He used strong language, blaming the lady Jin Zhi for interfering. She commented on how his carelessness and laxity had caused the current situation, and . . ." He shrugged.

"One might wonder if there was some past connection between Qing Song and Jin Zhi . . ." Kai speculated disingenuously.

"I couldn't possibly comment," Hu responded. He looked as if he would have liked to say something stronger, if not for his position.

Irene filed the whole past-liaison thing under *blatantly obvious*.

"Almost there!" the driver called over his shoulder. "Get ready to hop out fast."

The car drew up with a screech of brakes and the four of them scrambled out, followed by their escort. Kai took a deep breath of the river air and immediately looked happier. On one side of the street rose the buildings of New York, and on the other side lay the wide dark expanse of the Hudson River. Irene couldn't restrain thoughts about there being nowhere to run and nowhere to hide. Farther south, she could see the lights marking the ends of the piers, and the dark outlines of ships. Heat brought the stink of petrol rising from the concrete, overlying the smells of water and sewage. Several trucks were drawn up near where they'd parked, and Irene took care not to stare at them too obviously. If Lily had told George what she wanted, and if George had complied, they were one step closer . . .

Evariste licked a finger and held it up to the air. "There's going to be a storm if it gets any hotter," he said. "The sort with lightning."

"That's all we need," their escort muttered.

Then a distant roar echoed across the city, and the shadow of a tremor touched the ground beneath their feet. The surface of the river rippled in the glow of the street lamps, and distant alarm bells sang in disharmony with car horns and screams.

Irene looked at Hu and Kai: they both had the same expression of grave concern, as though an unmentioned line had been crossed. But it was Hu who spoke. "That was my lord Qing Song. He's begun to call the earth to aid him."

She didn't want to think what would happen to New York if the tremors became any worse. "Is there anything *you* can do?" she demanded of Hu. "I apologize if it's rude to ask, but is there anything you can summon?"

Hu's face was such a perfect mask that Irene realized she must have touched a very deep nerve. "Sadly a person of lesser ability like myself cannot command such power," he said, with the sort of forced politeness that came from extreme personal bitterness. "I could not possibly challenge the higher nobility on that level."

Irene pondered the taste of foot in mouth, and decided that apologizing further would only make it worse. Instead she turned to their escort. "Where are George and Lily?"

"Looks like that's them now," he said. She turned to see a cavalcade of oncoming traffic rumbling in their direction, a limousine with an escort of police cars.

"Right." She gestured for the others to join her. "Once Lily's in position for the shot, then we're good to go. Kai, are you ready?"

"Yes," Kai said. "At least they won't be bothering you. They'll be focusing on me." He glanced up at the skies. It wasn't quite nervousness. It was more the controlled readiness of a man preparing for a fight, where he knew the ground and his enemies, even if the odds were against him.

Irene touched his wrist. "Be careful."

"While getting between two of my kind who might be fighting to the death?" Kai was almost laughing. He caught her in an unexpected embrace. "Be careful yourself," he muttered into her hair. "If George thinks he doesn't need you any longer—"

"I know," she murmured back. "And you know what to do. Be

ready." For a moment she didn't try to pull out of his arms. His presence, his safety, was reassuring. It was far easier for her to handle risks to herself than to be putting him in danger yet again. *I am hopelessly compromised,* she thought. *Just as much as Evariste.*

She occasionally daydreamed about being the sort of character in a story who could faint and leave everyone else to sort things out.

But that wasn't going to happen.

"When we make a break for it," she continued, "you take Evariste and Qing Song—once he's in human form. Hu can't retaliate if you've taken his master hostage."

"I'd rather be carrying you," he murmured in her ear.

"We have to get everyone out and make sure Hu doesn't pull a fast one. Trust me." It was like one of those logic problems where the narrator had a single boat and had to get a fox and a rabbit and a bunch of carrots across the river, without having any of them eat the others. How else were they all supposed to get out of this world without leaving someone behind, or having Hu fly off with Irene or Evariste at his mercy? Kai could only carry a couple of people, and this was the best she could come up with. "Think of somewhere safe to take us, so we can finish negotiating. You'll be the one navigating, after all."

She gave him a last squeeze and let him go.

"Not interrupting anything, am I?" George enquired as he came strolling up with Lily behind him. Lily was now carrying an oddly shaped large rifle with an oversized barrel slung openly across her back.

"Getting ready to go," Irene said firmly. "Where will Lily be wanting to take the shot?"

"Behind those trucks should do nicely for cover," Lily said, without the slightest betraying flicker of expression. "You and the other Librarian can come across with me and set yourselves up."

They followed Lily, with Kai and Hu a few paces behind. Lily unslung her rifle and broke it open, demonstrating the cartridges.

"How come you found something like this so quickly?" Evariste said. He was developing a rabbit-in-the-headlights look again.

Lily gave him the sort of smile that would have suited a fox. "I'm a Girl Scout at heart, Mr. Jones. I'm always prepared. You should see my merit badge collection."

Irene was taking the opportunity to check the trucks. They were full of crates, which were laden with unlabelled clear glass bottles. "What's in here?" Irene asked, checking that she had what she needed.

One of the gangsters shrugged. "Gin," he said. "Straight from Holland—"

Another rumble drifted through the ground beneath their feet.

"Distilled downtown in a bath-tub, you mean," Captain Venner said with a snort. His cops were spreading out to secure the perimeter, but he'd joined what was technically, Irene supposed, the command group for this operation.

"I'm greatly disappointed in you, Captain," George said. "It's a proper high-class operation, even if there's a possibility it's not from Holland."

Irene took a deep breath and nodded. "Gin. Right. Very well, gentlemen. Please will everyone stand well clear of blast range. And stay back when things get messy."

Kai nodded to Irene and Evariste and stepped into the empty space between the trucks. The air around him began to glow. There were gasps from the assembled gangsters and cops, and they drew farther back towards the perimeter.

Irene could hear the sound of guns being cocked. "Stand down!" she called. "He's on our side."

And in a flash of light it wasn't a human standing there any longer: it was a dragon, perhaps ten yards long, horned and serpentine, like something out of a classical painting. He carried himself with a natural pride that made the humans around him look unfinished and pitiful. The street lamplight gleamed on Kai's dark blue scales, turning them into sapphires that glittered as he flexed his wings. Behind him the waters of the river seemed to flow faster for a moment, as if encouraged by his presence.

Irene raised her hand in assent, and with a single leap Kai swept up into the night sky, ignoring gravity and mass, moving like a calligraphic streak of ink across a scroll.

Captain Venner was staring in shock at where Kai had been. "Don't tell me he's one of them too."

"What did you think he was?" Irene demanded. "Given what we'd said he was going to do?"

"I didn't know," Captain Venner muttered. "I am not used to people in my city here who can turn off the lights by talking, or who can turn into *giant flying lizards!*"

"Are there more of you?" George asked. His tone was casual, but Irene didn't need warning signs to imagine the sort of thing he might be planning. "Are you all over the place?"

"Dragons exist," Lily said. Her voice cut through the mutters of panic that were spreading around the area. "So do dragon-slayers. That's what people like me do. Isn't that right, Jeanette?" Her smirk said *Contradict me if you dare.* She snapped her rifle closed again, moving to brace herself against the side of a truck. "Jeanette here's not a dragon. And the one that's just gone up there to distract the others—well, he's under her control. So as long as they behave themselves, they've got nothing to worry about."

Irene could feel how shaky the metaphorical ground under her feet had grown. Out of the corner of her eye, she noted that Hu was getting a light for his new cigarette from one of the guards. Now that was *really* impressive. It set a whole new standard of blending into the crowd for her to work towards in the future.

Thunder rolled above them, and all of them looked up to see the three dragons descending.

CHAPTER 26

Kai was doing a good job of acting as if he were fleeing in panic. At least, Irene hoped it was acting. Both the other dragons were bigger than he was—twice his size, at a rough estimate, possibly three times—and there was nothing playful about the way that they were harassing him. While Irene had no expertise in interpreting dragon-attack flight patterns, Jin Zhi and Qing Song were moving with authority, clearly setting the pace for the confrontation, and Kai was having to dart and ripple through the air to avoid them, like a dolphin dodging sharks. They moved like the after-flare of fireworks, and all three of them glowed with power.

"Everyone clear!" Irene shouted as they winged closer. "Evariste, over here with me!"

She wasn't the only one who'd been staring. She didn't take her eyes off the dragons, but she heard the sound of running feet as people stampeded in all directions. Behind her, Evariste said, "What's the wording?"

Hu was a safe distance away. "'Glass bottles, shatter,'" Irene said, her voice low. "Then 'Alcohol, rise to form a mass above the gold and green dragons, and ignite'?"

"It's a bit wordy," Evariste said. Then the actual meaning of the words sank in, and he gaped at her. "Did you say what I think you just said?"

"I was looking for practical criticism, not artistic commentary." Irene watched Kai barely avoid a body-blow from Qing Song. Jin Zhi moved in while Kai was distracted, stooping from a higher plane. Irene coiled her fingers into fists, feeling the old scars on her palms, willing self-control into her voice. "Any better suggestions?"

"Nah, it'll do. I like this. I like it a *lot*." The nervousness in his voice was being rapidly overlaid by vengeful pleasure. "Say when."

"In just a minute. Lily, are you ready too?"

"Sure I am." Lily sighted through her rifle's scope. "So, if I've got this right, you hit them with the fire and I shoot them with the drugs. And at some point your pet there drops the river on top of them?"

"Or drops them in the river. Whatever. I'll leave the timing of the shot to you, just don't hit Kai."

Lily didn't bother replying. Her finger caressed the trigger.

Kai had to drop from his current height to avoid Jin Zhi's claws. He fell towards the river like a trailing ribbon, the other two following him down at the same speed.

"Now!" Irene turned to face Evariste and raised her hand like a conductor, then brought it down, and they spoke in unison. "**Glass bottles, shatter!**"

Gin poured out of the trucks, gushing from the broken bottles and running through the cracks in the floor. The fragments of broken glass had been contained by the trucks, but the raw smell of the alcohol was so thick it was hard to breathe.

The air seemed to hum with significance—something to do with the Language's nature, gaining so much more power as their voices harmonized. Irene and Evariste looked at each other in surprise for a moment.

Kai curved just above the surface of the river, and it rose to meet and flow past him. The water glowed like molten metal in the burning light that emanated from Jin Zhi, and it reached for Jin Zhi and Qing Song as if it were alive. The two larger dragons beat against it, thrashing their wings as it grappled with them. Where the water touched Jin Zhi, it hissed wildly and boiled off as steam, draping veils of mist around her.

Lily's rifle cracked once, then a second time.

Then Irene gave the signal to Evariste again and they spoke together: **"Alcohol, rise to form a mass above the gold and green dragons, and ignite!"**

The spilt gin burst heavenwards in thousands of drops, rushing towards a space just above Jin Zhi and Qing Song. It didn't have the elegance of Kai's element. But the gush of alcohol surged in a straight line through the air to a point above its targets, cleaving through the surrounding waters without being diluted.

Hu's face was a mask of horror. He thrust aside the man he'd been talking to, shouldering towards Irene and Evariste. "No, you can't—"

His voice was lost in the boom of the detonation.

The explosion threw everyone at the waterside to the ground. It was eye-searingly bright, painting Irene's vision with aftereffects. The remains of the gin came pattering down in burning droplets.

It certainly distracted Qing Song and Jin Zhi. They went crashing down towards the river, as much from the shock of the igniting alcohol as from the force of the blast. Rivers of blue flame poured over them, briefly outlining their thrashing forms.

Then the waters rose to swallow them.

Irene pulled herself to her feet against the side of the truck, rubbing her eyes. The river heaved and rippled, as if about to flood its banks, with gouts of bubbles swelling up from beneath the surface. The wide expanse of water shuddered from side to side, shaking the anchored boats until they ground against the piers. Huge shapes moved beneath the surface, only their outlines perceptible. The smell of decaying waterweed mingled with the reek of alcohol as the river was churned up by the struggle taking place beneath its surface.

As they all watched, it began to subside.

The gangsters, drawn by the irresistible human urge to risk danger just to get a better view, began to move closer. Hu was in the forefront. Irene stayed back, and gestured for Evariste to remain beside her.

Then Kai rose from the depths of the river, his wings spread as he circled above it. The bodies of Jin Zhi and Qing Song drifted to the surface, still in dragon form, but unmoving, barely breathing.

"Holy shit," Evariste said. "It worked."

"Of course it did," Irene said. It would be a bad idea to admit to uncertainty in front of her current audience. She urgently hoped the attack hadn't gone too far: if they'd killed or severely injured Qing Song or Jin Zhi, they'd just exchanged one catastrophe for another. "Now we get to the difficult bit."

Evariste looked at the rising circle of gangsters and police, all of whom were armed, and most of whom were now openly holding their guns. "I think—" he started.

"You do it by talking, don't you?" George interrupted. Lily, next to him, had discarded her rifle and had a revolver in each hand. Irene knew it would be a waste of time to bring up her agreement with the Fae: it hadn't covered what would happen *after* they subdued the dragons. "So right now you don't say anything, either of you. Or you're going down as well. Me and my boys, we're just about to do some dragon-slaying. Or do you want to read them their rights, Venner?"

"Under the circumstances, I'll skip it," Captain Venner said. "Can't see them asking for a lawyer anyhow."

Irene shrugged. Then she glanced behind her at Kai and raised her right hand in the air, palm upwards, as though she were lifting something.

George, Lily, and the gunmen had seen Kai use the river to take down Jin Zhi and Qing Song, but they hadn't appreciated the full implications of his power.

Now the Hudson River surged and broke its banks in a wave several yards high. It rushed across the street, bowling over gangsters and policemen alike.

A narrow channel of dry ground still lay between Irene and Evariste and the water's edge. Irene ran down it to the railing that bordered the river. It would be impossible to get Jin Zhi and Qing Song off this world in their current form. "**Jin Zhi, Qing Song,**" she shouted, "**change to your human form!**"

She hadn't expected it to be easy, and it wasn't.

It was a good thing there was a railing. It stopped her going head-first into the river. She'd managed to change werewolves back to their human shape previously: that had been tiring, but manageable. She'd never tried to affect *dragons* by using the Language. Dragons were metaphysical heavy-weights when compared to werewolves. She gasped for air, and her Library brand seemed to press down on her as if it would crush her to the ground.

But when she raised her head to look at the scene in front of her, she saw that it had worked. Qing Song and Jin Zhi were in their human shapes now, though still—thank goodness—unconscious. The rising water had carried them onto the riverbank, and they lay there, soaked and crumpled like jetsam.

There was a bright flare of light along the bank to her left, and she turned to look. It was Hu: he had taken his own dragon form, and his scales shone like hammered copper as he prepared to launch into the air.

Urgency energized Irene. "Grab Qing Song!" she called to Evariste. "You're both travelling on Kai! Kai, pass me Jin Zhi—Hu must carry us!"

"But my daughter—" Evariste protested desperately.

"We'll get Qing Song to give her back, but we have to get out of here first! Come on!" She grabbed his shoulder and pushed him towards Qing Song.

The waters thrashed across the street again, knocking down those gangsters who'd managed to get to their feet. Hu reached for Qing Song, but Kai swung between him and the two unconscious dragons, forcing him back.

Lily had dragged the half-drowned George behind one of the trucks and was standing over him, her guns drawn, but she didn't seem inclined to fire. Perhaps she didn't want to start a war either. Or perhaps without George to give her the order, she was less eager to pull the trigger. "Are you leaving?" she called to Irene.

"Getting the hell out of here, and glad to do it," Irene called back. "All of us are going. We won't be coming back."

Kai backed against the roadside, dipping the arch of his back to allow Evariste to drag Qing Song aboard. Hu hissed furiously but didn't try to stop them.

About time I made my own exit. Ankle-deep in water, Irene stood over Jin Zhi on the riverbank and beckoned to Hu. "We can discuss the details later," she called, "but let's get out of here!"

Lily lowered her guns. "I hope you realize I could have shot you." Her voice carried over the noise of the water.

"I'll remember it!" Irene hooked one arm across Jin Zhi's chest and turned to see that Hu was directly behind her, his back curved so that she could clamber on with her own dragon cargo. Once aboard, she turned to raise her free hand in a wave.

"Just one question!" Lily shouted. "What's your name? Who *are* you?"

Irene weighed the possible consequences of giving her name against the fact that Lily might well be able to find out anyhow, with a bit of research. She mentally shrugged. "Irene Winters!" she called.

And as she spoke, Kai rose, followed by Hu, climbing into the night sky.

Irene lowered her head and clung on, pinning Jin Zhi face-down against Hu's back. She hoped the other woman would stay unconscious. It was much easier to handle her like that.

New York spread out beneath them, marked out in patterns of light and darkness, with the windows of skyscrapers gleaming in impossibly complicated grids, and the gleams of car headlamps moving jerkily along the streets. The oppressive heat had eased with Jin Zhi's unconsciousness, and Irene breathed in the cooler air with relief.

Ahead of Hu, Kai mantled his wings and roared, and Irene hoped he had a safe destination in mind. A rip tore in the night sky, glowing with a light that seemed to shine from the other side, in a shade that Irene couldn't name. This was how dragons travelled between alternate worlds: they somehow passed *outside* the regular flow of worlds, to where the air was like water and where only dragons could find their way. As Hu's passenger, Irene keenly felt her own lack of control. But as long as Kai had Qing Song, then they had a metaphorical leash around Hu's neck.

Kai angled his wings and swooped through the rift, and Hu followed.

Irene had expected the shadowy sky beyond, the endless currents of blue and green—she'd been there before with Kai. But she hadn't expected to find other dragons waiting.

The four newcomers, all of them larger than Kai or Hu, swooped on them in a blaze of wings that shone like gemstone and metal. The sounds that came from them were deeper than Kai's earlier cry as he'd opened the way. They were organ-tones that throbbed in Irene's bones and made her shiver in near panic, flattening herself against Hu's back. She saw Kai flinch in mid-air, coiling in on himself, trying to draw away from this display of threat and aggression. Hu jerked beneath Irene as though he would have liked to flee, but there was nowhere to go: they were in a great sea of emptiness, surrounded by four strange dragons.

CHAPTER 27

The desert was cold by night, and Irene was grateful for her coat. Evariste hunched his shoulders inside his battered jacket, staying behind her and Kai. The new dragons didn't object: they were far more interested in Kai than in his human followers. Hu knelt to one side, checking the physical condition of Qing Song and Jin Zhi—who, fortunately, were both still unconscious.

They had been forcibly escorted to a world of the strangers' choosing. Looking around at the flat sweep of desert and tasting the bitterly dry air, Irene had to conclude that part of that choice was to ensure that Kai couldn't call on any local water sources.

One of their four escorts had left, the moment the rest of them had entered this world, flying off on an unknown errand. Irene had a nasty suspicion that they were reporting in to receive further orders. But all the other dragons had assumed human form, as had Kai and Hu. And now the strangers wanted answers.

"Identify yourselves," a woman who appeared to be their leader commanded. She was robed in deep amethyst purple with light green collar and cuffs, and her rich dark hair was coiled up in an elaborate hair-style. "Why are you bearing unconscious nobles, courtiers from the Queen of the Southern Lands' domain?"

"My name is Kai," Kai answered, "son of Ao Guang, the King of the Eastern Ocean. If I have trespassed on the territory of another, then I will make my apologies. May I also know your name?"

Irene kept her mouth shut, hoping against hope that they might somehow wriggle out of this without her and Evariste being identified as Librarians. Their interrogator was clearly fixing on Kai as the obvious one to question. Perhaps they'd blundered into a standard patrol. Perhaps these strangers would accept a plausible explanation for Qing Song and Jin Zhi's state.

"I am Mei Feng, of the Queen of the Southern Lands' court," the woman in purple said, in a noticeably more courteous tone. She clearly hadn't expected to catch such a big fish. "A violent altercation was observed, which might have caused a change to the very reality of that world. Were you involved?"

"I observed these two dragons in dispute and intervened to stop them," Kai said. The twitch of his shoulders suggested polite boredom. "As you say, it might have been unhealthy for that world's stability."

"Ah." Mei Feng stepped closer, inspecting the two unconscious bodies. The other pair of dragons, robed like their leader but less elegantly, were too close for comfort. "I recognize these individuals. But where did you intend to take them? And who are these humans?" Her questions were polite enough, but it was clear that her attitude could very easily change if Kai did not provide suitable answers.

"Such questions are extremely personal and could be considered to be prying into my private affairs," Kai objected. But it was weak. Irene knew it, and she knew that Kai knew it, and she was fairly sure Mei Feng knew it as well. They'd been caught with the evidence on them. It was, as the English would say, "a fair cop."

"I would not wish to interfere, Your Highness," Mei Feng replied. "But perhaps you could provide me with some information?" Her glance fell on Hu. "Or maybe *you* wish to tell me what is going on?"

"I am servant to my lord Qing Song," Hu said quickly, "and may not speak on the matter without his permission."

"I see," Mei Feng said. "Well, then, these humans—"

"Are under my protection," Kai broke in.

And the other two possible witnesses are unconscious, Irene thought, *and let's hope they stay that way for the foreseeable future.*

Mei Feng paced thoughtfully, her face perfectly calm. The wind was picking up, however, and Irene wondered if that might be a more accurate representation of her feelings. "Your Highness, you must understand that your position here is rather dubious. You appear in the company of these two nobles. They appear to have been drugged, scorched, and half-drowned—and you wish me to believe that your involvement is completely innocent?"

Deny everything, keep your mouth shut, and demand a lawyer, Irene thought, remembering Kai's earlier advice. But did dragons have lawyers for this sort of situation? Or was it much less civilized?

"I couldn't possibly comment," Kai said. "And I must ask by what authority you are keeping me here. I am not under the queen's rule."

"You are within her domains," Mei Feng countered. "Are you here with your father's leave?"

"He is not aware of my current whereabouts," Kai said with great care. "I hope there will be no need to involve him in this matter."

As the two of them stared at each other—irresistible force and immovable object—there was a roaring noise in the sky above, and a rift tore open. The fourth dragon had returned. The newcomer dropped from the heavens like a stone, barely managing to spread their wings in time to slow their fall.

The dragon's form blurred in a burst of light, and then a young man was standing there—his breath coming in hoarse gasps, his forehead streaked with sweat. "My lady," he croaked, struggling to keep his voice even, "Her Majesty commands the presence of all involved, with the utmost speed, in order to resolve this situation."

"Excellent," Mei Feng said, clearly relieved by this solution. "Your Highness, let me invite you to the court of the Queen of the Southern Lands so that you may restore her subjects to her presence. As you perceive, she will be glad to know the full truth of this matter."

"A moment," Kai said, suddenly regal. He turned to Irene and Evariste. "Irene?"

Irene could hear all the undertones of his question. *What do I do now? What do I tell them? How can we go in front of the queen and explain any of this?*

Irene took a moment to silently curse her luck. But she answered in her most politically neutral tones, "Naturally we will be glad to comply. We wouldn't want to inconvenience the queen." She smiled at Kai, trying to reassure him.

But her stomach settled like lead. She'd failed. There was no way this could be explained without bringing the Library into it. Maybe if they were allowed to see the queen in private, then she could plead for mercy. She could explain that Qing Song had broken the rules . . . But would that actually work, if Qing Song denied everything?

If she needed to claim all responsibility herself—to save Kai, Evariste, and the Library—then she would. But she could lose everything that she cared about in the process.

There was no way to measure time on the flight to the Queen of the Southern Lands' court. Their "honour guard" had graciously taken charge of Jin Zhi and Qing Song, allowing Irene to join Evariste on Kai's back. Irene suspected it was because Mei Feng hadn't wanted to leave either of the two unconscious dragons in Kai's custody for a moment longer than necessary. But at least now they were all together, with Irene perched forward on Kai's back and Evariste behind her. Mei Feng, her subordinates, and Hu all flew at a courteous distance, allowing Irene and her friends to talk quietly and hope they might not be overheard.

"First things first," Irene said. "Kai, what you did with Qing Song and Jin Zhi was incredible. You didn't get hurt, did you?"

"Nothing to signify," Kai rumbled. "But we should be more worried about the future."

"Is there some way we can get out of this before we get there?" Evariste asked. He didn't need to define the *there*.

"Even if I could manage to evade our guard, it would do severe damage to our reputation," Kai said. "And it would leave the others with the opportunity to spread whatever story they wanted."

Irene considered that. "Do you think we're being offered a chance to escape—now that we're together—for just that reason? So that the whole affair can be blamed on us?"

"Believe me," Kai said, "it really isn't that much of a chance. I wouldn't bet money on it."

"Did Mei Feng's name mean anything to you?"

Kai turned his head slightly to one side, in a gesture that might have been uncertainty. "I can't be sure, but she may stand at the queen's left hand—in the same way that Li Ming does to my uncle."

"Meaning?" Evariste said.

"Meaning a faithful servant who gets things done—both on and off the books," Irene answered. "Rather as Hu is to Qing Song." She frowned. "For Mei Feng to be here suggests that the queen was keeping a close eye on this. Kai, how serious a threat do you think there was to the world's stability?"

Kai hummed thoughtfully, and Irene felt it vibrate beneath her. "Possibly very serious. I have been warned that a fight like that *could* shake a world in its course, but I've never been near enough to find out."

"Right. That's a positive."

Evariste took a deep breath behind her. "How is anything in this situation a positive? We're all prisoners, there's no way we can even get to the Library now, and my daughter's still a hostage . . ."

"It means that we did a good thing by stopping the fight," Irene said patiently. She kept her tone level, not wanting Evariste to realize just how poor she thought their chances were. "When this comes down to explanations, we helped. At severe personal risk. Even if it might have involved some minor inconvenience for Qing Song and Jin Zhi."

"An inconvenience . . . You co-opted a mob boss to blast a couple of dragons out of the sky with bootleg alcohol!" Evariste growled.

"We do the best we can with the materials available to us," Irene said. "Evariste, try to stay calm. I'm not asking you to be optimistic. That *would* be unreasonable. But there may still be possibilities. And Qing Song can't get to your daughter until we can get this sorted out." She nodded at the still-unconscious Qing Song, where he lay on Mei Feng's back. "I haven't forgotten about her. Believe me, I haven't. We . . ." An unwelcome thought struck her. "We have actually secured the book somewhere, right?"

Evariste bit back a snort somewhere between laughter and bitterness. "I am so tempted to say no right now, just to see your face."

"I might have deserved that," Irene admitted.

"It's safe in the Library," Evariste said. "Room B-349. Though is it actually any use at this point?"

Irene shrugged. "We might need it as proof to support our story."

"What sort of authority does the queen actually have?" Evariste asked. "Over us, and over Kai? She won't want to get into a fight with the Library over us, will she?"

"She has whatever authority she chooses to have," Kai answered. "If she considers that I have offended her, then my father . . . will accept her judgement over me. These are her territories. Her will is law. Lying to her is high treason. And she might send you back to the Library. Or she might send an apology for having you executed. It depends on her final decision."

"But wouldn't *that* start a war?" Evariste demanded.

"Not if we're found guilty," Irene said.

"So, what are we actually going to tell the queen?" Kai asked, returning to the crux of the matter.

Irene really wished she had a good answer. She'd sworn to help Evariste get his daughter back. But she'd also said *With the understanding that my duty to the Library comes above all other oaths* . . .

If she couldn't prove Qing Song was at fault, and he or Jin Zhi counter-accused, then her options were sorely limited. She'd have to say Evariste had been a rogue agent, and possibly so had she— and take the consequences.

"We're going to be economical with the truth," she finally said. "We—Kai and I—were sent to that world to find you, Evariste. While we were there we discovered the dragons fighting, and we stopped them, out of the goodness of our hearts. And if Qing Song and Jin Zhi have any sense, they won't try to push us, because it would incriminate them just as badly. And afterwards . . ." She was surprised to hear the restrained fury in her voice. "We contact Qing Song. We demand that he returns your daughter safe and unharmed, or the entire Library will know what he, and by extension his family, is willing to do to Librarians. And other dragons will learn that he'll risk war to get what he wants. The book won't be an issue any more by that point. He *will* hand your daughter over, or he'll be putting his family at risk."

"Will that work?" Evariste asked. His tone begged to be reassured. "You said *if they have any sense*. What if they don't? What if they think the only way they'll get out of this is by blaming us?"

"Then you both leave the talking to me. As far as possible." Irene's stomach was a mass of knots. She couldn't see any way out. With no proof, and no witnesses, she might just as well be voiceless and powerless again.

But she had to try.

Ahead of them, Mei Feng spread her wings and called—a long note, like a trumpet soaring above a lesser orchestra of whispering strings. A rip tore in the swirling currents of blue in front of her, and she plunged through it. The escorting dragons closed in on either side, a clear direction to follow her.

"Holy shit," said Evariste as the view was revealed.

Kai circled high above the land below, which was beautiful, regular, and almost *too* idealized. The mountains they were approaching reared up as if they'd reached the end of the world, framed by clouds and painted with snow. Directly ahead stood a fortress of concentric white walls, each one higher than the last and banded with gold. Green fields spilled out from the foot of the mountains like scattered fragments of emerald silk, bounded by the clean glitter of roads and rivers. This whole world was a place of order and control: mere humans were fragile, transient dust in the face of its power.

Mei Feng led the way down to one of the inner courtyards, and one by one the dragons settled to the ground and took on human form. Irene could see signals being exchanged between the guards on the battlements, and she had no doubt that the queen was being informed of their arrival.

Jin Zhi and Qing Song had finally regained consciousness. Hu was conversing quietly and rapidly with Qing Song, nodding attentively as his master spoke. He seemed almost more in control of the conversation than Qing Song.

Jin Zhi stood alone, her eyes flicking between the different groups. Irene almost felt sorry for her, until it occurred to her to wonder why Jin Zhi wasn't attended by her own servants. She'd been on her own throughout. Had she been planning something that she didn't want even her servants to know?

"I hope this inquest is going to be private," Irene murmured to Kai as he adjusted his jacket. "Surely the queen isn't going to want a public display until she's decided what she wants known?"

Kai was looking around with an air of polite interest, like any noble visitor admiring the scenery, ignoring the guards. "Some things are going to be easier to explain than others," he said quietly. "Like me."

And there was another elephant in the room. There were so many elephants in the room that it was getting positively crowded. Appearing publicly in Kai's company, as a Librarian, would not help Irene's argument that the Library was neutral and was staying that way. Still, if this was a very private audience, Irene might be able to give their relationship its proper context . . .

Hu broke away from Qing Song with a nod and walked over to the three of them. "Your Highness," he said, inclining his head to Kai. Then he turned to Irene. "You had a good run, but it's over now."

"I doubt that very much," Irene said pleasantly. "I will have a great deal to say when people start asking questions."

"You may—but who will believe you?" He turned to Evariste and produced a black-and-white photograph from an inner pocket.

The girl in the photo looked enough like Evariste that anyone could see they were related. Hu waited for a reaction from Evariste, then tucked the photograph away.

"My lord's word will outweigh yours," Hu said to Irene. But to Irene's surprise, *my lord* was said dismissively, as though Qing Song were his trained dog—his mouthpiece. As if Qing Song had been given his instructions and knew what to say. "You have stolen, you have lied, and you have committed assault on two of the queen's servants. If the blame for this matter is placed *properly*—" His gaze indicated Evariste, as clear as a pointed finger. "Perhaps with a suitable confession? Or simply a lack of defence . . . Either would suffice. Do you understand me? If you want the child to live, then you will comply."

Irene was searching for the words to tell Hu just how wrong he was, when she saw Evariste's face. Despair was settling in, bound up in a knot with desperation and hopelessness. All he had to do was sacrifice himself.

And sometimes, as she knew from her own experience, that could be such an easy thing to do. The easiest choice in the world.

"Get away," she said to Hu, and her voice made him step back. "This man is a Librarian, and he's not alone here."

"If you wish to fall with him, then you may do so," Hu said, moving to rejoin Qing Song.

"You were wrong," Evariste said numbly, his voice barely audible. "This isn't going to work. We've lost. Look, if I say it was my idea, then you can blame it all on me, right? It won't be the Library's fault—it'll just be mine. Just promise me that you'll make sure that she's safe—"

Irene grabbed his shoulders, turning him to face her. "Shut up and listen to me," she snapped. "I am in charge here, and I am telling you that we have *not lost*. Give me a chance. I am asking you—no, I'm damned well *ordering* you not to give up. Trust me, Evariste. I am not going to surrender to Hu and play his game while we have one ounce of hope left. If we let him win on his terms, then he's always going to have a hold over the Library. He'll try this again further down the line. I won't let that happen. *Trust* me."

A solid thud rang through the courtyard, and all eyes turned to the robed man standing in the central arch, who'd just rapped his staff against the ground. "Hear and attend!" he called. "Her Majesty the Queen of the Southern Lands requires your presence. Let all who stand before her speak truth, that justice may be established."

CHAPTER 28

Irene and the others were escorted through the halls of the palace. The part of her that craved distraction wanted to take mental notes on the decor, the lay-out, the works of art, and the hierarchies of the passing courtiers. After all, when would she have the chance to see such a thing again?

But her main focus was on something much more immediate, something she had only just realized. Something that cast an entirely different light on the last couple of days.

Hu was not *just* Qing Song's servant—the velvet glove over the iron hand. Hu was the brain behind Qing Song, the plotter and the intriguer. Irene was certain that Hu had been speaking on his own behalf when he threatened Evariste just now. And when Irene looked at events with that in mind, so much of it made more sense.

Hu had been coordinating the hunt for Evariste, and then for Irene. Hu had deduced that Irene was lying, and had restrained and drugged her. And he'd been out of the room when Jin Zhi and

Qing Song finally lost their tempers with each other—and things went badly wrong without him. Hu had been pulling the strings throughout, and allowing everyone to blame Qing Song. Just as Irene had been running around New York to draw people's attention, so Hu had allowed—had always allowed—Qing Song to be the public figure while he himself did the work. Possibly Qing Song didn't realize how much Hu was manipulating him. Hu wasn't powerful enough or nobly born enough to hold high rank himself—but that didn't matter, as long as he had a suitable puppet who'd listen to his suggestions.

She'd been deceived—no, she'd *let* herself be deceived—because she'd disliked Qing Song, and she'd seen an echo of herself in Hu. *Fellow professionals. Oh yes.*

There was something about Jin Zhi that was nagging at the back of Irene's mind too, but she put it off. Hu was the more immediate threat. Qing Song was a poor liar—too hot-headed to maintain the right facade—as she knew from her own experience. Events in the next few minutes might depend on whether Hu or his master was making the accusations.

But was it true that Qing Song's word would automatically be believed, over anything that Irene might say? If it was, then Irene and Evariste might have no chance at all. They'd have to confess personal involvement in order to save the Library's reputation—and even that might not work. It would leave both Qing Song and Hu with far too much knowledge about the Library. And they'd still be holding Evariste's daughter, and would be willing to use the same tactics *again* in the future . . .

The Queen of the Southern Lands, Ya Yu, sat in state in her private receiving room. If this was the less impressive room, Irene wondered what the main throne room was like. But common sense told her to be grateful the situation wasn't public enough to require its use.

Tessellated tiles cut from reflecting stones in tones of deep green and brown covered the floor in a complex pattern. The walls were decorated with panels of carved amber. A couple of dozen other dragons stood around the room, clearly members of the nobility from the richness of their silk and brocade robes. They were all in the part-human form that Irene had seen once or twice before. The dragons here maintained a human build and height, but their skin showed scales like a snake's, the colour of gems or precious metals. Their long, manicured nails almost resembled claws. The courtiers all wore their hair long, tied back in a single braid. And they carried themselves with an absolute authority that made their shape seem the natural, *proper* way to be formed. By comparison, human flesh seemed but a larval stage; weak, pitiful, and unfinished.

Irene realized this was going to take place in front of an audience, even if it was a collection of the queen's most trusted servants. The stakes had just gone up, and her options had grown even fewer. A private confession wasn't an option any longer.

The room might have looked at first glance like a medieval fantasy—but it was timeless. The guards with halberds by the doors also wore efficient-looking guns at their belts, and Irene had no doubt they knew how to use them. And everything and everyone in this room, in this castle, belonged to the queen. Irene could feel her power permeating the room. Even though sunlight streamed in through the high windows, there was still somehow a feeling of being deep underground. She could imagine herself in some mine vault that reached down to abysmal depths. The weight of earth was a terrible pressure bearing down on her, making her conscious of how tiny and short-lived a thing she was, and the light seemed very far away.

With an effort she lifted her head and focused on the queen. Ya Yu was the shade of willow leaves in spring, and was robed in the same delicate light green, bordered in pale gold. She sat on a throne—or at least a highly dramatic chair—that seemed to have been carved from a single block of onyx. There was apparently no cushion.

Irene made a private mental resolution that if she ever became a queen, her throne would incorporate a cushion. Also a convenient bookcase.

Their group approached the throne, led by Mei Feng, and all bowed. Qing Song, Jin Zhi, and Hu behind them all made a full obeisance, going down on one knee and pressing right fist against left shoulder. Kai made a deep bow of respect. Irene and Evariste bowed as best they could.

Ya Yu gestured for them to rise: her attention settled first on Qing Song and Jin Zhi. "I had not expected to see either of you without the book that I requested. It was to be proof of your fitness for office," she said. Her voice was sweet and low, but it filled the room and hummed in Irene's bones the way Mei Feng's roar had done earlier. "I desire an explanation."

Mei Feng took a step forward. "Your Majesty, I approached the target world with my servants when two dragons were observed in open battle. And we intercepted this group leaving. They have not yet offered an acceptable answer as to their actions or motivations."

Ya Yu looked at the six of them. "Perhaps one of you would care to speak?" she said mildly.

Under the queen's gaze, Irene's throat seemed to lock up in terror, and she had the urge to babble everything she knew. She managed to look away, and glanced at Hu out of the corner of her eye. She'd expected him to advance his case first, then wait for Evariste to back him up. But he was silent, standing behind Qing Song in perfect passivity.

Then Irene realized that Hu couldn't speak instead of his lord. It just wasn't appropriate here. The queen had requested answers from junior nobles of her court. It wasn't a servant's place to put himself forward and offer an explanation.

As the silence stretched out, it became clear that no one was keen to speak first, and the tension was building. But silence wouldn't save them. If the queen felt like resolving matters by declaring a universal *off with their heads*, she had the authority to do it.

So if Irene wanted to take control of the explanations, it had to be now.

"Your Majesty," she said, stepping forward. "I request permission to speak."

Kai twitched very slightly, one hand moving as if he wanted to hold her back. She knew him well enough to read his face. He looked as if he was preparing himself for a catastrophe. All she could think was *Trust me.*

"Do so, and identify yourself," Ya Yu commanded.

"My name is Irene, and I am a servant of the Library," Irene said. "As is Evariste here, who may be considered"—*if one squinted really hard in a poor light*, she thought—"to be under my authority. I was originally sent to investigate his current location and activities."

Ya Yu nodded. "Continue."

"When I arrived in the New York in question, I located him and heard his story. He had been imposed upon by dragons."

"In what way?" Ya Yu demanded. Her disapproval was clear in her voice, and echoes of it were visible in the courtiers' faces. But whether it was disapproval of Irene or of the accused, Irene couldn't tell. Out of the corner of her eye, Irene could see Qing Song standing a few paces to her right with his face set like stone, clearly ready to deny anything and everything.

"Evariste returned to his world of origin, intending to visit his old mentor," Irene said. "But he came home to find that the man was dead of a heart attack, and Evariste's daughter had been stolen by a member of your court." She turned her head to stare accusingly at Qing Song and Hu, ignoring the look of betrayal that Evariste was giving her. He stepped forward to interject, but Kai pulled him back. "He was blackmailed into compliance by a threat to his daughter, and ordered to find a certain text. Ultimately he fled from those involved, but he was too afraid for his daughter to risk returning to the Library. While I was trying to resolve this, I was assaulted myself, and the nobles here—Qing Song and Jin Zhi—engaged in open battle above the city. We subdued them and removed them from that world in order to save civilian lives."

Ya Yu tilted her head like a raptor considering a prey's last desperate attempts at escape, and the tension in the room tightened. "You make serious accusations against one of my servants," she said. "I trust that you can justify them." She glanced at Qing Song.

"This is all highly emotional and poetic," Qing Song said curtly. "Your Majesty, this woman has clearly learned her trade from the books she has stolen. She can spin a lie at a moment's notice. I ask her for proof of her story."

"Did you or did you not employ the man Evariste?" Ya Yu asked.

Qing Song squared his shoulders. "He came to me and offered his services."

A burst of muttering rose from the courtiers at his words. In a less well-regulated court, it might have been uproar. Here there was murmuring and short fierce gestures, and even then Irene could sense the shock and turmoil behind it. This was a place of law and order—and Qing Song had just admitted to breaking the rules.

The queen's eyes went wide with anger, and as she spoke everyone else fell silent. "He did what? And you accepted?"

"Your Majesty," Qing Song said, a hint of desperation in his voice, "I know the rules of your challenge forbade us to seek their help, but surely there is no harm in taking a gift when it is placed in front of you? Only the foolish general ignores the benefits of chance."

"Mm." The queen smoothed the folds of her robe. Irene couldn't read her expression. Was she approving this strategy as original and effective? Or was she merely deciding how serious the punishment should be? "And the rest of the story?"

"The woman has it the wrong way round," Qing Song said. He smiled coldly at Irene. "The man Evariste approached me seeking employment, in order to gain wealth to provide for his child. Apparently their Library does not pay well. He then walked out halfway through his task and tried to blackmail me for more money, threatening to reveal his involvement to bring disgrace upon me. Perhaps I shouldn't have agreed to his offer in the first place, but he was very persuasive."

It was a smooth lie. There were no obvious holes in it—apart from the exact location of Evariste's daughter—and it was indeed coming down to a case of *he said* against *she said*.

Ya Yu turned her attention to Evariste. "It seems the fulcrum of this case lies upon you," she said. "Speak."

Evariste's breath caught in his throat and he swayed on his feet, closing his eyes for a moment. Irene knew exactly how hard it was to stand under the weight of a dragon king or queen's regard. She wanted to reach out to support him, but she was afraid it might be a breach of protocol.

Then she thought, *Damn protocol.* It was harder than she'd expected to raise her hand under the weight of the queen's gaze, as if she were forcing herself to move through the pressure of multiple gravities. She touched Evariste's shoulder and felt the warmth of his body under his battered suit. Her squeeze tried to convey to him, *Trust me, don't give up yet.*

Evariste swallowed and opened his eyes again. Despair was written on his face. He couldn't turn away from Ya Yu. "Your Majesty," he said, barely audible, "I have nothing to say."

The murmurs from the bystanders were louder this time. Irene could catch the words *put to the question* and *forced to answer.*

The queen had to raise her hand for silence, and the growing wrath in her gaze suggested that she was displeased by such disorder in her court—and by those who had brought it there. "Then we must look to our other witnesses," she said, turning to Jin Zhi. "What have you to say to these serious allegations?"

"I know nothing of these accusations," Jin Zhi said calmly, but a pulse jumped in her throat. Was she weighing up the benefits of supporting Qing Song against the possibility of her own death if she lost the challenge? "I had been having little success in my own hunt for the book, though I have not yet explored all possible avenues. I chose to call upon Qing Song during my search, and I admit that during a discussion of current events we were both roused to anger. I am ashamed that we required intercession to remind us of proper behaviour."

So that makes all of us lying so far, or at least eliding the truth, Irene judged. *Multiple counts of high treason. But Qing Song and Jin Zhi are hanging together. Or at least she's not putting a noose around his throat by declaring she knew he'd hired a Librarian . . .*

The note of uncertainty Irene had felt earlier finally crystallized. *When we met for the very first time, in York, Jin Zhi already knew Qing Song had hired a Librarian. But how did she know—who told her? This was Qing Song's biggest advantage, his most important secret. If anyone found out about it, he and his family would be disgraced for breaking the challenge's rules. Were Jin Zhi's spies really that good? And if they were, why didn't she also know Evariste had escaped? And why has Jin Zhi been hiding her knowledge, rather than gloating about what she'd found out?*

"And you," Ya Yu said, focusing her gaze on Kai. "Youngest son of the Dragon King of the Eastern Ocean. I trust that you will present my compliments to your father when next you see him."

Kai bowed again.

The courtesies over, Ya Yu's tone grew sharper. "I am displeased to find you involved in this matter. It borders on interference in another monarch's realm. Can you explain yourself?"

"Your Majesty, I have taken no sides in this matter!" Kai protested. "I have no reason to reproach myself."

"Let us hope not," the queen said. "You are old enough to receive an adult's punishment. Tell me your perspective upon the matter."

"I can only comment on events I witnessed myself," Kai said carefully. "I would not wish to put forward my conjectures and claim they were the truth."

"We would expect no less from the son of Ao Guang," Ya Yu agreed. "Continue."

"It is true that the Librarian Irene visited this world because she was concerned about her colleague," Kai said. He gave no visible sign of nervousness, affecting the calm of innocent truthfulness. "I was present when he told us he'd been blackmailed—by threats to his child, and to his mentor's reputation. It is true that at the time he accused Qing Song and his servant Hu. I did not personally encounter Qing Song while I was present in that world, except when I intervened in the challenge between him and Jin Zhi."

"So you heard the man's lies as well," Qing Song said. "That does not make them truth."

Kai turned to look at Qing Song. "It is also true that *someone* administered a throat-paralysis drug to the Librarian Irene. I would be interested in knowing the facts there."

Ya Yu tapped her clawed finger against the arm of her throne. "No challenge may be given or taken during these proceedings. I desire the truth, not blood. Not yet, in any case . . ." Her voice rang in the air and hummed in the stone and amber, thickening through the room like an oppressive chord of music. For a moment nobody stirred.

Then Qing Song shrugged. There was an unpleasant gleam in his eyes. "I admit that I administered the drug to the woman, after it became clear she had concealed her identity and insulted me."

"I admit that I failed to give my true name on first introduction," Irene said coldly. "I do not recall insulting you. I did refuse your *offer of employment*."

"You misunderstood my words at the time," Qing Song said firmly. "No doubt because you are already bought and paid for."

He turned to Kai. "Tell me, what do you pay your Librarian? They are clearly for hire. I can see why Her Majesty wished us to avoid dealing with such petty, *venal* creatures during this challenge."

Irene bit back a furious comment justifying their relationship. It wouldn't be believed anyway. She could feel the other dragons looking at her and Evariste consideringly, assessing their worth. Again she was reminded that they were entirely within Ya Yu's sphere of power. The queen could decide to simply hush up the whole business by having all three of them disappear—even Kai. And none of them had the power to stop it.

Kai took his time before answering, as a lump of ice congealed in Irene's guts. "There appears to have been a misunderstanding here. Your Majesty, will you permit me to explain?"

"Speak, and be to the point," Ya Yu said. "I grow impatient." Her words sent a chill down Irene's back. But over and above that, she was dreading what Kai was going to say. There was something too formal in his voice and manner, in his glance towards Irene— as if he was already distancing himself from her. An unexpected chasm seemed to be widening between them. *No,* she thought, *don't sacrifice yourself for me . . .*

"When I heard of this mysterious Library some years ago, I was fascinated," Kai began. "I knew the Library was scrupulously neutral and that I would not be admitted, given my true nature. So I put myself in the way of one of their representatives and pretended to be no more than human. I was dishonest. I admit it, and I can only plead that I was young and foolish. When I was assigned to work with this Librarian, she believed that I was only a human, and I said nothing to disabuse her."

Irene could feel a ball of furious contradictions gathering in her throat. She knew that the older Librarians had identified Kai early on for what he was, even if he hadn't known that they knew. And she herself had realized Kai was a dragon within the first few days of working with him . . .

"When Irene became aware of my true nature, naturally she was disturbed," Kai went on.

Which happened several months back, Irene thought. *Neatly done.* But she could sense there was worse coming. The train of inevitability was bearing down on her and she was tied to the tracks.

"She is a reliable and honourable Librarian, who has always done her best to serve the Library's interests. And now that it is no longer possible for me to deny my true nature, or to claim to her that I am human, I realize she can no longer call me 'apprentice.' She knows her duty to the Library and its neutrality." Kai turned to Irene. "So for the sake of our friendship, before you are required to renounce me, I will remove the necessity from you. I regret that I can no longer serve as an apprentice Librarian."

She had seen what was coming. And she admired the way he'd done it—gracefully, intelligently, taking the blame and doing his best to leave her reputation untarnished. But all she could think as he finished speaking was *No, don't do this.*

But he had.

And now the only thing she could do for *both* of them was to accept it, just as he had.

Irene looked Kai in the face and saw the echoes of dragon-red in his eyes, even though he was still in his human form. "I accept your resignation," she said, "and I will inform my superiors of your true nature—and the reason why you have chosen to leave the Library."

There had to be something more she could say. Something that wouldn't ruin his careful separation between himself and the Library. Something that would tell Kai that she was grateful, that she trusted him in a way she'd never trusted anyone else. And that she *didn't want to lose him.*

But here at one end of creation, among a court of dragons, there was nothing she could say that could keep him by her side.

Her throat ached with unshed tears, with bitterness and fury and loss, and her fingers traced the scars on her palms. "I appreciate your honesty," she said to Kai. Something that he would understand, and that nobody else here would—because she knew how much of the truth had gone unsaid in his statement. She only hoped that he would know all the things she might never have the chance to say. That she cared for him. And how much she would miss him.

Ya Yu brought her hands together sharply. "Very well! Son of Ao Guang, I hope that you will apologize to your father for your lack of honesty. But this is a good argument in favour of the Library and its standards. I'm inclined to believe that as an institution it maintains the neutrality it has always claimed."

Meaning—Irene translated through her bitterness—*that this is an acceptable political excuse and nobody here will be allowed to debate it. And she's only talking about the Library as a whole. Not about individuals. Not about Evariste and me.*

Irene had thought she'd been angry before. Now she was *livid.* She had lost something—someone—whom she cared about very much indeed. She hoped that Qing Song, Jin Zhi, and Hu were prepared to pay, because the bill was about to be extremely large.

The queen turned to Irene. "And as for you, Irene, servant of the Library. Young Kai here must be a good actor for you to have been so thoroughly deceived. Perhaps you have also been lied to in other matters?" Her gaze flicked to Evariste. "If you will release your junior to our authority, we will see that he is questioned and establish the truth."

Again there was that thrum of power through the room. Out of the corner of her eye, Irene saw the guards by the entrance stiffen to full attention. She could feel the required response rising to her lips under the focus of the queen's attention, in a mixture of fear and obedience. She should be willing to hand Evariste over. She should be glad to get away safely and with the Library's reputation intact. She would have fulfilled her mission.

No, she thought. *I would fight all the way to the gates of hell itself to save a book. And I'll do just as much for another Librarian.*

"Your Majesty." Her mouth was so dry that the words came with difficulty. "It is possible that I may have been deceived about Evariste's actions and motivations."

To one side she saw Hu's shoulders lose a fraction of their tension. But if he thought she was going to let Evariste swing for this, then he was in for a shock.

The queen nodded, waiting for Irene to continue.

Irene took a deep breath. "My superiors will demand answers when I return to the Library. May I ask a few questions of the others present, in order to establish the full course of events?"

CHAPTER 29

The queen weighed Irene's request, in a moment that seemed as long as tectonic plates shifting. Finally she said, "That seems reasonable. I trust you will not occupy too much of our time in doing so."

Irene had to provoke an admission of guilt, and she had to do it *fast*. The truth might not save them, but it was the only thing she had left. She'd run out of lies.

The lever in her hands was the question of who had told Jin Zhi about Qing Song hiring a Librarian. And why.

Irene turned to Qing Song. "I believe you said that Evariste approached you, seeking employment."

"You have repeated my words accurately," Qing Song answered curtly.

"And he did so at exactly the time that you needed a Librarian's service?" Irene tried to make the question sound as if it might be incriminating Evariste even further.

Unfortunately Qing Song was cautious enough to see the possible trap there. "Apparently word had spread about the challenge. He made contact through my servant Hu. Hu, you have my permission to answer," he finished, with more than a little relief.

Nice passing of the hot potato, Irene thought. She looked at Hu. "Would you mind giving me more details? If Evariste is in the habit of selling his services to outsiders, this can only add to his guilt."

Hu's fingers twitched as if it would ease his nerves to be holding a cigarette. "To be precise, madam, it was an older Librarian who had spoken with me in the past. When he died, Evariste had our contact details. I believe you would say, in the local idiom, that he knew what number to call."

"You appear to be suggesting that the Library is staffed with people who would sell their services to anyone," Irene said coldly.

Hu twitched a shrug. "I'm sure these people are not representative of the Library as a whole."

"So when *did* Evariste contact you? Chronologically speaking."

"Shortly after Her Majesty"—Hu paused to bow to the throne—"made her request for a certain book."

Ya Yu inclined her head in acknowledgement. "That seems clear enough," she said. "There seems little need for further questioning."

Irene glanced at Evariste, but he had his mouth so firmly shut that he might have been biting his lips. He glared at the floor, refusing to meet her eyes.

She didn't look at Kai. She couldn't.

"This whole series of events has involved a number of poorly timed meetings," Irene said quickly to Qing Song before the queen could move from hinting to outright ordering her to stop. "The arrival of Jin Zhi in your hotel suite, for instance. I have heard that dragons can fly into an alternate world and appear in the sky above someone they know, but I didn't realize that it went to the extent of knowing which hotel room they were in."

The look Qing Song gave her was sharp enough to flay. "You would have to ask Jin Zhi about the time of her arrival."

"And the mechanics of it?" Irene said blandly.

The red light in Qing Song's eyes intensified. He turned to Ya Yu. "Am I to be submitted to this questioning in my own queen's hall, Your Majesty?"

"Yes," Ya Yu said. She might have been carved from emeralds or beryls, just as much a piece of stonework as her throne. "You are." Her face showed nothing at all, but Irene suddenly felt that her line of questioning had caught the queen's interest. She'd won herself a few more minutes before Ya Yu's patience ran out.

Qing Song's mouth tightened. "Then I suggest you ask Jin Zhi," he said to Irene, "since it was she who came to visit me, rather than the reverse."

"As you wish," Irene said politely. She turned to Jin Zhi. "Madam, would you care to explain your arrival at Qing Song's hotel suite?"

Jin Zhi had lost her expensive coat, but her dress was close to the robes of the surrounding dragons. With her poise, she almost managed to look like a member of the attending court, rather than a witness on trial. "I thought to visit my fellow competitor as a courteous gesture. As I said earlier."

"And might I ask how you located him?" Irene pursued.

Jin Zhi looked as if she would refuse to answer for a moment. Then her eye caught Ya Yu's and she gave in. "I have a token of Qing Song's," she said, touching a chain at her neck that vanished beneath the bodice of her gown. "We exchanged them, some while ago."

That did get a reaction. A ripple of murmurs ran around the room. Even Mei Feng stepped forward to murmur something to the queen. Both Qing Song and Jin Zhi avoided looking at each other.

"I was not aware that you were so closely attached," Ya Yu said.

"We are no longer so, Your Majesty," Jin Zhi answered. She glanced at Qing Song with distilled contempt. He returned a glare of cold fury.

Good. I'm onto something here. Keep going, keep pushing . . . "Was Evariste's approach to you general knowledge?" she asked Hu, trying to keep the question as casual sounding as possible. "Or did he confine himself to you and your master?"

"If he contacted others of my kind, then I didn't know about it," Hu parried. "He certainly didn't mention it to myself or my lord."

Irene addressed her next question to Qing Song. "When Evariste blackmailed you, what threats did he make?"

Qing Song shrugged. "He threatened to say that I had forced him to look for the book. He knew he could disgrace me and my family." He was clearly aware that he was repeating Irene's own threats to him, and there was a malicious satisfaction to his tone.

"So nobody knew that Evariste was working for you?"

"Of course not," he said. "I did not even trust my human servants with his identity. Only Hu and I knew who and what he was."

Irene saw Hu's eyes widen at that. *Yes, he's made a mistake, but you don't realize how big a mistake,* she thought. But she nodded, as if deeply impressed.

Then she turned to Jin Zhi. "Madam," she said, "will you admit that you spoke with me earlier, before we met in Qing Song's company?"

She could see the thoughts playing across Jin Zhi's face as Jin

Zhi considered her options. Then the dragon shrugged. "Spoke with you, certainly," she said. "Not more than that. Or do you intend to claim otherwise?"

"I agree that you didn't try to hire me," Irene assented. *Though you wouldn't have objected if I'd offered to work for you, would you?* "That would be ... let me see, two nights ago? Do I have the timing correct?" It barely seemed possible that it had been only two nights since then. But with the queen's deadline approaching, time had been running out for everyone.

Jin Zhi eyed Irene with the same wariness as Qing Song had earlier, trying to work out where the danger lay in that question. "Yes," she admitted.

"And you said, if I recall correctly, that you knew your competitor had also hired a Librarian. So you were merely evening the balance by making an offer to me."

"I understood that he had *lowered* himself to break the rules and do that, yes," Jin Zhi said. She looked down her nose in Qing Song's general direction.

Irene nodded. She was near the crux of it now. "It must have seemed a betrayal when you were told that Qing Song had hired a Librarian," she said, keeping the natural flow of the conversation moving smoothly. "No wonder you objected."

"I was far more honourable than he was!" Jin Zhi snapped. "I didn't try to hire one myself. I simply wanted to remove his advantage."

"I see," Irene said, nodding. "Thank you. That does clarify the matter. And may I ask who told you that Qing Song had hired a Librarian?"

It was the vital question. She'd been leading up to it very carefully, trying to keep Jin Zhi in the pattern of question-and-answer, and it *nearly* worked. Jin Zhi had opened her lips to answer. Then full realization sparked behind her eyes, and she shut her mouth with a click. After a very obvious pause she said, "My spies."

Hu's face was utterly blank. His freckles stood out like a scattering of copper across his cheek bones. *It must be difficult,* Irene thought drily, *having to keep silent now, when you would so very much like to speak.*

"So you were spying on me," Qing Song sneered. "I should have expected no less from you."

"Fine words from a lord who breaks his oath the moment it becomes inconvenient," Jin Zhi snapped. "I'm sure you'd have had my movements watched, if you'd been capable of it."

"You are too harsh, madam," Irene cut in. As both of them turned to stare at her, she continued. "Neither of you would do such a thing in person, after all. You would leave that to your servants."

And now the queen's attention was concentrated on Irene like the weight of a mountain. Qing Song and Jin Zhi were too focused on Irene—and each other—to pay attention, but the other dragon nobles around the walls of the room had caught Irene's implication. None of them made so much as a whisper to break the queen's silence, but they exchanged quick glances again, remote from the emotional drama in front of them.

Qing Song jerked a brief nod. "You understand that much, at least."

"Unfortunately I do," Irene agreed. "And it also explains why Jin Zhi came to see me alone and unescorted, and then did the same to you. She'd had a prior example of betrayed loyalties to warn her."

"What do you mean?" Qing Song demanded.

Irene turned to Jin Zhi. "It was Hu who told you, wasn't it?"

The silence that filled the room was like liquid ice.

Qing Song was the first to break it. "You have offended me by insulting my sworn servant," he said. Each word was laced with threat. "Even though I will not touch you in this place and time, this will not go unpunished."

"That you would defend him is the best thing I've seen in you so far," Irene said tartly. "I respect that. But you're putting your trust in the wrong person. Jin Zhi hasn't answered me yet."

"I have nothing to say—" Jin Zhi began.

Then Ya Yu raised her hand again. "You will speak," she said. This time her voice was like the tremors heralding an earthquake. "And truthfully."

Jin Zhi lifted her chin like an aristocrat going to the guillotine. There was panic in her eyes, and she had to work to force the words out. "I have told you. My own spies—"

"Your own spies couldn't possibly be that good," Irene broke in. "Qing Song has just told us that only he and Hu knew who Evariste was and what he was doing."

"But what would his motivation be for betraying me?" Qing Song said in a growl. Yet his defence of Hu was emotional rather than based on fact, and Irene could see that he was beginning to realize that.

Irene took a pace towards him. "There is a motivation. But you wouldn't have seen it. It's not the sort of motivation that a nobleman of rank *would* see. It's the motivation of someone who has gained everything by being your loyal servant, your right-hand man, and who loses his status if you lose yours. It's the motivation of someone considered weak by the standards of dragons, and who has to take power where he can get it. Your family aren't the only ones at risk if you lose this challenge. So are your servants. If you fall, then Hu falls with you. It was Hu who suggested you employ a Librarian, wasn't it?" She saw the momentary shadow of guilt touch Qing Song's expression. "I know that you'll say it was your idea. It's a nobleman's right to take credit for his servant's good advice, after all. And it must have seemed good advice, once you started getting desperate. Though it meant breaking the challenge's rules. Did he convince you that it didn't really count if you let *him* organize it? And if you didn't get caught?"

She turned to Jin Zhi. "And you, madam. I'm sure Hu told you a number of things. He could say whatever he wanted, as long as he made sure that you and Qing Song never discussed the matter." *Because one of you would be exiled or dead.* "If you'd found the book because of his information, would you have taken him into your own service? As a loyal servant who deserved a better master?"

"Do you think you can avoid the blame by putting it on me?" Hu said, speaking at last. He walked a couple of steps towards Irene, and she shifted her position so that she was facing him head-on. "You're spinning fantasies out of thin air. You tell stories just as easily as you steal them."

"When Evariste ran for it, you saw the key to Qing Song's success slipping away," Irene said. "After all the hard work you'd done to get him there. But Evariste had succeeded. He'd proven a Librarian could find the book. Then Qing Song sent you to Boston to destroy the library there. You took advantage of the situation—the fact that you were away from your master for a few days. You went to the lady Jin Zhi and suggested that she do something: hire a Librarian of her own, or expose Qing Song and win the challenge by forfeit. You were counting on her gratitude if she won the contest. And if that happened, Qing Song would be dead or out of power, so you could leave him and go to serve her. She'd owe you a debt of gratitude. Either way, you won."

"I was in Boston," Hu countered. "And I barely know the lady Jin Zhi—"

"You know her well enough. When she walked into Qing Song's hotel suite, you prepared a drink for her—without needing to ask what she'd like or how she'd take it," Irene said. "And you weren't in Boston that whole time. When I arrived, the gangsters—your local hired servants—said you'd been out of town. You were only just back from visiting Jin Zhi."

The queen had curled her hand into a fist. The room was taut with the stillness and pressure that came before an earthquake. That she was angry was beyond doubt, but who was the true target of her anger? Hu, for this betrayal? Jin Zhi or Qing Song, for letting themselves be fooled? Or Irene herself, for exposing it in front of the queen's court?

Kai's face held the faith of someone who had never doubted. Evariste was looking at her with disbelieving hope and the shock of a man caught and pulled back from the very edge of the abyss.

"These are lies," Hu said again. The practice of years served him well, keeping the mask of control on his face, but his eyes glittered like verdigris. "You're desperate. You want to save yourself and your friend, but you're simply making yourself look foolish. Can't you see that?"

"What I see," Irene answered, "is that it's very difficult to sustain a lie when you've been telling different lies to different people. And now you're caught out in front of all of them together. Believe me, I've been there. I've done that." Her mouth curled as she thought of those moments in Qing Song's hotel suite earlier that night. "And what I'm saying is that if Qing Song and Jin Zhi an-

swer my questions truthfully—if they obey the queen's orders—
then I would be very interested to see what version of events
emerges."

She paused for a moment. "Besides, I suspect there are two witnesses that we can call."

"Who?" Ya Yu demanded.

Irene turned to face the queen. "Your Majesty, I think it unlikely
that Hu visited Jin Zhi without a single person in her entourage seeing him. Her servants, her own bodyguards, her attendants—they
will have seen him. I understand that Jin Zhi doesn't want to betray
someone who claimed to be acting in her interests, but I believe that
in this matter she and Qing Song are both betrayed. And the witness
to Hu's other reprehensible behaviour? Evariste's daughter. If you
believe me, Your Majesty, then I beg you to have her found and
brought here. She is old enough to answer questions. She is old
enough to tell what happened to her."

And Hu's composure cracked. For a moment his face was dis-
figured by a brief flash of fury and utter despair. He had it under
control a moment later, but it had been long enough, visible
enough. Everyone had seen it.

A whisper of movement ran around the room. The weight
seemed to lift from Irene's shoulders, to be replaced by a vast
and improbable hope of success. *Did I do it? Is that enough? I think I
did it . . .*

"Stop." It was Qing Song who spoke. "Your Majesty. I request
permission to make my apologies."

The entire emotional tempo of the room changed. The tension
snapped. It was as if a cold wind had passed through it, cooling the
growing rise of earthquake anger and bringing a sort of release.
The courtiers had caught the emotional resonance as well: there

were sidelong glances and nods. Whatever Qing Song meant by "apologies," things were now falling into what the nobles considered to be the proper pattern.

Ya Yu sighed. She opened her hand again and extended it towards Qing Song. "You may do so. I grant you permission as a noble of the Winter Forest family and as a member of my court."

Qing Song bowed his head. He turned to Jin Zhi. "To you, madam, I . . ." He trailed off, as if certain things were outside his vocabulary. Finally he said, "It is true that I broke our pledge, and on my servant's advice I broke the rules of the challenge and employed a Librarian. I apologize for that, and for all other matters that are unresolved between us."

Jin Zhi's eyes glittered like gemstones. The fern patterns of dragon-scales showed on the skin of her arms and face. "I do not regret anything."

"I will take that with me," Qing Song said.

He looked at Evariste. "Your daughter is being held at my household in Zagreb: the queen's servants can take you there. My servants there will surrender her to an official request. I . . . realize that my threat may have been . . ." He looked for words again. "Unkind."

"Is that an apology?" Evariste rasped. Irene could hear the unspoken profanities, the sheer anger, behind the barely controlled snarl of his voice. But his sheer relief almost drowned it out.

"Yes," Qing Song said slowly, as though he could not quite believe he was lowering himself to apologize to a Librarian. To a human. "I believe it is."

He turned to Hu. "You," he said. "As you were my servant, I accept full responsibility for your actions, and for any advice that you gave me, and which I took. But I now dismiss you from my service." The scorn in his voice was just as much for himself as it was for Hu. His body was tense with anger, with self-disgust and despair.

Hu stood alone. He was as white as chalk. Nobody else was even looking at him or acknowledging his existence. He was, Irene realized, effectively a non-person amongst dragons now: he had no rank, no power, and he had been caught breaking what should have been his greatest loyalty. He'd played for the highest stakes and he'd lost. His petty ambitions had nearly started a conflict that could have dragged down the Library and involved both ends of reality. His life now hung on the queen's mercy, and Irene didn't think she was feeling merciful.

Qing Song turned away from Hu and glanced at Irene. "I make no apologies to enemies," he said, "and you have been mine, Librarian. However, I grant you my respect."

Irene bowed her head in response. She could guess what was going to happen next, just as she would have been able to do at any theatrical tragedy, and it didn't help. There was nothing she could do to stop the pattern of events she had unleashed. She knew that she'd done the right thing for the Library, for Evariste, and for herself, but at the same time she regretted what would come next.

Finally Qing Song turned to Ya Yu. He stepped forward and went down on one knee before her throne, in the same manner as earlier. "Your Majesty," he said. "I apologize to you and to my family for my failure."

"Your apology is accepted," Ya Yu said. She gestured, and one of the guards walked across from by the door. He drew a knife from a sheath at his side and offered it to Qing Song.

Evariste's indrawn breath broke the silence. He hadn't guessed how far the apology was going to go, Irene realized. Her hand clamped down on his wrist and she met his eyes, trying to communicate, *There's nothing we can do now. And Qing Song admitting his guilt has saved you—and saved the Library.*

This was someone else's story. The Library should never have been involved in it in the first place.

Qing Song took the knife. In the deathly hush, he set it against his chest and thrust.

The only sound was his body crumpling to the floor.

He lay there, looking as human as Irene herself, or Evariste, or Lucky George, or Captain Venner, or any of the people that Irene had met over the last few days. Death had no respect for him: it did not straighten his limbs, or restore him to a dragon's form, or stop the blood that slowly pooled on the floor. The assembled nobles were still, giving him some form of final acknowledgement.

"Jin Zhi," the queen said. "Attend me."

Jin Zhi knelt beside Qing Song's corpse. The hem of her gown trailed in the pool of his blood. "Your Majesty," she said.

"You will receive Minister Zhao's place." Ya Yu's glance flicked to Qing Song's body. "Since your fellow competitor has admitted defeat, and since you have kept to the rules of the challenge, you are the victor. I will take your oath in full court tomorrow." Her eyes hardened. "It is my wish that no vengeance be taken over any part of this matter. You will embrace our visitors and part from them as allies. Is that understood?"

Jin Zhi swallowed, and Irene could see her throat working. "Your Majesty. I lied earlier in court before you. Should I also apologize?"

Ya Yu sighed again. "I have already lost one servant today, child. Your work and your life will be your apology to me. Rise. Mei Feng, attend me: we must discuss the new minister's position. And let

Qing Song's body be removed and returned to his family for the funeral."

Mei Feng also approached the throne. The courtiers began to murmur to each other, inaudible from where Irene stood. The trial was apparently over.

Irene wondered what she should do next. Probably the best course of action was to wait for a chance to speak to the queen, to request that her servants collect Evariste's daughter. She released her grip on his arm. And . . . Kai had turned away from her and was starting to make polite conversation with a nearby noble. She blinked, trying to convince herself she didn't want to cry.

Then she realized that Hu was standing next to her.

"Why?" Hu asked. There was something very distant to his voice, as if he were looking at Irene from the end of a long tunnel, considering her with the dispassion of a man past all wishes and regrets.

"Why what?" Irene countered. Everyone else was now deliberately ignoring them both, just as they'd ignored Hu earlier.

"Why did you involve yourself in this?"

"Because *you* brought the Library into this in the first place," Irene said. She found that her anger had not left her. She throttled it back: she would not lose control, not now, not in front of the queen and her nobles. But she *would* answer him. She wanted Hu and everyone present to understand this. Even if they were pretending not to listen, she knew they'd hear. "You and your master tried to involve us in your private politics. You threatened the neutrality that the Library has always fought to preserve. You suborned and blackmailed an innocent man. You blew up the library in Boston and destroyed its contents. You let your master and Jin Zhi push a human city to the breaking point. And then you tried to put it on my fellow Librarian here and leave him to take the blame." She met his eyes. "We are not just 'book thieves.' And we are not your servants or your toys."

Hu nodded. And then his hand slid inside his jacket, and when it came out again, he was holding a small gun—dark ugly metal in the beautiful throne room. It was pointing directly at Irene.

Now she knew what that expression on his face had meant. It had been the decision of a man—a dragon—who knew that the game was lost and had chosen to take his opponent with him.

Ya Yu cried out, and the queen's power filled the room in a choking land-slide, weighing down on them all. It clogged voices and forced muscles to stillness. It compelled dragons just as much as it compelled humans and Librarians, and the very earth itself. But it wasn't quite fast enough to stop Hu's finger from tightening on the trigger.

Something hit Irene from behind at the same moment that the bullet hit her in front.

She tasted blood in her mouth.

And then there was darkness.

CHAPTER 30

A single point of fire blossomed in Irene's upper arm, and abruptly she was conscious.

Irene had always thought that some awakenings were better than others. For instance, waking up in bed on a morning with nothing urgent to do, a pile of books next to you, and a mug of coffee within arm's reach could be described as good. Waking up in the deserted tunnels of the London Underground to the sound of distant werewolf howls was bad. Waking up to find yourself hanging in chains in a private Inquisition Chamber was really bad. (And hell on the shoulders.)

She had no idea what she'd just woken up to this time, but it smelled of antiseptic and plum blossoms. She was in some sort of plain robe, by the feel of it. Her chest ached as if someone had kicked her.

She gathered her courage and opened her eyes.

"She's awake, Your Majesty," the man leaning over her reported. He was human rather than a dragon, and he wore a simpler version of the robes the courtiers had been wearing earlier. He withdrew a hypodermic needle from her arm. "Will there be anything else?"

"No," Ya Yu said from a position out of Irene's line of sight. "You may leave us."

The man bowed himself out of view, and the door clicked shut behind him.

Irene tried to sit upright, looking around her. It was a graceful room in shades of white and green, minimally furnished except for the bed and the table next to it. Afternoon light streamed in through the floor-length window, silhouetting Ya Yu as she stood looking down at the view below.

"I would offer to help you sit up," the queen said without turning round, "but I wouldn't want to embarrass you. Can you breathe freely?"

Irene sucked in a gulp of air, let it out, and touched her chest. Taking advantage of Ya Yu's back being turned, she pulled open the hospital gown's neckline and peered down at her chest. There was a small fresh red scar about halfway down, a few inches to the right from her heart, but that was all. "Yes, Your Majesty," she reported.

"Good. Fortunately Hu missed his shot. If your fellow Librarian hadn't thrust you aside, I believe the bullet would have taken you in the heart, and even the best medical science has its limits. As it was, you required repairs to your lung and ribs."

Irene touched the scar. It was tender rather than actually painful. *That close . . .*

"I'm like Ao Shun." Ya Yu turned round. "I see no reason not to use scientific advances. Especially when it comes to avoiding a diplomatic incident. Such as the representative of a neutral power being shot in the middle of my court."

"Ah," Irene said neutrally, desperately trying to think what to ask first. "But, Your Majesty, where is everyone? What *happened*?"

Ya Yu counted off details on her fingers. "Jin Zhi has been invested with her new position. Your colleague Evariste has been given custody of his daughter, and has returned with her to the Library to report on the situation." She watched Irene assessingly. "Ao Guang's son Kai has returned to his own affairs."

Irene tried to nod as if taking this in her stride. But she felt strangely hollow. For months she had been growing used to Kai, depending on him, worrying about him, caring for him. It might not be love, depending on one's definition of love . . . but she hadn't wanted to lose him. And now he was gone.

"I'm glad to see that you are in your right mind and capable of rational behaviour," Ya Yu said. It was like the edge of a knife being run very delicately along the skin: not enough to cut, but enough to remind the subject of how dangerous it was. "Let's both pretend that everything Kai said was true. He must get that from his mother. I respect Ao Guang and I've borne him children, but he is a stable ruler rather than an imaginative one."

Irene swallowed. Her scar picked that moment to ache. "The Library appreciates stability between the extremes, Your Majesty. It provides the best environment for human beings to prosper."

Ya Yu nodded. "Good. Now, have you any questions you would like to ask me?"

Irene shifted her position so that she was sitting on the side of the bed. It made her feel slightly less vulnerable. "I do, Your Majesty, but I'm not sure what it's politic to ask—and what I should pretend I never knew."

Ya Yu raised her hand to her mouth, hiding her smile behind a trailing sleeve. Her presence was subdued now, not weighing down on Irene as much as it had been in the throne room. "This is a private audience, child. It's the meeting where we *decide* what you should forget about and never mention again. That would be difficult if you can't talk about it now."

This was all pointing towards a relatively optimistic outcome, Irene tried to convince herself. *Except for Kai . . .* "So the Library is cleared of collusion or theft?"

"There were no such charges in the first place," Ya Yu said blandly. "There was an internal enquiry in my court, in the course of which two Librarians were requested to provide information. They generously and disinterestedly did so. The Library itself was not involved. Am I correct?"

Irene mentally reviewed the precise meaning of *disinterested*—not influenced by personal considerations, neutral, uninvolved—and decided she could live with that. "I believe my superiors would agree with you," she said carefully. "Though since this is your court's internal business in any case, it wouldn't be a subject for general discussion."

"It's certainly not going to be for *general* discussion," Ya Yu agreed. "But the families involved will need to be made aware of the facts."

Irene didn't want to raise the question, but she needed an answer. "Will the Winter Forest family hold a grudge against the Library, for the way events turned out?"

"I've ordered them not to," Ya Yu said crisply, "and Qing Song himself apologized for his errors. I think they're more likely to avoid Librarians than seek revenge."

"You ordered them, Your Majesty? That was very generous of you towards the Library."

"I am far older than Jin Zhi or Qing Song," Ya Yu said, "and certainly older than Hu. I know better than to discount the Library. I know what you do to stabilize our realms, and why. And while I will certainly take advantage of you if you put yourself in my debt, child, I do not wish to make you my enemy. Or the Library."

"Nor we you, madam," Irene said quickly. She chose not to think about the fact that Ya Yu apparently considered her worth personal mention. "If I may ask—what happened to Hu?"

Ya Yu's face drew into rigid lines, and her eyes glinted red with personal offence. "I have spared him, for the moment, in case you wished to be present at his execution . . ."

Irene tried not to pale at the thought. "No, Your Majesty. I don't."

"Then he will be returned to the Winter Forest family, to answer for his actions towards his master."

Which was probably the worst fate Irene could wish on him.

"You have time for one more question," Ya Yu said, watching her.

Irene weighed her options and decided to chance it. "Your Majesty, did you intend for Jin Zhi and Qing Song . . . well, for anything to happen between them while they were trying to find that book for you?"

Ya Yu was silent for a long moment, giving Irene all the time in the world to reflect on how she might just have said exactly the wrong thing, and to calculate her chances of walking out of this room alive.

Finally the queen said, "It would have resolved certain difficulties between their families if they could have found an . . . *original* solution to the situation. I reward solutions that work, Irene Winters. I was aware of their previous relationship. If they'd come to me together with the book, then I would have found some way to reward them both. As it is, I have lost one servant and another is mourning him. But I have you to thank that matters are not worse."

Ya Yu had assumed her role as queen again. The previous intimacy, fragile as it had been, was gone. So Irene rose to her feet and bowed. "Thank you for your time, Your Majesty. I am glad this issue has been resolved in a manner agreeable to both sides."

At the back of her mind she wondered: if Qing Song had successfully manipulated Evariste and found the book, then would the queen have punished him? Or would she have approved it as a *solution that worked*? And what would the consequences have been for the Library? Irene locked the thought away. After all, she wanted to leave this place alive.

She was more tired than she had thought possible. It wasn't just the weariness of recovering from a near-fatal wound: it was an exhaustion of the soul. She was tired of playing politics, of walking a knife's edge between danger for herself and danger for the Library. She wanted to get back to her books, to go back to being a Librarian. And she knew, with a cold, truthful bitterness, that she had cared about Kai. And she was going to keep on caring about him for a very long time—now that she'd lost him.

Ya Yu acknowledged the bow. "One of my servants will show you to a castle library. If you can't reach your own Library from there, then she will escort you to another world where you can do so. Oh, and ask your superiors if you will lend me that copy of the *Journey to the West*." She smiled as she left. "They do have two copies now, after all. And I still want to read it again."

The attendant who appeared a few minutes later led Irene to a set of interconnected rooms, which almost had Irene wishing she could stay a bit longer. The shelves brimmed with interesting possibilities, neatly stacked scrolls and well-organized books.

But with a nod of thanks to the servant, she touched a nearby door and said, **"Open to the Library."**

This was the highest-order world that Irene had ever visited. It was set in its ways, rigid and unchanging. It didn't want to obey the Language at all. But right at this precise moment, Irene wouldn't allow it to refuse. Her brows came together in a frown and she wrapped her hand around the door-handle, focusing her will on her own connection to the Library, on her certainty that all libraries could reach the Library and that this one was no exception.

The wood of the door shuddered and then relaxed, and she knew the connection had formed.

She opened the door and stepped through, closing it behind her.

CHAPTER 31

Irene managed to reach Vale's world a few hours later, after writing a number of reports and changing her clothing to something more appropriate. She hadn't yet been summoned by Coppelia or Melusine or any other senior Librarians to explain herself in person, so she'd decided to slip off to her current world of residence before any of them *could* demand an interview. There had been a very brief note of thanks from Evariste. He'd managed to combine gratitude with a subtext of hoping that he'd never need her help again. She couldn't blame him.

When she arrived, she found that Kai had cleared his possessions out of their shared lodgings. He'd left the furniture, but his wardrobe was empty. And his bed had been stripped, with the blankets left in a neatly folded pile on the end of the bare mattress.

It did nothing to raise Irene's mood. The lodgings barely felt inhabited any more, and her own books didn't fill the empty space.

It had been stupid to expect . . . What had she been expecting, any-how? A letter? A last chance to say goodbye?

Misery weighed her down like lead. She wasn't used to *missing* people like this. Routine kept her moving, but a part of her just wanted to sit down and cry.

She bit her lip. This was *stupid*. They were both adults and they'd both—eventually—done the right thing. It couldn't have lasted. Common sense told her to pull herself together and get on with her life.

Common sense, Irene decided, was absolutely bloody useless.

She shut the door on her empty lodgings and caught the next cab to where Vale lived. Part of her hoped that he'd be out. It would mean she could put off telling him about Kai for a little lon-ger. Kai was his friend as well. Vale might even blame her for Kai having to leave, and justifiably so.

The lights were on in the upstairs windows as Irene paid off the cab-driver and let herself in. She knocked on the door to Vale's rooms, waited for his call to enter, then pushed the door open.

Kai was standing there.

It was as if nothing had changed. He stood there looking at her, and his eyes gleamed as he watched the expression on her face as she tried to process what she was seeing. *Of course there's no reason why he can't visit Vale.* The thoughts cartwheeled through her head. *There's nothing to stop the two of them spending time together . . .*

None of it mattered. Irene stepped forward and grabbed hold of him, unwilling to let him go. She was conscious of Kai's body against hers, his arms around her as she clung to him, his con-trolled strength, the warmth of his cheek against hers . . . Every-thing seemed to come together in an impulse that made her slide her hand round the back of his neck and pull him down into a desperate kiss.

He didn't try to stop her. Quite the opposite.

Eventually she managed to release him. Her hands didn't want to let go of him. Her chest ached as if she'd just been shot again.

Kai took a breath. "Well," he said. "You did once tell me that if you took me to bed, I wouldn't be complaining. So far I have no complaints."

"This is a really stupid idea," Irene said, getting the words out with difficulty, trying to work out exactly how her brain had jumped from *We can't possibly do this* to *How do we do this without getting caught?* "For both of us. But . . ." And there her speech trailed off before she could construct a viable argument about how they should never see each other again.

Kai raised an eyebrow. "I happen to be visiting my friend here. He's being kind enough to let me stay with him. Isn't that correct, Vale?"

Irene belatedly realized that Vale was sitting at the table. He was poised in front of a confusion of scientific glass-ware, his eye fixed to a microscope eyepiece. "Yes, whatever," he muttered, not looking up. "By all means drag me into your political misconduct, Strongrock. I have a spare bedroom, and you're welcome to it."

"There you have it," Kai said fondly. "And you know something, Irene?"

"Yes?" she said, trying to come to terms with everything.

"I'm not your subordinate any longer." He gave her a thoughtful smile. "Just mentioning it, you understand. For future reference."

"I'll bear it in mind," Irene said. Her lips burned with the memory of his kiss. "Though even if you're not my subordinate, you're not my superior either."

Kai nodded as if he was following her train of thought. "No," he agreed. "But if you've taught me anything, you've taught me never to give up."

"That wasn't what I meant to teach you," Irene said. "Or what I was supposed to teach you either. But it'll do for a start."

She gave up on coming to terms with anything. It could wait at least a few hours. There might be urgent messages waiting for her back at the Library, but potential apocalypses could wait for a day or two. Or even three. This secret could stay between them—for now. And until someone actually came to order Kai home, he had every right to impose on Vale's hospitality.

There might be time to say goodbye properly. There might even be time for more than that.

ABOUT THE AUTHOR

Genevieve Cogman is a freelance author who has written for several role-playing game companies. She currently works for the National Health Service in England as a clinical classifications specialist. She is the author of the Invisible Library Novels, including *The Lost Plot*, *The Burning Page*, *The Masked City*, and *The Invisible Library*.

CONNECT ONLINE

grcogman.com
twitter.com/genevievecogman